FOREST GUARDIAN CHRONICLES

THE WHITE HOUSE CODE

BETH ROOSE

The White House Code

Copyright © 2021 by Beth Roose

All rights reserved

Published by Red Penguin Books

Bellerose Village, New York

Library of Congress Control Number:

ISBN

Print 978-1-63777-126-6

Digital 978-1-63777-127-3

This is a work of fiction and any resemblance to any person, institution or organization alive or dead is purely coincidental.

Contents

Characters

Forest Guardian marriages & kids

Dr. Morgan & Marsha King: Morgan-Barkly (Clay), Dorothy-Alice (Dorothy), Zoey, Liam, Wyatt, Tig, Gage, Emmi, Phillip, Iris, Idel, Idenna, Heidi, Paulie, Mickie, Galyn, Sparrow, Cornelia (Cordy), Tharus (TJ), Hawke, Donny, Charlie, Danny, Charlotte, Winnie, Kiaha, Billie, Hera, Garmen, Altair (Al),Wren, Lark, Tanager, Zoar

Dr. Jim & Bev Mottice: El, Dallas, Finch, John, Helen, Micah, Rue, Belle, Hazel, Mae, Everett, Celia, Morgan (Max), Kira, Kammi, Bronwyn, Bonnie, Abe, Noah,Star, Olivia

The Justice League

Bat Masterson, Wyatt Earp, Charlie Bassett, Luke Short, Wild Bill Hickock, Daniel Boone, Davy Crocket, Jim Bowie, Virg Earp, Annie Oakly, John Hughes, Bass Reeves, Doc Hollliday, Bill Tilghman, Kit Carson, Buffalo Bill Cody, Don Schrodel, Henry Brown, Jim Miller, Seath Kinmen, John Hicks, Abe Allen, John Allen,Jeremiah Johnson, James Roose, Sherman

Roose, Dave Allison, Ira Alten, Pat Garrett, Frank Jones, Chris Madsen, Heck Thomas, Dave Allison, , Betty Zane, John Adams, Andrew Alexander, William Allison, Red Angus, Harry Wheeler, Buffalo Bill Cody, Burton Mussman, Spikehorn Meyers, Henry Plummer, Jeff Milton, Sacagawea, Merriweather Lewis, Bill Clark, Bill McDonald,Blue Jacket, Tecumseh, Yellow Horse, Ralph Truax, Neil Brown,Thomas Smith, Judge Roy Bean, Chief Blue Horse, Porter Rockwell, Leander McNelly, Harry Love, James Hume, Wiley Haines, Lee Hall, Ben Daniels, Alfred Shea Addis. Tobias Norton, George Russell

---

1

The Messenger

Aggie stood abruptly; every hair on her body stood straight out. Her eyes held a fierce, startled look. Her fists were clenched tightly. The room swirled with time displacement waves. Morgan knew it was most likely a time traveler, but Marsha looked almost shell-shocked. Aggie took one tentative step forward.

Bev was in the kitchen, just coming back to the family pod with green tea for herself and a coffee for Jim. Morgan rose, looking at Aggie with a puzzled expression. He had never witnessed her react to anything with that magnitude. As he turned to face what was coming through the time portal, it looked for all the world to be a Bigfoot wearing a cape, its hood pulled up over his head.

Jim jumped over the back of the sofa, ran to Bev, and pulled her down the hall into the lab. He had seen the waves and swirls of time travel and knew he needed to get Bev as far away from it as possible because she'd had a severe, life-threatening reaction to the opening of the space-time continuum previously.

Aggie shoved the sofa—with Morgan—back against the wall, flipping it over backward so Morgan and Marsha were behind it.

Next, she stepped sideways and pushed the sofa where Jim had been sitting over into the hallway. Jim was beside Bev down on the floor, dragging her into the lab. Aggie looked like a bad movie version of King Kong; her teeth dripped with saliva, and the roar coming from her throat was deafening.

The audible alarm from the intruder alert in Dr. King's family pod was deafening, repeating "Intruder Alert." Marsha shook visibly, holding her wrist. Morgan stood up halfway, calling to Marsha to stay down. Aggie turned toward him and roared, forcing Morgan to jump to safety behind the sofa. He pulled Marsha close as she cried in his arms. Her fear level overwhelmed her to the point that she was now in a medical crisis. Morgan knew he had to get her to the medical bay.

They had had a peaceful, uneventful life the entire four years they lived with the Nordic Alien race on St. Pierre Island in Newfoundland.

Suddenly several eight-foot-tall, white-haired Nordic guards burst through the door. They shot protective shields that encompassed the time traveler along with Aggie. Both struggled to get free; however, the shields held as they transported both to cells in the brig. Aggie continued to roar, baring her teeth as she struggled to get loose.

The Nordics remained calm, seemingly unfazed by events. Olzing, the head of security, sedated both, then went to Morgan and Jim's family pod to assess the damage to the pods as well assess any injuries that had occurred.

Olzing entered the family pod to find both sofas smashed against opposite walls. There were shards of broken glass and some kind of liquid in the hallway from the kitchen to the family pods. He radioed for maintenance to clean up the trail of glass and fluid on the floor, then repair both sofas.

He could see down the hallway from the kitchen into the lab. All lights were on. Olzing continued back to the lab where he saw both Morgan and Jim working feverishly over Bev who appeared in critical condition. Marsha lay on another bed, holding her wrist and crying, "No, no, no."

She began calling to Morgan, who could not leave Bev to tend to her injuries. Olzing radioed a medical emergency to Dr. King's lab. Several additional injured lay on other medical bay beds.

Three Nordic physicians ran to the lab. One went to Marsha; the other two went to assist Morgan and Jim with Bev. Thar began work on Marsha, who repeatedly called out to Morgan. He lightly sedated her so he could look through the diagnostic screens, noting the broken right wrist. Her blood pressure was dangerously high for a human. Her sugar was critically low and her pulse rate was overly rapid at 144.

Thar dispensed meds to calm three of her most critical issues. He noted the break would need a pin, radioed for the surgical unit and someone to assist. Bev had stopped breathing and was in cardiac arrest. CPR continued as Jim inserted a breathing tube and attached her to the ventilator. They pulled the crash cart over to Morgan as the two Nordics administered meds. Jim stayed by her head after inserting the breathing tube. Four years ago, she had come close to death when exposed to time travel.

The Nordics, along with Jim and Morgan, frantically struggled to stabilize her. Morgan had to use the AED device on her twice to get her heart beating again. The Nordics tried an experimental medication that, thankfully, worked. Bev's blood pressure and heart rate gradually stabilized.

Morgan felt tears well up in his eyes as he walked away to let the Nordics and Jim continue uninterrupted. He approached Marsha as Thar and two others set the bone after placing a stabilizing pin in her wrist. She was still out but her vitals looked stable. They wrapped her wrist in a soft brace until the swelling subsided and placed a strap to keep her arm from moving.

Morgan and Thar discussed next steps for treatment. He told Morgan he would be back in the morning to do a follow up. Morgan lifted her other hand and cradled it to his cheek as tears rolled down his cheeks. He told her that he loved her and was so sorry that he had, once again, put her in danger.

Morgan gently laid her hand back down and looked over to Jim, deciding his time would be most usefully spent helping him. Both Nordics left the medical bay, assuring him they would return in two hours. They said they could monitor both beds from Security Control.

Morgan began flipping through the screens as Jim held her hand and stroked her hair. Jim looked to Morgan and asked, "Was that a Bigfoot with a cape?" Morgan raised his eyebrows and said, "Sure looked like it. I have never seen Aggie like that before."

"I thought I might pass out myself," Jim replied. Morgan told Jim he hadn't thought Bev could pull through this time after the terrible side effects from her previous brush with time-travel displacement. Jim remarked he was impressed at how much more the Nordics knew, and even their medications seemed superior.

"I wish we never had to find out how good their medical skills are compared to ours," said Morgan.

"Four years we lived peacefully with the Nordics. And I love this community, but I miss our own farm," said Jim.

Morgan shook his head and said, 'Yes, I think It is time to go home. Everyone knows we are not doing DNA splicing and focusing on the genes that cause Lou Gehrig's Disease.

Just then, Marsha began screaming at the top of her lungs, calling for Morgan. Both Jim and Morgan ran to her. Jim pulled up the screens as Morgan tried to quiet her. He climbed onto the bed with her as Jim gave her the medication. Morgan had difficulty keeping her still and nodded to Jim to give her more. As the meds took effect, she settled back, and Morgan assured her he would be right beside her.

Suddenly, she sat up and screamed, "My babies, oh, my god! Don't let him take my babies, Morgan." She struggled to get out of bed. Morgan glanced at Jim, who knew he needed to help her get back to sleep. Morgan felt tears welling up in his eyes. "She will take this hard. She won't be able to process what is going on now! She only sees our baby girl, Caci's, death four years ago," said Morgan, as he choked back tears.

He got out of the bed and stood by Jim, looking down at Marsha. "I know she will relive that nightmare of four years ago," said Morgan. He began to sob out loud. Jim put his hand on Morgan's shoulder and whispered, "We will get through this together—as a family."

Two of the Nordic physicians came into the room with Olzing, who informed Jim and Morgan that the doctors would look after Bev and Marsha while they went to speak with the time traveler. Neither really wanted to leave their wives, but Olzing promised the Nordic physicians would take care of them, and the girls would stay asleep while they were gone.

He explained the Nordic women would keep the children in school and guards had been stationed all around the school, along with Bat, who was armed, inside the school. "We have extra guards with Bat's wife. You, too, have been assigned guards. We fortified the shields even more so that intruders cannot enter, either by time travel or energy transporters."

Morgan took this news hard. He dabbed at tears that rolled down his cheeks. He, too, was reliving the kidnapping of Caci, his precious baby girl by Ciril, the Blue Alien, and which had resulted in her death.

Morgan, Jim and Olzing did not speak the rest of the walk to the brig. As they walked through the door, they could see Aggie asleep, lashed to the steel bed attached to the wall. Morgan and Jim glanced at each other. Morgan abruptly stopped. Olzing looked back at him. "It hurts to see Aggie tied down like that," Morgan explained.

Olzing assured him he would awaken Aggie as soon as they knew what the intruder's intentions were. All three approached the brig console where four Nordic guards operated the controls.

Olzing instructed him to maximize shield defenses around the intruder and wake him up. They entered the necessary instructions into the interface console. All three stood behind the console as a hiss, and then a fog filled the intruders' confinement cube.

A laser light safety perimeter surrounded the oval chamber. Morgan's brow wrinkled momentarily as the fog cleared. Two sentinel guards moved around the console to stand in front of the cube as the fog dissipated, revealing a caped figure standing illuminated near the front of the chamber.

Jim and Morgan now saw his leather-like face with its deep folds. He looked like a sinister villain from a cartoon. As their eyes fixated on his face, they noticed it held no emotion. He blinked his amber eyes and pulled his hood back.

Jim and Morgan instinctively stepped back. They felt as though this Bigfoot was seeing right into their minds. Olzing snapped, "SHIELDS UP NOW!" He turned to Jim and Morgan who stood speechless. He told them he had detected a mind probe from the intruder and had isolated everyone from it.

Jim blinked heavily while Morgan looked down, shaking his head in an attempt to clear the foggy feeling. Olzing asked if he should continue. Morgan shook his head while Jim told him he was so dizzy he didn't know if he could think straight. The guard called for Medical to get to the brig as fast as possible.

Morgan reached out for Jim as he slowly crumbled to the ground. Jim's face was pale and he appeared totally unconscious. That made Morgan angry. His face screwed up as he looked at the illuminated Bigfoot in the chamber. He screamed, "What the hell …" as he knelt beside Jim and medical arrived. Two others dragged a gurney to his side. Morgan instructed them to take Jim to his lab and he led the way. He didn't even glance back at Olzing as he left with the group.

"I can't understand why he tried a mind probe! It isn't logical," Morgan explained to Jim as he lay on one of the medical bay mats. Jim was slowly recovering but still felt too dizzy to sit up. Two Nordics flashed through screen after screen, performing a comprehensive diagnostic evaluation. Jim said, "Sorry we did not have time to question the Bigfoot, but I have no doubt we will find out what he is doing here."

Morgan shook his head as he looked up, pondering various possibilities. The Nordic named Thar told him there was some swelling in his frontal lobe, but he had no idea what had caused it. He asked for permission to try a medication and med bed repair.

Jim agreed but added, "Yes, and we need to plan a protocol to talk with this Bigfoot without anyone, Nordic or human, getting exposed to potential harm … and we need it right now!"

Thar told Jim to lie still, "Remain calm and quiet for the next hour while the medical mat does its repair." He added he would give him something to assist in that process. Morgan glanced at the screen Thar was working on, noting his blood pressure was very high as was his pulse. Morgan looked toward Thar and then to Jim. He knew what was coming next. He gave the shot just as Morgan remarked his blood pressure would have soon reached dangerous levels. "They ARE giving you something to help you sleep, so nighty-night, my friend." Jim made a feeble attempt at objecting but was out before he managed to open his mouth. Thar turned to Morgan and said, "A little bedside humor, Doc?"

Thar guided Morgan over to Marsha to give him an update on her progress. He told him their plan was to keep her in a light coma throughout the night to give the wrist bones enough time to heal better. He mumbled he'd glimpsed her "wildcat" side and thought it might be prudent to keep her sedated. Morgan laughed and told him he was spot on there. Morgan took her hand and held it to his cheek again, whispering he loved her in her ear. He leaned in to kiss her as he smoothed her rumpled hair.

Thar told him Bev was still critical and they were concerned. He said they had no documented cases of time-displacement waves having such a destructive effect on the human body. As they reached Bev, Morgan took her hand and leaned down to her, saying, "You got to fight, Bev! I need you to hear me, FIGHT." Thar could see the depth of Morgan's emotions. He asked Morgan if they could talk for a few minutes, so they crossed the room to Morgan's desk and sat. Morgan looked concerned as he thought it would be about Bev.

Thar asked Morgan to indulge him in a hypothesis about who the intruder might be. Morgan's eyes opened wide in surprise and told him, "I'm all ears."

Thar described that in Earth's ancient past there was a beast widely known to be capable of shapeshifting and invisibility cloaking—an immortal with time travel and a litany of other capabilities. He was a known Alchemist. Morgan began to laugh and said, " Alchemy—really?" Thar looked Morgan intensely directly into his eyes and said, "Yes. His name was Merlin."

Morgan's mouth dropped open and then he began laughing so hard tears ran down his face. He asked if King Arthur with the sword Excalibur would appear next? Thar still showed no emotion beyond his standard serious look. Morgan stopped laughing, composed himself and sat up straight, then apologized and asked him to go on.

Just as he did, the alarms sounded "Intruder escaped" and within minutes, the Bigfoot intruder stood in front of Morgan and said, "I am Merlin of the 6th century in Earth's past." Morgan jumped back with a look of fright and horror on his face as he felt the same symptoms as Jim and went down hard on the floor.

Morgan awoke to the roar of a Bigfoot and the vibrations created by that roar. He sat up to hear Marsha screaming as the Bigfoot stood next to her bed and was reaching out for her. Marsha was screaming at Morgan. "He killed Caci, my baby. MORGAN! MORGAN!" He leaped from the bed though Thar tried to hold him back. He pushed Thar's hand away and the medical gun fell and skittered across the floor. He stood right in front of Marsha and screamed in the loudest scream he could muster, "NO!"

Merlin stepped back and the guards were able to deploy a shield to encircle him and release a neurotoxin to knock him out. Morgan turned to Marsha who had climbed out of bed and crouched against the wall. Morgan went to her and told her she was okay now. He encouraged her to get back in bed. Marsha shook her head and said, "No, not the lab. No, Morgan—not the lab." He looked in her eyes as she cried.

Thar approached with the medical gun. Morgan looked at him and said, "No." He looked back at Marsha who would not look at Morgan. He waited patiently for her to process what happened. He was sure she rebroke the wrist. As she finally turned to him with a frightened look, Morgan touched his nose to hers, locking his tender gaze into hers. He did not speak but waited on her as he enfolded her in his arms.

Thar watched carefully for fear Morgan would collapse as he waited. Two other Nordic doctors surrounded them. Marsha, with tears streaming down her face, could sense the calm emanating from Morgan she needed so desperately. "He killed my baby—my Caci." Morgan kissed her tenderly and waited. She finally said, "Why do you always win?"

He laughed and said, "I love you. Let's get you in bed, because, frankly, you have an audience." She looked past Morgan and saw the three Nordic doctors. He helped her into bed and covered her. He asked for a gown. One of the Nordics ran to the cupboard, pulled one out, and handed it to Morgan. He helped her put it on. "TRUTH, pain in wrist, number please. TRUTH!"

He sat on the side of the bed while Thar readied the medical injection gun. Marsha saw it and Morgan could see the wave of fright wash over her. He pulled her chin around and said to her, "Focus on me." She looked at him, and he asked, "TRUTH, pain— what is the number?"

She started to look away but he guided her chin back toward him for eye contact. She put her head on his shoulder and sobbed saying, "Twelve." He nodded to Thar to give the injection. "Ok, they just gave you something for pain. We need to see if you rebroke your wrist."

"NO! I NEED TO SEE MY BABIES NOW!" One of the Nordic doctors quickly pulled up the screen so she could see the school room. They all turned to look as Liam, in the front of the class, was giving a report while Tig, in the second row, shot a rubber band at Liam. Morgan chuckled and said, "That's my boy!"

He turned Marsha's chin toward him again. She locked eyes with Morgan as he asked her if the pain was better. She did not answer him. "I need to look to see if it is rebroken." She nodded her head. He put his hand under her chin while looking at Thar, who nodded, indicating it had moved out of alignment, without saying it out loud which might panic Marsha. Morgan again waited on her, and five minutes later she finally said, "Okay, fix it."

Thar pulled the surgical device over as the other Nordic helped her sleep. Morgan told him, "She is prone to blood clots so please take…" his voice trailed off as he collapsed.

Morgan awoke with Jim standing over him, paging through the screens. He looked up at Jim and said, "Jesus, what happened?"

"Same as me buddy." Morgan asked if he was taking care of him. Jim looked at him with a raised eyebrow and said, "Uh, yeah!" Morgan grimaced, "Oh great, the last time you took care of me it was snip-snip … so, I am fine."

He sat up as Jim bent over laughing. "Yeah—real funny Dr. Snip-Snip!"

Morgan went directly to Marsha. "Why is she still asleep?" asked Morgan.

"They had to put in two pins because she fractured both the trapezius and the radial bone, with a hairline fracture across the ulna." Morgan shook his head. "She is still a spitfire." Jim put his hand on Morgan's shoulder and said, "In four years you have become a brave warrior to stand up to a Bigfoot. Wow, I wish I had been awake for that sight." Morgan looked at him and told him he would do the exactly the same for Bev.

As they crossed the room to Bev's bed, Jim told Morgan he was glad they were finally alone. They stopped halfway across the bay. "So, we are to believe this is really Merlin?" Morgan nodded his head with his brow furrowed, and said, "Yeah, and I am Phyllis Diller, too!"

Jim laughed. "Good to see you have not lost your rotten sense of humor." Jim's face took on a look of concern as he asked why Aggie had that horrific reaction to "Merlin." Morgan told Jim he had never seen Aggie react like that before. "Totally out of character. She obviously felt we were in danger." They walked to Bev's bedside. "She still looks critical, Jim."

He put his head down on the rail of the bed and let out a sob. "She is a fighter; we know she will not give up." Suddenly, the alarms went off, sounding "Intruder escape, intruder escape," and the Bigfoot appeared across the room, staring at Jim and Morgan. He was near Marsha's bed.

Morgan marched up to him and said, "Leave her alone and get the hell away from her right now, Merlin!" The Bigfoot stepped to the desk, asking them to trust him and not have him subdued again until after he told them his mission. At that point he promised he would go willingly.

Morgan looked first at Jim who collapsed on Bev's bed. He looked back at Merlin and demanded he stop emitting his mind probe that would eventually kill both of them. Merlin turned toward the guards rushing in as the doctors got Jim on a bed. Morgan demanded the guards stop and stand right where they were, then nodded for Merlin to tell him what his mission was and how it involved Jim and himself.

Morgan began feeling the effects of the mind probe and sat down abruptly. He again demanded he turn the probe off right now or the guards would be again forced to subdue him with even greater measures. Merlin stepped back and told him that, as an elemental, mercury was a major part of his body composition. He indicated the mercury was causing this reaction to humans because over the centuries, it had built up and almost overtaken any other elements.

Morgan asked the guards if they could put shielding around him to deter the mercury from affecting humans. The guard poked at the display screen and then a shiny clear barrier surrounded Merlin. He immediately felt better and turned to see Jim getting off the bed, going to the desk where he sat down. Two doctors tended both Marsha and Bev, as well as two doctors, including Thar, stood by Morgan and Jim.

Both Morgan and Jim felt relieved. Merlin sat across from them. He explained that what he was going to tell them would be difficult to believe and even more difficult to execute. "Very well, then, let's hear it," said Morgan with a scowl on his face.

"I have been charged with mapping out for you from the beginning, what is about to happen, and the part each of you need to play in preventing the Earth from a great extinction," said Merlin. A wary look crept across their faces but, though they were uneasy, they stayed silent, indicating their readiness to listen.

Merlin glanced up at the revealing glare of the overhead light. It felt warm, but he kept his place at the table. However, before he could begin, Marsha began screaming, "Morgan! He killed Caci, MORGAN! MORGAN! MORGAN!" Morgan ran to her and asked the Nordics to wait. He sat on the bed and comforted her.

He whispered to her, "I am here with you. We are okay, I promise," said Morgan. He allowed her time to orient to her surroundings. He finally pulled back from her, willing her to look at him. She was breathing heavily.

He nodded at Thar who began running scans. He asked how her arm felt. He couldn't wait; he took her chin, pulling it up so she would have to look at him. In her whiniest voice she told Morgan, "Hurts—Bad! What did you do to me?" Morgan laughed and told her she fell, breaking her arm which the Nordics had fixed for her. He nodded toward Thar and introduced him. Thar smiled at her and told her he would like to give her medication for the pain if she would agree. She looked at him and said, "Why are you standing there? Give it to me already!"

Morgan looked shocked as she spoke to Thar in that tone. "Marsha, that is not like you!" said Morgan. Thar smiled and gave her the meds. Then she saw Merlin. She pushed away and jumped out of bed, screaming "NO! NO! NO! NO! MORGAN!" Then, in a hoarse whisper she said, "Help me, Morgan—I can't breathe," as she collapsed on the floor.

Morgan pulled her to her feet as Jim came running. Thar told them she had a pulmonary embolism. Jim grabbed a breathing tube kit and told Morgan to push the drugs. The Nordic stepped back, letting Jim and Morgan handle her. Morgan looked toward Jim and the Thar handed the medical injector and gave her medications necessary for Jim to insert the respirator tube. Jim called out, "It's in, Morgan." Thar pulled up a screen and directed the bed to repair both the clot in her right leg and right lung.

Morgan looked down at Marsha, "I am here, baby." He looked at Jim and Thar, but suddenly everything was too much for Morgan; he felt overwhelmed with all the events in rapid succession. "I am at my breaking point, Jim!" Thar guided him to the other bed and told him to sit, then injected him with light anti-anxiety drugs. Thar told him to rest there for a few minutes and let it take effect.

Thar then went back to Marsha, flipping through the screens in another comprehensive scan. Jim sat next to Morgan, telling him she was stable. He thought Morgan should lie back and said they would continue the conversation with Merlin later. Before he could say anything, Thar injected him, and Jim helped him lie back. Jim instructed the bed to warm a further 15 degrees. Jim approached Merlin and asked him to go peacefully back to the brig with the guards and stay there until he and Morgan could see him. Merlin stood—not saying a word—and followed the guards, two in front and three behind him.

The next morning, Morgan awoke first. Thar and three other Nordic doctors were already busy at the screens, looking at each patient. Morgan sat up and Thar asked if he was feeling better. Morgan smiled and said "Yes, like a new man! So what miracle drug did you give me?" He snickered, looking at Thar. Thar replied, "Mostly a good night's sleep, and a few adjustments to your serotonin levels with light anti-anxiety meds thrown in for good measure."

Morgan jumped out of bed and walked over to Marsha. Thar reassured him she was much better, adding, "We removed the tube about an hour ago." Morgan asked if she had been awake. Thar told him, "We are expecting that any minute." Morgan did not ask anything further; instead, he lay down next to her. He ran his fingers across her hair, stroked her face and followed her jawline with his finger.

He felt her stirring then and, as if on cue, her eyes opened. Morgan told her not to move but that her arm was in a cast. She looked down at her wrist and told Morgan, "I hate the color pink!"

He laughed and asked how it felt. She told him it was tight on her fingers and rubbing her arm by her elbow. Thar ran a scan as Morgan continued to murmur gently to her. He told her they would take care of that. He looked at her and said, "Now, truth please, my precious; pain, give me the number." She looked at him and told him an eight. "Ok, let's take care of that."

"Next: how is breathing? And no fibbing, please!" She looked at him and said, "Struggling." Morgan looked at Thar who continued to comb through more screens. Morgan told Marsha they would take care of that. "Let's see what the bed says for repair." She smiled and asked if she had clothes on. He laughed, and told her, "Yes, for once you do." She snuggled closer and said, "That's too bad." His face turned pinker, and Thar actually smiled. Morgan asked her if she had a headache. She looked him in the eye and said, "No."

Jim came around the corner, drinking coffee and laughing. He got to the edge of the bed and said, "Yep, she is feeling much better. She will soon be on the prowl!"

She slept and Morgan got out of the bed. Thar assured him they would keep a close eye on her breathing. They would also do a brain scan to make sure she hadn't thrown any clots there. Morgan and Jim walked to get coffee where they met up with Bat.

The three sat with their cups of coffee at the kitchen table. Bat asked how they were doing. Both told him they were much better today. They told Bat about Merlin, about whom he had already heard and they planned to talk with him today. Bat asked if he could tag along. Both welcomed the thought of having Bat inject his thinking on what Merlin had to say. Bat assured him he planned to be strapped and loaded, and certainly would not put up with any aggressive behavior. Morgan said, "Well, you have watched yourself on TV enough. I think I have every episode on the DVR. 'Bat Masterson was a 'Legend of the Wild West and stands out above the rest; they call him Bat Masterson.' Isn't that how the song goes?"

Bat laughed and said, "Oh, you're good, Morgan." Morgan asked, "Which episode was Bigfoot?" All three laughed as they finished their coffee. Thar approached them and told Morgan he wanted to intubate Marsha again, this time keeping her under for three days. He asked if they could place an NG tube for a partial obstruction, explaining he couldn't keep her still enough for the arm as she fought him every step of the way.

Bat stood and told him, "That's a big NO! Emma will stay with her 24 hours a day, so NO!"

Morgan looked at Thar and said, "Well, there's your answer. Now, as far as the NG tube goes, Jim and I have that method down pat. We will do it." He asked if she was awake and Thar told them, "Yes, she fought the medication." Jim laughed and said, "That's our little hellcat." Bat told them he would be right back with Emma.

Morgan grimaced toward Jim, "Every time something bad happens, it is the same thing, fight, not tell us stuff, NG tube, breathing tube. It was a nice four-year break." Morgan approached Marsha's bed while Jim gathered his instruments. Marsha rolled facing toward Morgan. "Right now, we have a problem. No lab, no bed," Marsha said. Jim turned, saying, "Too late, you're already on the bed and in the lab. We need to put one of those tubes in again." She nearly jumped out the other side of the bed, but Morgan grabbed her just in time.

"Marsha, settle down! I know you hate this and so do I, but for you to get better, we have to do it." Jim pushed the tray over and Morgan pointed to each item telling her again what it was for.

She reached forward with her cast and dumped it on the floor. Jim said, "ONE." Morgan looked at him, laughed and asked what his bet was. Jim laughed and said, "Four and a throw. And this counts as ONE and the THROW." She slipped out of Morgan's grip and demanded her clothes to leave.

Jim said, "TWO." The Nordic doctors stood with their mouths agape, surprised by the goings on. Morgan got her back into bed but covered her with a sheet, without getting her dressed. He sat holding her face to face. He didn't say a word waiting on Marsha. Then he decided to speed things along. He ran his finger from the top of her throat to her belly button. She threw her head back, and he nodded at Jim who grabbed the tube and didn't bother with the cup of water. At the same time, Morgan slipped his finger down her body, along the inside of her leg and back up, then repeated it on the other side. She reacted and barely noticed Jim inserting the tube. It was an intense moment for Marsha, waiting for the next movement. It took almost nothing to arouse her. She laid back and asked for Morgan to do it again. He laughed and said, "Go to sleep, baby."

Thar injected the meds. Jim slapped Morgan on the back and said, "I would never have thought of that method, but it works."

Emma walked up to the bed. Morgan was glad his little distraction with Marsha was over before she arrived. Morgan introduced Emma to Thar, then got up and washed his hands before coming back to the bed. Emma sat down next to Marsha and asked for a gown. Jim went to the cupboard and pulled one out for her, then helped Emma dress her. Marsha murmured to Morgan to come back and do it again. Instead, Emma told her to quiet down and just sleep. She pulled Emma down to her and told her she loved her and not to leave. Emma swung her legs up on the bed as Jim told the bed, "Two human females on the bed now, please identify both females and keep separate."

She told Morgan and Jim to get going. "Bat is waiting in the kitchen having another cup of coffee." Morgan leaned over and kissed Emma, thanking her for taking care of Marsha. She smiled and told him to scram. Jim asked Thar to radio him if there was an issue. He waved the radio for him to see. He asked if he could radio Olzing and let him know he, Morgan and Bat were on their way to the Brig to speak with Merlin. "Please have the mercury shield up."

Bat additionally asked to have them record the entire conversation so they could have a copy of it to review. Morgan patted him on the back and said, "I knew we brought you for a reason. Which episode was that?" They laughed as they walked toward the Brig.

As they entered the brig, Bat walked with Morgan to Aggie. Morgan asked why she was being detained. Olzing explained that, because of her aggressive behavior, they needed to detain her until such time they could determine how to handle the situation. Morgan understood—he didn't like it, but he did understand.

Bat, however, pulled his pistol and told Thar to unlock the door and that they would deal with it inside the illuminated detention cube. Olzing was very surprised. He had never seen an antique firearm up close. Morgan touched the pistol and told him to put it away. Bat looked angry as he holstered his weapon.

Jim asked if one of the guards could have a doctor bring a medical gun with enough drugs to sedate a Sasquatch should that be necessary. Olzing radioed the request. Just three minutes later, Thar came with the med-filled gun. Jim took the gun, then lowered the shield momentarily so that all three could enter. As soon as they entered, Olzing put the force field back up. Thar whispered to Jim the entire gun held nothing but sedative.

Morgan asked them to awaken her. It took about five minutes for her to awaken. Morgan leaned down to her and told her they could only let her up if she could contain her aggression because they were all fine and wanted to remain in that condition. He explained that a Bigfoot called Merlin had traveled through time to give them some important information. Morgan leaned down and kissed her forehead, telling her he loved her. He asked, before they removed the restraints, did she think she would need some medication to help calm her. She nodded and Jim gave her an adequate amount of sedation. Bat put his cane across her chest, told her he would be here for her, and should she need to break anything in anger, here was his cane. He stroked her head and told her she was the strongest woman he knew, and he meant that literally.

She smiled and puckered, blowing a kiss to him. He told her, "Please, I am married." Morgan told him to stop stealing his lines. Jim turned and signaled to remove the restraints, still holding the medical gun in his hand. The restraints retracted and Morgan helped Aggie sit up. Then he told her to sit for a minute to get her bearings before she stood. She kissed Jim's forehead and hugged him. She stood momentarily, but Jim asked her to sit back down, because he wanted to check her eyes. She looked lovingly at Jim as she sat.

He explained to Aggie that in the next cube she would see Merlin and he did not want that to surprise her. She growled and stood. Jim immediately gave her a bit more meds. She looked at her arm and then to Jim and said, "Thank you." Bat took his cane and knocked on the containment field. Olzing lowered the field and Aggie stepped out. She did not look at Merlin as she exited the brig.

They determined that Aggie should go to the medical bay with Thar to be with Bev. Aggie ran ahead of Thar and was at Bev's side before he arrived. Emma was hugging Aggie as Thar walked into the lab. Aggie went to Marsha and stroked her hair, giving her a kiss. Marsha cupped her hand to Aggie's cheek. Aggie took the hand and kissed it.

She then crossed the room to where Olzing had moved a chair next to Bev's bed and Aggie sat beside her. Thar watched as did the other Nordic doctors for any increase in agitation or outbursts of anger. They would need to medicate her with a super dose if that happened.

Emma worked with Marsha all day. She was able to get her to drink some dandelion tea; then some hot water with lemon and honey after Thar removed the NG tube. Marsha had tried to fight them by turning her head and pushing them away. They wanted to medicate her, but Emma would not allow it. She made them wait until she told them she was ready. Emma explained, "That is her process and that is how we do it." It was about 30 minutes until she decided it would be okay. Emma held her hand as they prepared her.

Thar asked if she was ready, and she nodded. He told her to blow as hard as she could. He was able to pull it quickly in one smooth pull. She began to cry, and Emma tried to comfort her as she asked over and over for Morgan.

Emma looked at Thar and then to Marsha and back to him. He understood and gave her a light sedative to sleep. Thar moved the recliner from the family pod next to Marsha's bed so Emma could rest. First Emma went to Aggie and asked if she could go help with the children, making sure they had a bath and put them into bed. Aggie told her she would take care of it, then turned and walked to the children's pod.

Emma tucked Marsha's top sheet in tight under the mattress. That would assure she would at least hear her if she tried to get up. It was a trick she learned to keep her children in bed at night. Thar and two Nordic doctors stayed with Bev and

Marsha. Emma fell asleep and Thar covered her with a warmed blanket. She stirred for a second, then cuddled into the warm blanket.

About four hours into Emma's sleep, Marsha awoke and tried to get up. Emma scooted over to the bed with her and let her cuddle up to her. Thar bought another warm blanket and covered her. He programmed the bed for two human females. He was shocked to see Emma's blood pressure. It was 220/104. He radioed for Jim and he and Morgan ran into the lab.

Thar started apologizing immediately, shaking his head back and forth. Jim and Morgan ran to Bev. They began flipping the screens. Thar approached and said, "She is stable; it is not her." They turned to Marsha; but she was okay. Both turned to him as he explained it was Emma.

"She has a narrow artery in the brain and her blood pressure is 220/104." He thought it would be better coming from them. Morgan started to grit his teeth, but quickly realized what he was doing, relaxed and gave an inaudible sigh of relief when Jim said he would tell her.

Jim nudged Emma's shoulder and she sat up. Jim flopped into the recliner and asked how Marsha did today. She gave him a brief summary of what had gone on throughout the day. Jim told her they had been called for her. He looked concerned and struggled to tell her. She shot a questioning glance at Morgan who stepped forward, reluctantly, and swallowed away the ache that gripped his throat. His warm concerned eyes met hers and he told her that when she lay on the bed with Marsha, they had discovered the narrowing of an artery in her brain and her blood pressure was almost too high to give them an accurate number.

"This will result in a stroke unless we take care of that right now." He asked Thar to call Bat to come immediately. "We will finish with Merlin later." Bat ran in; he knew it had to be

Emma. Thar explained to Bat what was going on, and Bat asked if the reading could possibly be wrong. Jim told him the results were conclusive and there was no indication of a computer malfunction or failure on the part of the diagnostic screens.

Emma looked nervous as Bat sat by her side. He told her that if she would allow them to fix it, he would be here with Morgan and Jim by her side. She began to cry and asked Morgan if he would help to fix it. Jim muttered, "Hey what about this son, too?"

She laughed and said, "Of course, both of my brilliant sons will be assisting." Jim walked over to the other bed, powered it up and directed it to sterilize everything in the field and around it. Thar wasted no time waiting; his fingers moved lightning fast in a series of commands to the diagnostic and repair screen for her brain. It took just a half-dozen keystrokes more once she laid down on the bed. The other Nordic doctor gave her the sedation. Morgan and Jim donned gowns and were where Emma could see them as she drifted off to sleep.

Jim asked if she would require a central line and intubation. Thar looked at her and agreed. Jim told Morgan to do the central line and he would intubate. The surgery took nine minutes total and Marsha awakened to see Emma surrounded by the Nordic doctors with Jim and Morgan assisting. She jumped out of bed and ran to Emma. Bat caught her before she entered the sterile field. Marsha began screaming for Emma, but Bat managed to get her back in bed.

The other doctors worked to finish with Emma, so Bat knew it was on him to keep her confined. She tried to get up, but Bat laid his cane across her shoulders and gently pushed her back into the pillows. Marsha was stunned, wrinkling her face to convey shock and dismay. She then stroked a lock of her long hair from her face and tucked it behind one ear. Bat smiled, telling her she was beautiful, and he loved her fiery personality.

Marsha told Bat he had her personal commitment to stay put in bed and tame the personality down. She asked Bat if she could give him a truthful description of her pain. Bat lifted one eyebrow and said he would expect nothing less. She explained that her fingers felt numb and the forearm from the wrist to her elbow was "buzzing," and the pain was deep in the bone along her forearm. She asked Bat if he thought it was from her little episode of wanting to leave the lab.

"At present, Marsha, I don't know for certain if that's the case or not; however, as a gambling man, I'm going with a yes," Bat told her. "Let's wait and give Morgan an update." She turned her head to look at Morgan and her entire demeanor softened. She had a tender look of love in her face and body language. She looked back at Bat, and told him, "He is my everything, I love him with my heart, mind, spirit and body."

Bat took her hand and squeezed it giving her a nod of approval and a delighted smile. Morgan and Jim walked over to the bed as the Nordic doctors finished up with Emma and made sure all meds were onboard. Morgan settled down beside her on the bed, and she sat with one leg straight and the other curled back. Morgan reached and pulled her gown down. Jim laughed. Bat told him of his discussion with Marsha, and that, as a gambling man, I told her that her little fiery outburst may be the cause of her issue."

Morgan and Jim went from smiling to a look of concern. Totally not like Marsha at all. She looked Morgan in the eye and took Jim's hand. She apologized for the way she acted. She told the three of them it was just that it had brought back so many sad memories of Caci. She said she could and would get through it, "And I will make every effort to contain my fire as much as possible." They continued to listen to her as Morgan's expression turned to one of loving compassion.

She looked at Jim and squeezed his hand. "My arm," she sighed audibly. She explained the deep bone ache from her wrist to elbow. "Two fingers are numb, and I can't feel them. The others hurt so bad I would like to cut them off. Of course, then I couldn't teach Tig how to shoot rubber bands!"

They chuckled, but Jim ordered everyone off the bed so Marsha could lie back and he could complete his exam. Morgan touched her fingers. He told Jim they were cold as ice, and the circulation looked bad. Thar moved to the display screens Jim was flipping through while he listened to Morgan and Marsha, then sat down on the bed beside her. He smiled and told her how brave she was to accept responsibility for her actions and also deal with such a deep and painful loss. She hugged him.

Morgan watched this transformation take place in Marsha and felt relieved. Thar went on to tell her his best guess was she had several pinched nerves and a quick surgery to release them would be necessary. He asked if she would let Nor, a hand and arm specialist, fix it for her. "We do not need to put in a breathing tube. We can just numb it up and give you light sedation; how does that sound?"

She told him she liked his plan. "May I go back to my own bed tomorrow? Thar told her, "We don't make promises we can't keep, so ask tomorrow. How does it sound if I call Nor? She is very nice and has a personality similar to yours. You should both get along fine. She could do this for you right now. Your blood pressure is up which likely is from the pain. If you tell us right away, we can get out in front of it and keep you at a more even level. Is that something you would consider doing?" She nodded her head yes.

By now Jim and Morgan were staring at Marsha, wondering what had come over her. They had not seen this side of her before. Morgan motioned to Bat to jump up so he could sit beside her. Morgan took her hand and pulled her chin to face him. They looked at each other, locking eye contact. Marsha said, "Morgan, I am tired. Can we please go home to the farm as soon as possible? Mentally, I am ready for that." Jim moved to stand by Bat and Morgan, and all three placed their hands on her hand and said, "We are family and we're going home to the Cuyahoga Valley… of course, with the help of Nordic security and a couple of the gals for the kids' and our sanity." They all laughed and Thar was happy to see a family bond this strong.

2

The Weight of a World

Morgan, Jim, Bat, Olzing and Thar sat in the family pod. Marsha and Bev were both sedated in the lab; each had a Nordic doctor assigned to her. Olzing began by talking through the move back to the Cuyahoga Valley in the Cuyahoga Valley National Park.

Olzing explained over 75 Nordics were engaged in a variety of tasks from getting each house and barn in order and repairing them; grounds maintenance and preparing the fields for planting; security fencing, perimeter monitoring and cameras; barns and houses equipped with high tech security measures and cameras; and driveway gates including a guardhouse. All houses and barns would be set up to prevent time travelers and energy transporters. Additionally, they would have laser bounce technology.

The barn at Bev's would be rebuilt into a schoolhouse with a complete second story that houses four apartments for two guards, a nanny and a teacher. Morgan's barn would also have a second floor with six apartments for two guards, a teacher, and three nannies for the children. They were building two apartments in the basement of each house for two security guards which would have their own private entrance.

They planned enough room for two security personnel in the guardhouse with monitors installed to view the entire property. In addition, one guard would control two fly-over drones at all times for each property.

Since Morgan had the most room, they sent Nordic craftsmen and builders to put together a 30,000 square foot geodesic dome lab that would be set up similar to their Nordic base lab. In addition, it would have a bunker installed with an underground tunnel from the house to the lab. They would install a bunker at Bev's that would be in the barn with a similar underground tunnel from the house to the bunker.

Jim and Morgan would have complete control of the lab and their property with optimal security. They would also work with Thar in setting up the medical bay. He and two other doctors would be helping them with their work and advancing their understanding of technology. There would be four apartments for Thar and his two doctors as well as three guest suites, and four security apartments.

Olzing had been retained as Chief of Security for both properties with a total of eight guards for the houses and four to cover the lab, three security guards for the Nordic dome, plus himself. One of the guards would be in charge of communication oversight to make sure no one could tap into the cable lines or place listening devices and oversee their jamming technology. One guard was in charge of the electrical grid and transformers at each property. Their property would be highly secure so both families could feel safe.

The Nordics financed the entire operation by designating it as their base of operations for planet Earth. There would be a second geodesic dome of 18,000 square feet. The top floor held

12 apartments and, on the bottom floor, they had designed a lab with two monitoring rooms, one training room, and one communications lab.

Thar and Olzing told them they would have all the construction complete in four weeks. Jim and Morgan both burst into laughter. Jim said he did not know how that could be even remotely achievable. Thar rather patiently explained that the pods were prebuilt and easy to assemble. The bunkers and concrete floors would take a full week to complete but other than that they had built hundreds of the modular buildings across various worlds, each capable of withstanding a category 5 hurricane. Morgan told him it would be a huge upgrade for him. His present lab was only 8000 square feet.

Morgan told them his family needed seven bedrooms with six designated for the children and that he would like built-in beds with drawers under the beds and bookcases built for each bed with an open shelf above the headboard to optimize storage and, hopefully, encourage neatness.

Additionally, in the attic he needed a room for Bitty and Aggie with a bathroom upstairs for them. Olzing took notes. "For the kids we would like a playroom in the attic. There is plenty of room for the bedroom and playroom with a bathroom that would accommodate Aggie's and Bitty's size along with four stalls for the kids with a sink for Aggie and Bitty, and four more accommodating the kids.

"On the second floor with all the bedrooms, Marsha and I need our own and two other bathrooms on that floor, one bathroom on the main floor, and a bathroom for each apartment in the basement. We really need a large laundry room in the basement as will Jim and Bev." Jim spoke up and told him they needed a bathroom in their master bedroom and two more bathrooms on the second floor and one on the first floor in addition to one in the attic where they needed two bedrooms and a playroom and, of course, the basement apartments with bathroom and kitchens for each apartment.

"You're sure you can do this in one month with all the apartments and security, bunkers, and guard houses, plus a lab?" Olzing told them they had a full battalion regiment that was organizing now, with construction beginning in two days. Morgan asked if they could give their lab more room to put in a cafeteria for all personnel. "I would like to have a kitchen large enough to cook food for all, and that, of course, would require three more apartments above the lab for kitchen personnel." Olzing agreed that was a good idea.

Thar told them he would like to discuss Morgan and Jim's research, and more specifically that they would receive notification in the morning that they had each won the Nobel Prize for their work in research on Lou Gehrig's Disease. "You are both on the brink of true greatness with your research which will unfortunately be on hold as all of us work to keep this planet safe from the upcoming supernova event; however, the acceptance ceremony will be in conflict with Merlin's mission for you."

Morgan said they would carve out time for this. "The girls will want to go to Paris. It will be their first big event after returning to the Valley. Besides, they did not have the opportunity to explore last time we went."

Olzing told everyone they should talk about Merlin and that the information he had provided was spot on as far as the star Betelgeuse going supernova. Rigel, Saiph, and Bellatrix all have planetary defenses and will be protected; however, the Earth must activate its own planetary defense. "The last time it was used was with the Tunguska event in 1908. The activation codes have been lost, so the clues that Merlin gave us about American Presidents placing clues in the White House china is the only realistic hope for planet Earth," explained Olzing. "It was a genius way to preserve the codes in the event they were lost, as they have been."

He further explained that it made sense for the placement of the defense system to be on the Giza plateau. Osiris and Isis put the mechanism in place and aligned it to the Orion constellation. It was the same for Teotihuacan in Mexico and the Siberian Valley of Death Cauldrons. "This has to be activated before the Earth reaches perihelion in January. Our scientists tell us that in all probability the supernova will occur at that time, but we'll have more precise information on that later."

Morgan asked about the monastery in Portugal that had the Templar Cross from 1139. "Merlin told us that was the starting point. What do you think that he was trying to tell us?" Olzing told him that the Hermitage of St. Bartholomew in Space was rumored to have contained the Holy Grail and the Arc of the Covenant. It was eventually moved to this monastery in Portugal in Salzedas. That is also where the Spear of Destiny was said to have been located.

"Now, we looked into the Order of the Christ and determined the Templars rebranded themselves under that name. I believe we should start there. It must have something to do with the four pillars of the Templar Cross." Jim wished that Merlin knew more about this, other than the vague references to the Templars, and the American Presidents, there wasn't a whole lot to go on, he thought.

"In my era it was always rumored that Vasco da Gama and Magellan were part of the Templars and the astrolabe they used held clues to the Templars which would lead to the Arc of the Covenant and the Spear of Destiny," explained Bat. Bat also told them that even in his era Oak Island was rumored to be where the Templars moved the Arc of the Covenant, the Spear of Destiny, and the Holy Grail and that they had placed many traps and obstacles to protect the relics.

Olzing asked Jim to research Magellan and De Gama's astrolabe location. "Once we have that information, we should request permission to examine them." He then askcd Morgan to obtain permission for a private tour in the Monastery in Portugal. He also asked Bat to arrange a private meeting with the archeological dig crew on Oak Island. "Once we have those dates, we will align our schedules and be on our way. This first part of the investigation should point us in the right direction. I will work with our liaison to the White House to view the Presidential china.

"Morgan, you are well connected and already have clearance, so we will assign that to you," said Olzing. Morgan pointed out that 32 of the US Presidents were Masons who are rumored to be part of the Templar secret society.

Olzing reminded him, "Merlin told us to focus on Washington, Jefferson, Madison, Lincoln, Hayes and possibly Reagan." Thar stood and told Morgan and Jim they should go check on Marsha and Bev and pick this up again tomorrow.

Jim thought it was brighter than normal in the lab. Morgan looked up at the lights. Thar told him they had upgraded the lighting system. They walked over to Marsha's bed. Jim and Thar paged through all the relevant screens with the other Nordic doctor giving everyone an update. Morgan sat down on the bed with her, picking up her hand. To him she looked pale. Then he overheard what the Nordic doctor was telling Jim and Thar. They had adjusted her pacemaker because she had an irregular rhythm. Morgan stood with a furrowed brow and his teeth clenched. He fought back the urge to scream at the doctor. He swallowed hard and took a deep breath, Jim could see the anger rising in Morgan.

Jim asked—so Morgan would not explode at the Nordic doctor —why they were not notified immediately. "This is a serious condition; we are physicians, and we deserve to be involved."

Thar turned to the Nordic doctor and told him it was against their protocol to not send him notification instantly as they all had radios. The doctor looked down and told him he thought since he took care of it before it turned into a full-blown medical emergency, that it met the protocol standards.

Thar turned to Jim and Morgan and told him this doctor was new to his group and had only been assigned to him four days ago. He apologized, but Morgan and Jim were already flipping through the screens, drilling down on pertinent details. Thar pointed out several issues that they should have taken care of.

Thar then dismissed the doctor and told him they would continue with her care while he took a break. When he left, Morgan, who was still angry, asked if he could be an infiltrated spy or, worse yet, an assassin.

"Our names are in the forefront again with this Nobel Prize." Thar pushed a buzzer on his radio that neither Jim nor Morgan's radios had. Olzing and two guards came running. He told them what happened and had they not walked in something nefarious could have happened. "Question that doctor. He is new and I did not select him," Thar directed.

Olzing advised there would be two guards in the lab from then on. They left to go get the doctor for questioning. It had only been five minutes from the time he left that Olzing returned. They were surprised to see him return so quickly. He told them the doctor in question had stepped into the disintegrator before they could take him into custody.

Morgan slumped to the floor. The guards lifted him onto the table mat. His blood pressure was significantly elevated, so they gave him medication. Jim and Thar flipped through each diagnostic screen. Morgan came around and tried to sit up. Jim pushed him back against the bed. He told Thar and Jim he was fine. It had been overwhelming to hear they were in danger—

YET AGAIN! He clearly was fighting back the tears. He resorted to looking upward so his tears would not fall. He tried sitting up again and Jim once again pushed him back down. Jim knew he was feeling like himself when he screamed, "LISTEN DR. SNIP-SNIP, I AM FINE! GET OUT OF MY WAY!"

Thar glanced at Morgan and then to Jim, baffled by Morgan's statement. Jim told him it was an inside joke. Jim stepped back and said, "After you, my dear doctor."

Morgan went back to Marsha. He told them the adjustment was just plain wrong and was not needed. He turned the pacemaker back to the previous settings Jim and Morgan had given her. Thar asked if their cardiologist, who had been on his team for 11 years could look at her. Morgan snapped back immediately and said, "Only if we're here to observe and question." Thar told him that was fair and exactly what he would require.

Morgan laid down beside Marsha, apologizing that somehow they had been compromised with an inside job. "Security and Medical are on top of this and there is no need to worry." Morgan promised to take better precautions going forward.

Then another thought dawned on him, and he said it out loud. "Bev! God, go check her now!" All three ran to her bed. After 20 minutes going through the screens, they could tell that slowly over the past three days she had been given a drug that kept causing cardiac arrest. Thar administered meds to counter the dangerous drugs that had built up in her system.

Jim nearly collapsed, but the guards pulled him away and sat him on the medical mat. Morgan came and sat down beside him. He put his hand on Jim's shoulder while they both cried. Jim said, "Are we nowhere safe?" Olzing overheard that as he approached them. He knelt down in front of them and said "YES, YOU WILL BE SAFE! Our human resource person who falsified his clearance is being transported as we speak to the base on Mars. There he will face trial and execution. What we know is the person behind it is one of the original traitorous US Army Generals who was stationed on the moon base. He is also now in custody along with his assistant and they are being transported by the Galactic Police to the Mars base. There they will face trial and execution according to Galactic laws. Your compounds will receive the ultimate in safety monitoring.

"I would like to ask you, Jim, if we could move the farm to Morgan's 90 acres. Bev will still own her parents' property and could have it farmed by locals known to you. That way we are all more secure in one compound." Jim did not hesitate to say yes. He knew Bev would want her babies safe. "We will leave the barn and build an addition to Morgan's barn. That allows us to fortify it even more."

Morgan asked about the contractor and if they screened them better than the medical personnel. Olzing told him, while this was an unfortunate fluke, the answer is "Yes, this is the same crew that builds the embassies and quarters for all ambassadors galactically. We have a separate security crew who sweeps every day for listening devices and other more deadly things."

He further told them, "They have cracked the planetary defense mechanism that would help keep out the galactic trash that can come and go almost at will on planet Earth. For now all aliens are being stopped before they enter Earth's atmosphere and for those who elect not to stop, well, it is a fate they do not live to regret. Construction begins tomorrow. We will give you nightly updates in our review meeting. During the meeting is the time to make additions to the plan if you have any."

Morgan looked back at Marsha who had begun to stir. He tried to stand but still felt weak in his legs. Thar told both to sit tight; he wanted her to sleep a bit more so he could examine them for anything that could have been slipped to them unknowingly.

Jim looked frightened at his point and Morgan became visibly angry. His face was turning from pink to red; he was that angry.

They moved a chair over for Jim to sit next to Bev while they scanned Morgan. It took almost 20 minutes and Thar asked if they had anything to eat or drink in the last few hours. Both said coffee. Two security guards were dispatched to pick up the coffee and take it to the lab. "Also bring Bat and Emma Masterson to the lab right away." Morgan, shook his head, asking "Why?"

He told them they had discovered high levels of arsenic in his blood—life-threatening levels—and he was betting it would be in Jim's blood as well as Bat and Emma. Morgan demanded he check every one of the kids as well. Thar asked if the children could be scanned at their medical bay since it had 22 beds. Morgan agreed that would be fine.

"Okay, here it is, Morgan. You will need to be on the bed to clean your blood and repair your pancreas and liver. That will take three hours. Jim, we can't have you and, potentially, Bat and Emma waiting for Morgan to be done. I need you three at our lab at the same time. I don't make this request lightly. It is with the utmost urgency that I ask this." He radioed for a gurney to be brought to the lab with four guards.

He also requested four guards be dispatched to take Bat and Emma Masterson to the Nordic Medical Lab. He radioed to his lab to have the beds ready and that Dr. Tolsen was to be in charge of their care. They would also bring the children to that lab as well.

Morgan asked, once his bed was programmed, if they would scan Bev and Marsha for poisoning. Thar quickly agreed; he would scan them himself. Right now, they would be short staffed in the medical unit because of the children, Jim, Bat and Emma in their unit. He asked for one of the nurses to come to Dr. King's medical lab to assist him. As he was programming, he told them they could put two of the children in each bed as long as they laid still. Morgan looked at him skeptically and muttered, "You think that's going to happen?" He suggested they sedate them to get an accurate scan but Morgan vetoed that. Thar radioed those instructions to Dr. Tolsen.

The children had no issues except for Dorothy-Alice, who had an ear infection for which they gave her antibiotics. The rest remained in excellent health. "Bat, Jim and Emma have all been poisoned. They are all currently being treated," said Thar. "We also sent guards to check the one shop on the island that carried that particular brand of coffee. The shop was clean as were the other cans of that same coffee. So, we deduce everything happened here and was clearly planned."

"We have arrested the housekeeper who had access to the coffee. In addition, we currently have guards inspecting the entire pod for anything else harmful in any way. This admittedly revealed security holes which will be dealt with prior to your moving back home to your compound."

"After four years of nothing we became complacent. No excuses, we relaxed our security net. I apologize and you have my word this will never again happen on my watch," explained Olzing.

Thar interrupted, "Morgan, your blood pressure is up again. I think you need to consider taking regular medication for this. In the interim, let me give you some additional meds for that." He was clearly beside himself with embarrassment at what had happened. He felt the weight of it fall on his shoulders. He also felt responsible for the many mistakes that had created this situation in the beginning. Thar asked if he could please give him something to sleep for a little bit. Morgan just nodded his head yes, anything to stop reliving the events of four years ago and now this.

Morgan awakened with the lights low—just the beds and diagnostic screens illuminating the room. He looked around, then sat up. He saw two doctors around Marsha and two around Bev. He also noticed two guards in the lab and down the hall, and two more guards in the family pod. He swung his legs off the bed and stood. He still felt a little unsteady but walked over to Marsha's bed.

Thar saw Morgan as he approached. He greeted him but admonished that he should still be in bed. Morgan held onto the rails of Marsha's bed to steady himself, then asked how she was doing. Thar told him much better after the cardiologist had reset her pacemaker. However, there had been damage to the pacemaker from the poison given to her and Bev. They were prepping her to remove the old pacemaker and replace it with a new one with better functionality.

Morgan fought the feeling of nausea and dizziness. Thar could see he was on the verge of collapse and signaled for guards to help him back to bed. He walked alongside Morgan and told him he needed a few more hours of cell regeneration. Morgan protested, saying he wanted to be there for Marsha's surgery. Thar shook his head, telling Morgan he would just have to trust them on this because he was not well enough to stand nor think clearly, and did he really want to be the one who diverted their attention away from Marsha. Morgan's chin dropped to his chest, but he agreed to leave Marsha in their capable hands. Thar gave him sedation to sleep.

When Morgan next opened his eyes, the lights were so bright he had to squint to see. He threw back the covers and sat up rubbing his eyes. He saw Marsha sitting up. He couldn't run fast enough to get to her bedside. There, tried to calm himself as he sat on the bed next to her. She threw her arms around his neck and pulled him down on her. She gave him a heated kiss. Morgan readjusted the bed.

He pulled her gown down off her shoulders to see where they put him the new pacemaker. He could just see the outline so he felt around it.

Thar came over to the bed. He asked Morgan if he felt better. He told Thar he had just a little residual nausea. He pulled the med gun out, but Morgan declined any further meds.

Morgan asked about Marsha and what they had done. Thar explained the new pacemaker was far superior to the old one. However, it had pumped the poison through her body faster and she might have permanent damage to one of the kidneys, but they would know more tomorrow.

Thar then asked Marsha if she had any nausea or aches. She looked at him and then looked at Morgan. He grabbed her chin and locked eyes. "This is important, no kidding! It is imperative he knows exactly how you feel; that is why I told him that I still had nausea." With a look of resignation, she told them, "Okay, I feel like I have the flu and nausea. Thar told them, "Both of you can go to your quarters early this evening, though I want to keep you both through the day. I think that will help even your systems out. Now both of you in bed and resting."

"How is her arm looking?" Morgan asked. "The bone has almost regenerated, however, we will give it several more days in a cast."

Morgan next asked about Bev. Thar took in a deep breath and said, "She is far from out of the woods." Marsha jumped off the bed and ran to Bev. She yelled, "Damn it, Bev you fight! RIGHT NOW— FIGHT!"

She turned and asked where Aggie and Bitty were. "You go get them right this second or I will!" Morgan did not feel steady enough to go get her, so Thar guided her firmly back to the bed. As soon as she reached the bed, Morgan grabbed her arm and pulled her into the bed and Thar gave her a light dose of meds.

She turned and told him to stop giving her that stuff, she was sick of it. She attempted to get away from both of them, so they called security to give them the needed assistance getting her back into bed and put her back to sleep.

He reviewed the diagnostics and told Morgan she needed more regeneration time as well. Morgan nodded his head.

Morgan awakened feeling a great deal better. He sat up and could see Marsha was not in her bed. Thar came over to Morgan and asked how he felt. He told him he actually felt like a new man. Thar smiled and told him Marsha was already in the family pod with Jim, Bat, and Emma. "Before you go in, Marsha awoke screaming about how they killed Caci and began sobbing. Consider letting us help both of you with a block we can do for that deep pain. It will help your blood pressure and her suppressing everything. It doesn't remove the memory but blocks the pain message." Morgan looked at him and told him he would think it over.

Morgan next asked about Bev. Thar told him she had improved and perhaps if she remained stable for the next two days, they could awaken her.

As Morgan walked into the family pod, everyone there stood and hugged him. They were all glad to see each other. Morgan turned and asked how Dorothy-Alice's ear infection was. Thar told him she was fine. The chef came in and told them the family table was ready and all the children were more or less seated and ready. Marsha took both Morgan's and Jim's hands and walked into the dining room. They went around the table, kissing each child. Jim leaned over kissing Zoey just as Tig shot him with a rubber band. Jim yelled "Ouch!" He turned around to see Tig was trying to cover his mouth laughing. Morgan turned and knew exactly what happened. Jim stood next to Tig with his hand out not saying anything. Tig reached into his jean pockets and handed him about 10 rubber bands. Jim put them in his pocket and ruffed up Tig's hair. He continued on kissing each child. They all sat down.

On Bev's vacant chair was a picture of her drawn by Liam. Jim went back to Liam and thanked him for making a portrait of Bev so they would all be together. Aggie and Bitty came into the room. Aggie kissed Jim, Morgan, Marsha, Bat and Emma. Bitty followed right behind, kissing everyone as she went.

She stopped at Tig and gave him a high five. Jim said, "Apparently, Bitty is his partner in crime. I will remember that!" Morgan was very happy to have a cheerful dinner. It was good to have all the kids arguing, Tig playing pranks, Zoey crying, Bitty taking leftover food from the kids' plates. He was grateful for this moment of normality. His heart overflowed with joy. He asked Dorothy-Alice if her ear was better. She jumped up out of her chair, ran around the table and hugged him, saying "Daddy, I want you to look in my ear next time. You are softer." Morgan laughed and said, "You got it, princess!"

Morgan glanced up and half of the kids had finished their dinner and moved on to wrestling on the floor. Morgan, Jim, and Aggie got up, separated the kids and sat them back down. The biggest scrapper of them all was John. The way he moved and handled himself, they were sure he could land a tackle position on a football team. The five Nordic nannies came into the room and told the kids to line up. They ran and got into a line. Emma and Aggie went with them to get them ready for bed.

Marsha leaned on Morgan's shoulder and Morgan asked Jim how he was holding up? "Bev is doing better. I think I am going to go sit for a while with her. I have her Little Women book."

"Hold on," exclaimed Marsha. She ran and stopped the kids and brought them all back. "Let's go, everyone. We are all going to circle around her bed and sing her song." As they walked down the hall, they began to sing Bev's favorite song, "It is well, it is well with my soul."

They all stood for about five minutes singing to her. The nurses, doctors, guards, Morgan, Jim, Emma, and Marsha all choked up. Bat stayed back to speak with Thar. Morgan stepped back as Bat explained he wanted to know what time they planned on waking Bev in two days. "This wonderful chorus of angelic kids is what will awaken Bev."

Morgan couldn't hold back and became visibly emotional. He turned and walked to the empty bed and sat down. Thar went over to him and asked if he was okay. His blood pressure was up again, and he gave him a bit more medicine, telling him to come by tomorrow for a prescription to fill in their pharmacy.

Morgan shook his head and told him this past week had been overwhelming. Bat slapped him on the back and told him he was just getting old. "Buck up!" Morgan laughed as Bat walked back over to the group.

Thar then asked how he was really doing. He looked up and said if it weren't for Marsha, he would be in his bed another day. Thar told him he couldn't let that be what drove his common sense. "I feel another day for you would be good. You carry the weight of all this on yourself. It is delaying your healing." He walked away and got Jim who held his three-year-old twins, Rue and Belle.

Thar talked to him as they returned to Morgan. He asked Thar to hold the kids, then sat down next to Morgan. Jim told him to get back in his damned bed right now! Morgan admonished him not to use that language in front of the kids. "Let them finish singing to Bev."

Morgan looked at Jim and said, "Marsha has been aroused to a point I have never before seen. She will jump me in this bed if I don't get to our bedroom." Jim laughed and exclaimed, "AW, POOR THING!"

Thar heard, came over and told them he could make that go away for two days with a medication they gave their pilots when they were on two-day missions. "They never have a sexual urge during that time."

Jim stood, taking the kids back from him and told him to just shoot her with it and not to ask. "Tell her it is for blood pressure. I will tell her Morgan needs to stay one more day in quiet, and that Zoey has asked to sleep with her tonight. That should take care of that."

Morgan laughed and remarked, "Damn, you're good." Jim told Morgan he would make sure Zoey and maybe Dorothy-Alice were in bed with her all snuggled up. "Then I will be back to sit with Bev and check on you."

Morgan thanked him for taking care of the kids and Marsha. Thar picked up his med gun and loaded it, approaching Marsha who held Gage, her three-year-old. He put the med gun on her arm. She looked over to him, her eyes narrowed and lips pursed, so he put the injector in his pocket.

"This was just something for anxiety. Who is this little one?" He reached for Gage's hand as Marsha said, "His name is Gage; he is my youngest. However, next time you must me before you shoot me! I might just surprise you and say yes!"

He looked at her and apologized, then asked if he could give her just one more medication. She stuck out her arm. This time it was the anxiety meds for when Jim told her Morgan was staying one more night and needed quiet. He went on to let her know that Zoey and Dorothy-Alice, especially with her earache, wanted to sleep with her tonight. She surprised Jim and said, "Of course; my baby is sick."

Jim then gave her the news Morgan needed to stay one more day on the med bed. She looked at him sitting on the bed, so Jim jumped in, "He has to have complete quiet tonight for a cellular level healing he desperately needs. Go give him a kiss and tell him goodnight." She walked over to the bed and flashed him, saying, "Meow. Tomorrow, my precious. Tonight, you stay on the bed and sleep, baby. But tomorrow you will be very busy, meow." Morgan laughed as he gave Thar a questioning glance.

Jim walked over and told Marsha, "I forgot to give you this so you do not catch what Dorothy-Alice has, okay? Then I am going to go and get Zoey and Dorothy-Alice ready for bed so we can have TV snuggle time. I'm thinking it is a Mr. Rogers kinda evening." She turned as the rest of the kids, Bat, Emma, and Jim trooped out. Finally, Morgan laid down and Thar lightly medicated him. He fell asleep almost instantly.

Thar pulled up the diagnostic and could see his serotonin levels were way off. He still found arsenic in his liver, so he cycled that for repair. In addition, he saw he was dehydrated rather severely. He would ask Jim to start an IV for hydration, and that would also help flush the rest of the poison out of his system.

Jim walked back into the lab and across the room to Morgan's bed and began reading information from the diagnostic screens. He stopped on one screen, walked over and got out an IV kit, and retrieved a bag of fluids from the fridge. He sat down on the stool beside the bed and started his IV. He thought to himself that Morgan had rivers for veins and he wished Bev had those veins.

After he completed that task, he went back to the screens and saw his liver was still inflamed and had a good amount of arsenic left in it, but could see repair was underway. He gave meds to optimize his serotonin levels.

Suddenly, he heard a commotion behind him and turned to see Aggie carrying Bitty. She laid her on the bed mat as Thar came running through the door. He had seen her running with Bitty down the hallway to the lab. He instructed the lights to brighten. Jim had already asked the bed to program for a female Sasquatch. Jim spoke excitedly, asking what had happened. Aggie told them Bitty had just grabbed her stomach and fallen to the floor.

Thar flipped through the various screens like they were on fire. He then radioed for Dr. Tolsen and Dr. Cay to report immediately to Dr. King's medical bay. Both came on a dead run along with two other physicians, all of whom had Sasquatch experience. Dr. Cay told them she was pregnant and administered some medications. Jim felt like he might faint. Aggie roared her displeasure, and Jim took her by the arm, leading her away from the bed, and asked her if Bitty had been out by herself at any time.

Aggie thought for a second, then responded that yes, she did go out into the hills all the time. "She goes to the mountains and the woods." Dr. Cay turned to Thar asking if they had Sasquatch here. He responded, "Yes, of course." He looked puzzled and then asked if she had been in the woods or surrounding mountains by herself. Aggie nodded her head. Jim inhaled deep, swallowing hard, choking back tears.

Dr. Cay interrupted their conversation to say that she was in labor. Jim said, "Well, that explains why she was eating everyone's leftover food!"

"Aggie, now is not the time to be angry with her. Now is the time to give her all the love you can and support her through this. She has never known pain like she is about to experience. Do you think she knows she is pregnant?" Aggie shook her head no. "She has never asked for anything since four years ago."

"I need you to go get Emma and bring her here so she can explain, lovingly and tactfully, what is happening to her. I just know I can't be the one to do that," admitted Jim. "The father in me really wants to yell at her, but the person she really needs is Morgan." He asked Thar to awaken him immediately. Thar went to Morgan's bed and gave him a light nudge to awaken him.

Morgan opened his eyes and grumbled, "Nope, call me in the morning." Then, he saw there was something major going on with all the docs in the room and Bitty on the table. He sat up and asked what in the world was going on. Jim gave him the news that Bitty was in labor.

Morgan screamed, "Labor?" Thar gave him the short version as he unhooked the IV and went to Bitty. Morgan sat next to her, leaned over and kissed her forehead. She opened her eyes. He stroked her face, brushing the hair out of her eyes. He told her he was right by her side. "It appears you are having a baby, young lady." Her eyes got big, and it was obvious she had no idea. Morgan asked who the father was so they could let them know.

She put her arms around his neck and said, "Another evil man with red hair followed me while I was walking in the woods. He used a taser to stun me and he did bad things to me." Emma arrived in time to hear what she said and immediately elbowed everyone else out of the way, even making Morgan move.

She grabbed ahold of Bitty's arm and told her it was big girl time. "But all of us are here with you and we will help you. Are you in pain? Bitty shook her head no.

Emma said, "That is a good thing. Grandma is here and I will help you every step through this, and your Dad and Uncle Jim are here for you as well."

She glanced at Jim, mumbling, "Don't you need to start an IV or something like that?" Jim laughed and nodded his head as he turned to get the kit. Jim then sat on the other side of the bed and said, "Remember, this is Bitty the Brave!"

She nodded her head and he asked, "May I do this?" Unsure what he was asking, she again nodded her head. The other doctors motioned for Morgan to look at the diagnostic screen. The fetus was that of a deformed human.

Morgan turned and rushed to the sink, where he promptly and violently vomited. Jim stood and glanced at the screen. He sat back down and got himself under control so he could get the line started. Morgan washed his face as the others prepared to take the fetus. Thankfully, it was not alive and was a spontaneous miscarriage. They told Morgan and Jim what they needed to do. They would like to put her to sleep, intubate her and keep her under for an entire day to regenerate the uterine wall.

Morgan told them he and Jim would do it without all that. "Give her light sedation but let me tell her first. Emma and Aggie will help her." Morgan sat down opposite Emma. He told Bitty how brave she was to have told him the truth. "That evil man caused you to have a bad thing inside you that Uncle Jim and Daddy need to take out." All the Nordic doctors shot looks at each other when he called himself her daddy.

"Can you be brave? Remember four years ago what those evil men did to you? Remember we were able to fix that for you and for Aggie, too. Now, we need to do the same thing. Are you okay with us fixing you right now so we can make the pain go away?"

She roared in response and instantly he knew that she was having a contraction. Dr. Cay stepped forward and gave her pain meds. "Dr. Cay here is helping us today. Is that okay?" She looked at Dr. Cay who was smiling warmly at her. She smiled back and nodded yes.

Morgan and Jim stood to gown up while Thar asked for sterilization and Emma to go sit with Bev. Bitty roared again, and they could all feel the vibration from this roar. Dr. Cay medicated her so she would sleep. Jim asked the bed to go to the vaginal exam position. Jim decided to take the lead and directed the bed to expand the area and dilate her cervix.

Morgan handed him the surgical tool to grab the hideously malformed fetus. Morgan laid it in the tray and Dr. Cay quickly covered it, as Jim scraped the wall of the uterus, then allowed the cervix to close. Dr. Cay then input the settings for repair of the uterus, with rebalancing of Sasquatch hormones to dry up her milk ducts.

Thar had already notified Olzing who was waiting for them to finish. Dr. Cay topped off her medication to help her sleep through the night.

Jim and Morgan stepped back to remove their gowns and gloves. Dr. Cay approached them, asking if it would be okay to incinerate this monster. Morgan began to cry, nodding his head yes. Morgan then returned to his bed and Jim swung his legs up onto it. Thar asked if he'd like some medication to sleep as Jim reattached the IV. Jim directed the bed to bring the temperature up 15 degrees, then retrieved a warm blanket to cover him.

Morgan awoke the next morning to the sound of diagnostic screens being paged through and saw Jim standing over him. Jim started with, "Shut up and lay down." But Morgan replied, "Well, Dr. Snip-Snip is in a snit-snit today!" Jim laughed and then looked down at Morgan, who asked, "Ok, let's have it, Dr. Snip-Snip! How am I this morning?"

"You, my friend, need another entire day on this bed! They must have hit you with the largest dose possible. Maybe they wanted to shut you up permanently if you know what I mean. Maybe they're afraid you know something and maybe told me," teased Jim. "So let's have it; what are you holding out on me?"

Morgan didn't say anything, but rolled his eyes up to look at the ceiling. Jim sat on the bed. "What is bothering you? Come on, talk to me! Why in the hell are you keeping everything bottled up!"

"I feel like this is all my fault from splicing the hornet queen. That is what started this and now they are once again after my family. I should leave so that you guys are safe." Jim responded with sarcasm like Morgan would do, "Sorry you're stuck with all of us, including that baseball team you call your children and your horny wife!" Morgan looked to him and admitted he had a point there. "But really, Jim, I can't go on carrying this guilt with y'all being in constant danger. It is too much, Jim! I couldn't redo four years ago. Bitty getting raped again and all this! It's a heavy burden to carry. I am feeling like four years ago is starting all over! This is bad and, yes, I can't believe it happened to Bitty yet again!"

Jim retorted, "But we need to face things and tackle them one by one. Thar told me he can take the painful part of that memory away. He can't erase the memory, of course, but he can do something about the pain of it. Let him do it!"

"You lead all of us, Morgan. We need you! Hell, according to Merlin, even the Earth needs you! So let's get by everything that needs doing now, then hopefully, we can talk Marsha into this.

We can start by letting Thar dial her back on her female urges for the present. You need to be busy. You and I can be working through this star supernova while we are waiting for the completion of the compound. Please, Morgan, I would not ask if I did not believe this to be the correct path."

Thar approached the bed, looked at Morgan, then looked at the screen. He said two words, "BLOOD PRESSURE!" Morgan glanced up at him and said, "Okay, let's do it." Jim smiled and nodded. He looked back at Morgan and said, "One more day on the bed; agreed?"

Morgan reluctantly nodded. "I am giving you something for your blood pressure, some anxiety meds, and I need you to be asleep to take care of that pain; do you agree with that?" Morgan sighed, but nodded for him to proceed.

When Morgan next awakened and opened his eyes, Marsha was lying beside him, running her fingers through his hair. He wrapped his arms around her and realized her cast was gone. He told her he was happy to wake and find her in his arms. "How is your arm, baby?" asked Morgan. She told him it was fine and how great it was to lie next to him. Jim walked over and bluntly told Marsha to scram. He pulled her by her non-injured arm and then smacked her butt. She waved, telling Morgan she would be by later.

"Well that was uneventful! She did not try to jump my bones or undress me!" Jim laughed and told him, "She put up no argument. She let us give her the pain treatment and we medicated her for the other to dial her down for two weeks. That should give you time to catch your breath." He went on to ask how he was feeling.

Morgan replied he was much better. He sat up and swung his legs over the side. "I vote for a shower if you truly think Marsha will behave—and we all can have a cup of non-poisonous coffee!"

"I do feel you are safe for now from Little Miss Tiger Marsha."

"How is Bitty?" Jim lowered his head and replied that she had been in the corner facing the wall, not eating or drinking. Morgan said we will fix that. "I feel like I could take on the world again."

Jim handed him two bottles of medication. "To remain that way, you will need to take one of each once a day. And don't worry, I am on the same prescriptions. Go take your shower and I will be right in. Tonight, we wake Bev." Morgan's face brightened up; he got sparkles in his eyes and a smile of pure happiness crossed his face. He slapped Jim on the back and thanked him. Morgan walked down the hall and into his bedroom to shower and change clothes.

Marsha never entered but had coffee waiting for him when he came out. Morgan walked around the sofa and Marsha handed him his coffee. She told him he looked so good. She kissed him, then sipped her coffee and looked into Morgan's eyes, "My pain is gone, Morgan. It feels so good. I forgot what life felt like until now." Both put down their coffee cups and embraced. He told her his pain was gone as well. She told him that she wanted to be a good wife again. She and the kids needed him, and she whispered, "And you tell me when you're ready and I will be there for you in that way. I will let you tell me." He kissed her so passionately it took her breath away. She pulled back and asked if her tonsils were still in place. He laughed and picked up his cup.

Jim came around and sat next to them with his coffee. He smiled and asked how the King family was doing. He could tell they were both happy. That aura of perpetual tragedy was gone. Both of their eyes sparkled, almost dancing. Marsha looked up at Jim and thanked him for lifting the veil of sadness from Morgan and her. "I am so happy! I feel like I don't deserve this man! But—not to change the subject or anything—I hear we are going to Paris! I am so excited, and I plan on spending an obscene amount of money for a dress and in the boutiques. Thar fixed me up on that end of things too."

Jim asked if she thought it worked. She said, "Of course! I feel so good, virtually like I am a teenager again!" Morgan began to tear up. Jim leaned over and Morgan hugged him. "I am just overjoyed, that's all. My shadow of sadness is gone, and I feel like the old me. I may still need to find the right balance with the meds but I feel like I am almost there."

Jim slapped his leg and said it was like a fresh start for all of them. "Oh, by the way, since I heard Dorothy-Alice say she only wanted you to look in her ear, she needs a look-see. She keeps pulling on her left ear now, but she would not let Uncle Jim look." Morgan asked Marsha to go get her and bring his black bag in so he could examine her ear.

Jim said, "I am happy for all of us. The veil is finally gone. Did Marsha behave?" Morgan laughed and said, "Yes, however, I gave her the most passionate kiss as a test, and after the kiss she went right back to drinking her coffee and told me when I was ready, she would be there."

Jim's mouth dropped. "Well, I didn't think we dialed her that far back! Jeez, sorry buddy."

"It is all good, something tells me I only need to touch her in her special place, and she will still turn into a wild child!"

Jim moaned, "You have the best sex life, ever!"

"I love her so much and, honestly, sometimes it is embarrassing but then I take inventory of who else would love a teddy bear like me and love every inch of me." Both chuckled.

Dorothy-Alice ran in yelling "Daddy, Daddy!" Morgan enveloped her in his arms. He kissed her and asked how daddy's princess was. She said, "My ear hurts!"

Morgan made a sad face and told her to let Daddy look. He looked and then said, "Ewwww. Yuck! Ok, let's get you some medicine so that goes away. Ok, now, how is that?"

She asked if she got ice cream for being brave. He told her that, no, she just had her dinner, and he knew she had already had her dessert. He gave her a pat on the bottom and told her to go play. He sat back on the sofa and smiled. He said, "I love kids. I never thought I would, but I could have 20 and be happy." Jim made an offhand observation that he was crazy, and both laughed.

Jim then asked if he was ready to get started on finding the codes tomorrow. He said absolutely. Jim told him he would get Dorothy-Alice's prescription and for him to get in bed and rest the remainder of the evening. Both stood and Jim went back to the lab and Morgan went into his bedroom. Marsha was already in bed watching TV. Morgan asked about what she was watching. She said, "You are stripping, if you are ready." He took his clothes off and slipped under the cover to find her with no clothes on. She kissed him and asked how she could pleasure him. He kissed her and told her she knew what to do. Afterward, he told her he needed to settle himself down since he could feel his blood pressure was high. She rolled up under his arm and snuggled. He closed his eyes and held her tight. He inhaled deeply, telling her he loved her smell. She closed her eyes and said goodnight. Both fell asleep.

About 4:00 a.m. Morgan heard the door open. He sat up and saw it was Bitty. She didn't ask, she just crawled into bed with them. Marsha snuggled close while Morgan slipped on his boxers and a tee shirt, then went out for coffee. Jim saw him from the hall and came into the lab. "You okay?" he asked. Morgan told him yes, but Bitty had just gotten into their bed.

"She just opened the door and crawled into bed. Marsha cuddled right up to her." Jim told him they needed to talk to her tomorrow, then looked down and told Morgan he was bleeding.

Morgan looked and Jim told him to come back to the med bed. He directed the bed to repair the skin, after which the medical bed announced three minutes to completion of repair.

As he sat there Jim noticed the bed had repaired his snip-snip work. "Um, you know the snip-snip we did, well, the bed has reversed it. Is there any way Marsha could get pregnant? Do you know her cycle?" Morgan looked like he was going to faint; all color left his face. Jim told him to lie down.

Morgan told him, "No, this is not funny, no, no, this has to be a joke." He sat back up and said they would have to check it tomorrow. "Hear me! We check." He took in a deep breath and blew it out.

Then jumped off the bed and headed back to his bedroom. He laid against Bitty and pet the fur on her back until he fell asleep.

He awakened at 8:00 AM. Marsha was already up, as was Bitty. He showered and could see traces of blood on the sheets. He dressed and walked out in the family pod area. Everyone was up and having tea or coffee. There were bagels and cream cheese on the bar as well as fruit. Morgan grabbed a banana and a cup of coffee. He sat down next to Marsha and smiled. He leaned in and kissed her, telling her good morning. She smiled warmly and put her hand on his thigh. Morgan spoke softly to Marsha; however, Jim sat next to them and asked when her period was due. She said, "Not for two weeks."

Morgan knew exactly what that meant as did Jim. She looked up at Morgan and then to Jim, and she knew from their faces. She put down her tea and walked back into the lab. Jim and Morgan followed. Tears ran down her face as she turned to both. "Tell me that the bed did not fix your vasectomy."

Jim lowered his head and told her he wished he could tell her that, and Morgan asked her to get on the table. She didn't argue but got up on it and laid down. Thar watched, but had no idea what was going on. He approached and Morgan asked how soon the bed could tell if they were pregnant. Thar said, "Within four hours of conception." Thar pulled up the screen and told them, "Yep, and oh look—twins!"

Morgan began to sway. The two security guards grabbed him and laid him down on the other bed mat. Thar went to him and told him his blood pressure was still too high. "Twins," he remarked, and said, "Yes, looks like two girls." Morgan threw up on the floor. Jim gave him meds for nausea and some to Marsha as well.

Marsha cried hysterically at this news. She looked at Morgan and stopped, wiped her eyes, and stood. She crossed the room over to Morgan and told him it was meant to be, and they would love both with their whole beings. "You said girls, great! Iris and Idell." Morgan sat up and Marsha told him, "No worries, babe, we got this. That chick who has 19 kids and counting has nothing on us." She then kissed him and told him she was happy. "Zoey and Dorothy-Alice will be in love with two new sisters. And oh, babe! I will look fat in my gown in Paris. Will you still take me without a smoking hot body?"

Everyone laughed and Morgan pulled her to him, saying, "You bet, my little momma!"

Marsha asked if he was mad or upset, and he replied that no, he was as happy as if it were his first. He already loved Iris and Idell.

He looked back at Jim and told him he was ready today for a snip-snip again! Jim laughed and told him to get up on the bed. Thar was already rolling the surgical machine over and directing it to set up for sterilization.

Jim told Marsha he would be along this afternoon before they woke Bev. "And absolutely no, none, nada sex. Not even manual! Got it, Chicky?"

She told him yes and that he was cut off for two days. Jim looked and said, "Five days, you hear me, Missy?" She told him, of course, you got it! She turned back around and told Jim to make sure Morgan knew to keep his hands off the merchandise for five days.

Jim turned to Marsha and told her no more rough stuff or hours' long sex. If she needed help with that, he could give her medication to get her through the urges.

"This is so you don't lose Iris and Idell. You are still medically fragile and the roughness with extended hours of sex can cause a spontaneous abortion." She looked horrified and started to tear up. She told him he was to give her that shot right now. "I will not lose my babies!" He doubled up on what they had given her previously. She smiled and skipped down the hallway yelling, "Guess what everyone, I am prego with twins! They are girls, Iris and Idell." It was funny to watch, and Jim turned around shaking his head.

Morgan smiled as he lay on the bed. "We will have a softball fast pitch team!"

"You are amazing Morgan! And better thee than me as they say," said Jim.

Later, Morgan awoke and tried to sit up. Jim pushed him back down. "Time out! Lay back down for another hour. The bed is repairing your incision so you won't be in pain when you get up." He settled back down, but said with a smile, "Twins, Iris and Idell. Isn't that awesome?"

Jim shook his head and asked if he had lost count. That made 11 kids, "Let's see Morgan-Barkley, Dorothy-Alice, Zoey, Liam, Tig, Wyatt, Emmi, Philip, Gage and now Iris and Idell and, if we throw in Bitty, yup, that's 12!"

"That sounds like music to my ears!" said Morgan. Thar came over and gave him light pain and anti-anxiety meds. He asked Morgan if he wanted them to put in another bedroom addition with a Jack and Jill bathroom. "We could have Iris and Idell together and Dorothy-Alice and Emmi together, and they can share the Jack and Jill bathroom."

He continued, "Tig and Gage together and Wyatt with Morgan-Barkley. They share a Jack and Jill bathroom, then Liam and an empty bed together. We do an extra bedroom for overnight stays with friends. Each pair shares a Jack and Jill bathroom." He thought that was perfect for the family. "We keep babies with us in our room for the first three months in bassinets," said Morgan.

Jim replied, "You know, that is a great idea. Rue and Belle together and El gets a room to herself, and they share a Jack and Jill bathroom. Dallas and Finch together, with John by himself and they share a bathroom."

Morgan snapped back, "You have room for another boy and girl!"

Jim laughed and said, "I guess so." Thar told them this is the same set up for our families. "Most Nordics have eight to 10 kids like Morgan." Morgan sat up on his elbows and said, "See,

Jim, you need to get busy!" He pushed Morgan's face and told him to lay down as they all laughed.

Morgan sat up again and asked Thar if he had a family. Thar told them yes, two children. Morgan looked at Jim with his eyebrows raised. Jim knew exactly what to ask. "Thar, I have a request for an addition. You build a house for your family in the compound." Thar was stunned. He asked if they were sure about that. Morgan asked how often he was able to see his family.

Thar looked down and said, "Every three years." Jim was astounded and asked him to repeat what he said. Thar responded with, "That is unfortunately the way it is." Morgan now sat all the way up and turned with his legs and feet off the bed.

"Now, we will not take no for an answer. You are taking care of our family, so we will take care of yours! You will have them come to the compound and move in with the rest of us. What are your wife's and kids' names?" asked Morgan.

Thar said, "I will only tell you when you are lying down again in that bed!" Morgan quickly laid down. "My wife's name is Shri and my daughter is Lang. She is six, and my son is Vaughn. He is nine. Shri is a chemistry professor."

Jim smiled and said, "Outstanding! We got us a teacher!"

"By the way, I did forget to mention that there will be another house built in the compound for a couple with two kids that you know." Jim and Morgan both looked puzzled. Thar asked if they could guess. Morgan threw up his arms and said, "I couldn't begin to guess."

Jim was in deep thought and said nothing for a minute. Then he turned and looked at Thar and said, "I hope I am correct: Kron and Virg with Mottice and Grissom."

Morgan said, "Wow, Jim! Excellent! Virg builds and Kron should be finished with medical school."

Thar smiled and said, "Excellent deduction, and you are correct."

Morgan laid back and said, "Family—I am so excited for us to be all together." His smile turned to a concerned look as he turned to Thar and said "Bitty. We have to do the pain thing for her."

Thar smiled and told them Dr. Cay was doing that as they spoke. It had to be a special bed for her that could strap her down because that process for a Sasquatch is long and a bit difficult.

Morgan attempted to sit back up, but Thar pushed him down, telling him Aggie and Emma were with her. "They could not get her to leave the corner in the family pod and she had taken to putting a blanket over her head. She would not eat or drink anything and it became critical. Even Jim could not reason with her. So they had sedated her and took her for treatment. "She, like you, Morgan, will be much better now," said Thar.

3

Plans For The Farm

Morgan lay in the Medical Bay with a smile as he thought through everything now that he could process it all without the intense guilt and pain. He thought through the events and could logically put it all together and realize his mistakes, and then was able to say to himself, "Let's move forward. This is a new beginning for all of us."

Jim came over to his bed, "You've been smiling this entire time; you okay?"

Morgan said, "I'm happy for a new beginning and the family being all together. I am excited about this challenge and the race to save the Earth. It will be the most important thing we could ever do, Jim."

"Ok, you're outta here. Be back in an hour with the kids in tow. Emma and Aggie will not be done with Bitty until tomorrow; however, Emma will slip away to be here for Bev."

Morgan jumped off the bed. Jim caught him by the arm and warned, "Again, no sex for five days and easy going even then! Do not let passion take you to an unsafe place for Marsha—or for you!" Morgan nodded, not saying anything, and walked into the family pod where the kids were running wild. They ran to him surrounding him. Morgan was so happy tears welled up in his eyes. Marsha came and put her arm around his waist as the kids were playing ring around the rosy with them.

Tig was chasing everyone he could find with a frog. The girls were not having it and screamed. Morgan looked at Marsha and said, "I am so happy."

Morgan reached out and snagged Tig by his shirt as he attempted to run by him chasing Emmi, who was crying. Tig said, "AW, DAD!" Morgan stood with his hand out and Tig handed the unfortunate amphibian to him. Morgan shook his head looking at the frog, then looked at Marsha with a wry grin, and said, "That's my boy!"

She laughed, telling him to get that thing away from her.

Phillip approached Morgan and tugged on his shirt and asked, "Uncle Morgan, can we get a dog? I want a big dog and name him Thor." He was the first of the children to ask for a pet. Morgan squatted down to his level and asked who would take care of Thor? "Me and Wyatt. Come on, Uncle Morgan! When we get home, please? We will brush him and give him food and water and play with him—say yes!"

"What kind of dog are we talking about here, Phillip?"

"I want a big black lab. We studied about dogs this week and the book said labs are the best dogs for big families. Come on, give a guy a break."

Marsha burst out laughing. "You and Wyatt can have your big black lab. Just as soon as we get home, we will run down to the animal shelter and find us one. And how about we get a small dog for the girls?"

Phillip said, "Well, okay, but they have to feed their own dog." Morgan laughed. He asked Phillip if he liked animals.

"Oh, I want to be a veterinarian. I would love to have a Nordic pony; did you know they can tolt?" Morgan looked surprised and said, "No, I never knew that."

"Can we take one home with us so we can all share?"

"Ok, that sounds like a plan. Will you take the responsibility for the pony and its care?"

Phillip grinned and said, "I would not ask if I did not intend to be responsible." Morgan glanced up at Marsha and mouthed, "It's a mini me!"

He looked back down at Phillip and agreed, "Yes, of course. However, over the next few weeks, I need you to read up and study about the proper care of a pony and dog, and understand everything you can."

Phillip threw his arms around him and thanked him, giving him a kiss. Morgan told him to go wash up so they could go see Bev. Phillip stopped and turned around, and said, "Emmi will not ask, but she wants a bunny." Morgan murmured, "That's good to know! Now scram and wash up."

Marsha added, "We better put in an additional request to build some rabbit hutches and four pony stalls. And Emmi also wants a bird for our family room to make pretty music. Guess she is our girly girl."

"One pony would be run to death with our 10 kids, Jim's six, plus two of Bat's. And just what the heck is a tolt?" asked Marsha.

"Have not the foggiest," mused Morgan, "I will leave that up to you to find out. Go find four well trained ponies for us to take back with us as well as four rabbits. Oh, and all the equipment they will need.

"We will take Phillip, Wyatt and Finch to the local animal shelter to find a dog, apparently named Thor," said Morgan.

"I am going to make up a work schedule for the kids over the next couple weeks. They can begin while they are here getting into the swing of things," explained Marsha. Morgan turned to Marsha and gave her a kiss telling her she was the best Mom ever.

"Oh, and last thing, I will be teaching a twice-a-week gym class. So it would help to have hoops inside the barn for basketball practice. I'd like a balance beam and rings for gymnastics, of course with mats. Also six exercycles and four rowers, four gliders and four treadmills.

"Wow, that is great, Marsha!" He pulled her to him, but she just pushed him away. "Hands off the merchandise for five full days, got It?" Morgan laughed and went to check on the kids.

He was stopped by Liam who explained that in the attic he would need a telescope so he could keep watch out for that star that was supposed to go supernova. Morgan laughed and said, "You got it." He was happy the kids were excited to go home again and wanted to be part of the planning process.

Marsha picked up her tablet and added ponies and bunnies to go see and put in the request to Olzing on the additions, and guards to go with her when picking out ponies and bunnies with the equipment.

She also made a note for Morgan to take Dorothy-Alice and El with the boys to pick out three barn cats. In addition, she made a note to ask Bev about chickens, as well as guinea hens and peacocks to keep the snakes away. She looked for a dress for Paris that was a looser style. She heard the kids all coming into the room. As usual John was pulling Emmi's hair and Tig was flying airplanes at Gage who thought that was big fun. The Nordic women took Tig's hand and took the paper airplanes away. Morgan heard him say, "Jeez, give a guy break! Can't I have any fun?" He laughed.

The nanny snapped her fingers and John immediately stopped picking on Emmi. The Nordic women got them in two rows and asked them if they were ready to go sing to Bev. Liam raised his hand and asked if they should pray first. Morgan put his arm around Marsha's waist as they listened to Liam pray with his childlike purity. Marsha smiled as they all joined in for the "Amen."

The lead teacher had a beautiful voice and soon all the children sang "It is well with my soul." They sang the first verse and repeated the chorus while El and Dallas sang the first verse again and they all joined in for one round of the chorus with El and Dallas singing the first verse.

Bev opened her eyes to what sounded like a host of angels singing to her. She recognized El and Dallas' voices. When she looked, she saw she was circled by all the children, Morgan, Marsha, Jim, Bat, Emma and all the doctors singing. Jim walked over and sat on the bed beside her. Both were crying. It was a sight to behold. Soon El, Dallas, Finch, John and Emma paced Rue and Belle on the bed. They all embraced her with Rue climbing up to her face kissing her and holding her face.

When Bev managed to compose herself, she thanked everyone and told them how grateful she was for each and every one of them. Jim held on to her, but Rue would not let go of Bev's face. Emma picked up Rue and handed her over to one of the teachers. She told Bev how much she loved her and gave her a hug and a kiss. She grabbed Belle who was pulling Finch's hair and hitting him. Emma told her, "Let's go you little tigress!" The Nordics took all the children back to the play pod.

Marsha went right to Bev, saying that was the most amazing thing she had ever heard or seen. Morgan asked how she felt. "I am blessed."

"Yeah, but the question still is, 'how do you feel?' You need to stop hanging out with Marsha."

Jim turned to her, and Thar started paging through the diagnostic screens. He said, "We are going to break up this party. She has had all the fun she can handle for now."

Morgan took her hand and asked again how she really felt. She smiled, "Tired and winded."

Thar queued right in on that comment. Jim stood flipping through screens. Morgan asked if there was anything else she would like to tell them. "Did I lose the baby?" Jim looked at her and said, "I never pulled up that screen. It never crossed my mind."

Morgan laughed and said, "It crossed mine and NO! She is SAFE AND SOUND!"

"How far along?" asked Jim. Thar told him she was in the second trimester, probably five months." He said, "You're not even showing!"

"I love a husband that is blind," said Marsha, slapping Jim on the back. Bev laid back, Thar gave her a light sedative and told her to sleep now. Morgan and Marsha left. Jim sat with Bev for over an hour. Thar came back and told him he would like her to sleep as much as she could, if possible, for the rest of the day," and told him to go be with the family.

Morgan had his tablet and sat with Jim when he came back into the pod. "Okay, tomorrow we start, buddy. No more time to waste!"

"I found a picture of the plates of the presidential china and will look over them. You find out what you can about that star, the supernova and all planets that will be in that shockwave besides us; is that ok?" asked Morgan.

He nodded his head yes. Then he looked at Morgan and asked why he had said nothing about her being pregnant. He responded with "I assumed you knew, and I didn't want to bring it up. It's a girl and my twins are girls. We officially have enough for a girls' softball team now." Both laughed.

"Everyone gets a complete physical from Thar and staff before we leave, including all the kids."

Morgan told him, "Yeah, good luck with Dorothy-Alice, she lets no one touch her but Daddy. Well, she will just have to settle for Daddy holding her. We need objective opinions, including ours. Whatever meds are prescribed, we will take them willingly my friend."

"So you are accusing me of turning into a Marsha?" Jim slapped his shoulder as he laughed.

"Oh, speaking of Marsha, you have the med mix perfect, she pushed me away and told me hands off the merchandise for five days. I had to laugh. I would like to keep her at this level for the remainder of the pregnancy, agreed?" Morgan said.

"Most definitely. Tell her to saunter in here once a week for a checkup. And, please, keep her subdued!"

"Now, back to the project. That will require me to go to DC to actually hold the plates and check for signs and clues that are not obvious in the photographs. I want to see them through the entire spectrum of light."

Jim told him, "Just by looking at Washington's plate says a lot. Let's see… Gold as the number one element in Alchemy. The cyclical snake, 15 gold points on that starburst which is telling all by itself … and the 15 colonies."

"I bet you there is more to that plate than meets the eye," mused Jim.

Morgan told him that the Rutherford Hayes Ornament interested him, "The sleigh doesn't touch the snow but looks like it is flying. The back horse's hooves do not touch the ground either. I can't wait to see that in person. I think I should get you clearance so that we can go together. You see things I don't and vice versa."

"Two heads together are better than one. Merlin told us we would recognize the codes. Certain things will catch our eyes. Remember it has to go in the proper sequence." Jim went on to explain that Merlin had mentioned the number 12 at least six times. "Let's attack that. As we list events with the number 12, they may give us a focus as we look at the White House china. Let's work on that tomorrow."

Jim explained to Morgan that he would like to also run him on the bed to make sure we have your levels right. "Let's do that first thing in the morning. How about we start at 7:00 AM? I'll have breakfast ready for us. I would also like us both to increase our protein intake for the next couple of weeks to boost our immunities."

"I am adding elderberries along with oranges and bananas. Same goes for the kids' diets."

"Okay, boss, whatever you say! Really, this is to make us look svelte in our tuxedos for Paris, right? We will outshine the girls with our new svelte figures," said Morgan.

Jim lowered his head, shaking it back and forth. "That wife of yours needs to tone down her hot little numbers. Folks will be seeing her and Bev as mothers who are pregnant. So fashion should be in accordance with that!"

"Uh, Jim, just who is going to tell her that? Sure as hell not gonna be me, buddy! That job is all yours!"

He laughed, "Morgan, just let me dream, okay? Let's just hope that what Thar did works for her. I would like to test it before we go, so he can tweak it if necessary. We can test it when we go to the animal shelter to pick out Thor, our new dog and the three barn cats."

Jim cocked his head half smiling and asked who would be going on that outing. "Marsha, you, Bev and me with Wyatt, Finch, Phillip, Dorothy-Alice and El. We're gonna need a big security contingent, I know, and Thar and one other of the Nordic doctors, just in case."

"Good plan, I just am cautiously optimistic, Morgan. "We'll have one car for the kids, a new dog, hopefully a lab mix we name Thor, a small dog for the girls, three barn cats and if you guys want a dog, too?" Morgan explained.

"We are bringing back four Nordic ponies and four bunnies to get us started. Marsha is leaving the chickens, guinea hens and peacocks to Bev."

Jim laughed and said, "You are gonna love farming!"

Morgan laughed back, "Okay, okay, farmer guy! The kids have a SUV, You, me, Marsha, Bev and a security guard driving us in an SUV, then an SUV with security in front and one behind with a gurney in case anyone gets into any difficulty. We stock it before we leave. Good plan."

"Do you realize our every outing will require this level of security from here on out, Morgan?"

Morgan slowly nodded his head but told him he agreed. "Safety has to be number one. We have so much riding on this!" Morgan looked at Jim and felt happy as he smiled and told Jim it was amazing to be planning going home and organizing as a family. "It feels so right, and I am so at peace right now with our future."

"How are you feeling," asked Morgan. Jim's eyebrows arched slightly as he answered, "Need you ask? I am ecstatic to be going home as one big family unit, Morgan. I have the utmost faith in our family and in the plan as we have laid it out," said Jim.

Morgan gave an answering smile, "Me, too."

Jim slapped his knee and said they should get some sleep so they can begin again fresh in the morning. He started to walk to his bedroom pod when he stopped and turned to Morgan, "SLEEP ONLY!"

Morgan nodded his head, signaling he understood.

4

The Shape of The Future

Jim sat down with his coffee, eggs, bacon, banana, and orange juice. Morgan appeared, with a brief apology for being late, waited on his coffee pot to finish brewing, poured a cup, went to the table, and sat.

"I guess it's going to take me a bit to talk myself into a schedule."

Jim looked at him, then down at his coffee. He arose and went to the coffee bar, and returned with a plate for Morgan. It had scrambled eggs, bacon, a banana, and some apple juice. He placed in front of Morgan, who nodded his thanks. Jim looked at Morgan.

"Maybe we should cut back on some of your anxiety meds. You did just sleep, correct?"

Morgan looked at Jim, 'Yes, you're right. Eat up so we can get started." Morgan sipped his coffee.

Jim looked over at him and decided he seemed way off from his normal, bright, cheerful self. His fingers itched to get Morgan on the med bed so he could make whatever adjustments were needed.

"Ok, Mr. Tower of Intelligence, bring your coffee and let's get this party started." Morgan glanced at him and just nodded. They were standing at Morgan's desk in the lab, but he seemed riveted to that spot. Finally, Jim grabbed the cup from Morgan's hand and pushed him in the direction of the bed.

Morgan's face looked like he was thinking of refusing, but Jim told him it was obvious there was something off, so he didn't argue and climbed onto the bed. Jim had already been in with Bev and so the diagnostic screen was up.

Jim had become near light-speed fast at using the diagnostic equipment and was feeling comfortable with the layout of the various screens. He stopped on one screen, reached for the med gun and gave him an injection. Morgan was unfazed.

"Ok, it looks like you have a buildup of the anxiety meds. Don't take them for a while. I just gave you something to reverse the effects. You should be back to your sarcastic, semi-humorous self shortly."

He decided to let Morgan remain there while he went through several other diagnostics. Morgan looked healthy except for that buildup of anxiety meds, which were already dissipating.

After several minutes, Morgan sat up and said, "Man, was I in a fog this morning! I think we should cut back on the anxiety meds." Jim began laughing. Morgan glanced down and realized he was already on a bed in the medical bay.

He chuckled and said, "Oh, is this how it's going to go today, Mr. Wiseass?"

Jim smiled and realized his pal was back and ready for the day's research.

They walked back to the family pod and sat down at the table. Morgan poured a fresh cup of coffee as did Jim.

One of the Nordic nannies arrived at the family pod with Dorothy-Alice in tow. Both looked up from the table. "Dr. King, she is complaining about her ears and she is running a fever this morning."

Morgan scooted his chair back, which Dorothy-Alice recognized as an invitation, so she climbed up and snuggled into Morgan. "Does my princess not feel so good today?" She nodded her head.

Jim stood up and retrieved the otoscope. Morgan asked if Uncle Jim could look. Jim didn't wait for the answer; he quickly peered into one ear, then Morgan turned her head so he could look in the other.

Jim told her she had a humdinger of an ear infection. He looked to Morgan who remarked when this had cleared, she was a candidate for tubes. Morgan nodded as he comforted her. Jim told him he would be right back with medicine and shortly returned with an antibiotic and acetaminophen. He told the nanny how much and how often to give the meds. "Keep her in bed and the others away from her."

Next, Emma appeared in the doorway and, seeing Dorothy-Alice, approached. "I thought I heard my favorite granddaughter out here crying. You are sick today!" The little girl turned and went straight into Emma's arms.

Morgan acted a little bit upset, "Oh, a little turncoat, are you?"

Emma spoke to the Nordic and Morgan, telling them she would keep her in her room today, where it would be quiet, and she could rest. The nanny handed her the medicine.

Emma asked her if she wanted to crawl in bed with Grandpa, which got a big smile and she nodded her head yes. Hand in hand they walked back to Emma's pod.

Morgan scooted his chair back to the table, "Dorothy-Alice, Daddy will be by later to check on you. Stay in bed please, my pretty princess."

Jim looked at him and asked, "Isn't that from the Wizard of Oz?" Morgan grinned and laughed.

Jim said, "I got kids, too!"

Morgan shook his head as he tried to quickly eat. Before he could get the last bite in, the Nordic nanny returned with Dallas in tow. Morgan's eyes narrowed. "Uh-oh, the parade has started."

As Dallas ran to Jim, Morgan got up and put a sterile sleeve on the otoscope. Jim asked Dallas, "What's wrong?" Jim answered for him, "You have a fever, and—oh, there it is—a cough and snotty nose."

"Have you heard of using a tissue rather than your shirt sleeve?" Morgan laughed and asked Dallas if he could look in his ears. Dallas pushed at his hand and began crying, which caused him to cough even more. Jim stood and carried him back to the medical bed. He laid him on the bed and began flipping through various screens.

Bev awoke to the sound of her child's cry and struggled to sit up. Dallas jumped up and screamed, "Mommy!" Morgan grabbed the back of his shirt and swung him back onto the bed.

"You can't go close to Mommy, Dallas, you're sick."

Dallas held out his arms to her, and Bev felt heartbroken she could not comfort Dallas.

Jim said, "Okay, got it, he has bronchitis and an ear infection." Dallas sniffed and wiped his nose on his shirt sleeve. Morgan began laughing as Jim shoved a tissue toward him.

Dallas mumbled, "I don't need that; I already wiped it."

Jim chuckled but Bev said sternly, "Dallas, you will use a tissue! I better not see a snot-filled shirt sleeve in the laundry!"

"Ok, jeez, you guys!"

"Well, what do you want to bet on a few more?" Jim cracked.

"Just as that left his mouth, El and Emmi were towed in.

"Look at our favorite little princesses," El immediately snapped back, "I am no princess. I am a warrior. I will thank you to refer to me as such."

Bev, Jim, and Morgan exchanged amused glances but none risked contradicting her. "Ok, Ms. Warrior, jump up here on the table," said Jim. "No fever, but she does have bronchitis."

"Off you go my mighty warrior princess!" Morgan laughed.

She shot him a look and put her hands on her hips. Jim looked over at Bev who had rolled on her side, face away from them, as her shoulders heaved with ill-suppressed giggles. Jim said to himself, it is really great to see her laughing. That was a sure sign she was improving.

Thar came in and remarked, "Looks like a pediatric infirmary. Once one gets it, they all get it."

Thar told him he would send the pediatrician over to the children's pod with a couple of nurses to diagnose and treat the sick ones. "We should separate the healthy ones, if any."

"I think actually the sick ones should come to the peds medical bay. We have all the comforts of home and maybe Bat and Emma could spend the day over there. By the end of day, on the beds and continued medication we should have this contagion contained.

Jim, Morgan and Bev nodded their agreement.

"Great idea." Thar radioed for three nurses and gave the pediatrician the news that Drs. King and Mottice had sick kids and sent the trolly to get them to the pediatric ward. The Masterson's would help as expeditors for them today.

Jim then put Emmi on the bed. "Oh dear, you are very warm." She even looked sick. Jim flipped through the screens. He stopped and looked down at her and pulled up her shirt.

Morgan said "Oh, look—chickenpox!"

Thar radioed a nurse to retrieve Emmi right away. She arrived and Emmi wailed as she took her. She held her arms out to Morgan, begging for him to hold her. The medical bed sterilized the field, along with Morgan and Jim.

Morgan asked Bev if she had chickenpox before. She laughed and replied, "My mother took me to a chickenpox party to get it over with."

"Well, looks like we have one of those built in." Thar radioed for all the children to go to the pediatric ward. Then it dawned on Jim if Bat and Emma had had chickenpox in their time. Jim headed to their pod and knocked on the door. Emma answered and Jim announced that it looked like the kids were getting chickenpox so Dorothy-Alice needed to go to the pediatric ward. She said, "Oh no. We will go help."

Jim put his arm around Emma and asked if she and Bat had had them.

She answered, "No."

"Ok, for sure you need to go with the kids so you can get on a medical bed and it can fix you up before your symptoms start."

He headed back to the lab where Morgan was on the table and Thar worked the diagnostic screens.

Jim walked over and said, "Don't tell me you have never had chickenpox?" Morgan quipped, "Okay, I won't tell you."

Thar told him he had no evidence of it; however, he was giving him a vaccine to prevent it. They asked the bed to sterilize the room and all the people in the room. Jim asked if Marsha had them as a child. Jim saw a frantic look appear on Morgan's face as well as Thar's.

Jim said, "I will drag my little wildcat in here, you stay put, softy."

"Here comes Jim," Marsha was screaming. "Not the freaking lab — NO!" She was wearing a sheer nighty. Jim averted his eyes and said, "Let's go and stop bitching!"

She sat down on the floor but Jim continued dragging her down the hall. "I am not going. Let go of me. NOT THE LAB!"

Thar's face registered his shock. They picked her up, swinging her onto the bed. It took three of them to subdue her as she kicked and tried to get off the bed. Finally, Thar's outstretched fingers grasped the med gun and he quickly sedated her.

She looked at Morgan with fear and reproach, crying softly, "Not the lab..." as she drifted into sleep. Thar said, "WOW!" but Morgan and Jim laughed. Jim glanced toward Bev who was crying quietly. Jim quickly went to her. "That was awful! She has so much fear of the lab!"

Morgan somewhat nervously quipped, "Well, at least we don't have to go to the gym for our workout today. We're getting a complete workout wrestling our kids plus one spouse." They laughed but it wasn't wholehearted.

Thar thumbed through the diagnostic screens like lightning. "Looks like she already had them as a child."

Jim told the bed to warm another 20 degrees. "The babies?" asked Morgan.

"They are fine. And even with just the slightest traces of Blue these babies are ahead by three months already."

"Will they have Blue DNA?" asked Morgan.

Thar thought it through and replied, "More than likely, yes, however, we do have the technology to convert them to all human DNA, as you well know."

"What I am trying to say is right about the time to move, we may find we have twins to deliver."

Morgan chuckled, "Oh good, we meet Iris and Idell sooner than expected!"

Jim mused, it is like going to Walmart and hearing, "No waiting in checkout number 6."

"Stop stealing my lines!" Morgan playfully groused at Jim. They all sniggered. Thar told him they were looking healthy but were quite large for the dates given, "There will be no way she can deliver these without a C-section."

Jim grimaced, "Oh fun! Trying to drag a woman pregnant with twins into the lab!"

Thar shook his head as he walked away, musing "What a hellcat!"

"I will watch the ladies, well, one lady and one hellcat. You guys go to your desks and get started. Last thing any of us need right now is for Merlin to show up again."

Morgan decided he wanted to look into the number 12 and the various references to it, while Jim turned his attention to the

Iroquois and George Washington since there had been a dozen members of the Iroquois tribe sitting with the founding fathers as they constructed the Constitution.

Their tribe had spoken extensively about the Star People. In fact, he remembered, the woman at the top of the Capitol dome was fashioned after an Iroquois woman. He pulled up the Golden Lady and looked closely.

He noted she actually looked like she was slowly morphing into an eagle. She looked so much different than the original drawing and images he'd seen on the web. Jim asked Morgan to take a closer look at this. He showed him and said, "That has to be some kind of a clue! Bookmark and print that sucker."

Jim continued to research the Golden Woman on the Capitol Dome.

Morgan began by compiling a list of all the number 12s that appeared in the early history of the United States along with the cultures it had been drawn from:

Twelve sons of Jacob

Twelve gates of Israel

Twelve tribes of Israel

Twelve angels foretelling the future in Revelations.

MAJESTIC 12 and Project Blue Book

Vorlage 12 points entry and exit to Earth

Twelve as the symbol for completion of the mastery of the Universe.

Twelve knights of the round table

Twelve men carried the Ark of the Covenant

Twelve disciples until Judas committed suicide

Twelve particles; the number 12 is the God Particle (the Higgs-Boson particle discovered by the CERN supercollider).

Morgan read and printed what he believed might be pertinent as did Jim on the Golden Woman. They remained deep in thought until Emma came into the lab. Both looked up and stood immediately.

"What's wrong?" Both exclaimed.

"Nothing for you to worry about! Bitty is ready to be awakened and Dr. Cay would like you both to be there. Could you break away now and come to the lab?"

Both nodded and followed Emma. Aggie was already at her side. Morgan went right to Aggie and hugged and kissed her as did Jim. Morgan walked to the other side of the bed and told them to take off the straps. Dr. Cay released them.

Morgan sat on the bed next to her and picked up her hand. Jim looked at Dr. Cay and said, "Wake her." Everyone was quiet. Bitty slowly opened her eyes.

Morgan leaned over to her and told her, "Daddy is right here." She pulled him down and gave him a big kiss. The whole side of his face was wet from her slobber. He asked how she was feeling, and she told him she was good. She looked over and saw Jim and Emma and reached her arms out to both of them. Morgan stood so Emma could sit. Jim leaned over and she kissed and slobbered on him. Then Emma got a turn with slobber on both sides of her face. Bitty removed the bobby pins from her hair and threw them on the floor, fluffing her hair out and remarked to all she liked her hair to be free and breathe. They laughed. She sat up and stood hugging Aggie, burying her head into her shoulder and crying.

Morgan glanced over at Dr. Cay and caught Morgan's questioning glance. She nodded her head up and down with a smile. Aggie stood and picked up Bitty, carrying her out of the medical bay. Morgan, Jim, and Emma thanked Dr. Cay profusely for helping Bitty. She smiled and told them Bitty was all better now.

She added she had checked Aggie and Bitty both for chickenpox, and both were clear. Dr. Cay took them to the two-way mirror so they could see the kids. Six were on the beds but the others were playing quietly with the exception of Tig. Tig was being Tig—as usual, chasing the girls with what looked to be a hamster. The nurses looked frazzled by Tig. Morgan looked at Jim who simply shrugged and then said, "That's my boy!" Jim laughed and told him he needed to refocus Tig's energy. Morgan laughed.

He started to walk away when he noticed Emmi in the corner by herself crying. Morgan asked Dr. Cay if she knew what was going on.

She asked him to stay here, because she did not want the kids to see them and have the whole crowd in tears wanting to leave. She went in and went to Emmi. She pulled John off one of the beds and laid Emmi on the bed. The nurse came over, but on the way, had to break up an impromptu wrestling match between John and Tig.

Jim and Morgan watched as she browsed through the screens. They saw the Nordics gave her some meds and shortly thereafter she fell asleep.

Dr. Cay walked out of the room and said, "She just has not had her turn on the bed and her temp was 103, so she was feeling pretty bad. She is covered with pox, even into her scalp. She will need to be on the bed for 24 hours. She told them she felt all six on the various beds needed 24 hours.

Then she turned and told them Tig was the most precocious, ingenious, and smartest human child she had ever seen. "His IQ is 152 and he is only six."

Jim slapped Morgan on the back and laughed, "Oh, good luck with that, my friend!"

She told him the pediatrician would give them a list of things to start with, and continued, "As you said, Jim, refocus his attention and energy."

"In fact, John, Finch and Dallas are all about the same as Tig. All are college level and that makes them bored stiff with schoolwork at their chronological-age level. Tig is the only one spending his energy on pranks; however, the others will quickly catch on and will follow his example if they are not redirected." Morgan slapped Jim on his back and told him, "More good news for you, buddy!"

Jim stood still in shock. Dr. Cay told them their IQs respectively were 144 for John, Dallas was 146, and Finch was at 160. "Looks like you have some home-grown research assistants, gentlemen." Emma told him she would be staying to comfort the sick ones. Jim and Morgan turned to walk back to the lab. Morgan turned back around. He spoke in a soft and gentle tone as he explained to Emma that she should spend time with Emmi. "She is the most shy and sensitive of the bunch and would never ask for anything unless it is directly offered."

"The rest of my kids are not shy and, in fact, they're more like their mother, the hellcat. Try to get her to take more fluids in. If the pediatrician wants an IV, you tell her to wait, and Jim or I— or both, will come right over and put it in. The others will be fine if they need one, but for Emmi, that will not work."

Jim laughed and said, "Let's go." Jim told him he wanted to be there when he told the "little hellcat" her babies were all sick with chickenpox. "It will take four people to keep her from running to her babies. She's like a mother bear protecting her cubs, plus her memory of Caci is not gone. I do NOT want her to expose her little ones to the chickenpox. So we should keep her sedated on a bed in the lab, which will be a better solution. If we leave her with just her word, she will go to them. We both know how that will turn out."

When they walked in, Thar was trying persuade Marsha to stay in the bed. Thar must have told her since she screamed, "Let me up, damn you, LET ME UP!"

Then she cried out the words that went right through Morgan, "CACI, CACI, CACI," and she was sobbing but still kicking and pulling. Jim and Morgan ran to her. Thar called for help. Two other doctors came running as Morgan tried to settle her by saying, "The babies, Marsha, Iris and Idell, you must settle down!"

"I have to go right now to my babies!"

Jim did his best but she kept getting her hands loose. Finally one of the doctors medicated her and she fell asleep. Jim stood shaking his head. He had a big scratch down his face and was bleeding. Morgan had taken a kick to his crotch and was doubled over in pain, waiting for the throbbing to lessen.

Bev got back in her bed as another doctor ran in to her. Thar and a second doctor were programming the bed at lightning-fast speed. The other physician told Jim and Morgan to come and sit on the other bed. The doctor picked up the skin repair wand and waved it over Jim's face. The second doctor was running scans to make sure Morgan had not been injured since he just had surgery, but both checked out fine. Morgan sat there gazing at Marsha. Jim remarked that had been extreme, even for her.

They watched Thar continue giving directions to the computer. The other doctor picked up where he left off and Thar walked over to Jim and Morgan. "She obviously needs more time on the bed. The pain is much deeper than I thought. She will struggle with this the rest of her life, Morgan. We need to continue to tweak this."

"Somehow, it seems this same thread is what triggers her sexual urges. It is all part of what has intensified her sex drive with the roughness you encountered. In the future, you should take that as your cue that she needs another treatment."

"Again, if her sex desires become prolonged and rough, bring her in right away. I can see a deep trough in that area. My guess is she was sexually assaulted when she was young and has suppressed it. We will need to treat that deep trough, however, as it will continue to be an issue. She will relive it, which she believes she needs to do in order to deal with it. That will also help tame that little spitfire nature."

Morgan put his hands to his face and cried. Thar told him, "She needs to spend another 24 hours on the table completely sedated."

Jim walked over to Bev and asked if she was okay. She said "Yes," but asked to go back to their pod. She slipped out of the bed and said, "I am ready." Jim asked her to return to the medical bed. He and Morgan needed to be in the lab doing research and requested her to stay there while they were in the lab working. They would go back together.

Morgan and Jim went back to research and both focused on the Golden Woman. They assumed it was the first of the code. They wrote down every detail and highlighted areas they printed off.

Almost without warning, it was 7:00 PM and Bev was out of the bed and stood by Jim. She put her arm around his neck and said, "Let's go." Jim stood and picked her up, carrying her to their room. He told Morgan to go to bed and he would see him again at 7:00 AM again.

Morgan walked over to Marsha who was lying quietly awake. His eyebrow arched as he said to her, "I love you, baby." She looked him in the eye and apologized for becoming hysterical. He smiled and lay gently beside her.

The doctor came over and programmed the bed. Morgan smoothed her hair. She had tears running down her cheeks as she continued looking at the ceiling, telling Morgan that she was a fool, had acted like a fool, endangering her babies."

Morgan, still looking at her, hoped for her to glance his way, then told her, "We have to dampen down that urge to lash out."

She then made eye contact and asked Morgan if she could tell him something, and if so, would he still love her? His eyes melted into her eyes, and he told her she completed him as a person and there would never be anything she could say that would hurt him or make him not love her to the very core of his being.

At first, she maintained eye contact. She told him that when she was 12, her cousin's friend was over and while her cousin left to pick up pizza, they were alone and he… She hesitated, looking down into her lap. He lightly grasped her chin and turned her face toward him as he waited for her to continue.

She said, "He grabbed me, pulled my shorts down and… well," she gazed down again, biting her lower lip. Again he pulled her chin up , looking deep into her eyes as she described how he had raped her.

"It hurt me so bad, and I begged him to get off me. Finally, he heard the car coming back into the driveway and got off me. I ran into the bedroom and locked my door. I had blood running down my legs."

She began to sob uncontrollably. Morgan looked toward the physician and nodded for him to lightly sedate her.

When she asked if he hated her for being used and broken merchandise, his heart felt like it turned over in his chest. "Never! You are my all in all, my everything, and we will face this together."

"You are one brave woman with the heart of a lioness combined with the compassion of Mother Theresa. You have such a depth of love. I only want you, my Marsha."

She kissed him lightly and told him she adored him. She couldn't believe he could love someone like her, pregnant with Bat's twins. "I am again used merchandise."

He hadn't known she felt guilt about that. He looked at her and said, "We all have passion, Marsha. You felt a love for Bat then, I understand that. But it is our love that is so deep it encompasses both of our souls. Don't ever think that I ever considered anything but that. I never even felt it necessary to forgive you."

"But you have to forgive yourself. You, my wonderful wife, are not to blame for what that evil person did to you, and you are not to feel guilty because you gave your passion to Bat. I love talking to you and finding out little tidbits I didn't know before. It makes my love even deeper.

GOT THAT?"

She propped herself up on her elbow and looked him straight in the eyes, and said, "How do I ever deserve you—that's something I will never understand. I am grateful with every bone in my body. I love you. Please don't ever leave me. I will make you a good wife, if you can hang on through my falling short at times."

He laughed and said, "We ALL fall short, baby. And I see everything as a learning experience.

"Now, enough of that. I have good news." She smiled and looked excited, "Our precocious son, Tig, appears to be smarter than Albert Einstein and his old man as well. He has an IQ of 152."

Marsha asked if that was smart. He told her, "Brilliant, actually. They told me he should be in college classes. He is bored, and that's why he acts out with his pranks."

Marsha's forehead furrowed slightly, "Oh, please don't take that away from him; it is his personality. Leave that please."

Morgan laughed and said, "Ok, but for him to reach his potential, he needs to be redirected a bit. And, by the way, the rest of the kids are like you—spitfires!!!"

She laughed and asked if she could steal his line with one small tweak, "They're My Kids!" They both laughed.

"Let's walk down to see the kids through the two-way mirror. You can't expose Iris and Idell to chickenpox, so you can only look through the window. If they see you, they will all start crying and our extra smart kid will find a way to escape."

She laughed, "I think I need to stop and get a robe."

He looked her over, pretending to admire her backside, "Good idea. But after that, you have to get back to the bed and I will be right beside you in the recliner. You have to be on the bed by yourself, babe."

"Ok, deal."

He sat up and looked straight into her eyes, "TRUTH, you will do what we just discussed without any protest; TRUTH?"

She looked him in the eye and said, "TRUTH; YES, I will follow my husband's and doctor's orders. Do you really think I need more meds to keep me calm?"

Morgan said, "Do you want to try it without for a while and see how you do?"

She smiled, looked directly at Morgan, nodded, and said, "Understood. I will let you or Jim know if I don't think I can control things on my own. But… now I am ready to see the kids." He asked the doctor for a wheelchair, who told him she would meet them outside their pod bedroom.

Morgan sat her on the sofa in the family pod, went in and got her a long, soft robe and a pair of his socks. He put the socks on her first. He told her he knew she would love the socks. Then she slipped on the robe as she stood to sit in the wheelchair, "Ok, let's head on over."

He pushed her through their pod and down the hall to the medical pediatric pod. Two doctors stood and came from behind the desk. "Good evening. Dr. and Mrs. King." Marsha put her hand on Morgan's. "Right this way to the two-way mirror." Marsha saw all but the six eating and Tig was hiding the silverware. Marsha goggled at Tig. She shook her head and said, "That's your boy, Morgan."

He laughed, then turned and asked how the other six were.

She said that all but Emmi were doing great. Marsha heard that, stood and turned to the doctor. She explained they had intended after dinner to have Dr. Mottice and Dr. King come down to start an IV. "She will not drink." Marsha shot a concerned look at Morgan, but quickly regained control of herself and asked, "Morgan, where is Bitty?"

She explained to the physician that Emmi and Bitty were like two peas in a pod and she responds to Bitty. "Would you allow Bitty in with her?" Morgan motioned for her to sit down and he would go get Jim and Bitty.

Bev sat and looked at each of the kids. She was very glad her children had Jim's kids to play with. It was like they were her kids, too. Marsha saw the two Nordic kids playing with Finch. "Whose kids are those?"

"Dr. Thar decided to have a chickenpox party for his kids. The little girl is six and her name is Lang and the boy's name is Vaughn, he's nine. They will be coming with Dr. Thar and his wife, Shri, to live in the compound. So, it looks like you added two kids to your family."

She turned and said, "More kids are always a blessing!" She could tell Finch and Vaughn would be close friends. She hoped that Lang and Emmi could become best friends. Emmi was the shy outsider of their otherwise boisterous troop. It appeared Lang was a lot like Emmi. Bitty beat Jim and Morgan back to the pod. The doctors opened the hermetically sealed door after Marsha ducked behind the barrier. She heard Tig yell, "Chewbacca."

Bitty laughed and yelled, "Tig the Pig." Tig ran around on all fours doing his oink-oink routine. Soon all the kids were calling him Tig the Pig, and on all fours, oinking along with Tig.

Bitty went right to Emmi who sat up and they hugged. Bitty laid down beside Emmi. Jim and Morgan asked for a kit. The doctor gave them two in case they missed the first time, then handed them a bag of fluids. The doctor informed them she would go after it was in, so as not to upset Emmi.

Jim carried the kit and the bag of fluids. Emmi spotted them and began crying with her arms held out to Morgan. Marsha asked to hear what everyone was saying. She said, "Sure and set a barrier between the kids' and Emmi's bed, and turn the microphone on at her bed. Morgan held her and told her Daddy loved her to the moon and back. Emmi asked if he loved Bitty like that, too. He smiled, leaned over and kissed Bitty. "You know I do! How does my pretty princess feel?"

Emmi wrinkled her nose and said "Yucky."

Bitty said she thought she would feel better with her pink kitty and her pink nightgown and pink slippers. Morgan looked back at Emmi and said, "If that is so, Bitty would you please go get them for her?"

Bitty stood and solemnly told him she would run as fast as she could and bring them back.

Morgan touched her on the arm and asked her to promise him she would walk—both ways. Jim thought that very clever. Bitty nodded her head and they leaned over to kiss Morgan. "No skipping or running, my love."

"Ok, Daddy, I am a good girl."

He said, "That you are, my precious baby."

He looked at Emmi, "Now, listen, princess, you need a little more medicine so you don't feel yucky, and the polka dots go away." She shot him a frightened look under her lashes.

"I am going to hold you tight, and Uncle Jim is going to put in a tiny needle so we can give you the medicine; will you let Uncle Jim do that if I hold you and give you a thousand kisses?"

He asked her to turn around and hug him while Uncle Jim did the stick and pinch to slide the pediatric needle in. Jim pulled the tray over and got it ready, sat down on the bed, and asked if she was ready for a little pinch. Morgan nodded and Jim slid the tubing right on the first try. She screamed and cried out loud. Morgan began rocking with her and telling her it was okay, that he was all done. He needed to tape it in place and would give her a pink wrap around it. The doctor heard that and picked up a sticky wrap that was pink and ran it to them. Morgan continued to rock her and stroke her hair. The doctor gave her a quick boost of meds to calm her, but she pushed the med gun away and screamed.

Jim said, "Just like her Mommy with that shrill scream and pushing away. She is her mother's daughter for sure!"

Marsha heard that and giggled. Emmi was still crying loudly. Bitty came in with everything pink for her. Jim helped her into her favorite pink night gown and the pink fluffy slippers. He put her pink stretch bracelet on her as Morgan held her.

Bitty handed her Tootles the pink poodle and she relaxed back hugging Toodles.

She solemnly asked Bitty if she had brought her pink lipsticks, and Jim bent over, shaking with silent laughter. Bitty handed it to her and Emmi asked Morgan to put it on her. It was amazing to watch Morgan with her. He gently put it on her, smoothed it with his finger, and then told her to kiss him so he could wear her kiss all day. She smiled.

"Ok, princess, I need you to lie down and go to sleep," said Morgan.

"Bitty is going to lie next to you on the floor," and Bitty quickly laid down beside her. Morgan told Emmi if she needed anything Bitty would get it for her and the doctor would be back in to give her more medicine to help get rid of the polka dots. He promised it would not hurt nor would she feel it. Then he told her to close her eyes. He could see she was struggling to stay awake. He waited a few minutes while he watched the other kids playing.

He glanced down and could tell she was sound asleep as was Bitty. The nurses rounded the rest of the kids up to get them to lie on their mats.

Morgan and Jim helped gather them up and tuck them in. Dallas would not let go of the robot. Jim decided he could sleep with it rather than argue. Everyone was down and the doctor came in. Jim took the med gun and gave everyone light meds so they would all sleep soundly through the night.

Morgan and Jim finally came out and asked who the two Nordic kids were. The doctor told them they were Thar's kids, Lang and Vaughn, and he wanted to expose them to human chickenpox. "As soon as they catch it, we can treat them."

Morgan looked at Jim and said, "Congratulations it's a boy and a girl." Jim smiled. Marsha was watching the kids. The lights were low with only the display projection on. The doctor told Morgan Tig was something else. He had had all of them in stitches. Morgan smiled and thanked her for her kind words.

5

New Additions

The next morning, Morgan and Jim met over coffee and breakfast. Bev was still fast asleep in Jim's family pod and Marsha hadn't awakened on the med bed in the medical bay. Thar came into the room, grabbed a cup of tea and sat down across from them. Morgan asked how Marsha was doing. "She will be ready tonight when you're finished for the evening."

'"I hear you got kid duty last night."

Jim smiled, nodded and said, "Yes and we met your kids. Looks like Finch and Vaughn will be good friends."

He laughed and said, "That is all they talk about... how crazy fun your kids are, especially Chewbacca and Tig."

Morgan and Jim both smiled. Thar grinned, "I thought it would be a good time to start exposing them to human viruses to build their immunity over the next few weeks. So, if you don't mind, my kids will be hanging with your kids. Hope they pass as many germs as possible to my kids."

Morgan laughed and said, "Be careful what you wish for. Our kids are veritable petri dishes on the move."

Morgan then heard Marsha beginning to stir. He stood and said, "Wish me luck." Both smiled as Morgan walked back to Marsha's bed as she sat up.

"It's lonely back here without you. How are the kids?"

He told her, "Emmi is much better this morning, but we left the line in for a 'just in case.' The Nordic kids think our kids are crazy fun, especially Chewbacca and Tig the Pig."

Marsha gave him a warm smile. He leaned over and gave her a kiss, and then brought up the diagnostic screens.

Marsh made a playful grab at his zipper, which he lightly brushed away, "Why do you think I'm only interested in sex with you? That's just one part of our marriage and you bring so much more to our family."

"I'm not as smart or as accomplished as you."

"But, I'm a nerdy guy stuck in the lab all day. That's not the whole of life! People get together socially to get away from all that work stuff and talk about their everyday life and their struggles. That is you, Marsha, you're so comfortable in dealing with that family and friend's world! I don't ever want to hear you talk like that again! It is simply not true!"

"But as for the other, yes, we do have powerful chemistry that is like a magnet between us. We can't keep our passions for each other under control. But that passion sometimes gets a little rough and goes on for hours! That shows we both lack control and satisfaction in our carnal urges. Both of us—not just you. I am taking medication for this and so should you."

"We can have a lively sexual life but not all rough and constant. That is not what either of us is about. We both have full lives and need to live them to the fullest. And I do want you all to myself so no more going around without underwear or taking your clothes off and not thinking anything of it. I am not willing to share my beautiful wife like that. You are for my eyes only, got it?"

She smiled and said, "I love you more every second of every day. You make me a better person. I want to take that medication, too. I am so glad you picked me. I am sorry I didn't see how amazing and wonderful you are sooner. You have to promise me when we get back home the first opportunity we get, we will take an afternoon at Indigo Lake and a visit with Elias."

"And of course I promise to not be as rough, and we will have gentle passion. That is the place I feel safest, I can block out my worried thoughts and just be lost in your arms. Promise me. Morgan?"

"You got it, my lovely wife."

Suddenly, she jumped, then grabbed Morgan's hand to put it on her abdomen. He felt one of the babies kick and move. He flipped back the cover and lifted her gown. Morgan told her to look at the foot. They both could see an entire foot pushing out against her abdomen.

Marsha said, "I think we've got a pair of soccer players."

He laughed, covered her back up, then stood and pulled up the screen as casually as he could, trying not to show the shock he felt on his face. He left the screen up, then told her he would go get her some tea. She asked for two sugars, but he turned quickly and said, "You're a diabetic, think again! I'll find a sweetener that's not sugar." She laughed.

Morgan asked Jim and Thar to meet him in the coffee bar. He told them he had left the screen up but told them the monitor showed the babies were at eight months of gestation!

"I am making her some tea while you go in and look at the screen. We so need a plan!"

Jim went in first. "Always good to have a patient in our lab in the middle of research," he groused half-heartedly.

She asked if he was upset with her. "Okay, hormone-crazed prego person, not at all upset. In fact, I was being sarcastic; however, I am not as good at this as Morgan. So, can you be truthful and tell me how you're really feeling?"

"I can remember that cave and how difficult it was to pull the real truth from you." He sat on the bed and looked at her.

"I didn't jump his bones last night, Jim, I promise you!"

Jim laughed and said, "That's a relief, but that's not what I am trying to get at."

Her shoulders slumped, she gazed up at him and took a deep breath, slowly she blew it out.

Jim said, "Again, TRUTH!" as tears welled up in her eyes. She took another deep breath and blew that out.

With a start, Jim realized she was doing Lamaze breathing. He raised his eyebrow and asked if she thought was in labor?

"It's too soon, Jim." He stood and asked the bed to set up for a vaginal exam. As he was putting on his gloves, Morgan and Thar came into the room and saw what he was doing. Morgan told him the time was not now.

Thar said, "Maybe just let him do the exam if she is letting him."

But Marsha whimpered, "I promised Morgan I would keep my clothes on so only he could see me that way."

"Oh, you did, did you? Sorry, but that counts for all but me. Chicky, so spread 'em."

She complied. As soon as he could see her cervix clearly, Jim motioned for Morgan to look, "It's 5 cm dilated and spotting!"

Morgan ran to one side of the bed as Thar jumped to the other side frantically flipping through the screens.

Morgan, glanced at the screen and went right to Marsha. "Baby, you are in labor, and 5 cm dilated. Those babies are about to deliver naturally if we don't intervene now. It's C-section time."

"Morgan, I am scared; how can they be ready?"

"You leave that part to us and work on nothing but positive, loving thoughts."

Thar quickly shot her arm with the med gun.

Surprised, she looked at him and said, "Thought we had an agreement you were going to ask the next time, buster."

Thar looked at her, gave her a quick grin, and said, "I will remember next time, my little hellcat! But right now, we need to sedate you for surgery."

She laughed and that brought on another contraction. She breathed through it. They laid the bed down flat and Jim rushed back in with two kits, tubing and IV fluids. "With all the kids you have had, you know the routine almost better than me!"

Tears began to flow and she gave one loud sob. Morgan went to the head of the bed and pulled the headboard off.

"Morgan, no, I don't want that thing. Please, do we have to, Morgan?"

Jim laid three syringes on her chest and told her not to touch them.

"Morgan, I'm scared, please kiss, hug, and tell me you love me."

Holding her gaze, he walked back to her head, gave her a hug and a long kiss. "Will that hold ya' for an hour or two, babe?"

"Did you even leave her tonsils?" gasped Jim.

Morgan laughed, but Marsha cried out, "Morgan, I am not ready yet."

Jim told her not to move; he was putting the line in, then caught Jim's eye to tell Morgan they had access.

Two doctors arrived with incubators and Dr. Cay brought up the rear. Jim hung the fluids.

Marsha repeated, "No, Morgan, I am not ready yet. Let Jim do it while you hold me."

"Jim, will you?"

Jim got up and switched places with Morgan, then picked up all three syringes as Jim opened the first kit. Marsha had another contraction and breathed through it with her eyes squeezed tight.

Morgan quietly encouraged her and told her she was doing fine. When it began easing off, Jim told her the time was now if they hoped to do a C-Section before the babies moved into the birth canal. Morgan leaned over and gave her a kiss on the forehead. "You're doing fine." Morgan moved to her lips and gave her another but gentler kiss.

As he pushed the first syringe, he stood and told her to just close her eyes. She did, then he pushed the second syringe. He nodded to Jim who intubated her and attached her to the ventilator.

The cardiologist walked up to the bed as Morgan finished the last syringe. The cardiologist flipped through the screens. "Why didn't you guys call me sooner? With her heart, you should not have allowed her to go into labor." Jim told him she hadn't told anyone and then called for a crash cart to be brought in just in case they needed it.

Morgan, hearing that, got nervous and stepped back out of everyone else's way. The cardiologist gave her some meds. Jim had the surgical kit open and made the incision, then asked for the fascia to be retracted.

He could see one of the babies had her eyes open and was looking directly at him. Dr. Cay gasped, "Look at that! I have never seen that before, like ever!"

He pulled the baby out, Dr. Cay nicked the sac, clamped the cord and cut it. She laid the baby in the bassinet, quickly pulling up the screens and taking in all information as they rattled it off. Morgan and Jim heard a loud, strong cry.

Morgan's legs began to shake, and he discovered he could not stand. Jim rapidly and skillfully delivered the second twin. She had beautiful black curly hair. He laid her on Marsha's legs and Dr. Cay turned to clamp the umbilical cord, then cut it. She transferred her into the incubator, as the baby let out a loud, full-bodied cry.

Jim thought, "I'm not closing without a thorough search for another baby." He stopped when he felt a foot. He thankfully remembered Marsha had a history of 'hiding' babies. Jim said, "We need another incubator! Marsha was hiding a third baby."

The doctor ran and returned with the third incubator just as Jim pulled the last baby out. She was small with bright red hair and one blue curl.

He laid her on Marsha's legs and Dr. Cay saw the blue curl of hair. She clamped off the cord and cut it, then placed that baby into the incubator. "She's not crying. She needs lung cell generation. Her lungs are not yet developed enough."

Dr. Cay asked for an intubation kit and Jim turned around to look. She was moving, but not yet crying. Dr. Cay flicked her foot and the little redhead squeaked out a half a cry.

Dr. Cay quickly intubated her and attached the ventilator. Jim was just finishing with Marsha, then asked the bed to seal the wound and heal it and gave further instructions to tighten the abdominal muscles and eliminate any fat build up in the abdominal area, hips, and thighs.

Jim was then able to turn his attention to Morgan who lay where he had collapsed on the floor. Dr. Thar rapidly followed. Two security people lifted him onto a medical bay bed. His blood pressure was critically high, and the cardiologist walked over and began barking orders for the doctor to administer two drugs immediately. Everyone watched as his heart rhythm began to slow as his blood pressure stabilized.

Morgan was shaking visibly, so Jim told the bed to warm by 20 degrees. He grabbed a warm blanket from the cupboard and put it over him, then instructed the bed to raise his legs by 30 degrees. The cardiologist said, "I guess I would be in shock, too, with three more kids! But he is fine now, please let the man rest. God knows he will get no rest soon enough," he mumbled as he walked away.

Morgan opened his eyes and saw Jim; he yelled, "Are they all okay? And Marsha? How is she?"

"Marsha was a trooper. Two are full term and fine, and the third —" Morgan closed his eyes, "—a third?" swallowing hard.

"She has the same blue lock of hair that Caci had."

Morgan began to cry almost hysterically. Thar went to his side and gave him light anxiety meds.

"They are removing the Blue DNA, so that should go away, Morgan."

"I think I am going to throw up." Jim handed him a bag.

"We had this for Marsha but you need it more than she does at the moment!" Jim handed him the tissue box.

Morgan slowly stood up and steadied himself, "I need to see Marsha, then the babies."

He walked over to Marsha as the three physicians stood behind him. He leaned over and kissed her. "Jim, please keep her under for 24 hours, if not longer, and give her anticoagulants to prevent clotting." Thar told him they already have done that.

"Now, let's see my babies." He turned and could see two doctors hovering over each incubator. As he stood in front of the first baby, he said, "This is Iris; please mark her name plate so we know." Then he moved to the second incubator and said, "Idell," and spelled it for them.

He walked to the last incubator and the face gazing up at him looked way too much like Caci for his comfort. He felt himself sway and Jim and the other doctors grabbed him and helped him back to the second bed as he flopped down. Jim swung his feet up and another doctor brought him orange juice and a straw. Jim told him to drink it all so he would feel better. He sat up and drank it, but said nothing. Jim sat beside him on the bed.

Morgan looked down and said, "What on earth am I thinking! I am blessed to have three more kids. Let's give a name to the third. It has to start with an "I" or Marsha will be upset.

Jim asked about Iona or "Maybe, Ivy?" finished Morgan, "To Batman for me; how about Idena?" asked Jim. Morgan looked at him out of bleary eyes, then nodded and told Jim to tell them to call her Idena. Jim slapped him on the back and told him to down the orange juice. "Oh, how about you give them all middle names please," asked Morgan.

Morgan decided it would be better for him to stay on the bed overnight. He wanted to be there if Marsha awakened. They took all the babies to the pediatric pod. Morgan got up, walked over to Marsha's bed, and asked how she was doing. The doctor told him she was fine. "Everything looks great. We are monitoring her heart closely, on the lookout for clots. Personally, I would keep her under another 24 hours to give her mind and body time to recover."

He told her she was correct, to modify the orders, and then walked down the hall to grab some breakfast. Bat and Emma were seated with Jim. He poured a coffee and sat down. Emma got up and hugged him, and Bat shook his hand, saying, "You are a better man than I am, my friend. But Grandpa is so happy to meet and welcome three more to our clan."

Jim asked how he was feeling today, and Morgan could honestly tell them he was much better. "Kind of took me by surprise you might say. Anyway, I would like to get back to research today, while I still have some time and attention to give."

Jim agreed that would be a good idea, so he planned to work on the Jefferson plate.

"Ok, let's eat something and then we'll go check on the babies and the kids." They finished breakfast, then walked down to see the babies. They all looked good. Idena looked stable; her lungs were generating cells and she was at 68% capacity now. Everyone agreed that Idell looked like Elizabeth Taylor, especially with her black curly hair. Emma said Iris looked like the spitting image of Marsha.

Jim told them that when he opened Marsha, she was the first one and had her eyes open like, "Come on already, get me outta here." Morgan began to laugh but Bat and Emma were not quite sure how to take that.

"Hey, you better remember to tell Olzing you need two more rooms! Morgan told him "Ha-ha!" Then he stopped and shot a look straight at Jim. He knew exactly what he was thinking.

Then he asked about the rest of the kids and was told they were good for another 24 hours, if they didn't drive the staff crazy first. They told him Tig was a natural leader, smart and a real funny man. They emphasized he had told them he was a man! Everyone laughed and Morgan said, "That's my boy! Oh, I mean MAN!"

The staff had told them Finch had captured their hearts. He was so kind, considerate, and such a compassionate little boy. He helped them like Bitty, and wanted everyone to have everything they needed before himself.

"Must take after his Grandma Emma," said Morgan. Emma teared up and hugged Morgan, Jim gave Emma a hug and told her Morgan could not be more right. Bat looked at the staff and somewhat gruffly asked if there was one in there for Grandpa. The nurse stepped up to Bat and said Rue had looked for Grandpa all day yesterday. "She sat and cried, holding her little teddy bear calling for Grandpa." That brought a tear to his eyes. "I sure do love me some Rue!"

Jim watched and knew how difficult it was going to be for all the Mastersons to leave in a couple of years. He admired Emma's firm but loving hand in running the household and making sure each child felt equally loved. Bat and his funny way of sneaking the kids candy and teaching them how to play cards was fun to watch. Morgan slapped Jim on the back and told him, "Let's get to work; we have a planet to save for our babies!"

Through the rest of the morning Jim, Morgan, and Bev worked on their different avenues of research. Bev decided she would work on it from the perspective of the First Ladies and how the pattern selections had happened for each. Marsha was still being kept under for now which allowed them all to focus 100% on their assigned subject matter. Morgan and Jim spent much of their time on Washington and the multiple visitations he had. Each one was fascinating, and he noticed a pattern emerging in the manner in which each built in one way or another on the previous visitation.

Morgan kept feeling drawn to the starburst on the White House china and allowed himself to follow his instincts. There was something he could almost but not quite see in that starburst. He could not wait to fly to Washington next week. He went to the kitchen for some juice and a bottle of water. He brought back a bottle of the water Jim favored. He drank the small apple juice as he turned to look at Marsha.

As he went over to check on her, he saw a smear of red on her face. She was having a significant nosebleed! Morgan called for Jim, who looked up and saw Morgan lift a cloth with a lot of blood. He jumped up and looked down at her nose bleeding. He pulled up the diagnostic and saw a sinus infection.

Jim drew up the meds and administered them through the central line. He asked the on-call doctor if they had a spray for sinus infections like that causing the nosebleed. He brought over a spray for him and that quickly stopped the nosebleed. The doctor stayed with her while Jim and Morgan went back to their desks.

Jim said, "She has the same things the kids are getting over. I should tell that doctor to listen to… oh, never mind. Let's go listen the old-fashioned way."

Jim and Morgan grabbed their stethoscopes and Jim listened first, then told Morgan to listen. The attending doctor stood watching them. "Yep—bronchitis, and she needs suctioning."

They turned to the doctor and asked if she wanted to listen. She popped her stethoscope in her ears and was surprised how loud it sounded. The rattling of the bronchitis told her a large amount of suctioning was needed. She immediately pulled it around and began to suction her.

She injected some meds, then went to get an antibiotic drip. Jim and Morgan returned to their research, while keeping one ear cocked for the rattle that would tell them she needed further suctioning.

Morgan asked Jim if he had run across the Badland Guardian in his research of the Iroquois woman on top of the capital. Jim answered he had but thought it to be Ancient Alien stuff from the appearance of the guy with the weird hair. He told him to dive in if he felt pulled to it. Right now he was chasing down the Masonic-Illuminati connection. After an hour or so, Jim burst out laughing.

Morgan looked up at him as Jim exclaimed, "Get this! They say that Washington was assassinated and his body double took his place. Sounds like a Hollywood B-movie plot."

Morgan's eyebrow shot up. "I never heard that in my history class, but then again I slept most of the time in that class, so not surprised."

He asked Jim if this was the first he'd heard of that. Jim was so engrossed in his reading he failed to even hear Morgan's question.

Later Morgan stood; he was exhausted but felt he hadn't really accomplished much. He told Jim he was going to lie down on the medical bed for a while, and to call him if anything turned up. Jim never even acknowledged him; he was so deep in what he was reading. Morgan told the bed to raise the temp 20 degrees. He pulled out a warm blanket and covered himself, laid back and fell into a deep slumber almost immediately.

6

Strength From Within

Morgan glanced up at the monitor and noticed there had been an increase in Marsha's heart rate. He glanced over at the clock; it showed 7:30 AM. He took a syringe from his pocket and leaned over just as her eyes opened and filled with tears. He dropped to his knees beside her and took her hand, while pulling all the syringes from his pocket. She shook her head no.

She did maintain eye contact, but her tears overflowed. Jim walked into the room and took it all in. He picked up the syringes, at which Morgan said, "No, we take the tube out."

Jim looked at the monitor, still holding the syringes in his hand. He went to his knees at her head and began untapping the tube.

Marsha made eye contact with Jim. He smiled and asked if she was ready. She nodded but tears continued to stream down the corner of her eyes. He told her to blow, now, and pulled the tube.

Morgan leaned over and embraced her. Jim smoothed her hair and put his hand on her shoulder. She sat up and swung her legs around and turned to Jim and hugged him. He told her to lie right back down for an hour. She didn't argue and laid back.

She looked toward Jim and asked if she was okay. A broad smile crossed his face and he replied, "Tiger, nothing will ever keep you down for long."

"When you take this thing out of my neck, can you make the bed heal it, and make it look perfect?"

Jim touched her cheek wiping away the tears and told her, "You got it, Chicky!" Jim then noticed when she sat up there was spotting. He came around to the other side and went down to his knees. He picked up his stethoscope and listened. Morgan held her hand as he looked over at the monitor. Jim placed his stethoscope on her chest and Morgan picked them up to listen.

He took one of the syringes and put it through her IV, explaining, "This is for your heart! Now, one last thing Missy! No arguing, I am doing it."

She raised an eyebrow. "I see you are spotting still, so I am doing a pelvic exam." She looked to Morgan who squeezed her hand. She sat up, but Jim instantly pushed her back down. "No! Remember what I said about no arguing?"

He pulled his gloves on and flicked the light for the speculum to the on position. He grinned and said, "Legs up and spread 'em —you know the routine."

She hesitated and closed her eyes. Jim stood still, waiting for her to respond. Then she drew her knees up but didn't immediately spread them apart. He took her leg and gently pushed it out. She tensed. He leaned in against her other leg, "Ok, I am putting it in now." She jumped and the thought, "That was new," came to his mind.

When he completed the exam, he removed the speculum and smiled, "All done." He removed his gloves and wrapped the speculum, then stood and programmed the bed. Everyone was silent.

Jim knelt back down, he remained looking down and there was a long, silent pause, then he said, "Marsha," and paused waiting for eye contact. She looked at him as he calmed himself and collected his thoughts. Then he told her, "It's going to be very important that for the rest of your life both you and Morgan take this medicine to calm your urges to a manageable level."

He turned the screen toward them so they could see the 3-D image of her vaginal walls. There were deep wounds, some actively bleeding and some scabbed over. Morgan looked horrified and Marsha was clearly shaken.

Jim told them both, "A picture is worth a thousand words." He added she would be on the bed another hour so the bed could make as many repairs as possible. "I am giving you an antibiotic."

Morgan got up and grabbed a bag to mix the solution.

"In the meantime, your sugar is low. Let me order us breakfast, and I do not want to hear any bullshit about 'I can't eat because I won't fit in my hot new dress' from you!"

She laid back smiling. "How should I wear my hair? Loose and carefree or dramatic, slicked back with a low bun?" Jim stood and looked at her without saying anything, then tilted his head from one side to the other looking at her, and said, "For you, dramatic, with dramatic makeup to match. You will be the cat's meow!"

She smiled and closed her eyes. Morgan walked over and hung the antibiotic. She opened her eyes as he sat down next to her. Morgan took her hand and said, "I am so sorry for what I caused yesterday. I will never, ever let myself get that carried away again.

We will both take the meds and if we even think one of our meds needs increased, we will tell the other."

Morgan had fallen asleep on the floor next to Marsha. The breakfast trays arrived, so she sat up and carried her bag of fluids and antibiotics to the table. She sat with Bev and Jim as they ate together. Jim noticed she drank half an orange juice and ate a half piece of toast. He pulled up the app on his phone and walked around the table to scan her device.

Marsha looked down, knowing what was coming next. He put the phone in front of her, showing the number "51." He said nothing but sat back down and sipped his coffee. She tried to pick up her orange juice, but Jim saw her hand was shaking. He retrieved the rescue syringe out of his medical bag, and with one smooth move, leaned over her chair and pulled up her nightgown and injected it into her abdomen. He then picked up her orange juice and handed it to her, still silent.

Almost immediately, Marsha began to wretch. He grabbed the waste basket, silently handing it to her. He drew up nausea meds and put it into her IV. She looked at Jim and said, "I know I had a hysterectomy but there is no way at all I can be pregnant again; right? Bev jumped up, ran to her side of the table, circling her arm around Marsha's waist.

Jim was still in shock at the question. "I always have the thought of Blue in the back of my mind, Jim." she reminded him.

He looked down, and quickly shook his head, then steadily looked back up at her. "I need both of you to take a turn on the bed for a comprehensive exam."

Marsha asked him to be quiet so as to not wake Morgan. She laid back on the bed and as he programmed it, turning off the audio. Marsha watched as Jim's shadow towered over her. She looked at the shadow reflecting on her legs and body. It was like his personal protection over her; he always had her back. He was first to jump out in front of her, first with a plan of action both for her and Bev. She watched him stuck on one screen, peering at it, then he sat beside her on the bed and took her hand. She began to cry then screamed, "NO! NO! NO!"

Morgan jumped up in alarm to see Jim quietly sitting beside her and holding her hand. He got to his knees and said, "Gods! What now??"

Bev ran to her and smoothed her brow. Morgan breathed hard with a panicked look in his eyes. Jim turned to Marsha, "No, you are NOT pregnant, however, you have a large, active ulcer going, Missy!"

"You can thank me later for coming prepared for everything!" She sat up and hugged him. He helped her lie back and looked at his shoulder, "You didn't just wipe snot on me like Tig and Bitty, did you?" Their laughter broke the tension.

Morgan jumped up and looked at the image of her ulcer. Jim handed her a liquid and told her to drink it.

"Drink that ulcer beverage!" Morgan tipped the glass to her mouth and said, "NOW!" She scrunched her face as she finished it and looked horrified at the taste. "Put vodka in it next time! Lots of vodka!"

Morgan laughed and Jim silently handed him a loaded syringe, which he put in the IV.

She asked what that was, "A med to heal the bleeding and help that ulcer."

He pulled out his phone and scanned her sugar device, showing her the number had dropped to 38. He took her shoulders, sat her on the bed, then leaned over and swung her legs up onto the bed.

"Honey, I think Jim wants you to lie down." Jim, still silent, stepped in front of Morgan, pushing her shoulders against the bed. Marsha stuck out her tongue and called him a big meanie!

Morgan bent over, shaking with silent laughter. Jim went to get another rescue injection for her sugar. He came back to see Morgan still laughing. Jim tugged at her nightgown to lift it up. She yanked it back down, giggling, "Please, Sir, I am married!" Jim gave her a wry look and silently handed Morgan the syringe.

"We need to get up, dress and go shopping for our big day tomorrow" Bev reminded her.

"However, we will leave that access port in until tomorrow. Take a bath, not a shower, and Bev will help you wash your hair in the sink."

Morgan said, "Jim is right, my Marsha. No kidding, pinky promise you will comply with doctor's orders."

"Of course. I call dibs on the bath first, Morgan."

Morgan yelled, "Hear me, do not—repeat DO NOT!—get that site wet!"

She waved as she walked into the bedroom, shutting the door behind her. Jim walked to the table, selected two chocolate kisses and asked Bev to take those into her. "And see that she eats them! If you can, stay with her while she is in the bath."

"I—" Jim interjected "—WE, would feel better." Bev grinned and grabbed the bowl of Hershey kisses. "Later, boys!"

Both came out in towels. "I took a bath, too," said Bev. "Now we both will wash our hair. You two, scram, out of the kitchen!"

Jim and Morgan moved to the living room. Marsha helped Bev first. Marsha asked if she could sit down first. Jim and Morgan stood. They went to steady her and could see she was already winded. Her towel escaped her grasp and her eyes fluttered shut. "Sorry babe, I know I promised, but I'm too tired to care."

They laid her on the bed and Morgan pulled the blanket up to cover her. Jim noted her sugar was off the charts on the high end. "How many kisses did you eat?"

Bev told him they'd shared the whole bowl. Morgan drew up insulin and asked Jim how much he thought. Jim was quiet for a minute, then said, "Let's start low instead of hammering her. Make it 14."

Morgan drew it up and injected her. Suddenly, both Jim and Morgan's gaze shifted to her leg; she had a bright red rash. Morgan pulled the towel back and they both said, "Hives!" Morgan asked if they used something new in the bath water. Bev said, "Yeah, we used these new bath bombs."

Jim walked over to Bev and pulled her towel off. Hives. "Both of you two are having a reaction to those chemicals."

He gave Bev some Benadryl and Morgan gave it to Marsha, both getting one small dose. "Bev, go shower and wash that chemical off."

Morgan got a bowl and gave Marsha a sponge bath. "Morgan, what about my pee-pee, it burns there."

Jim said, "Let's see."

She let out a big loud sigh. "Spread 'em, Chicky."

"Wow and WOW." He asked the bed to heal and generate. The bed indicated it would take 20 minutes to heal and regenerate. "Bev gets on this bed after you."

Bev came out and said, "Jim, I am really burning down there."

He said, "I know, so is Marsha. Why don't you sit on the bed with her. The bed can do a two for one."

"I'm not kidding! It really burns, honey." Morgan programmed the bed for two. They sat together and mapped out where they would go shopping.

After a short time, the treatment screen indicated, "Repair is complete on both patients."

"Now—Shopping! We'll be dressed in a second."

"I'll put my hair in a scrunchy and wear dark glasses with no makeup."

Jim asked if they minded if he and Morgan showered. Both laughed and told them "Snap!"

Shortly they were all dressed and ready to go.

They made it as far as the lobby but there was a larger bunch of press and fans than security had anticipated. Marsha took one step back and tried to take another, but a security guard was right behind her and Bev.

Morgan heard her breathing hard. He moved into her with his arm around her waist. Jim didn't look but gathered Bev close to him and they squeezed into Marsha.

All the reporters started screaming questions at them which caused Morgan and Jim to smile. They walked to the bank of microphones where security and police surrounded them.

Marsha glanced at the policeman nearest her. He was in full riot gear, but behind all that, she could see he was a Blue.

She told Morgan, "Go, we have to go." Their security paved the way and two security guards helped support Marsha. They put her in first, laying her on the seat. The other opened, and Jim squeezed in, bag open so he could get what he needed.

Bev and Morgan climbed in with another security agent. Morgan picked her up with an arm around her waist and sat behind her. "Follow me, just breathe." Jim heard a strange deepness to her breathing and pulled his stethoscope out to listen.

She managed to get the word, "Blue," out as she closed her eyes and opened them again. She was breathing better, but Jim was still listening. He peeled back the bandage and gave her all three injections. Morgan was still asking her to follow his breathing and Jim listened again.

"My hand hurts." Jim picked it up and said, "This looks like a puncture wound!"

"He did it. That Blue man cop did it." Morgan let her sit up against the back of the seat, as he moved around in front of her. Jim pulled the stethoscope from his ears as security told the driver to stop.

"It was a Blue. He moved in close to me and made eye contact with me and that is when I felt the sting," said Marsha.

The security guard told him he saw him, too, but thought it was just the lighting. He did not see him stab Marsha, since his focus was on getting them out of there. Jim put some antiseptic plus antibiotic lotion on it and covered it with a band aid.

Bev held out her arm crying and saying, "Me, too." Jim turned as did Morgan. Jim grabbed his stethoscope, hooked it into his ears, and listened. She had the same strange breathing pattern as Marsha. Security asked if she had seen him as well. She nodded her head yes.

Marsha said, "I don't care—we are still going shopping! You just radio ahead and tell them to clear a block. We will go in for one hour, boys, and then we are all yours to probe as you want!"

Morgan looked at her and said, "I don't think that is a wise choice."

She told him. "Damn it, Morgan, I am sick and tired of living in fear. It is about time we face this!"

"Now, the driver should get going. Security radio ahead let them know about Blue..." As her words trailed off, she melted into Morgan's arms and murmured, "Caci, my Caci."

Jim told the driver to take them back to the hotel and clear a wide path and to make sure they looked over each and every security and police person. "I want two gurneys and pull into the delivery bay."

They had an elevator blocked off and ran in with the girls on the gurney. Morgan grabbed a piece of luggage and yanked out the other medical mat, directing security to help him set it up on the sofa.

Jim looked at him and Morgan shouted, "You are not the only one who plans!" Bev was already on her mat and Jim was running diagnostics. Marsha was unconscious as they moved her from the gurney to the mat. Morgan instructed it to warm 20 degrees. He brought up the diagnostics windows.

He still remembered them from the Blue Wars. Morgan hit the first screen and cried out, "NO!"

Jim looked at him as bent over and fell to his knees. Jim ran to look at the screen. The security guard helped move him to a chair in the kitchen. Jim knelt down and said, "Damn, the same for Bev!"

"We do not say one word until after we get home!" Morgan looked exasperated. Security handed him a tissue. A tear rolled down Jim's cheek. Morgan looked up at him and whispered, "Caci, this brings all that back." The security man asked why now after four years. Jim looked at him and asked his name. "Don, Don Scrodel. Sir, if I may present this to both of you."

Morgan turned, giving him his whole attention. "We're listening, go ahead."

"Both bathed in water with the bath bombs that were in the tub. The hotel doesn't provide those, so I checked and asked the maid if she put it there; she did not. Both needed that healing device…" Morgan glanced at Jim who was listening with one eyebrow cocked.

Don knew he had their attention. Morgan glanced back to Don. "It was then it regenerated their fertility again. I believe the Blue may have injected them with fertile eggs. And, after reading your dossier, my best guess is it was from your batch of fertilized eggs, Dr. King. My guess is they need more females."

Jim stood. "I'm afraid you may be correct. Don, I'm going to ask that you be reassigned to our personal service and stay by our side going forward."

Don nodded, "Yes, sir! Would you text Olzing and advise my duty station be switched, sir?"

Morgan was texting immediately; then exclaimed, "Done!"

Shortly, Marsha and Bev felt better. Marsha said, "You boys are not wiggling out of this. We are going shopping. Make it so, men!" Don radioed to have the limo ready in the loading bay in 10 minutes. "Make sure they run the mirrors and scan for devices on the limo. Have Kem run for any chemicals inside the car and anything sharp like a needle." Morgan instantly liked Don.

Marsha asked if both had their credit cards at the ready.

Morgan chuckled and said, "Yeah, and mine is already feeling the burn!" They laughed.

Shortly, they arrived at the designated boutique which had been closed for all but them. In fact, the surrounding area had been cleared for an entire block. First, Security went in and searched for anything out of the ordinary, then opened the door for the four of them.

Marsha instantly found a beautiful hair clip that would sparkle around her slicked back hair in a bun. Then she saw a sparkly red short skirt. Don suspected it might be just the thing she would wear and perfect for an adversary to hide a needle in. Don reached for it before Marsha could grab it and said, "Here, please let me get that for you."

The needle stuck him, however, he did not flinch and said, "Oh, it's torn; you won't want this."

He took it to Morgan, showing him the needle and where it had stuck him. "Please, let me inspect anything that catches their eyes before they touch it."

Don then approached Jim, showed him the needle and asked that he be the first to touch anything. Jim felt himself becoming quite angry but didn't allow his demeanor to show how much it upset him. He went right to Bev and when she reached for something, he took it first to look it over and told her he didn't like it.

Morgan quickly did the same to Marsha. He found her a short baby blue dress with black trim. Don took it back to a dressing room and scanned it. It was clean so Don told Marsha her dressing room was ready. She ran back and said, "I can't wait to try this on." She came out smoothing the dress down her shapely body and toned legs. She turned to Morgan and asked what he thought. "It is amazing and it would look stunning with those black heels with the sparkles on them! Especially because those heels give your legs more definition." He hoped that statement would deter her from trying on shoes. Bev tried on a deep green dress that was tight fitting. Jim's eyes lit up and told her she was gorgeous, and he was proud of doing a great job on the "perky boob job" she'd asked for. She laughed.

Don broke in, "Okay, folks, please finish so we can get you back to the hotel before Paris traffic turns ugly."

Jim appreciated how Don presented a very logical reason as the time limit on the girls. Morgan paid first, then stood watching Jim laughing as he shook, signing the bill. "How did that feel, old man?" asked Morgan.

Jim gasped, "Painful! I could have bought a tractor for that price!"

Morgan cuffed him on the shoulder and said, "Just look at their faces. They are so very happy."

Jim returned Morgan's look. "We will need to remember this moment when we get home."

They ordered dinner with a high-priced wine as recommended by the server when they returned to their suite. They asked the girls to lie on the mat until dinner came to make sure the allergic reactions didn't show when they put on their new gowns. Both did quick diagnostic screens, which thankfully revealed nothing.

There was a knock on the door. Don went to the door and asked if the chemical scan had been done. "Yes, sir."

"You scanned for any objects that did not belong, foreign objects included?" The response was, "Yes, sir."

Don pulled the cart in and set an array of marvelous dishes on the table. "Okay, folks, here's your dinner."

Jim was just pulling up the glucose app and scanned Marsha. "Your sugar needs some boosting, Marsha. Eat anything you like and have some wine as well."

They had just finished when there was another knock on the door. The security guard told him both bags had been scanned for chemicals and any foreign objects twice. He smiled and thanked him.

"Ladies, I have your gowns for the ceremony." Both jumped up as he hung them on the TV cabinet. They unzipped the bags. Marsha said, "OMG, I love it! I am putting it on right now!" She stripped right there on the spot and told Morgan to help her into it.

"Marsha, you promised!"

"Oh, you old prude; I can't wait." She lifted her leg and looked down to step into the dress and froze. Jim could see she was staring at her stomach. Morgan looked up to see what she was waiting for and saw it, too. Jim could see it from across the room.

She fell backward and Don caught her. They laid her on the bed. Don asked what that was.

Bev approached and said, "Blue infected us, didn't he, Jim?" She pulled up her shirt and said, "I saw it in the dressing room."

She hugged Morgan and told him how sorry she was that he had to relive such a painful moment in his life. "Jim and I are here for you. Marsha will come to accept it. She loves babies and will open her heart to any baby, blue or not."

Jim slid his arm around Bev. "Just so you know, the same goes for us. Every life is a blessing, that is what Jim and I feel."

Don said, "They will never—and I do mean never—slip by us again." He had already pulled his radio out and was calling Olzing.

Marsha came around. Her heart still raced and her blood pressure was critically high. Jim had hooked her to the heart monitor. She tried to pull the blanket up to look but Jim leaned across her chest. Morgan sat on the cot next to her.

Jim said, "You don't have to look, you know what it is and so do we. They got Bev too."

Bev knelt next to her head. Marsha closed her eyes, shaking her head back and forth, murmuring, "Caci, Caci, Caci" over and over, giving vent to her tears.

Jim gave her some meds but still laid across her. She would have to make eye contact with him. She tried to push him away, but Bev touched her shoulder gently. She looked at Bev who had a very tender expression on her face. She looked past Jim to Morgan, who held her hand cupped to his cheek softly crying with his eyes closed.

She turned back to Jim and gave him the eye contact she knew he was waiting for. Tears ran down the corners of her eyes. Jim had the most tender expression she had ever seen him give anyone.

"We love you, and you are what completes this family group. Now, yes, Blue got to both you and to Bev. Both of you are pregnant. It was a thoroughly calculated and executed plan by planting the chemical bomb, causing you two to sit on the bed, which neither Morgan nor I had programmed so it regenerated your reproductive organs. He stuck both of you. We are not sure how much he gave you or Bev. Now, we see just one egg anywhere in your body and one in Bev's. Both, thank God, are boys and we know they are after girls.

"So now, you have a choice right now which way you want to go." Her breathing became labored. She closed her eyes. Jim looked over at the monitor.

Morgan spoke to her, "Baby, open your eyes so I can talk to you, please." She turned her head and saw Morgan nose to nose with her. Jim was watching the monitor, not willing to let this go on much longer.

"Take in a deep breath—that's right—and now blow it out. That is good, baby. Now, there is nothing I would not do for you, you know that. But I need you, right now, to do something for me."

She dropped her head and began to cry. Jim questioned if he might have to medicate her. In fact, he stood and went to get what he needed. Morgan never broke eye contact with her. Bev continued to stroke her head. "What is in your heart?

"

She looked at him and asked without skipping a beat. "A boy?"

Jim turned around and double checked the monitor while Morgan looked nowhere else but deep into her eyes.

He said, "Yes, Bev, too."

She made everyone laugh, though a bit nervously, when she said "Andy and Barney! You know we are keeping him silly!"

Jim still brought everything over. He leaned across her again. "Now, can you tear yourself away from Mr. Teddy Bear?" She looked at him. He still had that tender look. "We have a decision here..."

She interrupted him with, "There is no decision! I am keeping this baby. And I'm happy about it!"

"I suspected you would feel that way. But your heart is skipping, your blood pressure is still high, and your pulse is too fast."

She looked at him and said, "Stop beating around the bush and do it. I need four hours to get ready for tomorrow."

Jim locked eyes with Morgan as he shifted to a position behind her. He pulled the gloves on and opened the kit. Jim laid five syringes on her chest and told her to close her eyes.

She said, "Remember four hours to get ready."

He touched her nose and murmured, "You got it." He pushed the first and then the second injection, then Morgan slipped in the breathing tube. He gave the last three and looked at the monitor. Morgan taped the tube down, then glanced at the monitor. Her vitals were looking better—not great but improved.

Jim turned and looked at Bev, "Your turn on the bed."

"Do I have to strip like Marsha?" She joked and they laughed.

He said, "Let's see how you're looking, because—like Marsha—you attempt to hide stuff from me."

Morgan said, " Oh, NOOOOOOOOOOOO, not our Bev." With a steely glare, she flipped him the bird.

"Well, I am offended, little Missy!" said Morgan. Their laugh was filled with relief.

"Morgan, come over here." He turned the monitor so he could watch Marsha.

"What do you think? Morgan looked and said, "Oh, no, not our Bev! She would never not tell you her pulse was racing, or—let me guess—nausea, and she's probably already thrown up, oh, and lookie, lookie here! Her blood pressure is higher than Marsha's!"

Morgan then got right down in Bev's face and growled, "Why did you not say anything? You have a horrific headache, right?"

She said, "Can I steal Marsha's line and say, 'Just do it?' I need four hours, too!"

"Oh, and can you have lunch here when we get up? I want a chicken thigh and oranges. Marsha will want salmon and a bosque pear. Both of us want a Coke Zero; got it?"

"Yes, ma'am!" Jim first accessed her vein, then put her under.

Jim and Morgan both opened a beer and sat on the sofa where they could watch the displays and Marsha's heart monitor.

"After four years of nothing, the Blue hunted us down and executed a diabolical plan. Can I say how relieved I am that these are boys?"

Jim looked at Morgan and mused, "Don't be so sure they didn't perfect their techniques so that the boys with your DNA can produce the same effect as just you with producing females."

Morgan looked mortified. He leaned back, color draining from his face.

"You okay?" Morgan shook his head no. Jim got up and came back with the medical gun. "I can't imagine going through the kidnapping again."

Jim told him their security will have to plan for a worst-case scenario with both Merlin and the Blue as the primary threats. "However, I don't think Merlin truly means us harm. He just doesn't have the codes to stop it himself. Or, maybe, because he is an Immortal that would be against his prime directive or whatever they have. Perhaps he can only give us nudges in the right direction."

"Look, it happened at the Louvre and we know that Easter Island is one of the places where we must enter the sequence. We also know—not exactly in order—Giza, Teotihuacan in Mexico, and the Metal Cauldrons in Russia."

"It also occurs to me there must be a place in North America and perhaps Canada or Alaska. If I were a betting man like Bat, I would say Oak Island, and/or that place in Malta called Ggantija. Remember, those pyramids in Malta are older than any in Egypt."

7

Paris

That evening, Jim took the first shift. He could occasionally see brief fibrillations of Marsha's heart, for which he adjusted medications. Bev was resting comfortably. He decided to look again for any other Blue eggs. There were none. He did find it odd there was only one. After some thought, he decided to instead check for blue DNA.

He reeled back in shock and horror. It was slowly but progressively turning her own DNA into that of a Blue. He calmed himself by telling his mind he could panic later, but right now he needed his mind sharp for them.

Next, he directed Don to radio Thar and put him on the first jet here. Or the fastest ship, or whatever he had to get him here along with someone who specialized in dialing back Blue DNA. He heard Thar say they were boarding a ship now and would arrive in an hour, He requested they have a car waiting for them at the private airstrip at Orly.

Don stepped over and Jim said. "I heard, thank you. Ask if they could bring another medical mat and any other equipment they will need—even possibly MIGHT need."

"Yes, Sir." He could see Morgan was struggling and it would do him a world of good to be on the mat, too.

Exactly an hour and a half later, there was a knock on the door. Don opened the door to let Thar and two other Nordic doctors in with a large array of equipment. He looked toward Bev and Marsha, then went to Marsha first.

It was clear she was the more severely affected by her struggle to take one breath in and let it out.

"Marsha has converted to 32 percent DNA Blue."

"Tricky bastards," said Thar. "Dr. Brock, dialing back now." They attached an external device to her line that began pumping in a clear fluid. Jim asked about the baby.

"This will dial him back at the same time, however, will make the baby sterile. So far, nothing too outrageous."

Jim asked, "What about the pregnancy? Usually they are accelerated to days."

He replied, "No, I'm dialing that back as this is early in gestation. It should be the normal nine months.

"We have seen a lot of sugar issues during these pregnancies as well as greater weight gain than usual. The babies are always too big to deliver naturally but are almost always in prime health."

They left Dr. Krill with Marsha and moved to Bev. Dr. Brock said "She's been converted to 49% Blue. She is close to the cusp of no return." They put the device on her and asked Jim to open the fluid drip and simultaneously give a bolus. Jim's concern for his wife—and for Marsha—was etched into his face. They put a monitor on her and put a monitor on both for the babies. Jim wanted to know how long this would take.

She answered, "About four hours," and sought to partially distract him by explaining how their technology had improved with the information shared by the Tellite race. "The Tellites were the first to use improved DNA for the Blue. They have tremendous knowledge."

Thar asked where Morgan was. Jim told him that was who he had ordered the mat for. "He is taking this badly, to the point it's making it hard for him to function. "Let's get another cot rather than the sofa and get him out here on it."

They set Morgan's mat up right beside Marsha. Jim had ready supplies for line-only access. Jim went into his bedroom to get him. He turned on the light for Morgan. "Okay, I am up," he groused.

Jim sat down. He could see Morgan sink. "What—Marsha, did she crash?"

"No, however, Thar is here with two others." Morgan struggled to get out of bed. "Sit down and listen, then react." Morgan looked down with his brow furrowed anticipating the worst. Jim continued, "I was flipping through the screens making sure the pregnancies were not speeding along so instead of a ceremony we had deliveries." Morgan nodded his head in agreement and to show he was following clearly. "I discovered that the bastard included a chip to reprogram their DNA to BLUE."

Morgan put his head in his hands, shoulders visibly heaving with sobs. Thar came in, sat beside him, and put a hand on his shoulder. Jim continued, "Morgan, we were able to dial them back—along with the babies—to 100% human DNA. It was a close call for Bev— she was almost at the point of no return—but both she and Marsha are doing so much better now."

"Now, about you, buddy. I want you on the mat and please, PLEASE!!! Let us help you rest. You are usually at least seven steps ahead of us, but now you are two steps behind. So, please, Morgan?"

"Okay but keep Dr. Snip-Snip away from me and make sure that dam mat does not reverse what Dr. Snip-Snip did." They laughed loudly in relief, and they trooped back out into the living room. "Well, you people were awfully certain I would go along with your plan."

Jim told him to just, "Go get on the damn mat."

"Pushy, Pushy!" growled Morgan.

Thar stepped in front of Jim and told him, "I got your back."

"Oh, by the way your diabolical son, Wyatt, fell on a rock outside trying to tackle Bitty. He fell mostly because she pushed him. He has three lovely sutures from Dr. Cay, because he, too, would not get on the medical table to heal it. No, he had to have the RED BADGE OF COURAGE!"

Morgan smiled, laid back and said, "That's my boy!"

"Jim, you want to start a line?" Morgan wanted to know why. "Because I said so," said Thar.

"Okay, jeez!" said Morgan. Jim quickly slid one into his upper forearm. "Run fluids and give me the med gun."

Jim injected him and he was out in seconds.

"Now, Jim, we have a surprise for you." They brought in another cot with a mat. "Get on it and not one word of argument." We will wake you and Morgan at 11:00."

He laid down and Dr. Brock started a line for him with fluids and Thar gave him something to relax. He had observed how high both their blood pressures so dispensed meds for that as well. The three monitored all of them.

Marsha as usual kept waking up as she continued to fight the medication. Finally, in desperation, they had security zip tie her arms to the cot so she could not pull anything out.

Later, Thar looked at his watch and announced, "It is 11:00. Go ahead and wake Morgan and Jim but pull their lines first."

It took about ten minutes for them to awaken. Morgan got up first and went straight to Marsha.

Thar walked over and said, "Your little hellcat kept waking up and trying to pull her tube out. So we fixed it so that would not happen."

Morgan laughed. "They want four hours to get ready tonight plus an hour for a late lunch. So, they need to be awake at 1:00. We will get you tickets to sit with us; you are all going. We are not dressed, but we can and will fix that."

Morgan picked up the phone and said, "We have three guests coming with us and they need to be seated right next to us. Two need to be fitted for tuxedos and one needs a gown. Thank you. And clear everyone through security before you send them up."

Jim remarked. "I see your nap did you a world of good."

Morgan smiled, "Yeah! Too bad Bat is not here. We could all play poker while we are waiting—as usual—for our girls." Just then, the door opened revealing Bat and Emma as if on cue.

Morgan crossed to them and gave each a huge hug. Emma went directly to Marsha. "Untie her this instant! I will sit with her. She is not an animal! Right now, you untie her."

"Well, now we know who the boss is around here, and it is certainly none of us." They all laughed.

"You, security, I need a basin of warm water and a washcloth."

"His name is Don."

"Oh, I am sorry. Don, please get me that, would you, son?"

Don smiled and told her it would be his honor.

She snapped back, "Listen, you smartass, I don't see you walking yet!"

Thar's knees failed him, and he sat down, choking on his own laughter.

"You, that's laughing, I need one of the doctors to sponge Bev." He stood and said, "Yes, ma'am."

She gently ran a sponge through her hair and then her face and arms. She slid the blanket down and saw her belly. "Hey, smartass, what is wrong with Marsha's belly?"

Morgan came over to her and told her that Jim would finish with Marsha. Jim sat down beside her, took the sponge, and finished giving the sponge bath.

Emma told him to not forget her back. Jim turned, smiled and nodded to her.

Morgan and Thar explained what had taken place. Emma cried, inhaled deep and stood up. "So we will have two new babies? Better have the names Charlie after Bat's friend from Dodge City and Bat's brother, Tom. She looked to Morgan and said, "You take Tom, and Jim, you got Charlie; any questions?" Both shook their heads no.

"I need a nail file and nail buffer to do their nails for tonight." Don radioed down for two nail files and two buffers. Morgan asked if Bat had a tux and she had a gown. She growled, "What's wrong with what I have on?"

Jim coughed. Thar turned away, laughing as silently as he could manage.

Morgan started with, "Mom, this is a formal affair. So, when they come up to take these three doctors' measurements, they will take Bat's and yours, too. You will look stunning in the gown they bring for you, I promise."

Emma said, "I am not wearing those shrink garments! They take me as I am naturally."

Thar could not hold it back; he burst out laughing and walked into the dining room.

"You guys would be lost without me running things, Morgan."

"Yes, Mom," he answered with a tender grin.

"Make sure you call right now and be sure we're sitting with you and these three nice doctors. Oh, and tell smartass not to be laughing through the ceremony."

"Mom, pretty sure he heard you," said Morgan.

"As I intended," Emma shot back. Then she asked if they had had breakfast. No one said anything. Emma picked up the phone and ordered. "Oh and have your security run checks on the food. If I find something, anything, I promise I WILL FIND YOU!" She hung up.

BY 12:30, they had just finished eating. Marsha was awake and Emma was at her side. She called for Dr. Smartass to come remove the tube.

"Yes, Ma'am."

"Call me Mom."

He smiled and said, "Thank you, Mom."

"I am only rough on the ones I like, and only expect what I know they are capable of."

"Thank you, for that kind vote of confidence."

Morgan came over. "Here, Mom, let me do it." He knelt at her head and pulled the tape gently. He told her to blow now, pulled it then turned and tossed it in the red bag in one fluid, practiced motion.

Emma already had Marsha in her arms. She told Morgan to go get a robe for her. She helped Marsha remove the monitor stickers. Morgan helped her slip on the robe. "Guess what, Honey? Emma named our baby Tom after Bat's brother."

Marsha told Emma she loved it and what an honor they could name another child after Bat's side of their family. Jim asked her to lie down so he could pull the line. And before she asked, Jim directed the bed, "And please repair the patient's wound so she will be scarless and spotless with a smoking hot body."

She laid back and watched Thar as he went through the screens fast as lightning. He told Morgan she looked great.

Next, they went to Bev as did Emma. Thar pulled her tube and Emma waited for her to wake.

"My lovely, you look so beautiful," said Emma.

Bev threw her arms around her. "Get her a robe, Jim."

Jim slipped the robe on Bev, then he told her to lie back down so they could pull the line. Emma removed the monitor stickers. They brought in lunch as Thar and Jim finished with Bev.

"Emma, did you do my nails?" asked Marsha.

Emma smiled. "I did yours, too, Bev. I hope that is ok." She came over and kissed her. "Let's sit down right now, all of us, and let's have a nice lunch."

Those without formal dress wear were measured and three tuxes and two gowns delivered in what had to be record time.

Bat laughed and said, "Still wearing my hat and cane."

Morgan said, "Uh, they might think you are Bat Masterson from the TV show," he laughed! "What episode is that?" Bat swatted his arm with his cane.

Thar and the other two Nordic doctors had not the faintest idea what they were talking about.

Marsha pulled out Emma's gown. It was a beautiful gold and black brocade with a silk brocade wrap and purse along with black flats with sequins.

Marsha told her she would be the belle of the ball. Emma blushed. "Let Bev and I do your hair."

She said, "My two daughters would do that for this old lady?"

They guided her into Marsha's bathroom. An hour later, she emerged with a loose curly updo and beautiful subtle makeup. She wore the clip Marsha had purchased for herself but realized it would be better displayed on Emma. Bat came right over to her and told her she was the most beautiful woman he had ever seen or known. She smiled and said, "I love you, Bat."

"Okay, people, we are going to our room. And, Morgan, thank you. It is a beautiful room," said Emma.

When they left. Morgan said, "Whoever brought them here and made the reservations, from the bottom of my heart, I thank you."

There was a knock on the door and Olzing stood in a very nice black suit with an earpiece in place.

"It was you who brought them here, isn't it?"

Olzing said. "It did not seem right for them not to be here for your big night."

The men were all dressed and ready. The doctors were clearly not comfortable in black ties. They were accustomed to the typical Nordic long loose gowns with linen pants underneath. They felt, and actually looked out of place with all their security and the three doctors with pure white long hair.

Morgan said, "They're cousins from Kentucky."

Jim laughed. The others just stood there.

Bat knocked on the door and he and Emma came in. She looked regal in her gown. Morgan and Jim both hugged her and gave her a kiss. They told her she was breathtaking. She said, "I know!"

Jim and Morgan exchanged a glance and laughed. Bev was the first out. Her dress was a tight halter style that had jewel tones with lots of sparkle. She had wound her hair up into a French twist and secured it with sparkle bobby pins. Her makeup was simple but so Bev. Jim walked up and twirled her around. Emma came over to take her hand and told her she was a real live princess.

It took Marsha another 10 minutes but when she finally swung the door open, literally everyone said "WOW!" Her gown showed off her fabulous figure and was cut so low in the front Morgan was worried that when she sat, it might slip down to reveal her breasts. Her hair was slicked back and done in a low ponytail that she wrapped with hair around the rubber band, which appeared metallic and shiny. She had long purple and gold earrings that touched her shoulders and her eyes jumped out at you. She wore false eyelashes that were thick but not overly long and added dimension to her eyes. She also wore a deep plum lipstick.

Morgan stood, holding his chest. Thar took a step forward but Jim pushed him back. He had tears welling up in his eyes. "You are magical! How am I so lucky? How am I to talk, looking at you? I will babble like a three-year-old. I am the luckiest man on Earth tonight! A beautiful wife, friends, family, colleagues and a Nobel Prize winner!"

Marsha stepped forward and opened her hand with a new crown with all the right birthstones in it. "And all your children, my love." She pinned it on him. "Are we all ready?"

Don radioed down and suddenly Nordic guards appeared everywhere. Morgan stopped in the hall and turned to Marsha, "We don't have to go, baby."

She said, "We are going. Usual tactic, ok? You guys hold me up and make damn sure I do not get poked again and neither does Bev!"

"We are ready," He extended his elbow for her to slip her hand through. As they all got on the elevator, security tightened around them.

When the elevator doors opened, it was so bright it was difficult to see. They saw what must have been over 200 Nordic guards, some in uniform and some in plain clothes. They all had batons with laser technology extended out, baton to baton. Anyone that tried to push forward or break through would receive a lasting injury.

Marsha stepped off the elevator but just could not move further. Thar gently touched her back and whispered he would be behind her, and Bat was behind Bev. Emma stood right beside Bat. Morgan and Jim recognized the sway as Don and another guard moved beside Thar, but behind Morgan and Bat, Jim could not help but look down at Marsha who had both her arms on Morgan instead of one on his arm. It was throwing her off her stride. Don saw that, too, and stepped in front of Marsha so Jim could reposition her arm and Thar held her from behind.

As one group, they all stepped to the microphone as people began shouting questions.

Morgan began, "We are glad to be back and so honored to do the work we do. The last four years we have worked with select doctors from the Nordic region." Of course he didn't say what Nordic region or even what planet.

He could feel Marsha struggling with the screaming and camera flashes. It was even disconcerting to Emma and Bev. Don spoke into the mic in his sleeve and a pathway almost magically cleared in a wide swath by the guards with their batons. One person tried to break through but Don stepped in front of the group and said stop, and a plain clothes guard subdued him and dragged him off.

One group including Thar's fellow physicians as well as Bat and Emma rode in one limo and Morgan, Jim, Bev, Marsha, along with Thar in the other with Don in the front providing security. They had almost thrown Marsha in first with Don on the other side pulling her through. There was even a mat on the floor in the middle.

Don positioned her so she was on the mat while the limo was surrounded and no one could see inside. The commotion had caused Marsha to have another panic attack. Thar drew a syringe full of a yellow substance out and mentioned it was from their technology, thinking it might be useful tonight. Jim sat back and injected her while Morgan knelt on the floor beside her. Almost instantly, she asked if she was in the car. Then said, "OMG, you're wrinkling my dress. Are my eyelashes on?"

Thar grasped her hand and said, "My Queen, you look ravishing," as he pulled her up to her seat. Morgan sat beside her and took her pulse, "My Queen has tachycardia." Jim did not ask this time; he leaned over to Marsha and removed the top of the vial with his teeth.

She said, "Please, not in my arm."

Holding the cap with his teeth, he mumbled, "Too late."

"Great, bet I have no sex tonight, either," she grumbled as she smoothed her dress.

Jim laughed. He pulled out another and held that top with his teeth, saying, "One more for the road!"

"Guess it will do no good for me to say NO?"

Jim replied, "You guessed right." Thar's face showed amazement at how they all functioned as one unit.

Don turned around and slid the window partially open. "We are pulling up to the entrance. Do NOT get out of this car unless you hear me, and I open the door for you."

Morgan said he understood, then turned to Marsha and grabbed her hand, telling her it was not too late to not go in.

"I have three men with muscles to hold me up. I will sit through that ceremony if I have to tape my eyeballs open."

Don opened the door and told them not to be alarmed at the size of the crowds or the number of guards and plain clothes that surrounded them.

Marsha stiffened, took in a deep breath and said, "Let's go get my baby a statue."

Thar got out first to throw them off a bit by shielding them with his body. Then Morgan, Jim, Marsha and Bev got out.

Marsha was first to see the Blue. She let out a yell and four plain clothes had him on the pavement in an instant. Two more jumped out of the crowd, one grabbing at Marsha and pulling her arm, trying to drag her away. She used her Christian Louboutin heel to stomp on the arch of his foot. The guards caught him and shoved him, none too gently, to the ground.

Don pushed her to the ground under him as two more Blues attacked. Jim felt something electrical surround them as Morgan pulled her to safety. Thar hoisted her to her feet as three undercover guards pushed them through the event door.

All doors were immediately barred and Marsha was down again. Olzing ran to them and directed the shields to go up. Morgan heard it as well. "The Committee said they would not allow the shield unless something happened first."

Thar responded, "Then we need to get her out of here right now." He instructed the undercover agent to please retrieve their Nobel Prize, but to tell the Nobel Committee that being attacked without a shield in place made it unsafe for them to remain a second longer.

Don ran in with blood dripping down the side of his face. "Let's get her in the car." Olzing promptly countermanded the Committee's order and yelled, "Shields up!"

Don spoke into his cuff mic and gave a code but Jim could not hear what he said. Instead of the car, a helicopter landed in front of the building, scattering the throng of reporters as it landed. "Let's go."

Don ran with Marsha and the others followed. There were two medical mats in the helicopter. The last undercover agent jumped on with mere seconds to spare, holding their Nobel Prizes, one in each hand.

Marsha opened her eyes and saw the statue. "Oh, man, I must have slept through your speech; I am so sorry, babe."

Don informed them that they were en route to Orly airport, and would board the Nordic ship, which was equipped with a full medical unit, for the ride to their base. Their ETA to the base was one hour, and the trip to the airport would take just 15 minutes.

Jim pulled out his stethoscope and listened as Marsha lay quiet with her eyes closed. "She is barely breathing. Grab that oxygen behind you, Thar."

Jim grabbed it from Thar, turned it on wide open, and slid the mask over her face. It worried Morgan that she was not protesting getting her dress wrinkled. She lay completely still. When they arrived at the airport, the agents grabbed everything from the limo and a gurney with two other doctors helped Don get her on the bed. They rushed her onto the ship where Thar and Jim were flashing through the screens, and Morgan spoke quietly and soothingly into her ear. They lifted off.

Jim abruptly stopped on one screen and lifted her dress. Morgan glanced over and immediately knew she was having a miscarriage. Thar barked to cut the gown off her.

Morgan said, "Please, I will do it! She'd never forgive anyone who cut this gown." She was quickly freed of her beautiful gown.

"Pelvic exam position," yelled Jim as he slipped on gloves. He looked directly at Thar and said, "It all comes out when we land. All of it!" She expelled the Blue fetus en route. It was still just a mass with no real shape. They slid a pad under her and covered her. Morgan told the bed to warm 25 degrees.

They had her hooked to monitors but still she failed to respond. Thar brought two kits; Morgan grabbed one to intubate her just as Jim announced, "I have access." They hung fluids as Morgan continued talking to her in a low voice about how beautiful she looked tonight.

Thar said, "She is having a reaction to the drug from earlier, plus her whole system is on overload. I need to counter that drug right now and reverse the effects."

"I do not want her awake. She must stay under a full 24 hours. Even then that is pushing the envelope." Morgan got on the bed with her and beside her, holding her to him.

In the confusion, no one saw Bev fall. She grabbed Jim, yelling that one of the Blues grabbed her wrist. She twisted and slipped free but that her wrist hurt quite badly.

Morgan heard that and jumped up. "Okay, let's go, Chicky!" He put her on the mat and told her to lie down. "Yep, broken! Pink or purple cast?" She laughed. Then Jim saw it, too.

Morgan lifted her gown and saw she, too, was bleeding. She screamed in alarm. Morgan had never seen Bev like that before. He didn't ask, but quickly shot her with the injector gun, putting her into a medically induced coma. Jim cut her clothing off, too, and slid a pad under her.

Jim grumbled, "She never tells me anything!" as he poked through the screens.

Thar jumped in with two kits. Morgan said, "You stick; I will place." Jim was visibly upset to say the least, and embarrassed. He told Morgan, "One, I didn't see her get grabbed, and, two, I didn't see her fall, and, three, she never said a word; no damned Nobel Prize is worth all of this!"

"Too damned true!" Morgan grumbled as he continued to work on Bev. He did a full pelvic exam, and she had also passed the Blue. They could see no other eggs, Blue or human. Morgan asked for DNA percentages. 100% human displayed on the screen. He went back to Marsha and asked; that screen also reported as 100% human. Both sighed in relief.

Don said, "Landing in five minutes but taxi to inside the mountain is another five minutes. There is an entire medical team awaiting our arrival."

When they got there, they could see the team was obviously very well versed in acute trauma care. They grabbed the gurney and ran with three agents in front and three behind along with Thar in the middle.

Four undercover agents along with Don surrounded Jim and Morgan. Jim and Morgan trailed them into Thar's medical bay. It was obviously much more advanced than anything they'd ever seen. They could see every vein and the ventricles and auricles of the heart in great detail—it was amazing.

They pulled the surgical unit over to Thar who placed it over Marsha. He performed a complete pelvic cleanout; uterus, tubes and ovaries, everything! One doctor scanned every artery and vein for hidden eggs. The cardiologist tweaked the pacemaker and added meds.

Bev's care was more straightforward. They set her wrist and put her in a soft cast, then moved her arm under a purple light.

Dr. Brock told Jim the light was used to build and solidify bone cells, and she would be able to use her arm in two days. Thar performed a D&C on Bev and made sure her uterus was scraped clean.

Morgan groused, "I hate sitting here as an observer." He stood up but Jim jerked him back down. "Now is not the time to lose your cool, Morgan!"

Morgan stood again, holding his hands up to fend off Jim, and said, "I need to see the kids. You coming to see Wyatt's 'red badge of courage' sutures?"

Jim told Dr. Cay they were going to see the kids and would be back very shortly. She told them that was a good idea; it would keep them out of her hair, so Jim and Morgan walked to the playroom where they were immediately surrounded by all the kids, everyone trying to talk at once.

Morgan and Jim sat down and said, "Please, one at a time.

"Wyatt, I hear you tried to arm wrestle with Bitty." He ran up and jumped on Morgan's lap, "Yeah, look what I got and I didn't cry at all!" Jim looked at it and whistled. "What a badge!"

Morgan smacked his behind and told him, "No more tackling Bitty!"

Dallas sidled up to Jim in his somewhat awkward and timid way, asking, "On the day we move into the compound can I…" He looked down, fidgeting. Morgan looked toward Jim who was listening patiently for Dallas to finish.

"Well, ah, jeez, can I say a prayer and dedicate the house?" He continued looking down.

Morgan grabbed him, giving him a hug and a kiss.

Jim pulled him over in front of him and told him it was the proudest day of his life! He and Morgan both would love that.

All the kids cheered him and clapped, except for Finch who shot a rubber band at him.

Morgan raised his eyebrow and looked pointedly at Finch.

Then El approached, saying, "I lost a tooth; where is my money, Daddy?"

Morgan laughed and said, "Well, Mr. Tooth Fairy?" Jim pulled out a dollar and handed it to her. She skipped back to her chair, and they all sat down in a half circle surrounding Morgan and Jim. Gage toddled up and said, "I got a boo-boo because Rue bit my finger." Morgan said, "Let me see that!

"Oh, that needs a really big kiss for sure." Morgan kissed it and moved his hand over for Jim to kiss. "All better."

He skipped over and sat down but gave Rue a kiss on the check first. Morgan laughed.

John had something behind his back as he approached Jim. "Daddy, promise me you won't be mad."

"I can't make that promise to you ahead of time," Jim answered.

"Oh, Daddy, can you not be practical just once and give a guy a break?"

"Deal," said Jim as John pulled a black pug puppy from behind his back. "His name is Button. We all voted on it."

Jim took him in his hands and said, "What a cutie! Where did you get him?"

"Mary, our teacher, brought him to us today. Can we keep him, Daddy, please?" Morgan looked at Jim waiting to hear an answer but knowing it before he spoke.

Jim smiled and handed Button back to John, saying, "Yes, of course." Then Emmi came up and gave them each a flower picture she had colored.

"Oh, this is so nice," said Morgan.

"Daddy loves this," Jim echoed.

Next, Tig came up, saying, "Wyatt pushed me down and now I have a big bump on my head and a headache. He is so mean. Daddy, make him be in a time-out circle."

"Let's see this bump." Morgan's eyebrow went up so Jim grabbed him, "Let Uncle Jim see! Oh, my, you boys! We should let Dr. Cay take a picture."

"Oh, good, so we can send it to Grandpa Garmen. He will put him in time out."

"Tig, have you ever pushed any of your brothers or sisters?"

"Yeah, all the time."

"Do you sit in time out each time you push them, making them fall down?"

"Nope, I am good at not getting caught," Tig admitted, somewhat proudly.

Jim rolled his eyes and Morgan shook his head, then grabbed his hand and said, "Let's go and take a picture. You and Wyatt may not push or pull anyone one down again; got it?" said Morgan. Jim added, "Seen or not, Tig!"

8

Tig Exposes A Plan

When they returned to the unit, they were careful to go straight to the pediatric unit so Tig would not see his mom or Bev. Dr. Cay greeted them, saying, "What do we have here?"

"Tig took an on-purpose from his brother's fall today," replied Morgan.

"Uh-oh," said Dr. Cay. "Come sit up here next to me and show me your bump." He sat up on the bed while Morgan ran a scan.

"That is a good size goose egg! Well, I bet Daddy has the picture up already. Looks like your brother did you wrong. You won a free ticket to stay with me tonight. How about some ice cream?"

Tig looked up at Morgan, who nodded his head that, yes, that was okay. "Go pick what you want from the freezer."

As Tig ran over, "It is a concussion, but boys will be boys. And with your rowdy group, you will likely see more of these as they grow up."

Jim bristled, "Hey! She called our group 'rowdy;' can you imagine our little angels being called rowdy?"

Morgan laughed and swung Tig up on the table, sitting next to him. "Please, son, listen to what Dr. Cay tells you. No running off. No playing tricks. Just listen and behave."

Jim sat on the other side of him and joined in, "Tig, I better not hear you were bad. Before I go, can I give you some medicine? It won't hurt."

Tig just shrugged his shoulders since he was too busy eating ice cream to answer. Dr. Cay handed the injector to him and quickly pulled the trigger.

Dr. Cay mumbled, "Out in five minutes—grab the ice cream!"

Morgan and Jim sat with their wives in the medical bay. Morgan wanted to move Marsha and Bev back to their home pod. Morgan stood and approached Thar. Jim looked up, then stood. "We want to move our girls back to our home pod."

Thar agreed, since they were stable and said his personnel would transfer them over.

"Go, get your beds ready."

Jim, on the other hand, hesitated, asking if Thar was certain they could be moved.

"Of course. Bev would most likely be disconnected from the life support in the morning. Marsha may be a bit more tricky, but we will come to your unit. I know having familiar surroundings will be beneficial for both of them.

"Oh, by the way, in the compound we intend to continue to support your own care for your kids and wives, as well as both of you. We have four doctors including Dr. Cay coming with us."

Jim started to walk, but turned back.

"Tig is in with Dr. Cay for the night. He took a fall and has a concussion. Could you please look in on him? He tends to pull pranks and wander off."

Thar smiled and said, "Great kid." Then Jim returned to their bay.

A short time later, both Marsha and Bev were wheeled on their medical beds by four doctors plus Thar. They moved their pod beds off to the side, leaving room for the therapeutic beds.

The team gave their briefings on both Marsha and Bev. The medical personnel left and Thar told them they would return in the morning. "Use the radio should they need any help."

Jim and Morgan sat at their desks. "The big move is in four days. I wonder if we should push it back a couple days to give the girls more time to regain their health? I think we should, but will our girls allow going home to be pushed back?" questioned Morgan.

"I would like for Marsha and Bev to help us with our quest to save the planet. Bev has proved her ability to abstract information and correlate it into individual tasks. Marsha has strong gut instincts and is not afraid to think out of the box. Bev, you, and I tend to be more scientific with our approach and Marsha could be our balance," mused Jim.

Morgan agreed, "It will be a welcome project for all of us. I'd welcome a break from the DNA project after the fiasco at the Nobel ceremony," said Jim.

Morgan nodded in agreement, "Not good memories."

Jim told Morgan to go jump on a bed, get some sleep and they would switch at 3:00 AM.

Morgan walked over and asked the bed to elevate the temperature by 20 degrees. He pulled a blanket from the cupboard and laid down.

Jim checked Morgan's vitals before he awakened him. He was doing perfectly. Jim barely touched his shoulder and Morgan sat up, swinging his legs off the bed. "How're they doing?"

"Bev looks great. She can come off everything when I get up. And Marsha is, too." Jim flopped down on the bed Morgan just vacated. He felt beat.

Morgan walked over to Marsha and pulled up her diagnostics. She was holding her own, but he wished her blood pressure would stabilize. He asked for the DNA percentage again, and it read 100% human. He hadn't realized how tightly he had been holding his breath until he let it out with a sigh of relief. He'd directed the bed to pull her abdominal muscles tighter and to repair her newest scar.

At 9:00 AM, Thar came in and Morgan stood to greet him. He asked how everyone was doing. Morgan nodded, "Bev is ready. Jim has been sleeping since around 4:00 this morning. And Marsha, well, she seems better, but, frankly, that is probably a bit optimistic." Thar went directly to Marsha's bed and flipped through the diagnostic screens so quickly Morgan felt like a rank amateur.

"I would like you to consider another go at our medicine for her. I will sit with her, and we'll bring our monitors down. This drug targets inflammation anywhere in the body. Morgan, I personally believe it would be a giant step forward in her regimen."

Morgan stood with his arms crossed and asked, "And the downside is?"

"Admittedly, we don't have a total understanding about humans. We use this mostly for our soldiers. Like those who were hurt in Paris when they were brought here. It stimulates healing and reduces the body's inflammatory response to trauma."

"But you understand she can't continue on like this, Morgan. You know it, Jim knows it and I surely know it. Our team has learned much working together, specifically while working with Marsha. She has a unique metabolism and a body that releases chemicals that we can't yet explain. I can't tell if this was something left over from when she was Blue or not."

"When did her sexual appetite become so exaggerated?"

Morgan thought about that, "And yours, too?" He glanced at Thar.

"I believe you're right and it could involve the Blue. The timing is fairly close. But you know Marsha will not like being studied under a microscope, though I do understand your line of thinking; it's very logical, of course."

"Shall we give our treatment a go this morning? I would prefer it is done just by you, Jim, and I. The fewer in the mix the better."

"I have to admit I am struggling with trusting people a bit. I am asking that, prior to moving in three days, a complete and thorough background check be performed on all doctors and security personnel."

"Please don't be offended by my wanting to see yours, and Olzing's, from the top security personnel of your planet."

"Done! I would have asked for this a long time ago. You and Jim are far too trusting; I am actually more comfortable seeing you tighten your security. Who does your gut tell you to trust on my team so if we run into a snag while using our technology, we can fall back on them."

"Actually, Dr. Cay, your arrogant SOB cardiologist!"

Thar laughed, "And Dr. Zoff. I have a check in about the two you brought to Paris."

He shook his head and said, "They came from another planet and were just assigned to him."

Morgan's eyebrows raised. "We don't want that to happen at the compound."

"In America, our secret service never brings personnel just assigned to anything or anyone. At least for your compound, I have selected trusted physicians who have been physicians to planetary and galactic leaders. They will go through a complete physical and psychological examination with truth serum testing, financial reviews of each as well as their extended families before they are brought into the compound."

"Now, are you good to try Marsha on this medication later this afternoon?"

Morgan's head nodded. "We should first bring Bev up and make sure she is stable. Give her a few hours to accept the miscarriage and then we can focus our attention on Marsha."

"How is Tig? You certainly have a handful with that one."

Morgan smiled and rocked back on his heels and said, "That's My Boy! Seriously, I believe he may outshine us all. He's not afraid to try anything and his thinking is way outside the box."

"Well, Mr. Unafraid will be ready, or should I say WE will be ready for him to be released to your care once more this morning."

Morgan laughed. "We need to hold onto him until Bev is completely cleared. And, by the way, your kid can pack away the ice cream. He must have snuck out of bed several times. Dr. Cay found him under the table with three empty cartons of ice cream!”

Morgan shook his head. “Sure hope he doesn't spread the word to the rest of the brood or you will have a procession of my kids in and out of your pediatric bay.”

“You know, Vaughn also made that discovery the other day, so, not just your kids.”

Morgan grinned. “Good to know Tig will have some competition for the goodies.”

Thar smiled. “We hope that when we move to the compound, your wife will consider teaching our kids your language. Since Earth is becoming a Galactic member, our kids need diversity and language skills.”

“She would be honored to teach them, Thar!”

“Most Nordic children, by the time they are your kids’ age, know at least three other languages. Your kids will have some catching up to do!”

“I will be back in an hour and we will awaken Bev. But please give Jim a little more time to sleep.”

Morgan looked over at Thar and nodded. “Get everything ready to bring Bev back up and make sure she is stable, and maybe a little ‘just in case scenario’ wouldn’t hurt.”

He reloaded the med gun. He was almost certain Bev would need some anti-anxiety help once she heard that she lost the baby. He glanced over at Jim and thought, “He should get a dose right now before he is awake. He will need to be a rock today for Bev and Marsha both.”

He put the injection into Jim’s arm. “He must be tired; he never even budged.” He then decided to take another glance at the diagnostic screens before him. Everything looked good, but he hesitated and backed up one screen. His vitamin D and iron showed low levels. He input instructions to repair all vitamin deficiencies into the bed.

Morgan went over to Marsha's bed and looked at the same screen, which reflected the same deficiencies. He input instructions for the bed to make the necessary repairs to her vitamin levels.

As he stood by Bev, he saw hers were more severely off and in many different categories. He input instructions to repair all her vitamin levels and sat on the bed, his own readings reflected the same condition. He input the repair for all his vitamin levels and made a mental note to run each of the children's vitamin levels later that day.

Jim awakened, sat up and jumped off the bed. He said he was going to the bathroom and would be right back. Within a short few minutes, Jim had showered and changed into fresh clothing. His thick black hair was still damp.

He indicated Morgan should hit the shower before Thar came to wake Bev. Morgan left, returning in 15 minutes. "It felt good to shower and change clothes," he remarked.

Thar arrived back in the medical bay. He smiled and told Jim good morning and noted they both looked well rested.

"I see you have everything laid out for us and the 'just in case' stuff as well."

Jim looked at Morgan and asked, "Am I finally rubbing off on you?" Morgan chuckled but ran the screens on her again for Jim and Thar.

"She looks ready, gentlemen. Let's begin the assent." It took all of 20 minutes to re-awaken her. Her eyes fluttered open and the first thing she saw was Jim's face. He had raised the bed up to his chest level.

She looked around and noted, "Back in our lab? Thank God!" She reached for Jim and put her hand to his cheek. His face reflected a look of tenderness that was quite rare for him. He told her she needed to lie on the bed for two more hours. She nodded and settled back.

Jim looked toward Morgan. Somehow he had known he would have this task. "Hey, Princess, how is your wrist feeling?" He raised the medical gun where she could see it.

"Well," said Bev.

"Just what I thought! Little-miss-I-am-not-going-to-say-anything finally tells us what we need to know." He injected her.

She closed her eyes as she murmured, "Wow."

Morgan laughed. Morgan placed the gun down on the bed and picked up her hand. A flash of pain crossed her face; and he could see she already knew.

As her tears trickled down her cheeks, Morgan asked if she would like some help and when she nodded, he gave her an injection. She wrapped her arms around Jim and half sat up, grasping him and sobbing. Morgan lowered the bed so Jim could sit beside her. Thar picked up the gun and gave her a synergistic drug, watching the display screen carefully. The sound she made was so deep and heavy, almost wailing. It felt like it was from the pit of her soul. Jim looked toward Morgan, then to Thar.

Morgan touched her back and said, "I want you to sleep."

She turned her head and snapped just like Marsha would, and said, "No, I need to feel this pain, not medicate it!"

Jim closed his eyes as tears trickled down his cheeks. It was heart wrenching to hear and to see.

After 40 minutes, Jim laid her back on the bed. Thar and Morgan stood by. Jim signaled for Morgan to come back, relieved him of the medical gun, saying, "Sleep, my love, just for an hour. You need your strength to get through this. See you in an hour. I will be right here." She closed her eyes and drifted into sleep. Morgan walked around the bed and embraced Jim. Thar waited and hugged him as well. Thar turned, wiping a tear away as looked through the screens.

Marsha awakened and ripped out her breathing tube, yelling for Morgan. All three ran to her. "You know not to do that, Marsha!"

"Just shut up," she barked at Jim. Jim held her shoulders back against the bed. "Let me go, damn it! Do not shoot me with any more of that crap. I will slap the shit out of the next person who does that to me!"

Thar drew back in surprise but Jim and Morgan stood their ground. Jim threw himself across her chest so she couldn't go anywhere. "I feel fine! I want out of this damned lab."

Thar gingerly approached the console and looked through all the diagnostic screens. Jim's eyes were wet as he looked down at her; she could tell he had been crying hard. "Bev? She lost the baby?"

Jim nodded and she threw her arms around him. He whispered to her, "And so did you."

She closed her eyes and began to cry but quickly and visibly gathered her strength, then yelled, "AND DON'T YOU DARE SHOOT ME WITH THAT DAMNED THING AGAIN, YOU HEAR ME?!"

Thar looked at Morgan leaning on the bed. He sat down beside her, but she abruptly sat up and knocked him over, lying across him crying and sobbing.

Jim held her back as her stomach began to heave. Thar grabbed a waste basket and managed to get it in front of her as she threw up. Jim picked up the medical gun and gave her meds which he assured her were only for the nausea.

She gave him a stern stare, and said "I will kick your ass if you give me anything else! Take this thing out of my neck right now! Morgan and I need to go grieve our loss and I don't need an audience!"

Jim turned to Thar. "We can agree to disconnect it but it's too early to be completely removed just yet."

Her eyes took on a fierce look and she hissed at him, "Well, just do it!" Jim disconnected the tube but as she tried to stand, she collapsed back onto the bed. Jim rounded the bed, scooped her up and carried her into their bedroom. He laid her on the bed and covered her.

Morgan followed, sliding in next to her and nuzzled her as she cried. Jim left, closing their bedroom door behind him. It was noon and Jim waited for Bev to wake.

Morgan arrived back in the lab, noting, "She is sleeping. I knew it was going to be hard but not quite that hard." He gave a deep sigh.

He turned when he heard running footsteps and Tig burst into the room. Jim scooped him up, giving him a big hug. "How is that goose egg, little man?"

"All gone, Uncle Jim."

Morgan was thanking Dr. Cay. "I heard you ate all kinds of ice cream."

Tig laughed and whispered, "They are so easy—what patsies!"

Jim reared back, looking genuinely shocked as he asked Tig where he had heard that term.

He said, "Grandpa Bat's TV program about him." Jim slowly shook his head.

Morgan came over and asked, "Hey, how is my ice cream thief?" Tig repeated, "They are so easy; such patsies."

"I will be speaking with your grandfather about letting you watch his show," declared Morgan, clearing his throat.

He reached his arm out to pull Morgan and Jim close. "I love you," he said loudly, then whispered, "I have to talk to you outside. Now! Please this is not a game. I will get Buttons and make up something! Please, they are listening!" Jim's eyebrow shot up and Morgan's brow furrowed.

Tig was not known to lie. Yes, he could and did find his share of mischief, but not like this. Tig ran into the lab and told them in a loud voice, "Emmi wants to play with Buttons and the others won't let her. They told her Buttons would eat her arm. Please come out and make them let Emmi play with Buttons."

Jim picked up Tig along with Buttons. "Let's go. My Emmi will get to play with Buttons." He asked Morgan to stay with Bev. As they walked out, he noticed Buttons had a faint bluish cast to his coat. He made a mental note to check the dog.

Bev sat up and Morgan went directly to her. She said, "I am okay now; it was just a shock. Jim and I will have another—all our own." Morgan smiled.

"Do you think I could go shower now and get in my own bed?" Emma rounded the corner just in time to hear her, and said, "You bet."

Morgan turned and said, "Mom's home!" Emma hugged him. "I love your statue prize." He laughed at how she easily dismissed it as a trophy. "Come with me, darlin'. I will stay with you. Bat is out indulging the youngsters with the candy he bought." Bev laughed.

Morgan groused, "Great—hyperactive kids for dinner! I can hardly wait."

Morgan went outside with Bat and Jim who were with Emmi, Tig, Wyatt and Buttons. All the kids were screaming and chasing each other loudly. He thought it was a perfect cover for Tig. They chased Buttons while Bat was holding Emmi, so Morgan picked up Rue as Wyatt and Tig stood talking.

Bat was clearly angry but was making an effort to hide it. Of course—that is why he was an excellent poker player! Jim had his back to the door but picked up Gage. The kids were so loud it was deafening.

Morgan said wryly, "Gee, thanks for the gift of hyperactivity! You know how we're all going to enjoy it at dinner time." They all laughed.

Gage leaned over to kiss Emmi and Bat as they continued to talk at whisper level. Gage hit Rue with perfect timing, then leaned in, kissed Rue and she swung her fist, connecting with his arm.

The distraction gave Jim time to lower his voice, and tell Morgan, "Get that damn dog; he is Blue! I can smell it a mile away." Bat put Emmi down and scooped up the dog.

Showing it to Emmi, he said, "Check my boy, Tig, for that puncture on his hand."

Morgan glanced down and his face reddened with anger.

Bat immediately caught his eye and said, "Bring Tig, Wyatt, Emmi, Gage and Rue in for a checkup. I think they all have sore throats." Then he smiled and tipped his hat to Morgan.

They walked in together with Bat carrying the dog, shepherding them all into the lab and swinging them onto the table. Jim gave Rue and Gage a stethoscope to play with and told the boys to play along.

Jim first singled out Tig on the scanner, ran a scan, then pulled the screen down. Dr. Brock walked into the lab, asking where Marsha and Bev were.

Morgan responded, "They're in their room, grieving the babies, and Emma is with them. What is going on here?"

Jim responded, "Nothing much, just the usual with our large group. One has a sore throat, so several others also have it—real or not. One little partner is inciting a riot about where they can get some ice cream and how."

She smiled, but glanced straight at Tig and said, "The cafeteria is closed!"

Tig instantly caught on with her ruse and played along, "AWW, JEEZ, give a guy a break!" She laughed, turned and left.

Bat tightened his gun belt buckle. "Keep these kids in the back school pod. This might get ugly."

"You have at least one fox in this hen house."

Jim took them back and asked Ang and Star to take the kids, then gave the others the day off. "The kids have sore throats and we do not want it passed around any further," he covered.

He woke Marsha, telling her, "The kids have sore throats and they're in the back school pod," so she would go and comfort them. She got out of bed, and Jim turned his back, saying, "You might get dressed first; don't you ever wear clothing?"

She threw him a grin, shrugged her shoulders, and headed for the bathroom. He yelled at her disappearing backside, "You don't need makeup to be sick and throwing up on your kids." He wanted to make it loud.

She cracked the door open, "And you don't have to scream!" She threw a dress over her head and slipped her feet into well-worn flip flops.

Jim stopped her and said, "Come on—at least some underwear, please!" She rolled her eyes and slipped into a pair.

"Happy now?" she asked.

He smacked her butt as she passed him. "They are in the back school pod."

He went to Bev, still dripping from her shower. "We could use your help. Six have sore throats and we sent them to the back school pod. I do hate to ask, but I need both of you to go and mop up some tears."

Bev threw her brush down and was out the door.

Emma was in on it and knew. "We got it." Emma brushed his side, and he knew she was packing some heat. He smiled his thanks.

Jim walked back into the lab and began cleaning the beds as did Morgan. Neither spoke as they worked. Then both clicked through diagnostic screens, clearing them, and Jim went to Tig's diagnostic. It revealed 20% Blue. He clenched his teeth and quickly deleted the screen. Thar walked in with Dr. Cay at his side. "I hear we have sick kids." He itched his ear and looked up under his brow at Jim and Morgan.

"Just sore throats."

"Dr. Brock has let me know." He rolled his eyes, so Jim and Morgan could understand he was onto Dr. Brock.

Dr. Cay took Morgan's hand and cried, "I failed. You warned me and I did not take it seriously enough. He stole all that ice cream and ate every last bit. That poor little guy didn't tell me he had a tummy ache but I guess he wouldn't."

Bat came around the corner and said, "She is NOT the fox in your hen house and nor is he. Doctors, you will find the children in the back school pod with Emma, and Marsha with Bev.

"Maybe you want to take a few things with you and check EVERYONE. Bev and Marsha still look under the weather."

Morgan, Jim, Dr. Cay, and Thar threw mounds of supplies onto a bed and Thar, with Dr. Cay's help, pushed the bed down the hall to the school pod.

Bat had one pistol strapped to his leg and another stuck in his belt. Don, Olzing and Bat waited in the shadows of the family pod for the culprits to expose themselves. Dr. Brock, Dr. Clez, Dr. Hadad and Dr. Jadon all headed for the lab.

Suddenly, Morgan and Jim heard bursts of both lasers, punctuated with the sound of Bat's pistols.

Don ran into the lab, "Are you okay?" Morgan and Jim ran in behind Don. "These are the foxes in your hen house working for the Blue. Two were dead and the other two were in restraints. They're going to give us a very thorough debrief!" said Olzing, and shoved both of them forward.

A team of guards arrived with body bags and zipped the two dead into the bags as another cleaned the floor and wall. Bat stepped forward, holstering both weapons. "Wish Wyatt had been here for this; he would have LOVED it."

Morgan stepped over to Bat, "You can never leave. We're sending body doubles back for you and Emma! Do you hear me!"

"I was hoping you would feel that way. We never want to leave our family."

Morgan smiled as he replied, "Let's go see how the women and children are doing!"

Olzing approached Morgan and Jim along with Bat. He told them that he and Bat would be gone for the day at the compound. Bat would be doing an inspection looking for holes in perimeter security that needed fixed or tweaked. Bat had every guard fitted with a pistol worn in a shoulder harness and an additional laser-guided gun at their belts, along with knives in their boots and cuffs.

Those walking the perimeter were given a baton and shown how to take down someone who was running and how to use the weapon as a deterrent to resistance.

"They'll return after dark. We'll load in the morning and the ship will have them at the compound in under an hour. Our target is no later than 2:00 PM."

"There are names above each child's bed and on their doors. It should be simple for the older kids. The little ones will be assigned two children per nanny. We understand that the children were upset with the dispatch of Buttons. We have rescue dogs coming the day after tomorrow that will be scanned as will the handlers."

"There's a black lab, a black Gordon setter, a black collie, black Afghan hound, and we decided to throw in a bloodhound for something totally different. For small dogs, we opted for no pugs as that might bring back sad memories. We have a beagle, a mini pin, and a rat terrier which are all full of energy and highly recommended for your group, along with a basset hound, and a toy poodle dyed pink…"

Morgan said "Emmi," and laughed.

"... as well as a cairn terrier and a Japanese chen. They're all sturdy enough to handle your group. We found four barn cats—sorry, they were a set—so we had to take the brothers and one sister. They are being fixed today. All food is in the proper bins and hay is in the barn. Rubber mats and sawdust are already in the stalls."

"Netting goes up today on the chicken coop and over the big tree for the peacocks. The delivery of chickens—pre-scanned—along with two geese and four multicolor peacocks arrive the day after tomorrow."

"The school room is complete as is the gym and all equipment is stowed. Baseball diamonds are scheduled for installation in the spring. In the interim, we put up soccer nets behind Bat and Emma's house and there are swings and slides for the little ones."

"The round pen for the pony just needs fresh sand and that should be happening as we speak. And that's the update! All your homes are complete."

"Bat, myself and our team will do a sweep before your arrival."

"Once you're in, we ask you to maintain a list of fixes and requests."

Morgan nodded and smiled his approval. "Wow, that's efficiency for you! I know we neglected to discuss this, but our friends the pukwudgie and other Bigfoot, where will they go in and out?"

"There is a tower at the back of the property with five guards on duty at all times and there's a large and somewhat formidable gate. They will be scanned and come in and out of that gate. They may be friends, but they will be escorted by at least three security guards. No one can roam free, I'm afraid."

Morgan shook his head. "And our shapeshifter, time traveler and immortal Merlin, do you have precautions for him in place?"

"We are testing it with KiKi, who can shapeshift and cloak. Time travel even at our level of technology can be contained in less than a second but does not prevent it. We realize the danger to Bev, so our lab on the planet developed an undergarment for her to wear that will give her a light shield protection immediately, and, of course, a guard will grab and shield her head to toe as he removes her from the environment should there be a breach."

"In addition, there is a clip she must wear in her hair at all times. It is transparent but once placed, it's good for a week. It will activate a shield immediately when time waves are detected. Many of our soldiers wear these clips for their own safety. The clip turns red and is both visible and audible when activated. Thar will be by later today to show Bev how to wear both devices."

"I would also like to update you on the intel for the Blue. We intercepted two on the planet and another in orbit around the planet, along with four arrested on Rigel who had nefarious intentions for females on that planet."

"The Galactic Federation of Planets has issued their leaders ultimatums with severe consequences for any continued pursuit or kidnapping of females and children from other planets."

"Now, if there are no questions, we need to be on our way." Bat tapped his hat with his cane and revealed two pistols strapped on his gun belt. They turned and headed for the ship."

Morgan found Marsha packing their clothing and personal items. Morgan walked in and she smiled. She pushed everything to the other side of the bed, turned back the covers and got in.

"I am tired, Morgan. Wake me in an hour so I can finish packing. Is that okay?" she asked with her eyes closed.

He smiled and decided he could work while she slept.

He had nearly all the clothing in boxes and labeled when he heard Marsha stir. He put the last box on the floor and lay beside her on top of the covers. She turned and was mumbling. He propped himself up on his elbow and watched her face.

"No, leave me alone, no." She rolled again, obviously having a nightmare. "Morgan, the pony got away from me. Why—oh, it's flying," she moaned.

Morgan decided to wake her. He rang his finger down her cheek, her neck and her arm.

"Morgan, make him let me go! Don't let him take me. No! Don't take me."

"Marsha, you awake?"

She rolled over to him, "What, uh, yeah, let me get going."

"You look so beautiful as you sleep."

"I see we need to fit you for glasses, old man!" retorted Marsha. She sat up and gathered her hair in a scrunchy. He put his arm around her waist.

"Did you have a nightmare, love?" She didn't answer but stood up to get an empty box and tape it together.

"We sure did gather a lot of crap over our four years here. I can't wait to see our old stuff."

Morgan got off the bed and put his arm around her waist standing behind her.

"Your hair smells good."

She turned to him, saying "How about a little hanky-panky one last time in our room?" She pulled off his shirt, pulled off her own and backed up, pulling him with her onto the bed as he kissed her with every ounce of the love he felt for her. She laid her head on his chest and he flipped her over, making deep passionate love. His eyes opened and was startled to see her sweaty face grimace in pain.

He stopped, feeling he had been too rough. "Babe, I am so sorry!"

"I am cramping, Morgan." He saw she was bleeding. "I am fine, just give me a second."

"Ok, let me get dressed and we need to pack."

"Truth, lovely! I am bleeding, too, so I know you must hurt. Truth level?"

"Don't worry about it, Morgan. Just get dressed and we can put these out by the door."

"Stop it, Marsha! You tell me this instant!"

"Okay, Jim-wanna-be." He took a deep breath, then glanced down and saw the blood through her shorts. He pulled them down and took them off. He told her to get in the shower and put on a pad. She went into the bathroom and started the shower. He followed and watched her.

He couldn't help feeling so much love for her so he took his clothes off and slid in with her. He grabbed her hair and kissed her. "Mmmm, okay this is more like it." He picked her up and let the shower rain down on her back, dripping down the front of her body. When she arched her back, he saw the blood flowing freely. He stopped "OMG! What am I doing?"

"What did I do wrong?" asked Marsha.

"No, it is me. Look at you. Put panties and a pad on and let's go fix this. We have not had meds since Paris." She came out with panties and a pad on. He looked at her and said, "Really? Could you put a shirt and pants on, too?"

"It's such a bother!" She reached in the box and put on a shirt. He held a pair of shorts for her to step into, then took her by the hand and led her to the lab. "Get on the bed." She started looking like she was going into a panic scenario, so he gave her anti-anxiety meds immediately. She didn't protest.

"Morgan it is an eight!" He added pain meds and asked the bed to repair without regenerating reproductive organs.

She slid off the table saying, "Yes you will! I want my own baby with you. Yes! You must."

"Honey, we have a whole baseball team of kids already," said Morgan.

"But I have an empty hole after the miscarriage. You will regenerate this for me, Morgan."

He took her in his arms, "You are too medically fragile to even attempt that. Our kids need their Mommy!"

She asked him to think about it, but he instead lifted her up on the bed and asked her to lie down. He took a dose for himself as well.

He led her back down the hall and into their bedroom. Morgan shut the door, putting the dirty sheets into the laundry bag along with Marsha's gown. He laid a clean blanket down on the mattress and climbed in bed, pulling her down toward him. He knew she was upset. "Come lay down, my love, we have a big day tomorrow. You are still recovering from everything and need to rest. I can go get you something if you need it."

She swung her legs up and sat there with her head resting on her knees. She was just staring at the bed. Jim knocked on the door and Morgan called out, "Come in."

Jim saw Marsha's face, and went to the bed, sitting next to her. "You guys ready for tomorrow?"

Morgan looked down but didn't say anything. Marsha turned her head and closed her eyes.

"Bev and I are feeling it too, the miscarriage, leaving our mostly safe living space and taking a leap of faith we will be safe there, too. It's hard to not have second thoughts."

Morgan shook his head. Marsha said nothing and simply kept her eyes closed. Jim reached over to touch Marsha's arm.

She leaped out of bed, saying, "Let me go, no, no, let me go, don't hurt me!"

Jim and Morgan stood, glancing at each other, then at Marsha. She covered her head, crying, "Don't hurt me!"

She turned toward the wall and sunk to the floor, hugging her knees to her chest. "Don't wrinkle my dress!"

Jim looked at Morgan, alarmed. Morgan knelt beside her, careful not to touch her. "Baby, it's me, look at me Marsha! You are fine. You are here with Jim and me. We have you safe."

He waited on her. Finally, she said, "Safe?" without looking up but keeping her eyes closed tight.

"He pushed me hard. You cut my beautiful dress, Morgan!"

They both waited without saying anything nor touching her.

"Am I dressed, Morgan?"

"Yes, baby you are dressed," Morgan replied. "You want to take a little walk with Jim and me?"

"Are you getting me a new dress?"

"You know I will."

"Just the last one; he pushed me hard."

"I know, baby."

"He tried to take me."

"I know, baby, but you are safe now! We will keep you safe."

"I want to go home." Morgan shot a glance at Jim.

"Marsha, I want you to walk with Morgan and me. We'll go to the lab for some medicine," urged Jim.

"Lab? No, no, no! He pushed me down and got my dress all dirty. You cut my dress off; he cut my dress off!"

Jim got her to stand, but she said, "Don't let him push me down to take me."

"We won't."

"Don't leave me by myself; they will take me and hurt me! No, I don't want to be alone, they hurt me so much! Morgan, I hurt. I hurt. I hurt, Morgan!"

"Jim, please take me to my bed. I want to go to bed! I am afraid! Please don't let them hurt me!" She tried to pull away and get into the bed."

Jim tried to direct her to the medical bed, but she jerked away and got in bed with her knees pulled up to her chin. She closed her eyes and started rocking.

Jim signaled to Morgan to come outside the door with him.

Marsha yelled, "No, don't go! Don't leave me by myself." She closed her eyes and rocked back and forth.

Jim asked what Morgan wanted to do. "Let's leave her in the bed but I don't know if she will let us near her with the medical gun again. I hate to bother Emma—she is packing up Phillip and Emmi right now. Let's sit with her and give her an hour to come around. If not, then we need to declare a medical emergency," urged Jim.

Marsha sat another 15 minutes rocking while Jim and Morgan sat with her. Then she laid down and pulled the covers up. She reached for Jim who took her hand.

"I hurt, Jim; make it go away!!" He stood, gathered her into his arms and murmured, "Let's fix it, Princess!"

He carried her to the medical bed while Morgan turned it on. Jim tried to put her down, but she clung to him as though her life depended on him. Jim turned and sat on the bed still holding her to give her more time.

"How about I put you right here and let me hold your hand while Morgan fixes the pain."

"But no tube and no sticking my neck! Promise me, Jim!"

Jim really did not want to make that promise. "Princess, you are sick. I need to make you better. Will you let me make you better?"

Morgan held the medical gun, "I am right here." He sat next to her, and Jim squeezed in as did Morgan.

"Am I going to die?"

Morgan and Jim's eyebrows shot up. Jim answered, "No, why would you ask that?"

"Blue wants me dead!"

"Now you know we would never let that happen," Jim soothed. Morgan took her chin and moved in close hoping and praying she would make contact.

"They keep trying to take me!"

"We have a safe plan worked out for all of us," said Jim.

"But I hurt," Marsha whispered.

"What is your pain and where? Tell me, princess," quizzed Jim.

"Stay with me, please! I am begging you!"

"You know we will never ever leave you, babe."

"I am such a burden to this family."

"No, you can't help what they did!"

Finally she opened her eyes and looked directly into Morgan's face. "No more sleeping, I need to work my way through this. It is hard, but please don't throw me away for being a burden."

"You are not a burden! You know I love you from the bottom of my heart."

"I hit my head when they pushed me. My head still hurts. I am putting the family at risk. They tried to take your statue, Jim."

Jim said, "I know." He began to think they needed to declare that medical emergency after all.

Then she looked at him and sat up. "Do you think I am crazy?"

Jim put his arms around her, saying "Of course not! You are just scared, and it is catching up to you."

"Don't drug me! Just sit with me and let me talk—or do you want to shut me up so I don't act like such a baby!"

"If you don't want the drugs, we will not give them. But I need to tell you your blood pressure is very high—too high!

"Let us give you some anti-anxiety medication, and we will sit close by, and hold you, so we can talk as long as you want," Jim replied.

She nodded, laying her head on Jim while Morgan gave her the medications. Afterwards, they both pressed tightly into her, putting their arms around her.

"I was so scared. I have never been that scared, ever!"

"I know. Bev felt like that too, and believe it or not, so did I!" said Jim.

"Morgan said that to me, too." She kept her head on Jim's chest.

"Do you think I am a good Mom?"

Jim replied, "Yes, silly, everyone adores you, except Tig when he is making wrong choices."

She laughed, "I do see me in him."

Morgan said, "Yeah, so do I and that's one of the reasons I love him so darned much!"

She smiled. "My head hurts if I lay down. Will you hold me tight, Jim, while Morgan looks? I am begging you not to let go, I am so scared!" He scooted down with her, and she snuggled into him. Jim noticed she was shaking and told Morgan to warm the bed 20 degrees.

On the screen, Morgan discovered a blood clot. "I found it! Resolve blood clot in the front lobe of the right hemisphere, and repair..."

"...Understood! Repair time: 30 minutes."

She turned her face to Jim and asked if he could stand to hold her for that long.

He said, "Absolutely."

"But why am I so scared?" she asked.

Jim told her that her brain was having a hard time processing and that it could take some time.

He went on, "Morgan and I really love you, and so does Bev as well as Bat and Emma."

"Am I always going to be so scared?"

He replied seriously, "To some degree, all of us will, Marsha."

She remained calm.

"Are you both mad I take up so much time?"

Morgan sat down on her other side, and told her, "Never! I love every second I spend with you!"

Jim said, "Me too."

"Although I do wish you would wear enough clothing!"

She nuzzled him and told him she would try and work on that.

She said nothing more for the next 15 minutes; they just lay tight against her and finally she closed her eyes and drifted into sleep.

The meds kicked in and would keep her asleep, Both Jim and Morgan stood up stretching sore and tired, cramped muscles.

"That was too damned close, Morgan! Look at me! I'm sweating bullets here, friend."

"I know you saw my hand, buster, right above the red GET-YOUR-ASSES-IN-HERE-NOW-Medical Emergency button! I was a fraction of an inch away from setting it off!"

"My hand was right there, too! GOD, JIM, I am glad that is over for at least the time being."

"As soon as I stop having palpitations and I can breathe normally, I will go tell Bev what we are dealing with. I know you promised her you would stay with her, and God knows, if she wakes up and finds you're not here—well, let's just say it was nice knowing you," he laughed but it was a sound devoid of any joy.

Jim's laughter was no less nervous. "Would you get going and tell Bev her Teddy Bear—he made sure Morgan saw him roll his eyes—will be back as soon as I can?" He laid back down and held Marsha tightly. He willed his bodily closeness to help her regain her mind and feel safe.

Thar strode into the bay, "I saw a bit of a possible emergency on the bed, Jim…"

"…Yes, Marsha had a complete mental meltdown. She was scared out of her mind, and that's for sure."

Thar stood silent as he flicked through the screens selecting meds to improve her serotonin levels. He added oxygen and put a mask on her face.

"Jim, your hands-on therapy along with both you and Morgan holding her tight to help her feel safe was spot on and the right treatment for her. I would never have thought of this method, but it worked! But if there is a next time, you two better not wait that long again. This outcome could have been much different!"

"Go with your instincts and stop second guessing yourselves. She needs to feel safe. Too many things have happened to her lately. Her processes shut down and, well, here you are. Jim, she is really brittle right now! She needs to feel love, security, and a sense of worthiness in her contributions to the family unit as well."

"I definitely encourage you and Morgan, too, to stay close to her — assuming Bev doesn't object—for the next few days to give her serotonin levels time to equal out. Don't leave her alone. That could trigger a complete breakdown, of that I am sure! Jim, we have plenty of people to help you unpack and get settled."

"For now, I'd encourage you to add a medical bed in their bedroom. I don't want her separated from you or Morgan even if you feel you need to be in the lab. She needs both of you right in her home giving her security. And that will take understanding from Bev but knowing her as I do, I would say she's up for that! She loves Marsha completely, and I can see she feels a deep compassion for Marsha."

To which Jim nodded yes.

"Involve her in your star research; and for that, thank you so much! We will keep her busy and give her the security she needs.

9

A New Beginning

Everyone and everything was onboard the ship, including four ponies, four rabbits, and two goats, yet somehow Tig had managed to bring in some contraband. Morgan leveled his eyes on his son. "What did you smuggle on board?"

"Uh, Dad, well—it's a frog."

"I am sure you have a marvelously interesting explanation as to why you are chasing everyone with this frog." Morgan held out his hand.

Tig groused his usual, "Give a guy a break!"

Morgan handed the amphibian to Thar to scan.

Tig went to Marsha and—giving his mom a hug—said, "Mommy make him give back my frog!"

She laughed and grabbed him by the waist. "Did you ask Daddy if you could bring him? Tig looked puzzled, "Why would I do that? I wanted to gross the girls out and he would have told me no!"

"But did you ask the question about keeping it?"

Tig looked down and shifted his weight from foot to foot. In a very remorseful voice, drawing out the words, "Nooooo, Mom."

Morgan pulled him over to stand in front of him, "You know we have to be extra careful. Now here is your pal. We just had to scan him to make sure he was okay. So, what is Mr. Frog's name?"

Tig broke out in a grin, self-pride evident, "Bubble Guppie."

Morgan laughed, throwing his arms in the air, "Of course it is!"

"Hey, everyone, look at my frog! "Don, I'm gonna gross out all the girls! You just watch how grossed out they get. They scream and run."

He laughed as he held the frog up to his face and kissed it.

"Tig, my man, you really should rethink that." Don shook his head as he walked away.

Seemingly in no time at all, they arrived at their renovated compound. As the ship hovered overhead, Olzing stood by the window pointing down.

"Please join me here at the window. I want you to watch how truly amazing it is as it unfolds beneath you." They ran to the window, not willing to miss anything Olzing called "amazing." They gasped as an enormous holographic image went up and around the landing pad, revealing the landscape as it was prior to the ship's coming in for a landing.

"Would you look at that!" Jim turned from Morgan to Olzing. "Is this holographic image mirroring the landscape?" With a broad smile, Olzing approached them and put his hand on Jim's shoulder as said, "Yes, what do you think of our magic?"

Jim turned to Morgan who was silent, but continued watching as the ship glided down, pulled into the hanger bay and then self- sealed itself as the hanger lights came up.

Morgan's face revealed a broad grin as he pointed, "God, look at this, we can see the ship, but we are in a sort of shadow. The cloaking makes it invisible on the outside—even to us. God, how I love this technology."

He laughed and walked in front of Olzing, extending his hand. Olzing took his hand. "Olzing, thank you for allowing us to see this unfold. Your technology obviously is amazing and I'm sure I speak for everyone how very grateful we are for the added safety and security."

Olzing asked Jim, "Any concerns?"

"Nope, not one!" Olzing smiled, turned, and said, "Let's unload, everyone." They all followed Olzing, almost sprinting off the ship. Tig ran up to Olzing. "May I have this technology for my homework? I could just project what is in the book and won't have to do the questions!" Jim glanced back at him. "Really, Tig?"

"Jim, isn't it good to see our home?" asked Bev. She looked up to Jim with excitement. "I can't wait to get inside the house."

Morgan looked to Jim with a huge smile. "Jim, I do feel safe." He grinned back, "Morgan, so do I." The kids were like cats as they ran off the ship and scattered in all directions. Marsha stood still, looking afraid. Everyone had been alerted to stay as close as they could to her.

Bat reached his arm around her, pulling her to his side, "Marsha, isn't this amazing? I can't wait to see your face light up when you see the amazing inside of this home. Let me be the first to escort you to your home." She still looked afraid and didn't move.

"Marsha, take your time. Look at how magnificent this is! You'll be safe here." Don took a position in front of her, and two other agents triangulated them from behind. Jim stood on the other side of her, sliding his arm around her waist and pulling her close against his side. Morgan walked up, gave her a quick kiss, then handed her Heidi who was crying. She looked down at daughter.

Morgan said, "She wants her mom to feed her, Marsha." Morgan glanced at Jim, who smiled, shaking his head as if to say, "Good job distracting her." She looked down at her daughter lovingly and smiled. "Heidi, let's go see our new home."

She continued to look at Heidi as she gave her a bottle tucked into her arms. Jim and Bat guided her off the ship and into the house. Don's plan was working flawlessly. He had known she would need help and a distraction. Thar watched; he too had a plan in place if she melted down mentally. He was impressed by what Don had set up. They walked through the house, Morgan had switched places with Jim so he and Bev could go through their own home. Thar and Dr. Cay followed behind Marsha, Morgan and Bat. Everyone was waiting on Marsha to speak, however, she was quiet as she moved through the house. Morgan nodded to Dr. Cay. She moved in front of Marsha and said, "Let me take Heidi so you can look at the house. I am so excited for you and Morgan!" Marsha smiled and handed Heidi to Dr. Cay.

She stood in the kitchen and looking to her right, she could see Morgan's office. His furniture looked the same except for a gigantic 75-inch monitor for his computer.

"Look, Morgan!" pointing to the monitor, "Someone told them you refused to get glasses." Everyone laughed, and Morgan kissed her. "Princess, thanks for embarrassing me right off the bat!" She kissed him again.

"No problem, baby!" She stepped away from them, running her hands over the countertop. "I love this choice of granite."

"Hey, babe, you would think we had a bunch of kids—two dishwashers." The others stood back and let her explore. Thar and Morgan exchanged glances and smiles.

"Oh, and two ovens! Think they are telling me I will be busy? Unless, of course, you thought of getting me a chef!" she laughed. She turned and looked at Morgan then as she jumped up on the counter and sat.

Don stepped forward, "Marsha, you are in luck. You'll have a wonderful chef; her name is Lidia, and she will arrive shortly. We wanted you and Morgan to go through the house first." We're keeping the kids busy outside looking at their new dogs."

She jumped down off the counter and Morgan could see she was upset. Morgan grabbed her as they walked back out on the porch.

Bat walked over to Emmi who already had the pink poodle gripped firmly in her arms. "Mommy, Mommy—look she is pink and all mine! And guess what, Mommy! Her name is Toodles."

Marsha looked down at her with great love and warmth. "Emmi, she is pretty and pink, just like you!" Emmi beamed with happiness. "She loves me already, Mommy." Bat gave her an unseen nudge forward to Marsha. "Mommy, hold her! She is so soft." Marsha looked at the dog and Emmi's broad smile, then picked them both up.

"Marsha, as your assigned guard, I made sure all the dogs have been scanned and thoroughly checked out."

She smiled up at Don, then back down to Emmi. "Sweet pea, Toodles will need lots of love and lots of walks. Now, Toodles will need to see her room in the house." She looked to Morgan, "I guess we have a dog."

Bat laughed, "Wyatt would be rolling on the ground if he knew our family had a tiny pink poodle." Finch was fixated on the rat terrier but El liked the beagle. Pushing and shoving ensued. Jim quickly grabbed both by their collar and the two dogs took off. He sat both down, kneeling down to talk to them.

"El and Finch, this is not how we act. Now, what do you think we should do here—and only one answer at a time?" Instead of answering, they continued to bicker.

"I want the beagle," said El. "Yeah, 'cause you're selfish!" pouted Finch. The handlers retrieved the dogs and Bev came over, taking both leads and handed one lead to each of them, along with a silver bowl for feeding. The look on their faces was priceless as they realized they each got to keep a dog.

"Now, what do you say to each other and to your Mother?"

Finch looked at El, "My dog is faster than yours!" and they both took off running.

Marsha pointed out to Morgan, "Here comes our parade of dogs." Dorothy-Alice and Rue were leading an English bulldog over to them. He was slobbering all over with his tongue hanging out the side of his mouth.

Marsha looked at him. "Oh, God, Eeewww!" She wrinkled her face, shaking her head no.

Morgan bent down and said, "I love him or her, as the case may be. What's his name, guys?"

Dorothy-Alice looked down and shrugged her shoulders. "It is Giles, and we like that name." He nodded his head, "Girls, that is a great name."

They hugged Morgan, saying, "Thank you for letting us have a dog," then asked, "Can we go show everyone our new dog?" Marsha still had a furrowed brow, sticking out her tongue and her body shuddered at the sight of Giles.

"Girls, all that disgusting slobber, hold up…" She pulled a tissue out of her pocket and tried to wipe it off. The girls ran to show Bat and Emma.

Marsha stayed where she stood. "Morgan, really, that is disgusting." He laughed and kissed her. "You will come to love him, Marsha."

She stood watching the girls with Giles. "God, are you kidding me? That disgusting slobber and you did smell him, right?"

Tig came running over with the bloodhound in tow. She got in Morgan's face. "Oh, NO! One of those slobbering messes is enough!" Morgan turned to see Tig, "What kind of dog is that?"

"Um, Dad, he is the king of slobber so I can wipe it on everyone." Morgan pointed to return him without saying anything. Tig turned away, saying, "Give a man a break!" Marsha, turned to Morgan and then ran over to Tig. "Wait." She walked around the pitiful looking dog who was now flopped on the ground. Tig pulled on the lead trying to get him to stand up. Everyone behind them was laughing. She put her hand on Tig's shoulder, saying, "Okay, he is all yours, but you have to take care of him and that includes cleaning up all the slobber." She put her hand out and demanded, "Deal?"

He shook her hand and said, "DEAL!" Tig turned to run but couldn't get the dog up. "What's the dog's name?" asked Marsha.

Tig thought for a minute, then said, "Lazy Bones, Mom." Marsha burst out laughing. Tig yelled to everyone, "His name is Lazy Bones." He let go of the lead and Lazy Bones immediately got up and loped after him.

Marsha said, "Look, here comes Morgan-Barkley and Wyatt. They have a mop to clean up the slobber." Marsha stood in front of them with her arms crossed. "What the heck is this mop of hair?" Wyatt grinned up at her, "I thought I wanted a lab 'til I saw Omar," Morgan-Barkly said, "He's magnificent don't you think, Mom?"

Morgan stepped forward, "Who is going to brush all that 'magnificence' every day?" The boys looked at each other and then to Morgan with giant toothy smiles. "We will, Daddy, and we will use Mom's scrunchies to put it in ponytails so it doesn't get tangled when we are running and playing."

Marsha's jaw dropped in shock, "MY SCRUNCHIES?" Then she laughed, "Morgan, I can't wait to see that sight! That'd better be the cover of your first book." Marsha walked by herself to the handlers and took the collie. She asked her name and was told it was Lassie. "We will take her, too." Marsha walked back with her and said, "Meet Lassie. She is my dog and will stay here in the house." Everyone was happy she had walked by herself to the handlers and back. She looked at Don, "Please find us a groomer that comes once a week to clean off the dirt AND slobber off all the dogs."

Then Marsha spotted Liam standing by himself and crying. She ran to him and knelt down, "What's wrong?" She signaled for Morgan to come over, too. "No one wanted the droopy, sad one, like you Mommy." Marsha took in a deep breath and let it out. "Liam, no more will Mommy look like that. Show us Droopy, Liam." It turned out to be the saddest looking dog ever. "Liam what kind of dog is this?"

Liam looked down at Droopy. He said, "This is a dog that is for me, please Mommy and Daddy?" Liam looked frantic that Droopy might be left behind. He pleaded, "I never ask for anything. Please know I am responsible and probably will have to take care of all of them, but I don't mind. I love dogs." He looked on the verge of tears.

Marsha looked at him, touched his face and turned to look at Morgan. She put her arm around his waist. "Well, shall we take pitiful Droopy into our pack?"

He laughed and said, "We will need Cesar Milan to come train our pack." She laughed. "Okay, Liam, he is all yours." He leaned over and said in his ear as if he were telling him a secret, "Welcome home, Droopy."

Morgan went to each handler and thanked them. He gave each a $5,000 dollar check. He also gave the same amount to each of the rescue groups. Then he took two steps back and grabbed the black lab. His name was Rufus. He walked up to Marsha and said, "My dog, Rufus!" Marsha shook her head, "Softy!" She leaned over to pet him and called for Liam to come get Rufus so he could be introduced to the other dogs.

She looked at Morgan. "I am happy and so are the kids. Let's go look at the house." They approached the house and Lassie jumped up on Marsha. "Look, she likes me already." She was petting her when a car backfired. She jumped and screamed. Morgan grabbed her as did Don, but Lassie pushed Morgan out of the way and jumped in front of Marsha. Don and everyone else looked surprised, it was like she was a trained guard dog and therapy dog all in one. She grabbed onto Lassie, seemingly frozen but Lassie began licking her hands and face, jumping up until she had Marsha's full attention. Morgan went around behind her and to her side so she could hang onto Lassie as Don took the other side. Lassie went back down on all fours. Thar asked if she wanted some anti-anxiety medication, but she shook her head.

"I can't be fully functional with that stuff." She told him. "Maybe Morgan or Jim can give me that before bed, but right now I need to be available to my kids."

They went inside and sat her at the table. Lassie put two legs on her lap and licked her face. She looked down at her. "Well, it appears we have a bond, little lady." She petted her and gave her a kiss on her long nose. "Sorry, everyone, that scared me."

Morgan knelt in front of her, petting Lassie, "You are fine now, princess. Shall we go see the rest of our place?"

She laughed and nodded yes. They stood and Lassie took her place at her right knee, glancing up to see where they were headed.

Marsha looked at Don, "All the dogs will need bowls, food, collars, tags, licenses, leads, beds and toys. I would like to keep my furniture and shoes intact!"

As they walked away, she watched him speaking into his cuff. She turned around, reached for his cuff and spoke into the microphone, "And thank you, everyone!" Morgan and Don laughed.

Marsha was happy to see her living room furniture and two wonderful new sofas. The TV was mounted up out of reach of kids' hands, with the remotes stored on a high shelf. She looked toward Don and said, "Is this is a joke? Do you guys honestly think Tig will not figure out—within one hour flat—how to get a hold of that remote and take total control of it?" Don looked surprised. She laughed, "You must not have kids!"

They toured the rest of the house. The only thing she didn't like was the cubby with the medical bed in their bedroom. Lassie had jumped right up on it. Morgan said, "Don't think you have to worry! I believe she thinks that is her bed." She stopped and leaned into Morgan. Thar turned to her, "You look tired. Why don't you and Lassie lie down for an hour while we give the kids a tour of the school."

"Oh, wait, add on a few minutes for rounding them up. That will be like rounding up your barn cats! We will be lucky if that is only one hour!" Morgan pulled down the covers and Lassie promptly leaped the distance from the medical bed to their bed. "Princess, uh, while we are in here making whoopie, we better make sure she is not in the room." Marsha laughed, "You got it, lover boy!"

She lay down and Morgan covered her. Lassie curled right up beside her.

"Thar, you are hovering!"

"Please let me give you something to keep her blood pressure in check." She closed her eyes, turned on her side toward Lassie, and mumbled "Make it so, Number One!"

Morgan shook his head laughing, "I knew it; you are a closet Trekkie!" Thar dispensed her medications. She turned half over, asking, "You will not leave me alone?" Morgan said, "No, you have Lassie." She still had the panicked look on her face. "Princess, of course not, if Lassie doesn't mind moving over." She gave Lassie a push and she quickly scooted over for him, then turned back toward Lassie stroking her soft hair. Morgan looked back at Thar, mouthing WATCH HER! He nodded as Morgan pulled her to him tightly. Lassie got up and readjusted with her head on her legs.

A short while later, Marsha was sleeping soundly, but then Jim came up and knocked on the door. Lassie immediately went ballistic barking. Marsha sat up screaming. Jim came in and Lassie went to Marsha, licking her face, but still she screamed. Jim went around the bed and pushed Lassie down to the foot of the bed. Morgan and Jim sat in tight to her. She was breathing in panic mode. Lassie jumped on her and laid down on her lap dropping her head on Marsha's chest, looked up at her face and kept licking her. She stopped screaming, relaxed a bit, and closed her eyes again.

Morgan glanced at Jim who was watching the dog closely, and that is when Morgan realized he was the one who had arranged for this therapy dog. Jim looked back at Morgan and smiled. After a few minutes, Marsha put her hand on Lassie. "I have a replacement for you, Morgan." Morgan smiled and then looked down at Lassie, "I wish I had her hair."

She looked at him and ran her fingers through his hair. "You have amazing hair."

Jim pouted, "What about me?" She laughed, "You know you do, and you know you are handsome, too, Mister-I-need-a-mirror-please!"

Jim laughed. "You know I only asked that one time." Marsha rolled her eyes and said, "Good thing, too, you still had Bev's lipstick on your face." Jim held her direct eye contact, "Okay, how are you doing? Do I feel you shaking?"

Marsha shook her head with a troubled look, "I have to admit I feel so scared, Jim. I can hardly breathe."

Jim decided she needed encouragement and in a positive tone of voice said, "You look like you are doing okay." As he turned to her, he could really feel her shaking, harder now. "But, I gotta say, I am not comfortable with all this shaking, Missy!" Marsha looked directly at Jim. "Well, then, why don't you take something for it?"

He and Morgan laughed. They both understood she was doing somewhat better but had a ways to go. They did not want to back off on his current plan yet. Even with Lassie, it would still take time. Morgan and Jim scooted closer to give her a safe feeling as Lassie continued to gaze at her with her head on her chest. Marsha stroked the dog's silky hair, which they could tell had already slowed her breathing.

"The kids' dogs are a muddy mess already!" groused Morgan. "Oh, no, not in my new, clean house! They stay in the barn, especially the slobbering ones."

Marsha leaned back, wiggling in between them. Jim laughed, " Why don't we test the boys and see if they will hose them off in the barn. It has hot water and there is a large silver metal tub in the barn where they can give them a bath. And there are even some old towels out there so they can dry the dogs."

"Can't you just see what a matted mess Omar will be?"

"Oh, Jim," she sighed, "You'd better take them out some scrunchies."

Jim told Marsha, "By the way, I learned Dallas is looking forward to giving the dedication and prayer. He actually has worked pretty hard on this. Frankly, I can't believe he is doing this. It is something like Finch would do." He looked over at Morgan and added, "You better search Tig for rubber bands!"

Marsha laughed, "Let me guess, 'That's my boy!'"

Morgan laughed and shrugged his shoulders. "What can I say..."

"We should ask if that could be one of Don's regular duties, searching that boy for rubber bands," Morgan laughed.

"Can we just stay here a bit longer until I stop shaking?" Marsha asked.

Morgan looked at her, grabbed her chin and pulled it toward him, saying, "You let me know when you're ready," and kissed her lightly.

Jim said, "Ah, do you two need some medication?" They both laughed.

Abruptly, Lassie picked up her head and faced toward the door; then immediately stood up with the hair on the back of her neck slightly raised.

Morgan stood, ready. But it was just Zoey who came in crying for her mom.

Marsha got out of bed and knelt down to her, hugging her, "What's wrong?"

Zoey spoke through her tears, "They spelled my name wrong." Marsha looked at Morgan, then back to Zoey. "I am so sorry, baby, Daddy will fix it. It was just a little mistake and it's easy to fix."

Jim could see her breathing again and it was almost like she was in a panic. Jim asked her if she saw the kitties. She nodded her head, yes, with her thumb stuck in her mouth.

Marsha asked if she had a favorite, and again she nodded yes.

"Which one?" Zoey still sniffed from crying, so Morgan reached behind her to get a tissue; however, she had wiped her nose on her shirt sleeve. Morgan remarked, "Well, at least she didn't eat it like Bitty does."

"Mommy, she is spotted with yellow and white dots. She is a little girl, like me."

Marsha gave her a kiss and hug. "What's her name, Zoey?" She removed her thumb from her mouth and smiled. Marsha suggested, "Butterscotch?"

She put her arms around Marsha's neck, "Mommy, can I keep Butterscotch in my room?"

Marsha looked to Morgan.

Morgan gathered Zoey in his arms. "In a couple days you will be able to, but we have to get a litter box first and get her used to using it in the barn; is that okay?"

She jabbed her thumb back in her mouth and nodded her head yes.

Morgan gave her a kiss, turned her around, and nudged her to get going. She turned in the doorway and said, "Mommy, I like your dog. Can she sleep with me sometimes?"

Marsha looked at Lassie and then to Zoey with a big smile. "Of course, if you're willing to brush her sometimes." She smiled and ran down the steps. Marsha yelled, "WALK, PLEASE!"

Marsha slumped against the bed and closed her eyes. Jim and Morgan lifted her right to the medical bed and began paging through the screens.

Thar saw the notification that someone was on the bed and ran up the steps into their room. He nudged Morgan out of the way and joined Jim in paging through the screens. Morgan pulled the oxygen mask from the side of the bed and slipped it on her. Lassie sat at attention at the side of the bed, toward the foot.

"What do you think, Thar?"

He turned to face Morgan, "She is showing signs of exhaustion."

Jim looked to Morgan, "I hate to say the word 'dehydration,' but I'm going to," said Jim.

"I would like her to rest," added Thar. "And I also want you to get her to drink a full glass of Pedialyte."

Morgan shook his head, whispering "DO NOT show her the bottle!"

Marsha opened her eyes and said, "No, not today."

Thar said, "You are just exhausted. How about we take you downstairs and we can sit on the porch while Dallas does his thing? After he has finished, I want you in bed for the night and —I'm gonna say this and you won't like it, but you will do it— you will allow us to medicate you for sleep."

Jim interrupted, "I am not going to listen to your whining about it! You will allow it, period!"

She said nothing but closed her eyes. Shortly tears fell as she said, "I failed even today."

Thar held up his hand to the boys to not say anything, "Enough of that BULLSHIT TALK!" She opened her eyes and looked at him in shock. Morgan and Jim's eyebrows shot up like they were synchronized. She looked at Thar for a moment, shrugged one shoulder, then said, "When you're right, you're right!"

Everyone looked at her, partly in shock and partly in disbelief.

"We need to give Dallas his moment to shine! Can I eat with everyone before I go to bed?"

Thar scowled, "No dawdling; you have 30 minutes at the table." Jim put in his two cents, "And for God's sake, actually eat something, will you?"

She sat up and Lassie stood at the ready. Thar said, surprised, "You have a friend, I see."

She smiled, "Her name is Lassie and, yes, I do have a friend!"

They helped her off the bed and Lassie tried to wedge herself between Marsha and Jim. Jim didn't move nor did Morgan as they squeezed in tight to her. Lassie decided the next best thing was to lead the way, but she glanced back at her frequently.

Morgan, Marsha, Bev, Jim, and Thar came out the side door with Don in the lead. Everyone clapped. The kids were at one long table and all the employees were at two other tables. Jim and Morgan sat at the head of the table with the kids and Marsha sat on the side of the table beside Morgan with Thar next to Marsha, and Tig on the other side.

Beside Jim was Bev with El next to her. On the porch were three chairs. Marsha asked why the three chairs. Morgan was puzzled as were Jim and Bev. Then out walked Dallas, and everyone stood and clapped. Dallas looked startled and ran back into the house. Bev started to go after him, but Jim took her hand and looked at her softly, "No, let's give him a minute."

It was only a few moments until he came back out and stepped up to the microphone. He started, "Hello, I am Dallas. My Dad is there," as he pointed to Jim, "And that is my Mom. Stand and wave so we can embarrass you!" Jim laughed and stood up taking Bev's hand. He sat down and smiled at Dallas.

Tig leaned over to Thar, "I told him to say that," he said proudly.

Thar laughed, shaking his head, "That's a great punchline, Tig." Dallas continued, "Since this is our first meal together, in our new compound, and with all our new friends, I thought we should stand and join hands in prayer."

Dallas began, "Lord, we pray to you for your emotional, physical, and spiritual protection over all of us. Keep evil far from us, and please help us to trust you as our refuge and strength. I pray you will guard our minds from harmful things and help us recognize truth. I pray you will make all of us strong and courageous when in danger. We know that we still have much to overcome, and one day you will set right all bad and wrong things that have hurt our families. Help all of our families and new friends to find rest in your shadow, as we live in the spiritual shelter you provide. Help all of us know that the only safe place is in Jesus, and that we only need to ask you for help. Amen."

Dallas looked up, taking in a deep breath and letting it out, then continued, "Oh, I have set a prayer bowl on the table in the cafeteria. Please put your prayer requests in there and I will come every day to collect them. My brothers and sisters will pray for every request every day."

Everyone said, "Amen," and Dallas walked off the porch and sat next to El. Bev stopped him first and gave him a kiss. Finch walked out next and in a shy voice said, "Hi," and waved. Everyone laughed and clapped. "Um, Dallas was too chicken to give a talk, so here I am!"

Everyone laughed. "My name is Finch, or some call me Finchy, if I have been a good boy. We are about to embark on a journey that will test our mettle, wits, courage, and faith as we race to save our planet Earth. This is the trial of our lifetime—the trial of the highest importance, and if Daddy and Uncle Morgan fail, then the supernova of the star Betelgeuse in the Orion system will destroy our planet. But when they succeed, we will survive for more journeys on this world".

"All of us kids and many of our new friends like Vaughn and Lang want to be smart like Daddy and Uncle Morgan. They are teaching us the ways of those that have walked paths similar to what we walk now. We are all working to grow in knowledge and help our planet Earth in our own journeys."

"Vaughn wants to help feed millions of hungry people. He hopes to use old techniques like cross-pollination with replicators and make wholesome foods in once unsurvivable climates and conditions."

"One thing all these children of my Daddy and Uncle Morgan have learned is to 'Never Give Up' even through our struggles.

The path we walk will not always be easy or smooth. We all have bumps, but it is how we approach those bumps and either go through or around, it is always our decision."

"My Aunt Marsha and my Mom teach us to be aware of the gentle movements that babies like on their backs. We apply that when things are hard; gentleness can cause happiness and helps us to know each other better. It teaches us kids to be kind and help our brothers and sisters and cousins."

You could see the crowd agreeing and nodding their heads. "We try to always listen to each other, but, uh, hey, we are kids, and we fight sometimes, especially Tig." Everyone laughed but Tig turned and shot him an angry glance.

Finch continued, "So from day one, I have always known he is the special one of all of us. He dreams, and dreams of bigness, and sometimes he does not make any sense. But he is a genius and I hope one day he appreciates it so both of us will help the universe in many great ways. I know—I just somehow know— he will have a great idea that can and will honor many. I can't wait to grow up and see what it is. We will have a future together, even I have known that from day one."

"Daddy and Uncle Morgan, each with their own special talents and abilities will be what saves Earth and our future." Finch bowed. The grownups told him he had done a good job. He was so cute as he thanked everyone. Everyone stood and clapped. Bev ran around the table and grabbed Marsha's hand and Tig's; together they ran to Finch. Bev and Marsha hugged him and Tig stood there waiting.

Bev stepped back for him and Tig punched him in his arm, Bev leaned into the microphone and said," Tig's way of thanking him." Everyone began to clap again. Lassie ran to Marsha and jumped up on Marsha licking her face. Jim shot a look at Morgan and together they ran to the porch, grabbing Bev and

Marsha to stand on each side of Marsha pushing into her. She was swaying and shaking.

Thar ducked in through the kitchen, heading straight for the bed to power up the screens and get the temperature right.

Kron stepped from around the corner and to the microphone. She said, "How will I ever top that; so why try? My name is Kron, and I know this group. Today we begin our combined future. Let our paths be paved with togetherness on this journey."

10

Tig's Prank

It was morning; Marsha sat up, stretched, and looked over at Morgan in bed. She stepped down and off the med bed and crawled under the covers, snuggling into Morgan. He opened his eyes, "Morning, my beautiful wife."

She smiled, "I love you." She gave him a kiss and smiled again. She ran her hand over his chest and began kissing it. He was very gentle with her as they made love. She could feel his love and tenderness today. She loved snuggling with him after such tenderness. As she snuggled, he ran his fingers through her hair. She closed her eyes and fell asleep snuggled into him. She slept another two hours. Morgan made sure Lassie stayed with her while he showered. He retrieved Baby Iris and a bottle, bringing both to Marsha who had just sat up.

Morgan said, "Somebody was looking for her Mommy." She took the baby in her arms, looking down as she talked to her. "Aw, you are just the cutest! Mommy loves you." She fed her, then let Lassie sniff her, finally laying Iris against the curled-up dog. Lassie licked the top of Iris' head.

Morgan picked her up and took her back to bed. When he returned, Rufus the black lab followed him into the room. Lassie raised her head and looked toward Marsha, then laid her head back down.

"It looks like you have a friend, too." Morgan told her the lab had been glued to his side.

"Want to take a shower, get dressed and go see the lab?"

She began to cry and shake and said, "Lab? Oh, God." Morgan sat down next to her, and Lassie moved to her lap. Morgan pressed a button that let Jim know Marsha was on the verge of meltdown. "Not the lab, Morgan," Her breath came in heavy, painful gulps. "OH, GOD, NOT THE LAB." Morgan heard a knock on the door as it opened.

"Are you ever coming to work?" Morgan laughed. Jim walked around the bed and took a flying body leap, landing on the bed. "I've always wanted to do that!" He laughed.

By now, Marsha was in a full-blown panic. Lassie had her head on her chest licking her skin.

Morgan pulled her over on him sitting on the bed, and Jim moved close.

"Well, when you do come to the lab, Morgan, remember we got a planet to save, you know." He waited, looking at Morgan, then Marsha.

"Marsha, how about you and Bev help us full time on this project?"

She never heard him. Instead, she kept saying, "Not the lab, no, not the lab!"

Jim said, "Lips are blue. She's getting cyanotic."

Morgan looked, "Oh, yeah, she could definitely use some O2."

Jim sat up, reached over, grabbed the mask, and tried to slip it on as she pushed it away. Jim pushed Lassie back and straddled her, taking both hands, trying to force her to get some eye contact.

"Stop, Marsha! STOP! NOW!" Finally her eyes found his, though he could still feel her shaking.

"I just want to give you some O2; you are too low! If you do not get some oxygen in you, there will be consequences, and you won't like them one bit!" Her breathing sounded more like an asthma attack.

Morgan mumbled, "In the dresser drawer." On Morgan's direction, Jim got up and retrieved the stethoscope out of the drawer. He brought that and the med gun back to the bed. He sat on her again.

He listened carefully, "It sounds like she has bronchitis. Will she take an oral antibiotic?"

Morgan nodded yes. "Marsha!" She made eye contact again. "I want to give you meds for anxiety."

She covered her neck with both hands. One eyebrow went up, "Really?" And gave her the next prescribed dose from the injector into her arm.

Jim whispered, "Good, she is fighting back. Get her up and showered! She is going to face that lab today!"

"I'll tell Kron to meet us here in 30 minutes. She'll help us get her there."

Then… "Where is Tig?"

Morgan looked startled, "Your guess is as good as mine … wait, bet the whole crew is in the barns with the dogs."

"I'll go get him and see if he can help coax her into the lab, too. Be back in 30 minutes with Kron and Tig."

Through a combination of cajoling, wheedling, and outright ordering, Morgan finally got her to take a shower. He helped her pull her hair back in a ponytail.

All the nannies were with their assigned charges. He took her downstairs, with Lassie and Rufus trailing behind. He made her coffee and made sure she at least got a piece of toast with apple butter down.

"Morgan, are all the dogs fixed?" He told her yes.

"Good, cause Rufus is awfully friendly with Lassie."

He laughed, "Well, even a lab knows a beautiful lady when he sees one."

Jim walked in first with Tig and Omar trailed behind. Marsha stood and said, "OMG." Morgan turned and his mouth fell wide open. "I really thought you might want to see Tig's handiwork."

Morgan shook his head as he approached for a closer look. "OMG! TIG!!!"

Tig lowered his head with a look of remorse on his face. "You didn't seem to like his hair so I thought he would be better with shorter hair…"

Marsha walked around Omar with her hand covering her mouth. She kept shaking her head back and forth. "Oh, Tig, his beautiful coat."

Jim laughed and told them, "Omar's beautiful hair is lying on the barn floor." His coat had been chopped into all different lengths like a typical kid would do.

Morgan shook his head and turned to Don, "How soon can we get a groomer here today to fix this mess?"

Don stepped back and spoke into his cuff, Marsha again pulled his cuff to her and said, "Thanks! And Tig also says thank you in advance of a more personal thank you!"

Tig shuffled his feet, shifting his weight back and forth. "Aw, I just can't get a break! I was trying to make it easier with the mud and brushing it out of him. I just can't catch a break."

Morgan crossed over to him, "Your intentions were honorable, Tig, but next time, ask a grownup—let me rephrase that. Next time you ask Daddy or Mommy first; understood, Tig?"

"Of course, I am not three years old!"

Morgan shook his head. "Tig, let's take Omar to the lab and show off your talents." Marsha said, "Morgan, that would embarrass Tig. He was, after all, just trying to resolve a problem."

"Yeah, what Mom said." He grinned, pointing to Marsha.

Jim was laughing so hard he was nearly crying. Morgan said— and Jim was just waiting for it—"That's my boy!" Tig had a smile and look of pride.

Tig asked if he and Omar could go, school would be starting, and he didn't want to be late.

Morgan said, "No, you are not taking the dog. Leave him here so the groomer can fix your 'artistic work.' See ya' after school and you can see Omar after school." Jim was still laughing as was Marsha. She was still trying to figure out a way to make him look better... "You poor, poor dog. How did you luck out and get our rambunctious boys"? Bev came through the door and saw Omar. "OMG—was it TIG?" Everyone nodded their heads yes. "His beautiful hair?" Jim looked at Bev and told her, "It's on the floor of the barn." She shook her head back and forth as she looked at the bewildered creature from every angle. "There is just no way on God's green earth to look at this hot mess and believe it is maybe going to look okay!"

Marsha said, "A groomer is coming to fix it."

Bev looked at it again and mused, "I see the spiky hair on top of his head, that was once beautiful and flowing. But, well, you know what Tig might like?"

They looked puzzled as she ran her fingers through it. "Have them dye this fluorescent blue and spike it so it stands up. Take it all the way down his backbone and his tail. Now that could be a dog Tig could be proud of!"

Marsha smiled, "DONE! I love that idea."

Morgan and Jim shook their heads back and forth with a look of chagrin. "This dog used to be beautiful; now, Omar, you are destined to be a punk rocker!" said Jim.

They laughed, then Bev said, "Well, shall we all go and save planet Earth?" Marsha and I are going to focus on the number 12 and correlate it to locations. Marsha has better gut instincts than all of us together. So, I need her today, boys." Marsha smiled and looked excited. Jim stepped up by Marsha, "Tell me you ate something before we have to scrape you up and give you a rescue pen."

Marsha glared at Jim, crossing her arms across her chest with a look of defiance. "Yes, I ate, Captain Smartass!" Her tone was sarcastic.

Bev asked, "Are there tea and coffee over there because I can't think without it." Morgan laughed, "I would sure hate for you to have a senior moment without your tea and caffeine."

Bev shot him a look of pure "Just you wait! You are so going to pay for this," as she shook her head and grabbed Marsha by the arm.

"We, of course, will be the ones to pave the way. It takes a woman for that, you know."

"Come on, Marsha! Let's go show these arrogant boys how it's really done!" She shot a hot look of "There will be hell to pay later!" in Jim's direction, then smiled sweetly and took Marsha's arm. They sailed out the door with heads high and shoulders squared, leaving Lassie and Rufus trailing behind.

Don followed behind all of them. Marsha abruptly saw the armed guards walking the fence line and hesitated.

Jim stepped up, thinking to approach her, but Morgan put his arm out, holding him back. It was difficult to believe she had made it all the way to the lab door with no outside assistance, except for Bev's arm, chattering to distract her as they made plans for the computer search for locations.

Bev opened the door and that is where Marsha froze—but just for a moment. She took in a deep breath that was audible to all, as was her almost forceful exhalation as she blew it out. She took two steps inside as Bev kept chattering about their search.

She again stopped and Bev could see, and even feel her shaking as she threw a glance back over her shoulder.

Morgan and Jim stepped in beside her as Bev let go. They moved in so close that Jim thought they might crush her.

Kron rounded the corner with a cheery, "Welcome all! I hear we are working on finding a way to save the planet Earth! Marsha and Bev, I am assigned to your team. I see, Marsha, you are a bit apprehensive as am I. We have been in tight spots before."

"How about I just carry you the rest of the way in since you don't know your way around yet?" Kron did not wait for an answer and picked her up, feeling for the first time how violently she was trembling. "Marsha, what is wrong with your men folk? You need fixing!" She turned, her tone was near to an accusation, "Shame on you! Does it take women to take care of women?"

Kron felt her sink down into her arms. She looked down and smiled as she saw her relaxing. Her eyes were closed.

Kron shot a look back at Jim and Morgan. Bev held Kron's arm as she looked back and smiled. Their plan had worked.

Inside, Kron laid her on a medical bed and glanced up to see Thar watching from afar. Kron touched Marsha's head as she paged through the screens and gave her medication.

In a moment, Marsha opened her eyes and Kron grinned, "Look, it took me to fix you! Men!"

Bev laughed. "Okay, ladies! No slacking now! We've got a planet to save and, without us, it ain't gonna happen! Let's get to work! The computers are this way," she gestured toward the computer lab.

She gave Marsha a hand off the table, feeling a bit of hesitation from her, but tugged her along, gently but firmly. "Who wants which computer?" asked Kron.

Marsha said, "I will take the middle seat."

Kron turned, "So may I have the one closest to the door? I've got an experiment in progress and will need to get up a couple times."

Marsha patted the seat for her to sit next to her. Kron knew it was going to be fine. Marsha had not yet caught on that she wanted to be on the outside to protect Marsha with Bev in the middle so they could make her feel safer.

Bev mused, "I seem to gravitate to inside chairs—less work. Learned that one back in high school."

"If my dad were here, I would tattle on you, and my dad would not like that, Bev."

Both giggled, then started, "All right now, 12 is the number of the Universe, according to our hairy friend, Merlin."

Bev quickly realized what she said as soon as it slipped out of her mouth. She shot a quick glance toward Kron. "Yeah, he knows a bunch, but it's the wrong approach. What a troublemaker!" She glanced at Marsha.

"What does your gut say, Marsha?"

Marsha grabbed the wastebasket and almost immediately lost her scant breakfast.

Kron slid off her chair, grabbing the med gun which Thar had thoughtfully preloaded for Marsha. Kron gave her the shot and remarked, "You have always had a sensitive stomach. You need an iron stomach like mine." I had chipmunk for breakfast and bet you had a single piece of toast." She said "Jeez, I need to retrain you!"

She got up, disappeared for a moment, then strode back in, carrying an egg and another piece of toast for her and Bev. She had pre-poured Pedialyte for Marsha, handing Bev the water. She sat down with some sort of mush for herself.

Marsha put down the wastebasket and looked hard at her plate, then at Bev's who had started to eat. She glanced at Kron, picked up her fork and took a bite of egg. She asked Kron what she was eating. Kron looked at her and said, "Eat first; ask me after you're done."

"EWWW," breathed Bev.

Marsha laughed and took another bite. Kron picked up her water as did Bev and said a toast to their hoped-for success. Marsha smiled and picked up her drink. "To the forever friendship of the three amigos." Marsha laughed and they downed their fluids as they kept toasting, Thar was amazed at what was happening. Jim and Morgan watched from afar as well. Everything was on track. Adding Kron was brilliant as was adding both dogs. Lassie and Rufus were both well-trained therapy and guard dogs, which had been Jim's idea.

Marsha mused, "Maybe we women should look at anything that points to the Orion system, like the Giza Plateau."

Kron began nodding in agreement. "Marsha, good place to start!" Kron told them she had been to Mintaka, one of the stars in the belt. "It is beautiful there. There are five colors in the sky, and it was a beautiful sight to behold."

Marsha and Bev listened in awe of her description of how colorful it sounded. Both said, "Wow," at the same moment.

"How I would love to see that!" said Bev. Kron could see both trying to visualize it and told them she would bring pictures tomorrow.

"Oh, Grissom and Mottice want to meet their new aunts and uncles!" she added in a cheery, almost lyrical voice. Both smiled and agreed they couldn't wait for them to meet their kids.

Kron smiled, "Well, it's happening today! They will all be in class together."

"Now, there is a picture! Wouldn't you love to be a fly on the wall?" asked Marsha. "The kids learning with Bigfoot and Aliens." They laughed at the pictures in their minds.

"And what do you guys think of Skinwalker Ranch in Utah where all that weird stuff happens, and you can hear something underground?" asked Bev.

Kron turned to face Marsha and Bev. Wrinkling up her nose, she said, "There's bad stuff there. The Hopi put a curse on that area and Star beings got upset; they're seeking revenge. It is said to be a base. Hopi leaders have told all of us Tiger People to stay away." Marsha asked with a puzzled look, "Is that the name they call your people?"

Kron was happy Marsha had engaged and fed her more information, "Only in the Old West. It's mostly native Americans who call us by that name."

Marsha turned to look at Bev and asked her what she thought.

"I will take this one, Marsha, if that is okay? It intrigues me, and I would love to learn more."

She shook her head, "Can't wait to hear this one!"

After they had been there four hours, Jim and Morgan walked over and both dogs promptly stood.

"Bet these two mutts need to use some facilities," Jim said.

"I hope you're referring to outside." Everyone laughed.

"The groomer has finally finished with poor Omar; wanna take a peek? She is in the barn."

Marsha laughed, "This should be a treat!" She stood, but nearly crumpled to the floor. Kron stuck out an arm and righted her. Marsha balanced on both feet and straightened her shirt.

"I hope you're all as excited to see this as I am! Let's go see this transformation!"

Morgan and Jim walked closely on either side of her while Kron walked just behind. Both dogs took their positions in the lead and Don fell in beside Morgan.

Morgan and Jim could feel some excessive shaking and Lassie felt it as well. She had backed up to Marsha, her graceful tail swishing against Marsha's leg.

As they rounded the corner toward the barn, there he stood!

Bev was first to gasp, "O-M-G! WOW!"

Everyone else froze where they were, mouths wide open. The groomer was obviously into punk rock. Omar had a purple stripe with spiky hair all the way down his spine and extending out on his entire tail, which in itself was edgy. She also dyed silver lightning bolts on each side and dyed his legs a brilliant turquoise blue with black paws.

School had just let out so the kids poured out of the classroom, surrounding Omar, clapping and cheering. They obviously highly approved. They waited for Tig's reaction. Then finally Morgan asked, "Where's Tig?"

Dallas muttered, "He didn't mean to do it."

Jim turned and asked, "Just what is it that he didn't mean to do?"

"Uhmm, well, he put his peanut butter and jelly sandwich on the teacher's chair, and it was kinda open, and well, you know, she accidentally sat on it, and darn it all, we laughed."

Morgan looked at Marsha, as she said, "I know," and everyone joined in, "That's My Boy!"

Kron grinned and said she would be happy to retrieve him.

A moment later, out she walked with Tig, Mottice and Grissom trooping behind her.

The kids parted like the red sea and Tig caught sight of Omar. He was so excited he dropped his books, and slowly walked around all the way around him, admiring him from every angle. "He is so amazingly awesome!"

The kids all loved it but Liam sat off by himself with Droopy and Giles. Morgan could hear him saying, "Don't worry, boys, I would never let anyone humiliate you like that."

Jim leaned toward Morgan, "Now, that is the one you should be saying, 'Now That's My Boy' about."

Mottice looked up at Kron and asked if he could have his hair done like that. "Let's talk about that later—after your homework is done!"

Mottice told Tig how lucky he was to have a dog like that, then said he should cut his hair like that and dye it to match his dog. Jim shot Kron a meaningful glance. She put her hand on Tig's shoulder and said, "If you do that, not only will you be in big trouble, but Mottice will be in trouble as well for suggesting it to you. And he, of course, will be participating in any consequences you get for such a horrendous and stupid idea."

Morgan laughed and told Tig he better listen to Aunt Kron.

Tig turned to Mottice and said in a proud tone, "We are related! I knew you were like a brother!"

Mottice grinned back, "Yeah, me too!"

Jim muttered under his breath, "I smell trouble with a capital 'T' here."

The groomer asked if, while she was here, did they want all of them groomed with a normal groom and blowout. Morgan said, "Yes, but, please, no other artistic endeavors with any of the dogs… except the pink poodle, Toodles."

The groomer's eyes lit up and she said, "A PINK POODLE? AWESOME! Can I take pictures for my album?"

Kron put her hand on Jim and Morgan's shoulders. They glanced at each other, then at Marsha. Kron pushed them away and picked her up and took her back to the lab, laying her on the medical bed. They followed, almost at a military quick step.

Liam followed with Droopy and Giles trailing behind in their slow and methodical progress. Liam sat down on the floor between Droopy and Giles watching them work on Marsha.

Thar noticed Liam watching and pointed it out to Morgan. Morgan stepped over to him and sat down in front of him to block the view.

He asked how school was going. "Other than Tig's pranks?"

"I love math and history."

"You know what, your old Dad at your age thought it was super cool, too." Liam turned and stroked each dog.

"It looks like you have two buddies."

"I don't mind the slobber; it doesn't bother me. Droopy and Giles are best friends. You can't separate them, so the three of us hang out together. They both like sleeping on the porch. It is too hot for them inside the house."

Morgan looked at both dogs and tilted his head to the side as he thought about what Liam had said. "Really? I didn't know that, Liam."

Liam scooted into his dad's side and asked, "Is Mommy still sad and sick?"

Morgan put his hand on Liam's crossed legs and explained, "She is making progress on getting better. It won't be long now, Liam."

"I am sad, too," Liam told Morgan. He picked Liam up and set him on his lap. "It's okay to be sad. You know you can talk to me or Uncle Jim anytime."

Liam glanced up at Morgan, saying, "You are too close to the situation. As advanced kids, we know that. Do you care if I talk to Dr. Cay a couple times a week?"

Morgan mentally gasped and reached to hold him close as his eyes started to water.

"Of course you can speak with her. May I tell her what days and times to expect you?"

"Tuesday and Friday after school. I promise to do my homework as soon as I get home and will feed Droopy and Giles when I finish my homework."

"Or—maybe Tig can feed them for you those days?"

Liam smiled, nodded, then added, "Tell Tig to not make fun of Giles; it hurts his feelings. He was born with slobber and it's not his fault."

"Okay, I will take care of that tonight! Anything else, Liam?"

He sat up straight and peeked over Morgan's shoulder. Morgan asked if he wanted to see her up close and he began to cry and shook his head no.

"Okay, I understand. She really is getting better. It is just taking some time."

"Why don't you go do your homework on the porch with Droopy and Giles? I am sure they would like the company."

Liam stood and looked toward his mom, then walked over to the porch with Droopy and Giles following him without his calling them. He ran into the kitchen and then came back out, sitting on the porch and took a drink of water. He then offered it to Giles who slobbered all over it as he drank and then Droopy whose ear wound up in the cup. Without another thought, Liam drank the rest.

Morgan laughed, "My perfect trifecta!" He returned to the lab and looked down at Marsha who was awake.

"Is Liam upset?"

Morgan glanced at her, trying to decide how much to tell her in this moment, but she demanded, "TRUTH!"

Jim laughed out loud, then answered her, "TRUTH. Liam did see everything, my love, and was back with me while I sat in front of him with his two new pals, Droopy and the King of Slobber, Giles."

"He has decided he would like to talk to Dr. Cay twice a week and work through some things."

Marsha cried, "OMG, my baby!"

Kron told her, "This is a reality for a lot of children. He at least has realized he needs to talk to someone. He will be absolutely fine, Marsha. I don't believe you should hide how you're feeling from him. He could easily feel betrayed and lied to; do you agree?"

Marsha turned her head. Morgan pulled her chin toward him and waited for her to look at him. They made eye contact and she said, "I am a terrible mom! Why can't I just be normal, Morgan?"

Jim touched her shoulder lightly and said, "You have been through an insane amount of real trauma and Dr. Cay will help you work through those feelings and the reality of the situation. You are not to take on that burden."

She tried to sit up, but Morgan immediately pushed her back down, saying "Time out! Another 20 minutes. When your pulse drops to 80, we will consider letting you out."

Thar walked over and glanced at the screen. He looked at Marsha and told her, "Frankly, you look awful! If you were my patient, you would not leave this bay for 24 hours!"

She closed her eyes and tears trickled down her cheeks.

"Tell you what; will you agree to stay on the medical bay bed in your bedroom for 24 complete AND consecutive hours? And yes, I do know how your mind works on twisting things around to work for you. So total and consecutive hours along with medication?" She looked at Morgan and then to Jim. She stayed focused on him.

He leaned in and murmured, "I will be with you and Morgan tonight. Bev knows the routine and, besides, she has play practice with the kids tonight anyway, plus two piano lessons."

Marsha looked at Bev and asked, "Can you take on—or should I say, will you take on Wyatt? He is certain he is called to be a jazz pianist."

Bev laughed. "Shall we place bets on how long he lasts? Loser cooks dinner for both families!"

Jim guessed two weeks, Morgan bet one month, but Marsha said. "He will stick with it."

They all laughed. Bev said, "I give him three months and he will be on to the next big thing, although I could teach him saxophone." A slightly wicked smile crossed her face and Morgan's eyes got big as he shook his head back and forth, adding a loud, verbal, "NO! Way!"

Marsha glanced toward the screen and said, "79," as she sat up.

"Okay, let's get you into bed."

"I want to talk with Liam sitting on the porch and talk about him drinking after Giles and Droopy! EWWW, that is just too disgusting to even think about. Can you and Morgan hold me up?"

Morgan told her, "We are your experts, no problem."

Jim turned and kissed Bev, "Finch will be waiting for his piano lesson."

"Yeah, Mr. Analytical, I can hardly wait." They all laughed and Marsha stood, with Morgan and Jim offering her their arms, and she put her arms through each of theirs as they moved in tight. They got to the porch and Marsha was smiling.

She beamed, "Liam, wow, look at you! Two new friends! Let's see Droopy and Giles." He beamed back at her.

"Will you do me a big, giant favor?"

He nodded and Marsha said, "Please don't drink after the dogs! EWWW!"

He laughed, "Okay Mom," then added she should be careful to not make fun of the drool. He stood and whispered, "He told me he is sensitive about his drool."

She nodded, and told him, "I got the secret, and mum's the word!" Then asked what he thought of Omar?

"Poor dog is so humiliated. I would never do that to these two. Totally embarrassing. But, in all fairness, it's perfect for Tig and looks like Mottice, too."

Liam laughed, "Is he a chip off the old block, Uncle Jim?"

Jim gasped, nearly biting his tongue. "Liam, really?" Then, he laughed and told him he is probably right, "Okay, buddy get your homework done and we are going in."

"Do you need anyone out here with you?" asked Marsha. He looked down at Droopy and Giles, who were looking up at Marsha. Liam cleared his throat and tipped his head toward Droopy and Giles, "Oh, Oh, you're right! What was I thinking? You have two friends sitting right here with you!"

Droopy licked his face. Morgan cleared his throat, "Liam, make sure you wash your hands and take a shower tonight!"

Liam scrunched up his face and said, "OH, JEEZ."

They had walked in the house and had gotten just around the corner when she collapsed. They got her up the stairs and onto the bed. Thar had received notice from the remote monitoring system that she was on the bed, and he was already paging through the diagnostic screens remotely.

He went right to the house with the med gun in his coat pocket along with a few syringes for good measure. He stopped and said, "I heard about Tig's dog! Embarrassing, huh?"

Liam smiled, "Yes, and humiliating!"

Thar asked if his dad was home.

Liam replied, "Yeah, they just went in."

"Can I go in? Droopy and Giles won't try to bite me, will they?" Liam laughed, looking at their faces. "Not got one of those bad bones in their bodies!"

"Good to know, Liam. Thanks. How goes the homework?"

His face scrunched up, "Boring."

"You should talk to your teacher about moving you up to a little more difficult work."

Liam looked up at him surprised, and his eyes got big, "I can do that?"

Thar bobbed his head up and down with a big smile, "Yes, you can. Why wait on the others to go for it?"

Liam jumped up with such enthusiasm his books flew clear off the porch. "WOW, come on Droopy and Giles. Let's see if she is still there." Thar laughed as he took off and ran inside, scampering up the stairs.

"She is severely dehydrated, get a line in her now!" He gave her meds. "This was way too much for her, guys. While it is a decent plan, you need to cut activities by at least two-thirds."

"Morgan and Jim, I will have no kids in the labs. That's the Number One rule!" Jim asked if that included dogs. Thar just glared at him. "Okay, got it now."

"Let's not put her under. I would rather she remember today and how much she did. So, if you are both staying with her tonight — which I hope you are—she must stay on the table or if she starts melting down, put her between you on the bed."

"Talk about the project and what you guys found today and let her tell you what she thinks about it. But when both of you are aware that she drifts off and is quiet, then let her sleep. BUT, if she starts screaming, push that button, hear me? PUSH THE DAMN BUTTON!"

"Of course," said Morgan.

Marsha roused as Jim accessed her vein.

Thar said, "You are not drinking even a fraction of what you need, little lady! We will leave this central line in until you prove you can drink what a normal person would!" She held still while he stuck her.

"Bath only! Do NOT get it wet! And have Bev help you wash your hair in the sink."

She asked where Liam was and if none of the other kids were playing with him.

Thar's expression shifted, "I sent him to talk to the teacher about advancing his schoolwork."

She sat up and said, "It is dark; who is with him? NOW—get someone with him NOW!" She went into full panic mode.

She saw Don talking to his cuff and she yelled "NOW!"

Don left the room. She was sure he went to go get him. "All kids have to be in before dark until we see how this goes!"

Thar returned, "Yes, that is fair, Marsha." She was breathing heavy and rough. Morgan took her hand and put it gently to his chest, telling her to follow him. He spoke softly to her and within 10 minutes she recovered.

Thar had shut the bedroom door, so Liam did not become concerned.

Marsha closed her eyes and slept for an hour, then sat up and looked at Jim and Morgan working on their tablets. She laid back trying to not make a sound as tears rolled down her cheeks.

Jim thought he heard something and glanced over. He put his tablet down and nudged Morgan's arm. They both approached her bed. She was shaking and crying.

"What's wrong, baby?" asked Morgan. "Come lay between Jim and I while we work. We won't tell Thar you were out of bed."

Her teeth chattered. He asked if she was cold, and she nodded. "Silly, I should have turned your bed up."

They helped her to the bed as Lassie and Rufus both jumped up. "Guys! "Look at all this dog hair! I have enough to knit a blanket!"

They laughed as she snuggled under the blanket and quilt but could see she was still shaking. They both got in close to her.

Jim asked, "Wanna see what we are working on?" They showed her an equation they were obviously really proud of. She closed her eyes as they spoke to each other across her. Within a few minutes, Marsha was back asleep.

Jim pulled a quilt up over himself and told Morgan good night. He laughed and did the same.

Jim felt Lassie get up, then move by Marsha's chest, licking her face. Rufus tried to lay across Jim to get to her hand, and he was vigorously licking her.

Morgan heard it and called Marsha's name. She did not respond. Jim felt for the pulse in her neck; and abruptly sat up. "Ring that damned bell, Morgan!"

They almost slammed her on the bed doing CPR. The medical team of four ran up the stairs after Don let them into the house. Thar declared, "No more! She stays in the medical bay where she has 24/7 care!"

The AED finally converted her and a good rhythm returned. The guards came and carried her on a litter, running across the compound into the lab.

Morgan bent over, braced on the bed as he cried. Jim put his arm around him but urged, "Save that for later! We gotta go!"

By the time they reached the lab, she was intubated and on the ventilator. Several different fluids hung by her bed, along with a few other bags.

Thar said, "Had those dogs not done their job, it would have been all over. Morgan, please get up on this bed right now," ordered Thar.

"I am fine."

"You don't decide that; I do! Now get on that bed!"

Morgan tried to sit up and Jim shoved his shoulder back down and said, "Will you listen to the doctor, please? Let us give you something for your blood pressure. Then, you go back to your own bedroom and get on the damn medical bed and, Jim, you are to make him sleep!" He shoved the medical gun into Jim's hand.

"We have Marsha! If there is any change, no matter how small, Jim will wake you."

"Jim, you are assigned to him tonight. Sorry, it's an all-night duty for you. But… what are friends for?" His face broke a rueful grin.

Jim helped Morgan sit up and did not let him linger beside Marsha. He pointed him directly to his house, up the stairs, and helped him lie on the bed. He told the bed to raise the temperature 25 degrees and tossed him the quilt.

"Sorry, it is a little on the hairy side," he laughed.

Morgan turned, trying to cover himself and Jim caught him off guard, giving him a light dose of sleep meds. He had no time to object; he was asleep.

Jim finished covering him and invited Lassie up on the bed along with him, then instructed the bed to differentiate between them and not to repair either species' reproductive organs.

Morgan awaked at 8:15 AM. He sat up, shook his head to clear remaining cobwebs, and groused in Jim's direction, "Why the hell did you let me sleep this long?"

Jim said, "Dr. Thar's express orders."

"Have you been up all night?"

"I repeat, doctor's orders! You may be interested to know that you do not snore; however, Rufus rattles the whole darned house!"

Morgan laughed and said, "Am I even sorry I missed that?"

"Your blood pressure is normal this morning."

"I am going to go shower. You might want to do the same and then we can head over to the lab."

"You will never believe what I found last night!"

Morgan said, "I hope this is good news for once."

"Don't be surprised if he makes you do this for a week! Just sayin'. Marsha is much improved this morning, but he still plans to keep her under for another full day, and she stays in the lab for four more days."

He smiled and said, "Get your shower and I'll meet you there."

Morgan jumped off the bed and first went downstairs to let Lassie and Rufus out to do their business. He made coffee, then let them back in.

He ran upstairs and jumped in the shower. The hot water felt wonderful. The urge for Marsha hit him as he showered. "Ask for medication before it gets out of control! Right now it is the first twinge. Stop it in its tracks," he thought to himself.

He dressed in jeans and his Cleveland Browns shirt, then slid into his tennis shoes. He drank his coffee, brushed his teeth and then was out the door. He opened the lab door and it asked him to scan his thumb print.

Now that was new! He put his thumb down on the reader and the inner door popped open. He walked in and Jim was at his desk. He walked over to his desk and rolled his chair over.

"Okay, let's have it. But before we get started, I felt the first twinge of an urge for Marsha."

Jim said nothing but got up, pulled out the med gun, and shot it into Morgan's arm, saying, "Thanks for telling me."

Just as Jim pulled up a site on his computer, Thar approached. "Hello, Morgan. I monitored you through the night and that sleep did you a world of good. You will do the same for the next four nights."

Morgan stood, and crossed his arms. Thar asked if he had an objection.

"Only that Jim should not have to babysit me if you have the capability to monitor."

"All the same, Morgan, he will continue. He will go get sleep at home or here, but we will make sure he will get a minimum of six hours sleep sometime today."

Jim said, "I will grab a table and get some sleep. He said some six to eight hours of sleep, correct?"

He nodded his head. "When you finish, Morgan, come over and we will talk about Marsha."

Morgan sat down as he walked away. Morgan laughed and said, "Damn, I feel like I am back at medical school again."

Jim said, "I was thinking the same thing, except we were younger and able to go with almost zero sleep for months on end. Sucks to get old!" Both laughed.

Jim said, "Okay, look at this."

He was interrupted by the loudspeaker system. "Dr. King, please pick up line one. It is Tig's teacher."

Morgan threw his head back and shook it back and forth. "Good thing he can't see my pressure right now."

Jim asked, "You want me to take it? It certainly would be my honor and pleasure to go and have this discussion."

Morgan shot him a look and said, "Certainly, all yours! I will continue looking through this information to catch up."

Jim picked up the phone and said, "Dr. Mottice speaking."

He heard, "This is Miss Tazzy and, well, did anyone see him before he came to school?" Then, "Apparently not, what is the issue?"

A moment passed, "Well, I believe seeing would be much better than me trying to describe it. Can you come over?"

"Be right there." Jim shrugged off his lab coat. "This outta be great," he murmured as he rubbed his hands together.

Morgan waved to him as he read.

Jim walked into Tig's classroom and stopped, cocked his head to the side and his eyes narrowed.

The teacher walked up to him. "Need I say more?"

"Nope, seen enough! May I have him, please?"

"All yours, doctor."

Jim said, "Tig, would you join me, please?" as he clenched his teeth.

Tig was looking down and knew he was in hot water.

Liam stood and said, "Sir, he just loves to shock people and does wild things. He really is a sweet, kind person."

"Thank you, Liam, for your overly kind review of Tig."

Tig stood in front of Jim. "Let's go young man."

He marched him into his house for Bev to deal with. Bev was in the kitchen and turned to see Jim smiling … and then she saw Tig.

"OMG, TIG! You went to school like that?"

He nodded his head. She walked over and kissed Jim, then with her hands on her hips, "I will handle Mr. Tig."

"But wait, let me snap a picture to show his dad."

Bev told him to turn around and smile at the camera "… or you WILL find yourself in a most unfortunate situation!"

Jim returned to the lab, slipped into his coat and Morgan was still reading. He pulled up the picture and put it in Morgan's line of sight. Morgan grabbed the phone and looked, then dropped his head onto the desk. He began laughing so hard he had tears in his eyes. Jim burst out laughing, too. Tig had glued Omar's cut off hair on top of his own hair—with superglue!

"Bev will probably have to give him a buzz cut."

Morgan was still bent over, laughing. Thar came over. Jim held up the image, still shaking with silent laughter. It took Thar a minute, then he said, "Tig, right?" and started to laugh.

"Wow, that kid is certainly one of a kind!" he said, laughing. As he walked away, he said loudly, "I hope he doesn't rub off on Vaughn."

Bev buzzed for Jim and Morgan to come to the lab door. Right away Morgan started to chuckle. They trooped out of the lab and into the outer hall of the lab and… there stood Tig. His head had been buzz cut and where the super glue had been on his scalp, were completely bald patches.

Morgan said, "Well son, that is quite the unique haircut. At least you match Omar in uniqueness.

"Your mother will be heartbroken when she sees this! You do realize that, Tig? What do you think we could do so that your mother won't be so upset?"

Tig thought for a moment, "Could I maybe try the plant root stimulator? That might make it grow back faster."

Jim laughed, "Well, Tig, that is one option, however, your hypothesis will not work; so try again."

"How about I take colored sharpies and make silver arrows like Omar?"

Morgan rolled his eyes and said "…Next?"

"How about I beg for forgiveness and take on extra chores and write a paper on how stupid it was?"

Morgan said, "BING, BING, BING. Now get yourself back to school. There are always consequences to our actions both good and bad. This choice resulted in bad consequences.

"And you need to thank Liam for trying to stick up for you."

"Yes, sir."

"Now get going!"

"But they will laugh at me!"

Jim stood with his arms crossed, "Consequences! Tig."

"AW, SHUCKS. NO ONE CAN TAKE A JOKE!"

Morgan yelled after him, "Consequences, son!"

"And you people wonder why I have high blood pressure!"

Jim slapped him on the back and said, "Okay laugh break over. Let's get busy looking at what I found."

Back in the lab, Morgan pulled up an article on Zecharia Sitchin. "He was reputed to be extremely knowledgeable in the area of ancient aliens and he translated the Sumerian tablets. However, the credibility of his translation ability remains an open question."

"The Anunnaki folklore had many roles in relation to humanity. But one of those roles was as our creators. Essentially, maintaining creation was a lot of work. The so-called gods had all the chores of existence and some of them went on strike. Obviously, this would have led to a disaster, so a solution had to be found. One of the Anunnaki, Enlil, told the others he could end the strike—but the gods must name him their ruler."

"So the Anunnaki came up with the idea of creating workers of inferior beings. Enki thought he'd had a brilliant idea and suggested to the Anunnaki that they create a race of slaves. They all agreed, so he got busy with a mixture of clay and blood from a slaughtered Anunnaki. Working this together, he managed to create the first human beings."

"It is way too easy to label all Anunnaki as evil, cold, heartless, and sadistic creatures. But Anunnaki are individuals, just like us. Some of them would have had different motives and personalities. Enki was actually reasonably friendly and benevolent toward humanity, even going so far as to save the human race from Enlil's flood. So, when and if the Anunnaki return, we can expect some surprises in their interactions with us."

"At our present time, we have identified at least two resources that the Anunnaki value and which we possess:

Gold: The Anunnaki require this to protect Nibiru from destruction. This is a basic survival need.

Labor: The Anunnaki don't enjoy physical labor, preferring to hand it off on to an inferior race."

Morgan read through the details but just printed the summary. Thar came into the lab and approached Morgan. "Can you come with me to see Marsha, so we can talk about her treatment?"

Jim was sleeping in the bed next to Marsha. Morgan approached Marsha's bed—it was always tough to see her lying there so vulnerable and helpless.

Thar approached and stood beside him. "She looks better, Morgan. Her vitals are stable; however, I want to keep her under until tomorrow. She will spend four more days here with us to evaluate her mental stability."

"We have many different medications that could help her. Let's figure out what will work best. I am a bit hesitant because of her issue with reactions to the different new drugs we have tried. And if she reacts adversely to any of those modalities, that will delay her recovery a few days."

"I want you to realize this and be prepared should it happen." Morgan stood with his arms crossed and his brow furrowed.

"I am concerned that she would not survive an adverse reaction. Could we wait for her to gain some strength first?"

"I have been leaning toward that myself, so long as this rest produces an improvement in her mental status. I believe that your theory of 'power to the women' might work. She just was not strong enough physically and she had been pushed to complete emotional exhaustion."

Morgan mused, "I would like to pursue that path again, but at a slower pace, obviously."

Morgan looked down at her. Her hand moved to him. Morgan said, "She hears me talking. She fights any medication with such ferocity!"

Thar gave her next scheduled medications and told the on-duty doctor to keep a tighter watch on her consciousness levels.

Morgan sighed, "I am done for the day. I need to go back to the house and deal with Tig."

Thar added, "You know, they have a nanny, Morgan! I had better see you on that medical bed. I will send Jim over when he awakens. You are in dire need of rest, my friend, so if it seems like I am being a tad bit on the gruff side, it is because that is the only way I've found to get through to you!"

"You are literally carrying the weight of humanity on your shoulders. All eyes are on you to find a solution. That is the heaviest of burdens, and, of course, you would never admit it, even to yourself."

"Without rest, you can't physically carry this burden, Morgan. I want just a week and to give you a medical vacation for five full days."

Morgan nodded his head in agreement, but looked him straight in the eye and said, "You are absolutely, 100% correct! But I will have to see you tomorrow."

Thar's shoulders slumped as he watched Moran leave the lab.

11

DNA Theft

Morgan got back to the house and pulled out some grapes to eat. Kulo, the chef, came from the pantry.

"Oh, Dr. King, let me make something for you. I didn't expect you this soon. How about a hot vanilla latte and maybe I'll whip up a mushroom omelet and a citrus salad? It'll take about 15 minutes, just enough time to drink your latte."

He thanked her as he sat down at the kitchen table where they could talk. She handed him the latte. Morgan took a sip and told her it was incredible. She replied that she always adds some Himalayan salt and hazelnut.

"Wow, that is good!"

She looked back at him over her shoulder and, with a grin, said, "I noticed Tig has an unusual haircut."

He laughed and agreed. She told him, "Boys will be boys."

He told her he was going to go lie down for a five-minute power nap. She told him she would come get him when his food was done. Morgan had a hard time getting up the stairs to lie on the bed.

Kulo turned the burner under the omelet off and quietly mounted the stairs. She cracked the door open and peeked in. She looked around and noted there was no security. She entered the bedroom, shut the door and bolted the lock. She slipped out of her pants and took Morgan. She was BLUE! She mounted him and began the transfer process. She loved the human way. It was ecstasy for her, over and over.

Don suspected something was up when he found no one in the kitchen, so he used a magnet to open the bolt and entered. He was shocked, told her to stop and put her hands up where he could see them.

She turned and said, "Go ahead, I already have the DNA." Don called out an emergency code; moments later, guards burst into the room, nearly knocking Don off his feet. The medical team was right behind. They lifted Morgan to the medical bed. Thar flipped through the screens, which revealed he had been drugged quite heavily but did not immediately identify the agent used. That would take further analysis.

By design his reproductive organs had remained functional, and he had been drained of semen. Thar radioed for a gurney immediately and told Jim to stay put in the lab. He told Security to bring her to the lab, "We have a few tests to perform," he told her with a grim expression.

They put Morgan on a litter and ran him across the compound to the lab, where they moved him onto a medical bed and covered him. Jim ran to Morgan and asked what happened as he grabbed an IV kit.

"Security in the compound has been compromised and the Blue was somehow able to trick Morgan into believing she was the chef."

"She drained nearly all Morgan's sperm after she drugged him. She had her way with him—that we know for sure. Give that bolus and we will do another."

Security entered the lab with the imposter, hands zip tied behind her back. Jim looked at her. He pulled off his gloves and kicked a chair out of his way, jaw clenched, as he ran across the room. He shoved her down and threw himself on her, choking her.

Security pulled him off and Thar gave Jim medication to calm him and stabilize his blood pressure. Olzing arrived just in time to help pull Jim off her.

"Strap her down on that table." Security threw her up on the table hard and Jim asked the bed to restrain her completely. Thar told one of the doctors to cut off her clothing. The see-through panel in her stomach glowed with the sperm fertilizing her eggs by the hundreds.

Morgan awakened, "What the hell am I doing here?"

Then, he noticed HER, that she was Blue, and that her stomach glowed. He jumped up with white-hot rage firing from every pore in his body. He was so angry he was not even aware he had no pants, but Thar yelled for someone to get Morgan some scrubs.

Morgan yelled as he pulled the scrubs on his naked legs, "Olzing, how in God's name did she slip by. How, How, HOW?"

"ANSWER ME NOW, DAMN IT!"

Olzing said in a calm, careful voice, "She told us she has been hiding in the trees at the back of the property under a squirrel's nest. The tree was hollow. She saw the chef leave and managed to make a duplicate of her identity."

Morgan started for her bed when Thar tried to inject him. Morgan shouted "NO, AND I DO MEAN NO," as he shoved the med gun away.

Morgan screamed at her, "WHY?"

She answered with no remorse in her voice. "We are desperate! Half of our children were killed by our enemy a few months ago. And, we have lost all but two of our females."

Morgan turned, walked away and straight out of the lab. He went into the house and cleaned up the eggs and threw out his cup, washing everything thoroughly. It helped him to work through his pent-up emotions and think the problem through as he cleaned.

After an hour, Jim appeared as Morgan was cleaning the living room from the kids' TV party the previous evening. Morgan looked up and saw him but continued to work. Jim sat down and said nothing, just waiting expectantly. Finally, Morgan came over and sat down beside him. "She raped me!" he began to cry.

Jim looked at him, as he said, "I know they need their planet saved. Jim, surely there are ways to help them. I need to go up and get on the bed and make sure this is reversed again. I also need skin repair. It looks like chopped beef."

Jim followed him. Morgan got on the bed as Jim programmed it. He told Morgan to lie down. The control unit read 30 minutes for repairs. Morgan sat up and said "OMG, Marsha and I had intercourse the day she came in!" He put his head down and shook it back and forth. He looked at Jim and said, "While I lie here, go over and check Marsha right now. You also need to go get Bev and see if they reversed her and also check you."

Jim got up and left, still not saying anything. The look on his face was concerning for all.

Morgan's bed turned off and he headed straight to the lab. He went right to Marsha. He looked at Jim, who nodded his head yes. Morgan said, "Bev?"

He nodded his head yes.

"Well?" asked Morgan. Thar came to Morgan, "Marsha and Bev conceived first before Blue could insert those eggs into either of them."

Olzing looked sheepish, angry, and more than a little ashamed, "Security failed to scan inside of those trees, but that is being completed now. We have Cleg, Virgil, Kron, Aggie and Bitty looking at every square inch of the woods with equipment to handle any that might be camped in the park."

Morgan shook his head. He looked toward Jim, "How did Bev take the news?"

"Happy beyond belief."

Jim looked at Thar, "Bring Marsha up."

Thar looked down. "Not so sure that is a good idea."

Jim repeated firmly, "YOU WILL DO IT!" He glared at the Nordic physicians, and they quickly began the process of awakening Marsha.

Morgan climbed in bed with her, running her hair through his fingers. She opened her eyes and Morgan squeezed her tightly. "Why are all these people around us, Teddy Bear?"

Jim approached the bed and pointing to himself, asked, "Room for one more? We have made lots of progress and can't wait to catch you up so you can jump in full throttle."

Thar cleared his voice, "Not full throttle, Jim, but after a few days more here she can begin with two hours at a time per day."

Marsha smiled broadly. Jim moved in as tight as he could as did Morgan. Morgan looked into her eyes and propped himself up on an elbow and kissed her lovingly when the urge hit.

"He gave her a passionate kiss. He put his arm around her waist pulling her to him. Jim grew uncomfortable as she threw her arms around him, pushing against him and moving her hips into him."

Jim said, "Okay that is enough for now. Break it up, you two! We are all standing here watching."

Marsha laughed. Morgan smiled, "We have some good news, honey."

She looked at him, "Wait, before you give me any good news, I have a headache. Can we do something? Thar leaned over and injected her twice and Morgan once. That will take care of the urge and the headache."

She looked at him and said, "Gee, thanks!"

He grinned, "Okay, what is the good news?"

"WE ARE PREGO!"

She looked stunned, afraid to believe what she was hearing.

He then asked if she had been on the med bed.

Her face looked puzzled. "Other than when they put me on it, NO!" She looked at Jim. "Is it a boy or girl?"

Jim shook his head, well the mass producer you are, it looks like twins—AGAIN! Two boys."

She clapped her hands in glee. "OMG, I'm so excited!" she said as she trailed off throughout the word.

Her breathing quickened and she mumbled, "Dizzy, Morgan! Dizzy!"

Thar saw the emergency alert light up, so hit the emergency security button. Fifteen responders—more or less—encircled where two were coming through. Their devices were pointed and ready to shoot the containment field as it deployed around the bed.

They shot, but Morgan screamed, "Wyatt Earp and Charlie Bassett!" Nearly everyone looked stunned.

"Go get Bat now!" snapped Olzing.

Shortly, Bat arrived with his pistol strapped to his side, his cane and bowler hat at the ready.

Marsha began to shake so hard she looked as though she were having a seizure. Morgan sat up, looking down at her.

Thar frantically ran the diagnostics. Morgan called Marsha's name, but she did not open her eyes. He then felt for the pulse in her neck. It was fast and thready. He wanted to jump out of bed but stayed in place, pressing into her to give her a feeling of security.

Bat ran in, walked up to Wyatt, and said, "Your tailor is slacking off on his work habits." Turning to Charlie, he continued, "Charlie, nice to see you! Mind telling me how you got in here?"

Wyatt looked somewhat shell shocked, "That thing—whatever you call it—brought us."

Marsha sat straight up and screamed, "DIZZY! NOW!"

More security streamed into the room at a dead run, armed and ready. Then, walking upright, proud and defiantly determined, came a Native American woman.

Wyatt looked at everyone and said, in a low, slow voice. "This looks for all the world like an Iroquois Indian Prophecy!"

The woman stood still, shoulders squared, head upright, looking calm but determined.

Morgan yelled, "Jim, Marsha needs us." He turned and ran back to the bed, jumping in and holding her tightly as did Morgan. She was struggling to just stay conscious.

With her teeth clenched, Marsha repeated, "No, No, No, No!"

Morgan began speaking to her in a soft and gentle voice. The Native woman tried to approach her, but four security officers blocked her way. Instead, she slowly reached over and touched Marsha's foot.

Marsha suddenly sat up in bed, jumped out, landing on her feet and faced the Iroquois woman.

"Are you one of the 12?"

"Yes, I am!"

"Let me hear what you have to say! I know that is why you are here, so please speak to me!"

"You must go to Serpent Mound in Ohio. It's the first location and you must not vary from this! The sequence is there for you to locate. Your success rests upon that. You are all protected, as we protected your President Washington so he could birth this nation."

"Morgan, you are the protector of this galaxy, a mantle not easy to bear. The 12 of us will stand with you clearing your path as much as we can, but you must be strong enough to take up this burden, along with the willingness to walk forward!"

Morgan rose from the bed and stood, straining intently as he heard her speak.

"You and your family are divinely protected along with your human protectors. These men I brought with me I will leave with you for the next 30 days to assist Bat in protecting this family. No harm will come to any of you. This prophecy has been told since the last star child left Earth 125 years ago."

"Marsha, your path is a divine appointment. Though it has been long and arduous, you will come out of the darkness and into the light soon. You have an appointment with destiny to be the mother of a new nation and a new galaxy."

"Now, I must return to the stars. Take heed." Within seconds, she dematerialized and vanished, as though into thin air.

Marsha collapsed. They got her back in bed and gave her meds. Morgan and Jim jumped in bed with her grabbing her tight as she was almost in a seizure-like situation.

Marsha whispered, "Mother of a new nation?"

She turned her head toward Jim. "Thank you for pulling me through this! You have sacrificed so much for Morgan and me, and you never complained."

He looked at her, saying, "I know you would do the same thing! It is our faith in the heavenly father, and his teaching that tells us to comfort one another."

She smiled, "I want to, and I will engage with both of you. Now I want to go home tonight and take my place at your side. We need to not walk but run towards saving this wondrous planet called Earth."

Thar stepped back. As they stood, he told them, "Press that button when you need an extra pair of hands."

Jim took her hand, putting his arms around her, "Marsha, every day before you and Bev begin in the lab, I'm asking you to jump on the bed for me so we can give you whatever meds you need."

She looked directly at Jim, "I am ready now if you are still willing."

Then she turned to Morgan, "I need you more than ever and I know you need me, too. Hold me tight and let's take our first steps."

They walked out as Thar yelled, "Put some clothes on!"

Jim glanced back over his shoulder and laughed.

They got her up the stairs and into the bed with one on each side supporting her between them. Lassie assumed her on-guard position at her feet, with Rufus on the floor facing the door.

Marsha turned to Morgan, "I need something to drink, my throat hurts! Do we have ginger ale?"

"I'll find you something." He opened the door and Rufus followed him downstairs. He filled a cup of ice, grabbed a ginger ale and brought them up to Marsha, waiting until Rufus came in, and shutting the door behind the dog.

"Teddy Bear needs you to sit up and drink the whole 16 ounces."

Don radioed to one of the guards to warm a plate of leftovers and bring a bottle of the black water up.

Morgan glanced at Don with one eyebrow arching up, "What's black water?"

"Yes, Sir!"

"Dallas suggested it because of its high pH and balanced mineral content."

Morgan shot a quick glance at Jim, "Maybe you should bring each of us a bottle as well."

After he radioed down, he added , "Don, would you please get me a nightgown out of the middle drawer and hand it to me."

Don stood with the nightgown as they removed the covers and Jim and Morgan assisted her in sitting up.

With averted eyes, Don handed them the gown and Jim and Morgan slipped the nightgown over her head. Morgan laid the covers back over her and tilted the bed up at a 30-degree angle.

"Don, please check on the tray and wait outside for it. Also scan and check it, including the water."

He responded, "Of course, sir," then exited, shutting the door behind him.

"Okay, Princess, let's get this oxygen mask on you and you can rest with your eyes closed until the tray comes up." He went into the bathroom and came out with a warm washcloth and wiped her face. He hoped that might help her feel better.

She opened her eyes, looking at Jim, then turned to see Morgan and smiled. "I am so sorry! I was so tired I couldn't hold on." "Marsha," he smiled warmly at her, "What do you think of Jim's two brilliant kids and shockingly, our Tig and Liam?

"Teddy Bear, I could picture Jim's brilliant bunch, but our Tig advanced to college level work? Frankly, I am in shock."

Jim laughed, "Well, I have to say I am not. He's been bored, and that's the reason for all his pranks, though I have to say gluing hair on his head was one of the funniest things I have ever seen. Straight out of the old Red Skelton show!" They laughed, happy, relaxed laughter.

Then Jim said, "And their career choices! Yes, I can see Tig as a gamer for sure. But Finch as a preacher? Dallas as a neurologist? And Liam as a veterinarian? Wow, so young to know what they want to do with the rest of their lives. I did not know until after my undergrad."

"Jim, I am so proud I could bust a gut."

Immediately Morgan and Jim swiveled toward her and in unison, cried, "Please, don't do that." Jim added, "Princess, Finch's selection… I guess I shouldn't be surprised now that I think about it. He always volunteers to say the prayer at meals, he put a prayer jar in the cafeteria, but I guess somehow I just didn't connect it."

"Morgan, can I get off this medical bed now and lie in our bed?"

Morgan deferred to Jim. "You guys, I know you want me to say yes, but no, not yet. You finish what's on the tray coming up and we will talk."

She smiled. "Jim, I understand." She reached for Morgan's hand as he leaned in to kiss her, but she pulled him into the bed. He lay next to her, and she gave him a passionate, long kiss.

Jim had turned and walked out of the bedroom to give them privacy. He knew it would be 30 minutes or so before a tray came up.

She rolled toward Morgan and put her arms around him, kissing him again with force and passion. As she lifted her head to look at him, Morgan pushed her back on the bed and got up. She called for Morgan to come back and said, "I am not done!"

"Marsha, my love, yes you are."

Morgan went into the bathroom, returning in sweatpants and a tee shirt. He brought her a pair of socks and helped her put them on. He smiled at her as he made his way back to her.

"Marsha, please cool your jets. We must wait until you are better."

She laid back and closed her eyes, "Morgan, in a few days can we go visit Indigo Lake and Elias? Will you make the arrangements for that to happen?" She opened her eyes, "PLEASE?"

"Marsha, I don't know but I will try to make it happen, if you promise to eat and drink enough, and tell Jim everything you are feeling BEFORE it becomes a crisis?"

"Yes, I promise."

Shortly, Jim came in with her tray, putting it in front of her. "EAT, MARSHA!" he commanded.

Her eyes flew open, "Jim, I feel like I am going to throw up!"

Jim got the med gun and gave her anti-nausea meds. "Marsha you are all set. Now EAT!!"

She picked up her fork and ate the chicken salad. She put down the fork, but Jim handed it back to her, "EAT!"

She looked up at him and her eyes narrowed.

I said, "EAT!" She ate a piece of red velvet cake, then put down the fork and looked at him.

Both Morgan and Jim were drinking the black water. Jim handed her a bottle, "Do I really need to say it?''

She took the water. "Princess want Boom-Boom!''

"This is a conspiracy, so not fair." She drank most of the water.

"Morgan, this tastes good!"

He gave her a smile, took the tray and put it on the dresser."

"Princess, scoot over so I can sleep, too."

She rolled away from him and closed her eyes.

Jim growled, "Morgan, change places and get up on the medical bed like you are supposed to!" Morgan smiled and without a word switched beds.

Jim sat up with his tablet. He wanted to study Washington's dinnerware as well as Madison's and Monroe's plates for clues. He was intrigued by what he saw.

He heard Marsha muttering and turned to her. Lassie's head went up. She began to thrash in the bed. Morgan sat up, then Marsha sat up repeating, "DIZZY, DIZZY! Keep him away! DIZZY!"

She screamed those words over and over. Jim looked but saw no time-displacement waves.

Morgan jumped in bed as Don rushed into the room. Both Lassie and Rufus jumped onto the bed facing the door, growling and baring their teeth. Morgan and Jim grabbed Marsha from both sides, holding her tightly between them.

Suddenly, there, right in the middle of their room, Merlin materialized, seemingly like out of thin air!

Jim banged his fist down onto the emergency button as Don yelled into his cuff on one side and in the other held a gun. The outside alarms blared.

Merlin said, "Focus on Washington, Madison, Monroe and Lincoln! You will find your answers there as well as what your children have said."

Rufus leapt from the bed and, latching his teeth firmly into Merlin's shoulder, growling and snarling, shaking his entire body. Merlin could hear the guards running toward them. With one arm, he backhanded the dog into the wall, reached over and yanked Marsha up with him, in an effort to drag her into time travel. However, Don grabbed her out of his grasp as Merlin disappeared into time.

Without thinking, Morgan and Jim grabbed her and threw her on the med bed with some force, reacting automatically to the urgency and unexpected nature of the situation.

Don went to check the dog and discovered he was dead; his neck had been snapped.

Morgan-Barkley ran down the steps followed by the rest of the kids in the house, but the guards intercepted him, assuring him everything was okay, and he and four other guards ushered the frightened kids upstairs.

Thar and Kron came running. She put her hand on Marsha's head and urged her down into the bed. Morgan wanted to jump in bed with Marsha, but Kron put out her arm and shook her head no.

Thar and Jim paged through the screens and asked the bed for multiple readings. "Bed repair, repair burn marks on skin and analyze what burned the skin."

"Thar, we need to put her shoulder back in place. If we do it here now and..."

Kron picked up the med gun, giving her pain and sleep meds to help her through the procedure. Jim held her arm steady and Thar expertly maneuvered it back into the socket. Marsha screamed as Thar and Kron completed the manipulation. Olzing rushed into the room just as they finished setting the shoulder. Kron covered Marsha and she slumped back into sleep.

Morgan erupted with pure rage shooting out of every pore. He grabbed Olzing by the collar, shouting incoherently. Don did his best to pull him back as did Jim.

"Olzing, why is my family still not safe? Answer me, damn it— WHY?" He sat down on the bed and began to weep in sheer fury and frustration.

Jim sat beside him, glaring at Olzing. "Now! We are waiting for your answer!"

"Morgan, Jim, you have to understand Merlin has the ability to vary the oscillation of his travel through time. There are literally thousands of those frequencies, and they can be changed moment to moment.

"We put in a request to the Pleiadians for help with full and mobile coverage. We are awaiting their final solution which they've said will be installed next week."

Bitty had sneaked down the steps and slid into the bed with Marsha, as Olzing continued. Kron turned to see Bitty; this was the first time she had seen Bitty in quite some time.

Bitty smiled and whispered, "Shhhhh." Kron smiled broadly and nodded.

***

Throughout the rest of the night, Jim and Morgan tried to puzzle out why Merlin wanted to take Marsha, particularly at this time.

Olzing interrupted their process, declaring both families should immediately move into the lab bunker which was equipped with modulating disruptors until those could be installed in both houses.

Marsha refused any more medications and announced she would not tolerate any further meds given to her unless she was informed and agreed to it, in advance.

Without waiting for any further response she switched to discussing the findings of the research done by Bev and Kron. They compared notes and sent them along to Jim and Morgan.

The White House had sent them plates, cups and saucers, delivered to them by the Secret Service, from the presidencies of Washington, Lincoln, Madison, and Monroe for them to go over with a fine-tooth comb.

Morgan was still drawn to the Rutherford Hayes' ornament. They decided to put the plates through x-ray, CAT scans, MRIs and swabbed each for color chromatography on the plate. They also studied the light spectrums of each plate. All had interesting things hidden.

Shortly after those disrupting events, the day planned for Marsha and Morgan to leave for Indigo Lake arrived. A tent had been set up for their use. Security seemed to be everywhere they looked. The train would not run during their visit; no drones or planes were allowed in the immediate airspace. The car was parked close by and up the road an ambulance parked in front of the lead car, but all were out of the eyesight of Morgan and Marsha.

Marsha skipped to the tent and Morgan ran close behind, both kicking their shoes off before they got inside. It was decorated with a white shag rug, pillows, a bucket of champagne and two glasses on a metal tray. Morgan poured two glasses for them and handed one to Marsha. "To my beautiful wife," Morgan toasted, and they both drank it until it was gone.

Morgan took Marsha's empty glass and turned to her. He drew her to him and slowly pulled her dress off over her head. He laid her back, slipping out of his clothing. They spent the next three blissful hours in the tent enjoying their freedom and each other. Marsha sat up and pulled her hair up in a ponytail. Morgan ran his fingers through her hair and then down her neck and her chest.

She laid back again. "Morgan, you started it! Let's have it, big boy!" They spent another hour lost in each other until it started to get dark. She sat up and again put her hair in a ponytail.

"Teddy Bear, it is getting dark."

He smiled at her, "Princess, thank you for a day I will never forget. We need more breaks like this!" She smiled and dressed, and as she stood, Morgan noticed droplets of blood.

"Just a minute. Marsha. Come down here, I need to look at you; lie down and spread 'em."

"Morgan, it is getting dark. Let's do this inspection at home."

"Princess, you are spotting!"

She saw a spot on her dress and looked with surprise toward Morgan. She laid back as he fished a flashlight from his pocket and tried to see. "It is not bad spotting. Princess, will you let me look at it when we get back home?"

When they arrived home, both were relieved to be back in their own home and in their own bed. Marsha jumped up on the bed and Morgan grabbed the lighted speculum. He slid it in, quickly examined her and then removed it. "Princess, it's a small tear, nothing to worry about as far as that goes."

She looked at him and sat up. "Morgan, what the hell does that mean?"

"Marsha, my love, it means you are prego. Last time you were on the bed and I was on the bed, I reversed it. You wanted a baby, so, well, we are having a baby. "Let's see if it shows yet. You can only be about seven weeks along."

Within minutes, he spoke again. "Well, Marsha, true to form you're having multiples: three babies. That means no more sex like we just had and complete bedrest. I want you to do bed exercise..."

"Teddy Bear, my lover boy, great suggestion!"

He laughed. "Marsha, seriously, you must eat, and especially hydrate, or Jim will put in a central line and a feeding tube to feed you." She shot a disgusted look in Morgan's direction.

"I would like to know the sex of these three." He queried the bed diagnostics and it revealed two girls and one boy.

Suddenly, Marsha looked frightened. "Morgan, BLUE; they won't try to get me again, will they?"

"Oh, Princess, NO!"

There was an urgent knock on the door. Jim opened the door and asked to come in. "You two do know the cat's outta the bag the minute Marsha got on the bed? Lay back and I will do the exams in the future. I am going to say this, every day if I must: Limited sex, manual if possible. Eat, drink lots of fluids or I will —and I mean it—put in a central line."

"Three babies. JEEZ!" Jim inserted the speculum, then said, "I want to feel the abdomen and the babies."

She tensed up and began to shake. He leaned against her leg and said, "Okay, here we go, Marsha." He felt her abdomen thoroughly. Minutes later, he told her she could sit up, removed his gloves and pulled up the diagnostic screen. Shaking his head, he grinned, "We would have all missed this—you have four babies! The machine can't yet see the gender of the fourth, which is hidden."

"Okay, complete bed rest. You are actually just under eight weeks. I want Bev to come over here and I am requesting a bed for her here because, yes, we are pregnant with twins as well! She is right at four weeks, both girls."

"During the day, you both hang out here because that will be the most comfortable for you both, and we need you to finish your work on the access sites."

He handed Marsha a bracelet and showed her both Morgan and he had one on their wrists as well. "They monitor both Bev and you at all times. Anything off, we are notified as is Thar.

"You are only out of bed for the bathroom, and when we are with you guys to wash your hair and take showers. The kids are all on schedules to spend time with you."

"So, they all knew? Well, hell! Everyone knew but me?"

He laughed, "I hope you enjoyed Indigo Lake because that is not happening again till six weeks after the babies come."

She looked shocked, "Jim, really?"

"We will not allow another miscarriage!"

She closed her eyes and took a deep breath.

He knew after he said it that it was the wrong thing to say to her. She released the breath slowly. Jim put his hand on her shoulder. "This will not go that way. No one will be throwing you across the room or jumping on you. Now, I want you to allow me to medicate you as I or Thar see fit, particularly for your blood pressure. Keeping that under control is critical. No arguing. Follow these rules for a safe pregnancy."

She nodded her agreement and smiled at him, giving him a big hug.

"Now, into your bed and let Lassie up as much as possible. She soothes you and I can clearly see she is your friend as well as your protector."

Marsha got into bed and Lassie immediately curled up at her feet.

"Ok, Morgan and I have to go back to work."

"Jim, this room is huge, why can't we put two desks in here and you two work here along with Bev and me? I DON'T BITE and, last I checked, neither does Bev!"

Morgan laughed, "Marsha, I will agree to that if you agree to come to the lab for a more in-depth look every single week!"

"The lab?" Her face turned into a fearful, worried expression and as she began to cry, the shaking began. Jim patiently waited on her, letting her work through her thoughts and after 10 minutes, she had stopped crying, but continued to shake. She nodded, so Jim and Morgan climbed onto the bed, one on either side of her, holding her tight between them. Finally, she put her head back, closed her eyes and let out a sigh.

Both felt her breathing pattern become accelerated. Morgan picked up her hand and put it to his chest. Jim reached across the bed and grabbed his stethoscope, listening to her heart.

Morgan looked at Jim and smiled. Morgan felt relief. She opened her eyes and said, "I am tired. You two, can I lay down?"

Jim pulled up the blood glucose app on his phone and scanned her. "Marsha, we can't let your sugar keep bottoming out!" He jumped up, retrieved his rescue pen, and injected it into her stomach. "No sleeping till you eat lunch."

She snuggled down against Jim as he sat on the bed. "Morgan, can you get her some high calorie food?"

She slept for 20 minutes until Morgan returned. "Ok, Marsha, sit up and eat!"

She sat up and Morgan put the tray in her lap. "We are not leaving until you finish your meal."

Morgan interrupted, "Peanut butter and strawberry jelly sandwich, with some fresh cantaloupe, and your favorite chai tea."

She drank all the tea and ate half the sandwich and all of the cantaloupe. "Boys, I am really tired. It's been a long, long day!"

Morgan laughed, "Princess, that is an understatement."

She looked at him and scooted down in the bed. She reached out and began rubbing him.

"Whoa, princess, that is enough."

"Morgan, Jim said manual, so that is what I was doing."

Morgan turned red and walked away with the tray. Jim stood and came back to the bed and injected her.

"Let me guess, Jim, the anti-sex medicine!"

He laughed and told her, "Go to sleep!"

She rolled over on her side and said, "Could you have someone get me some pickled beets, watermelon, green olives, and yellow peppers."

Jim laughed, "Seriously? But yeah, sure thing."

Morgan-Barkley was giving Gage a piggyback ride, taking him to see Marsha while Dorothy-Alice cared for little Heidi. She put Heidi into Marsha's arms and handed her the bottle.

She gave her mom a big hug and said, "You look so happy, Mommy. I can't wait for more babies! I hope one day I will be a great Mommy like you."

Marsha began to tear up and told her she was the best daughter a mommy could hope for. She asked what girl's name she thought the new one should be called. She said immediately "Elise."

"Okay, then that is her name, and we can start using it now, as we talk about her. You spread the word, okay?" She nodded her head.

Morgan-Barkly was in all ways a kind, shy and studious child. "What should we name the little boy?"

"You promised Uncle Bat, Tom or Charlie."

She said, "You're right, I did. Thank you for reminding me. Which one would you like?"

After a moment of thought, he said "Tom, after his brother. You could even name him Thomas Charlie King."

Her face lit up and said, "That's perfect! Pass the word."

She had them tell her how school was going, and Morgan-Barkley told her he and Mottice were best friends.

He said, "Mottice is so much smarter than me!"

She corrected him and said, "No. He has a passion for science and math, and you have a passion for English and writing. Bet you are better at those things."

He flashed a big smile and said, "Oh, yeah, I certainly am!"

Marsha explained, "You should never compare yourself to others. Everyone has a different passion and a different method of processing learning. You just can't measure that."

Her smile was so big it almost lit up the room. Dorothy-Alice asked if that was true for her, too, because she wanted to be a mommy and cook, and they didn't teach that.

Marsha looked at her and said, "They will now, love. You need to learn all the other stuff because somewhere down the line you will have to use it. But, as soon as they can slide it into the regular schedule, they will offer cooking for all of you and, for whoever is interested, how to run a household and care for children."

Dorothy-Alice threw her arms around Marsha and kissed her. She then asked Heidi and Morgan-Barkley if they heard that.

He looked down, shuffling his feet, and said, "Yeah, I heard. You do know Dorothy-Alice, we will now have to help more around the house and with the kids once they teach us?"

She responded, "SO??" He slowly shook his head and looked down.

"Okay, kids, time for school but Dorothy-Alice, please take Heidi and change her then take her to the playroom with the nannies."

Gage climbed up on the bed with Marsha and lay down sucking his thumb, holding his blanket. He curled up with Lassie, who gave him a few licks, then laid her head back down as Gage fell asleep snuggled into her with his fingers entwined in her fur.

Marsha laid back, cuddling into Gage and Lassie. Morgan came up the steps and saw how cute they all looked, so pulled his phone out of his pocket and snapped a picture of them snuggled together.

He needed to measure the area for the desks, so he did it as quietly as he could, but Lassie raised her head to look at him, then dropped her head back down. He thought to himself, "That was close."

Then Marsha called out, "Morgan, what are you doing here?"

He whispered, "Measuring for the desks."

She murmured, "That's nice." Laying her head back down on her pillow.

The thought crossed his mind, "That's not like her at all." He pulled out his phone and brought up the app to scan her sugar level. Sure enough, it was 29. He mixed a syringe and rolled her toward him to give her the shot.

He told her to sit up and shoved a Coke under her nose.

She rolled back, saying, "I'm too tired, Morgan. Can you come back in five minutes?"

He groused, "I guess you might feel better if I sent Jim over."

With that, she sat up and looked at Morgan, "You don't have to get nasty about it!" She chugged the Coke but choked, started coughing, then sprayed it everywhere and finished by throwing up.

Morgan was laughing so hard his sides hurt, but Gage roused and began crying, then Lassie stood and licked Marsha's face.

She stood, picked up Gage and told Lassie to get down while she changed the sheets and blanket. Morgan was still laughing when he took Gage. He told her to go lay on the medical bed and he would take care of the bedding as soon as he took Gage up to the nannies.

He returned in a flash and pulled clean sheets and a blanket from the linen closet. He got it all made and looked at Marsha who was sound asleep. He instructed the bed to raise the temperature another 20 degrees and went to get a blanket for her. She responded to the warmth and snuggled down into the pillow and bed.

He was glad that now he could monitor the bed. He sent the dirty linens down the chute and ran to the lab to complete a small piece of the puzzle.

Thar still refused to release Jim from night duty. He instructed him to go home and sleep for eight hours starting at 7:30 AM.

He had to be back at the lab at 4:00 so he and Morgan could work together till 6:00.

Jim then went home to have dinner with his family and Morgan did likewise. Jim needed to be back to Morgan's by 9:00 PM. Both Morgan and Marsha were to be on the beds at night, unless Morgan stayed up for a while with Marsha between them for the security she needed but she was finding she did not need that as much as before.

Her fears appeared to be under better control. During the day, she and Bev could lie on the bed and work on their portion of the project, but this was totally optional if they were having a bad day. Jim held up well to the pressure of finding the answers they needed, and Morgan was doing better with Jim handling the weight of this project. The teamwork had developed a rhythm that worked for the four of them.

12

Attempted Murder

The next morning, Marsha heard a commotion in front of her home and yelling from multiple voices. She went to the window and saw people picketing her home. She could not see far enough to make out what it was all about.

She slid on her robe and was just about to open the door when a woman wiggled out of the laundry chute and looked at her. Marsha could not reach the emergency button. Neither said a word. Marsha backed up to the bed and sat on it. She knew her racing pulse meant someone would come running quickly.

Marsha swallowed hard and managed to get out, "What do you want?"

The woman said, "To cut those things out of your belly! How could you have more children? I am going to give you an abortion right now."

Marsha backed up to the head of the bed and hit the diagnostic screen. Jim and Morgan saw the alert at the same instant. Both, along with Thar, ran and Thar yelled for guards to surround and secure the house.

Jim was first through the door, finding the woman holding a knife with which she had already cut into Marsha's abdomen. Don tackled her and slammed her into the ground. He zip tied her and yelled, "Medical emergency in Dr. King's master bedroom!"

Jim stepped over Don as the woman bit down on his ankle. Jim's face blackened with rage and, drawing back his foot, he kicked her square in the teeth. Satisfyingly, she began to bleed profusely and screamed in pain, while spitting out a bloody tooth.

Marsha did not respond to his frantic cries. He looked into the screen and discovered none of the babies had been damaged. The rest of the medical team along with Morgan burst into the room as Don dragged the assailant out of their way.

Two doctors tended to her, one held her while the other mopped up the blood. The litter was rolled into the room and they threw the prisoner on the litter, zip-tying her down and securing her firmly as she continued to scream, spewing words of hate. The second team arrived with a different kind of litter that had attachments for life support. Jim pulled out a breathing tube and central line kit while another doctor pulled the bed out to give greater accessibility for Morgan and Thar, as they frantically moved through the diagnostic screens.

Morgan said, "The babies are safe. She missed the sacs and the babies, but Marsha has a nick in two places along her bowel."

Thar said, "Her right lung is punctured," just as Jim yelled, "Access!"

Dr. Cay hooked up the fluids as Jim intubated Marsha. Dr. Cay hooked up the portable ventilator and Don radioed instructions to security to put up the barriers and line the way down and over to the lab.

"All the children need to be in school, including the preschoolers." They used the tunnel this time. It was a lot easier.

The crowd continued their attempt to breach the fence and security activated the electric current. Four immediately fell backwards off the fence, just as the local police arrived on the scene. One police vehicle was let through the boundary to take the prisoner.

Cleg and his tribe came running, scaring off the protestors who ran with two turning back to fire their weapons. Cleg took a fatal bullet to his head. Medical arrived and grabbed him, taking him into the lab in an attempt to save his life. The entire tribe surrounded and isolated the man who shot Cleg and security arrested him, but not before one of the tribe crushed the hand that held the gun, looking deep into his eyes with frank rage. The park police arrested him and threw him in the back of a second patrol car.

The scene was one of utter mass confusion. No one recognized that another woman who had come in with the last laundry delivery had not left yet. She wiggled her way up the chute. She carried a regular citizen's ID, which looked similar if you just glanced at the badge. She was not only armed with a knife, but she carried a pistol as well. The national park police took her into custody, arresting her on federal charges since it was within the national park.

***

Thar and Jim finished surgery on Marsha. Now, they had to wait to see if infection would set in. They gave her prophylactic antibiotics and set the bed to repair as well.

Dr. Cay sat with Morgan and tried to divert his attention until Gage was brought in after a fall from using a chair to reach the counter, and from there, into the cupboard after cookies.

Morgan held Gage so that Dr. Cay could look him over. He wasn't injured, just shaken up. Dr Cay offered him a cookie and he grabbed the entire bag from her. "Oh, God, not another Tig. One of those in any family is enough!"

Morgan laughed, "That's My Boy?" Dr. Cay shook her head, "Let's keep him here on the bed, if we can, just to watch him overnight."

Morgan laughed, "Yeah, good luck with that."

Dr. Cay told two of the doctors to stay with him at all times since he was a natural born escape artist like his brother, Tig.

Morgan sat beside Marsha on the bed and smoothed her hair back with one hand, holding one of her hands with the other. They had already pulled the tube and were waiting for her to awaken. She was actually doing very well. Morgan's eyes widened as he felt her squeeze his hand. He leaned down to kiss her and she opened her eyes.

Jim came in and approached the bed. "How are you doing, my second favorite princess? Of course, you know Bev has to be my number one!"

Morgan, calmly and softly asked her for the Truth saying, "I need to hear everything you are feeling, and I do mean everything, baby."

She was able to maintain good eye contact with Morgan, his eyes gentle, soft, and caring.

"Such tenderness! But I hurt so darned bad, and I don't want to hurt the babies."

"You let us worry about the babies."

"I feel a lot of pressure."

Jim asked her to show him where she felt the pressure.

"Under my rib," Marsha responded.

Jim pulled up the diagnostic screen and asked, "Anything else? Truth, baby."

"I can't remember why I am here Morgan."

Jim sat on the bed and explained, "What you're feeling is from when we worked on your bowel. We used gas to make sure there were no other holes, so it is just air and that will go away in time."

Morgan lowered his nose down to hers and said, "You're safe and we are here with you."

"But I can't remember, Morgan!"

"Who cares, all I know is that you are going to be fine."

"But the babies," cried Marsha.

Jim took her chin and turned her to face him. She looked at him as tears filled her eyes.

"They are all safe and snug as bugs in a rug."

She felt relief flood her emotions. Dr. Cay handed him the med gun and he told Marsha she needed a lot more rest to let her body heal, so he needed to give her something to sleep.

She looked from one to the other, saying, "I am begging you! Don't either of you leave me. PROMISE!"

Morgan told her, "I am right here with you," as Jim asked if they could use the bathroom.

Morgan laughed, "Hey, stop stealing my lines!"

They smiled and she relaxed, looked at Jim and said, "Okay, ready." He gave her the injection and she drifted into sleep.

After she had been pronounced fit enough to return home, Marsha was glad to be back in the familiar surroundings of her home. She carefully climbed the stairs and stood at the bedroom door with her mouth open, taking in what she saw in her room.

"Bright yellow sheets, you're kidding!"

"I wanted it to be sunny and bright for you."

She laughed and kissed Morgan. She told him it was very thoughtful of him. Jim came in and announced, "I am assigned to you as your doctor."

"Yeah, I am sure you are enjoying that assignment!" She shot back.

"Emma and Bat are moving over to our house to help the nannies with the kids and get that house running efficiently. Charlie and Wyatt are walking through security protocols with Olzing."

"Morgan, you forgot you had to talk to Emmi."

He glanced over at Marsha and told her to get in bed as he had something Liam asked him to do with Emmi that seemed urgent.

Morgan knocked on Bat's door and Bat told him to come in. Is Emmi here? Bat nodded. "I would like to have a quick word with her in the kitchen. You can listen from afar but no yelling at her after I leave."

Bat laughed and said, "Who me? You must be referring to the big boss, Emma."

Bat called for Emmi. She came out with the dog in the messenger bag strapped across her body. Morgan said, "Hi, princess, can we talk in the kitchen just for a second?"

They walked into the kitchen where he knelt beside her. "So, how is Toodles?" She unzipped the bag and revealed the little dog who was panting hard.

Morgan took her in his hands. "Princess, Toodles can't breathe in that bag. You see how she is panting? She needs water and air. If she doesn't get fresh air and fresh water, she will be very sick."

The little girl began to cry. "She needs to stay at home with your Mommy and Daddy while you're at school or you could leave her in the barn with Droopy and Giles."

He picked her chin up and she looked at him skeptically. "You love Toodles, I can tell, so it is hard to leave her, I know, but it is important that she be able to drink water and breathe."

"Okay," Emmi said, frowning a bit. "Yes, I will leave her with Giles and Droopy in the barn if Toodles has her own bed."

"I will make sure of that. All right, princess, Liam will be happy Droopy and Giles have a pretty pink princess to keep them company."

Emmi smiled through her tears and skipped back to her room. Bat and Emma stood and said they had no idea she had been smuggling the dog to school. They had thought the dog was in the barn with the others.

They both thanked him for looking after Emmi and the pup. Then Emma asked if she could come over the next day to help Marsha shower and wash her hair.

"Oh, that would be very helpful; yes, thank you."

She told him she would be over as soon as the kids left for the school rooms. He gave her a kiss and hug.

Morgan walked the kids to school and all the dogs except Lassie were in a big stall with fresh sawdust and beds. Droopy was sleeping with Toodles, Lazy Bones was curled up with Giles and both were snoring loudly. He found Liam and told him to get to school, and that he would finish watering and distributing food. Morgan filled the bowls and Giles swooped in after him, eating everyone's food.

Morgan watched the dogs, and muttered, "This doesn't work." Then the rat terrier, whom Morgan secretly called Trouble, wandered in and laid beside Giles. Morgan added another bowl of water, looked around and wondered where Omar was. He went outside to find him lying outside the school room door.

Morgan found him a bed to lie on outside of the school room, then let the ponies out in the field along with the two goats. He fed the cats, then decided to empty the litter box. He thought the cat could probably come inside. He picked her up and carried her inside where a litter box was set up inside of Dorothy-Alice's room. He put the cat in her room and shut the door to keep her from roaming the house.

Next, he washed his hands and went into the kitchen to make a plate of eggs for himself and Marsha, with orange juice, chai tea and vanilla lattes.

Morgan opened the door to the bedroom. In a barely audible whisper, he said "Hey, sleepy head, let's eat before everyone gets here." She sat up.

"How are you feeling?"

She told him, "So-so."

He glanced over at her and put the tray in front of her, then sat on the bed next to her and picked up a fork.

She asked how come she couldn't remember, but he told her to stop focusing on it. He explained it wasn't important, and that keeping the babies inside as long as possible was the focus.

"Now, EAT!"

"Morgan, I have morning sickness this morning." Jim heard that as he rounded the corner. He grabbed the med gun on his way past it and gave her meds.

"Sip on that tea, young lady," he said. He stood beside her, so she reached up, grabbed his shirt, pulled him toward her until they were in direct eye contact.

She said, tersely, "You better not be keeping anything from me! If I find out you are, I will kick your ass!" With that, she let go of him.

"Fine, now drink your damn tea and hop up on that bed when you're done so I can look you over."

She sipped her tea and Morgan drank his latte.

Suddenly, Marsha lashed out, "I know you're keeping stuff from me! What is it I can't remember? It's total bullshit you won't tell me!" She crossed her arms and sat there, alternating glaring direct eye contact from one to the other.

Morgan moved the tray and sat. Jim was on the other side of her, with the med gun behind his back.

She went on, "I am tired of being this fragile thing that everyone's afraid will break! I am a fighter and will fight with everything in me. I want to know! Right damned now! You will tell me this second!" Morgan and Jim both moved in tighter to her. She sat with her arms folded across her chest; jaw clenched.

She glared at Jim, "I am waiting!"

"Marsha…" She reached over and took Morgan's hand. "So tell me already!"

"Marsha, there were picketers out front that are pro-abortion and they were picketing you because you are pregnant with multiple babies. Somehow Dorothy-Alice posted it. She didn't know, so don't be mad with her. She is an innocent child."

Marsha went rigid. She could almost feel her blood pressure and heart rate rising.

"Someone slipped through the laundry delivery area and wiggled up the laundry chute. She took a knife and tried to cut our babies out of you."

Marsha's mouth fell open as she stared, first at one, then to the other. She slowly moved her head from side to side, trying to process the information, then blinked, and stood up on the bed and, stepping over Jim, to the medical bed, got on it and laid down.

Morgan and Jim arose as one and went to her. Still she said nothing. The monitor showed her pulse was racing as was her breathing. Morgan went to her head and softly whispered her name. Still she did not answer.

Jim felt alarm rising in his own body. He gave her medication to bring down both her pulse rate and blood pressure, then motioned to Morgan to get up in the bed and pull her to him. He hoped letting her feel his breathing and holding her hand to his chest would help her calm, matching her own rates to Morgan's.

They'd been working with her for 20 minutes when Emma came in. She went right to the bathroom, wet a cool rag, and put it on her forehead. Emma asked no questions, but spoke to her tenderly, "Marsha, honey, you are safe here with all your family. I want you to look at me."

Marsha turned glassy, glazed-over eyes in her direction. "Feel Morgan breathing and sync your breathing with his. You have to slow your breathing down."

She took the hand Jim had been holding and raised to his mouth. "Feel his air going in and out. Slow your breathing so it matches what you are feeling."

Jim held her hand by his mouth, slowly she matched Jim's rhythm. Suddenly, she yanked her hand away from Jim and turned to bury her head in Morgan's shoulder, sobbing. Jim gave her a little more medication, and a dose to Morgan to calm him.

Eventually, she relaxed back against his arm on her side, nuzzling against his chest. Finally, she lay sleeping on Morgan's chest. They let the meds take full effect, then he gently slid out from behind her. Emma asked if it would help if she got in bed with her and held her.

Jim said, "Yes, that might help." Marsha adjusted and snuggled into Emma. Her blood pressure had slowed to nearly normal, and her breathing was perfect.

Emma hummed to her and rubbed her back. Morgan and Jim exchanged relieved glances, then sat at their individual desks to work.

Four hours passed and Marsha began to stir. Emma continued to hum as she stroked her hair. Jim and Morgan both approached the bed as she opened her eyes.

She sat up, smiling at Emma. Next, she looked at Jim and thanked him for telling her. She could remember the incident in all its horror now.

She turned to Morgan and asked if they had fixed the security hole. With a relieved smile, he nodded that yes, they had.

"Are we safe? Will my babies be safe?"

He smiled and answered a firm, "Yes."

Emma said, "Why don't we take you and get you showered now that the line is gone. But first, let's get the clothes you want to wear today." Emma helped her lay it all out and stayed with her while she showered, then helped her towel off.

Emma glanced at her belly and said, "With that tummy, I don't think there's any way you're going to fit into those jeans."

Marsha put on her cami and underwear and walked into the room. Morgan sighed, "Marsha, you promised!"

Emma shot back, "Hold on there. This girl needs some clothing. Northing in her closet fits her now!"

They both looked as she raised the hem of her camisole; their faces reflected their shock as they first looked at her stomach, then glanced at each other. Calmly, Morgan got up and took a pair of his sweats out of a drawer. "This should hold you until you order some clothes. Lovetts delivers, so call in your order and have it brought over today, baby."

She grumbled, "I am FAT!"

"Come on, YOU are not fat! Our four precious babies have to have room to grow!"

Jim suggested she get on the table so he could see the babies on the scope. She slipped on Morgan's sweatpants only and kept the cami on.

"There must be just enough of the Blue alien DNA left over to accelerate this pregnancy," she mused.

Jim and Morgan both shot a glance at each other and then back at the screen.

Marsha grumbled, "I am not stupid! Why do you think I can't see your faces? Are you going to tell me the truth or do I have to ask Thar?

"My guess is you and Bev are in the same boat with the leftover Blue alien DNA and it's accelerating both your pregnancies."

With a chagrined look, he replied, "Okay, right now you are at seven months."

"Emma, would you please go and ask Bev to come over?"

When Bev arrived, they motioned her up onto the bed. The screen revealed she had perhaps one week left until delivery. Her emotions overflowed and she cried.

Jim held her and told her, "They are both fine! They look perfectly normal."

Bev sucked in a deep breath and blew it out in a giant sigh of relief. She went to Marsha and they hugged each other, then Bev turned to Jim and asked if the Nordics had come up with another nurse for them, plus two more for Marsha.

"Yes, I think they just completed vetting them. Their last assignment was for the President of the Lazka planet outpost."

Jim told Bev from now on she couldn't stay by herself, then asked if she would join them in the Moticce household until her delivery.

"… but the kids, Jim!"

"It is only one week, Bev."

"Our house will be a wreck without me picking up."

"About that…" Jim began, "Isn't that why they have a chore chart?"

Bev looked down and grudgingly said, "Okay, you're right. We should go pack my bag right now. We can let the nannies and nurse know where we can be found."

"But we need to lay the law down with the kids on keeping up with their chores." In unison, both said, "We shall return," then giggled at each other.

Morgan called Morgan-Barkley in and asked him to go to stay with Phillip at Bat's house for the duration. That way, Jim could sleep in his bed, and they could put the extra med bed in the room for Bev. Emma took Morgan-Barkley and his backpack back to their house.

Morgan then pressed Don about what he meant by "If something was wrong with him." Jim hesitated and looked at Don; then both ran for the house and up the stairs.

He assisted Morgan to the medical bed, where he saw what looked like a TIA (stroke). He paged Thar who came immediately. They both looked at the screens, then nodded agreement at the obvious diagnosis. Thar dialed in the indicated combination of meds, including a blood thinner.

"He must stay in bed for 24 hours. No discussion. Then, assuming no residuals, after 24 hours he can get up."

Morgan looked at Don with relief plain on his face and thanked him. Jim told him it never dawned on him Morgan would have a problem.

Don said, "Happy to contribute. Now, he is okay so why don't you get in bed and if he wakes up, I will come get you."

Looking relieved, Jim's face reflected his exhaustion. He crawled up on the bed and almost immediately fell into a deep slumber.

At 7:00 AM, Jim awakened to find Morgan still asleep. As he arose and began going through the diagnostics, Don walked in bringing coffee for them both.

Morgan slowly opened his eyes. Jim looked down and said, "Why the hell didn't you say something was wrong with YOU!??"

"Don and I went to the lab and..."

"… Was it a TIA?"

Jim nodded and they gave him more meds.

"You are to stay in that bed for a full 24 hours. Do you have any weakness or difficulty swallowing?" He demanded, then began the neuro exam by telling him to squeeze his hands. With relief, he noted they were strong and equal. He easily followed his finger, so that checked out. He scraped the bottoms of his feet, and both sides reacted equally. Next, he held out some water and told him to take a sip. He choked slightly and had to swallow a second time to get it down.

Jim took the glass from him and said, "Nothing by mouth until that clears."

He told him to lie back down, adjusted the dosages, and added just enough meds so he would sleep again.

Next Jim went to check on Bev; she had just sat up and her face looked like she wasn't entirely comfortable. He asked how she was and she told him, "My back hurts!" He had her lie back and ran through the diagnostics. After a brief time, he stopped and putting his hands on both shoulders, said, "My dear lady, you are in labor! Let me see how far you are dilated."

He gloved up and had her put her feet in the stirrups. He looked and said with astonishment, "You're at an 8, Bev, why didn't tell me sooner?"

She shrugged her shoulders, then a wave of pain crossed her face and she screamed. He could feel the baby was rapidly descending. He ran back, smashing his fist down on the emergency button, then returned to Bev who now was screaming at the top of her lungs. He gave her meds for the pain, and by that time the baby crowned and slid right out on the table.

By now, Bev was crying hard. Jim wrapped her in his arms as he waited for the afterbirth. As that came out, he saw the other one crown immediately. To his relief, the medical team ran into the room.

As Jim handed them the first baby, Bev screamed, pushed hard, and the second baby slid out. He wrapped her and the afterbirth delivered, so he handed the baby off to them to deal with.

The team grabbed the bed off the ground, and, arrayed around it like an honor guard, walked it down the steps and across the compound.

Jim followed, telling Don over his shoulder to hit the emergency button if Morgan woke up and tried to get up.

Don's face reflected his surprise. "Yes, sir, I will."

In the medical area, the team had already lightly sedated Bev and gave her something for the discomfort, so she was a little groggy.

Jim announced, "We have two robust, healthy little girls. What names have you decided on?"

She replied, "Hazel and Mae."

"Okay, sounds good." She took Jim's hand and asked what he thought the boys would think about having sisters.

He laughed, "You know they will adore them!" He told her to close her eyes, and no sooner had she closed them, than she drifted off.

Thar congratulated him and told him, "Great job, Dad!"

He informed him their names were Hazel and Mae, beaming a huge smile. Then he told Thar he was going back to bed; all the excitement had worn him out. Jim returned to Morgan's household and crawled into bed. Don shut the door so the kids would not bother either Morgan or Jim. Finally, he awakened at 2:00 that afternoon.

Morgan was sitting up in bed, working on a tablet. Jim sat up and inquired what his patient was doing.

Morgan answered, "Looking for a few answers."

Jim got up and told him to see if his swallowing was better. He first took a dry swallow, then picked up some water, took a sip and smiled as it went down fine. Morgan then drank several swallows in rapid succession.

Jim smiled broadly and congratulated him that he seemed to have returned to normal, but to start with soft food.

Morgan looked at him and said, "I'm craving a hot vanilla latte and some Maple-brown sugar oatmeal." Jim laughed and gave his order to Don along with some coffee for him. Forty minutes later Don knocked on the door and brought breakfast in. Jim handed Morgan his food, then sat down and drank his coffee.

Morgan sipped on the latte. Jim watched his face, finally asking, "Okay, what's wrong?"

"Nausea." Jim got up and gave him a quick injection.

"Any weakness?" he asked.

Morgan flexed and relaxed various muscle groups before saying, "Nope, none, and no symptoms other than nausea."

Jim sat back down drinking his coffee but glanced surreptitiously over at Morgan occasionally. He could see Morgan felt a bit off, so put down his cup and walked over to Morgan. "Damnit, what is wrong? Don't tell me nothing. Right now, tell me!"

Morgan glanced at him, then looked back down at his tablet. "If my math is right, we have four weeks tops to save this planet! I am ashamed of myself for letting this slide onto the back shelf, no matter what was going on here."

"This week and into the next we had better have every answer, then get to the locations. Give me the tablet so I can recheck the formula and my math."

"Lay down this minute!" Jim shot back, "We need you at full throttle tomorrow!"

Morgan shook his head, "Give me something right now, start an IV and give me fluids." Jim put down his tablet and got out a kit. His aim was dead on as he slid the needle into his vein and quickly ran a bag of fluids, then put Morgan back into sleep.

Morgan was right. He had to be on top of his game tomorrow; they both did! He laid back down and slept himself.

The next morning he awakened at 6:00 AM and felt so much better after a full night's sleep. He asked Don to walk across the compound with him to the lab. He went directly to Bev who was sitting up breastfeeding Mae. Jim lovingly ran his hand over her little head. He kissed Bev and asked how she felt.

She admitted, "My breasts are tender, and this will take some time to get used to again."

He asked her to just bottle feed.

"Are you sure?" she asked.

He answered, "Yes, this is crazy; you do not have time, nor I think enough milk for two hungry babies." He asked the nurse to take the baby and make sure Dr. Cay knew to switch them to bottle feeds. He sat back down beside Bev. "What do you think, Daddy?" she asked.

"They are beautiful like their Mommy." He kissed her. "Now, how are you feeling?"

"I am bleeding pretty heavily."

"Have you told Thar?"

She looked down. "You haven't told him?"

She shook her head no. "Lie down and let me look."

He pulled on a pair of gloves and put the bed in pelvic exam mode. The bleeding was heavy; this was not normal. He called one of the doctors over and asked her to run the diagnostics. There it was, just a small bleed but it was not clotting.

"Honey, you need a small repair and I'd rather do it now."

"Am I going to feel this?" asked Bev.

He assured her, "Of course not. Doctor, pull the bed over to the surgical unit and sedate the patient."

He made the incision and immediately saw a baby boy. Jim pulled him out and the nurse ran him directly to Dr. Cay. He finished Bev's repair and returned to the pediatric unit.

Dr. Cay approached and told him the little boy was dead before he was delivered. "He had no lungs."

Jim asked her to make sure she did footprints and handprints, and with a heavy heart asked if she could wrap him and try to get a sweet picture of him to give to Bev. "Name him Cody, please."

13

The Loss

J im was sleeping on the bed when Morgan awakened. He got up, jumped in the shower, then exited the master bathroom and down to the kitchen where he made a hot vanilla latte for himself and a coffee for Jim.

When he came back upstairs. Jim was at the door, demanding "What are you doing? Who said you could be up?"

"A coffee for you, good doctor…" handing him his cup, "… and a latte for me. That's being a good patient, if I don't say so myself."

"Get back on that bed," Jim pointed.

Morgan shot him a look, saying, "That may work with Marsha or Bev, but not me, buddy."

"We are going to go see our wives this morning along with our kids."

They sat on their beds and drank their beverages.

"So, really, how are you doing this morning, Morgan?"

"I feel so much better, like I could tackle the world! I'm rested and feel rearing to go."

Jim said, "Meds, please."

Morgan nodded as he drank his latte.

Not entirely satisfied with that response, Jim reached over and picked up the med gun. He gave him three different meds, then picked up his own coffee and finished it.

Morgan asked if he was medically okay to walk across the compound, but Jim replied, "Not just yet. Let me take a shower and we can go together.

"Maybe you can work on the access locations while I shower," he suggested. Jim went down the hall and was back with wet hair in 20 minutes.

Morgan put his tablet down and stood. "You ready? Maybe do the planning for Bev first? What are your thoughts?"

Jim said, "Well, let me catch you up. Instead of two kids last night we had three."

"Ha-ha!" Morgan said.

"No, Morgan, Bev actually had three, but one was stillborn. I named him Cody. They took footprints and handprints, and I asked them to do a dressed image of him for both of us. He was born with no lungs."

Morgan's face fell as he shook his head, sighing deeply. "I am so very sorry for you two."

"I want to keep her focused on the two who lived. They're going to be in the medical bay for a while. One was 1.5 pounds, and the other 2.7 pounds. These two little girls we named Hazel and Mae."

Morgan slapped him on the back and gave him a congratulatory hug. "We really are two very lucky men," said Morgan. "Let's get over and see your two newbies."

Don walked with them across the compound and into the lab. Morgan and Jim entered to see Thar and Dr. Cay with Marsha and two other doctors with Bev who was already feeding one of the twins. Thar turned to Morgan and Jim, and said, "Good morning."

Morgan wiggled past Thar and sat next to Bev. He kissed the top of her head and said, "You never cease to amaze me!" He gave her two more kisses, "One kiss for each new baby. Are you happy?" Morgan asked.

She told him yes and that their names are Hazel and Mae.

"How are you feeling?" asked Jim.

She answered, "Of course it hurts, but the joy overrides the pain."

Thar handed the image to Morgan and Jim went around to the other side of the bed and sat down. Jim put his arm around Bev and told her how brave he felt she had been last night, and that he was happy for them.

Marsha pulled the curtain back and revealed she and Emma were standing in the bed. Morgan and Jim ran around the bed to her and Emma. Jim asked how long they had been here.

Thar said, "Since right after you left, Jim. Emma is fine; just some first-time pregnancy jitters."

Morgan leaned in and kissed her as did Jim.

Morgan turned to Marsha and asked, "All by yourself, baby?"

Thar smiled as they both glanced up at him. "Well, I wanted to see the new babies, and Emma and Bat had just arrived so, well, here I am. You guys aren't mad, are you?" They both hugged her. Thar said, "Emma can go back to her house as soon as Bat arrives."

Morgan went back over and pulled the picture out of his pocket. Marsha, standing behind him, saw the image. She tensed and Thar moved behind her, ready in case she needed support, but letting her do as much as she could on her own.

Morgan looked at the image. It was like Cody was just sleeping. Jim took the image, but he could clearly see Morgan was not able to tell her.

He looked directly into her eyes and said, "I delivered a total of three, Bev. This is little Cody who did not even weigh a pound." Bev took the picture and looked at Jim, who gave her the direct, sympathetic eye contact needed.

"He was stillborn, with no lungs."

Bev took a deep breath, let it out slowly and said, "Jim, we will have a funeral for everyone to say goodbye. We can make arrangements for him to be buried with my mom in with her casket. We will send Cody off to be with your parents and mine. Will you do that, please?"

"Yes, of course," he replied.

"I want to hold him for a minute, and no, I will not take no for an answer. Go get him."

Thar left and Dr. Cay came back with him. She placed the very small bundle in Bev's arms.

Bev spoke to the little one with great tenderness. She got out of bed and sat down next to Jim, putting her arm on Jim's. "Cody, Mommy and Daddy love you. You keep grandma and grandpa company. I know your grandparents are fighting about who is getting to hold you and pour out their love on you. We have a hole in our hearts right now, but I know you are getting plenty of love. We will be lonely and grieve your passing, but I have such comfort knowing you are with your grandparents."

Then Jim took him in his arms. "Hey, little guy. I know you can feel our love and grief, but please know you are now and always will be part of our family. I know your brothers and sisters will draw you some pictures and write you letters to take with you on your journey to be with your grandparents. They already love you, too."

Jim handed him to Morgan whose tears spoke his emotions, "You have your Mommy's eyes and your Daddy's fat cheeks." Everyone smiled. He stared down at Cody and said, "I hope you can feel the love in this room for you."

He handed him to Marsha and put his hand on her shoulder.

"Thank you, little Cody for letting us all experience the love that supersedes time and space. This love we will always know is you. You are precious to all of us here now, and to the members of our family already in heaven. We know they welcome you with outstretched arms as we give you into their love and care."

She turned and walked to Emma, handing the tiny bundle to her. She kissed him and said, "Until we meet again at Jesus' feet. Godspeed, my little bundle of pure love and joy."

She returned him to Marsha, who began to sway. Morgan ran to her, taking Cody as Thar helped her sit down. Morgan handed Cody back to Bev, planting a kiss on the top of his head. She, in turn, returned him to Dr. Cay. They all hugged together, and their tears ran in mutual grief.

With the funeral behind them, everyone put their energy into revealing and understanding the code that would save the planet.

Morgan and Marsha visited the new babies after the funeral, then Aggie arrived, nursing both Idell and Iris.

She told them about the Hopi Hall of Archives which was located where the oracle was. She told them they could talk to the voice through a secret compartment, a compartment that reached the unseen and where thoughts could be read.

She told them she knew where the speaking tubes were located. It had been a temple and before that had a beam of light that once pointed to Orion's belt during perihelion.

They asked where that was, and she told him it was located on a ranch in Utah called Skinwalker Ranch but warned that strange things were known to happen there, and that many people used a special kind of radar to see a city under the ranch.

She went on, "It is actually an underground base for the Pleiadean race. They are known as the Benders of the Light."

Morgan told Jim, "We need to take a trip there tomorrow. I will ask Don to make the arrangements."

Aggie asked to go along, too, saying they needed to bring something of importance as an offering—something of love and importance. "This shows your willingness to share your heart and love. It also assures we are not betrayers of the Oracle."

"The Oracle requires you to inhale its essence in open air. It is the fragrance of the sweet desert rose."

Aggie then looked to Marsha and told her, "You MUST go, too. The Oracle will show you how Caci is doing on the other side. Same for Morgan. Take something with you that is special to each of you."

Marsha opened the drawer of her bedside table and pulled out Caci's teddy bear. She held him to her nose and inhaled. "I still smell her."

Morgan went to her, put the bear down, and held her tight. "Are you sure you are up to this?"

She smiled sadly and replied, "Do you think a herd of wild buffalo could keep me from this Oracle?"

Jim said, "While we are out, I want to see the old star base at Mt. Baker."

Marsha said, "Hold up there; first we need to go to the Serpent Mound in Ohio. It also points to Orion. Then we should visit Giza, Easter Island and Teotihuacan. We'd better also plan to visit Malta and the church in Scotland, Rosslyn Chapel grounds, and Oak Island."

In preparation for their trip, they inspected some plates from the White House china collections. They looked at Washington's, Madison's, and Monroe's. All three had one thing in common: a starburst in the center of the White House china plate, yet Washington's plate had one important variation: The gold starburst in the plate obviously depicted a supernova.

Neither Morgan nor Jim understood the 15 points and 15 stars. The ouroboros—a snake eating its own tail—is often interpreted as a symbol for the eternal cyclic renewal, or the cycle of life, death, and rebirth referred to as the mystery of cyclical time flowing back into itself. Constantly evolving and regenerating, it is known to be the oldest allegorical symbol, representing the concept of eternity and endless return: time's beginning and time's end.

"It is also said to be the cosmic dichotomy of light and darkness. Some stories foretold that the prized philosopher's stone of the alchemists would bring 'bling' to the world. Merlin overcame that struggle and became immortal. It is to break the cycle and, I believe, we need to consider how we view the moments that pass, then string this together."

"We have a lot of work to do on just this piece to break down the code. Now a circle with another, like in the middle of the starburst. A circle has no beginning and no end—so eternity. Circles hold and contain energy," explained Morgan. "The motions of time moving us along."

"So—timelines?" asked Bev.

"Yes, I believe that is correct," Marsha said. "It moves us forward and keeps us in an upward motion in the shape of a circle, also called an upward spiral," Marsha continued. "Everything in the universe moves in circles, and the planets are spheres—again a circle.

"It represents completion of cycles, transition, potential, and movement that never ends. I really think it protects against chaos, unpredictability, and invites an element of trusting in the universe."

Bev added, "It is like it's trying to inspire us to keep going."

Jim stood and said, "That's a lot of great ideas and thoughts."

Morgan added, "A circle also means maybe we are thinking linearly. I want us each to make sure that it is not a lack of direction keeping us in that circle."

Marsha added, "Right. There are 12 zodiac signs that all form a circle around our solar system, 12 houses partitioned in sections to complete a circle. Never-ending cycles of movement through each sign, without beginning or end."

"Hmm, similar to how heaven is described in the Bible," said Bev.

Marsha told them the circle is known for healing and invites strength into your life. "It is a life force. Energy moving in a circle," said Marsha.

"So, we have Life Force, Evolution, Completion, Ending and Beginning, Eternity, Infinity, Wholeness, Perfection, Focused, Centered, Higher Perspective, Heaven, and Cosmos?" Jim mused, then asked if he had missed anything. They all agreed that summed up the circle and its symbolism.

Jim continued, "Let's have lunch and tackle ideas for the code."

They trailed down to the kitchen for lunch. There was grilled cheese and fresh fruit with black water. Marsha picked at her food, really just moving it around her plate and taking small sips of water. Jim glanced at Morgan then to Marsha; catching the signal, Morgan looked over at Marsha. Morgan got up and took the cut watermelon from the refrigerator and put it in front of Marsha. She smiled and looked back down at her plate, but then got up and went up the stairs to their room. Morgan glanced at Jim, who put his fork down and followed her upstairs.

She was already on the medical bed. She laid there quietly as Jim paged through the screens. He stopped and looked down at her and said, "Really? You two couldn't keep your hands off each other? This is bad for you, but I suppose you knew that and knew I would follow you up here to see what the issue was. She wouldn't look at him and stood. He told her to get back on the bed but to remove her underwear first. He pulled the gloves on and directed the bed to go into a pelvic exam position. "I only feel one baby like the bed says."

He told her to get dressed. "You were not to have sex for six weeks, not six days. So, I'd bet it is safe to say you and Morgan have not taken your meds."

She told him, "Morgan did, but I thought I was safe." He gave her nausea meds and directed her to "Get downstairs to EAT and DRINK right this second!" She hugged him and thanked him.

"You are one batshit crazy chick, but one I do love dearly," Jim laughed. They both came down the steps. Bev asked if everything was okay. Marsha picked up her fork.

Jim said, "Only if you consider BATSHIT CRAZY being okay, then she is."

Bev said, "Jim, that is horrible!"

He shot back, "CRAZY is a correct diagnosis; she is pregnant." Morgan dropped his fork and began coughing. He took a drink of water, then got up and went to the sink and threw up. He washed his face and turned on the garbage disposal and ran water to wash it down.

He turned and Jim thought he was going to faint on the floor. He jumped up and helped him to sit down. Marsha threw her fork across the table and went upstairs crying. They all trailed her up the stairs. Jim sat down beside her on the medical bed, handing her a bottle of water, which she promptly threw across the room. She began to cry and said, "You have to know I didn't plan this."

Morgan sat back thinking he'd let Jim fix this since he and Bev both thought he was wrong for what he said. Jim then put his arm around her waist and told her he was wrong saying what he did. He loved her like she was his sister, and sometimes siblings say stupid things to each other. "You are medically fragile. and I am over the top concerned for you."

She was still looking at the tablet. He waited on her. He sat for almost an hour rocking his legs back and forth holding her at the waist. She cried out for Morgan who went to her and called for Bev. They all hugged. She told them, "I love you guys and would be dead if it wasn't for you."

She finally turned to Jim. "I'm telling you now, I can never drink enough water to stay hydrated. It is gagging me right now."

Jim pulled her to him and pulled her head down to his shoulder. "I will never let anything happen to you, Marsha." He helped her lie back and said, "Let's fix it and then we can go back to code breaking. You have some really insightful ideas." He leaned over and kissed her forehead.

Morgan retrieved a kit from the cupboard for him. "I am going to ask them to place a port, so I do not have to keep doing this. Then we always have access, and you can shower with a port. We can give you twilight and some anxiety meds when we place it."

"We can do it first thing in the morning, so nothing to eat after midnight. I'll text and ask them to add you to the schedule," Morgan offered.

Jim slid in the central line and started fluids. "Okay, confirmation to be over at the lab"–Marsha immediately tensed and began shaking –"at 8:30. That gives you time to go early and feed a few of the babies."

As he finished, Marsha's teeth were chattering, and she was shaking quite hard. Jim helped her sit up and warmed the bed by 30 degrees. He told her to sit there and mentioned he had turned the heat up.

They all had their tablets and Marsha started but it was difficult to understand her because she was shaking so hard. Without a word, Jim and Morgan both got up and squeezed in on either side of her.

Morgan asked where Lassie was, and Don said the groomer had her. Don came around the corner with a huge dog. It had been scanned and came out clean.

"This big girl is to replace poor Rufus. She is an Irish Wolfhound, and her name is Wolfie."

Marsha smiled, "Wait until Liam sees this giant. Better order more food, Morgan! Bet she eats a 40-pound bag by herself every week! She needs a twin bed just for her."

"Just so you know Morgan, Liam asked to do an internship with the Nordic Vets after school."

Everyone laughed as Don brought her to Marsha. With just a small hop, she put her front legs up on Marsha's shoulders standing up and licked her face. Marsha gradually crumpled back under her weight until Wolfie laid on her as she gradually dropped back and hit the bed.

Marsha muttered, "Will somebody get this mutt off me?"

With a laugh, Jim managed to get her down, but in her determination to be at Marsha's side, she curled around her feet.

"Wow, I've never seen a dog this big! I hope she doesn't knock the little ones over. Bet Gage screams when he sees her," said Marsha.

Jim smiled, "You better hope Tig doesn't invent a saddle and start charging for rides!" They all laughed.

"Maybe we should wait on Liam taking on an internship." They all laughed again.

Marsha was still shaking but she gamely started over. "We know gold is the number one element, silver is number two, and there are 15 points to the starburst, 15 states. Washington was the 1st President. So number order:

One for president

One for gold

Two for silver

Fifteen for points on the starburst

Fifteen states

What are your thoughts? I feel like we could be missing things."

Jim pushed her shoulder back, so she was lying flat, and then laid beside her. Morgan got a blanket for her and gave her anxiety meds.

Morgan mused, "Shouldn't Merlin's number 12 actually be number one in order?"

Everyone nodded to that as a possibility.

"Let's measure the circumference of the plate, the snake circle and the ring of states and the small circle in the middle, Bev proposed. You math people, figure that one out."

"Let me go down in the toolbox and get a tape measure."

Don interrupted, "That is what we are here for. Someone will bring it up."

Jim could feel the shaking had lessened and turned to Marsha to ask if she was okay.

She answered, "I am hungry and could use some of that watermelon."

Don heard her and said, "On it." He then sat the bed up to 45% as Morgan was measuring.

"The other tests show a variance in intensity between the golds by 12%."

Don handed a bowl of watermelon to Jim who passed it over to Marsha and told her, "Eat what you can and don't worry about the rest."

She looked at him and suddenly began shaking so hard she could not hold the plate. Jim called for Morgan, who told them to scoot over, "Teddy bear coming through!"

He sat almost on her as he measured the plate. She turned to Jim who was working on a formula and realized she was looking at him.

He looked up and made eye contact with her. She said, "Feels like this is going to be accelerated like the others."

His eyebrow went up with a wary look and said, "Most likely—but are we talking days?" Morgan stopped and put his hand on her belly. As did Jim.

"We will check a couple times a day, so we know where we are all the time. Any change, and I mean the smallest insignificant change, we want to know."

"Could it be hours?" She asked with a tremor in her voice.

Morgan and Jim jumped off the bed and pulled screens.

"OMG, why didn't you say something, honey? You're in labor, right now!"

Jim said, "Calm, Morgan, Calm. Go sit down with Bev."

He told the bed "Pelvic exam." He checked and said "Three."

She grabbed Jim's arm as he took off the gloves. "Am I going to be burying this one?"

"Not if I can help it. Let's go."

She sat back, saying "NO. You can have them come get me after I deliver the baby, but I am delivering right here with you guys helping."

"You should be in a hospital setting," Jim said.

"NO! My way or no way."

Morgan came over, "Baby, it is safer in the lab."

She crossed her arms across her chest and said, stubbornly, "NO, I am not saying it again. I mean what I say, and I say what I mean!" She began to shake and was definitely feeling the labor pains.

"Morgan, please come hold me!" Morgan sat up on the bed with her. She was not progressing very fast. She was still at 3 after four hours. She had her head on Morgan's shoulder, but suddenly screamed with the next contraction.

Morgan said, "Let him check you."

He laid her back and Morgan sat back with her, still holding her. She screamed again.

Jim said, "Oh, there's a big jump! You are at a 7."

She breathed in and blew it out. Bev stood by her with a cool rag on her head.

"She is three minutes apart. Blood pressure and pulse both up," Jim cried out. He gave her meds for that, then asked again about pain meds.

She told him no, she wanted to feel this birth, every single labor pain. Her next contraction was only one minute from the previous and she began to bear down.

Jim told her, "Not yet." I see the head, but the cord is around the neck.

She screamed, "Not this one, too. NO!"

"I got it free! Marsha, now push with all you got." She pushed and out popped a girl. She laid back and Jim laid the baby on Marsha's chest. Morgan jumped down and got a blanket for her. He turned her over and clamped and cut the cord, then wrapped her tight, covering her head to keep the heat in.

The baby had bright red hair and a blue curl. Marsha looked at Morgan and said "NO! Not a blue and a female. They will try to take her from us, Morgan." The pitch of her voice rose as she became hysterical.

Jim put his hand on her as he waited for the afterbirth. "I need to medicate you and YOU WILL BE IN THE LAB WHEN YOU WAKE." He gave her a dose just large enough to knock her out.

She awoke to Jim and Morgan lying in bed on either side of her, both on their tablets. Jim felt her move and sat up. She laid there with her eyes open not saying a word. She stared straight up at the ceiling.

Jim jumped up and looked at the screens. Morgan arose, then came back to the bed asking it to come up 40%. He handed her the baby and told her the name he had picked was a bit old fashioned, but he knew she would like the name Paulie, after her Grandma Pauline. She looked down at her with Jim on one side and Morgan on the other. She said, "Hi, Paulie, I guess you already met your Uncle Jim and your daddy, I am so happy you picked us to be your family. We will protect you, little Paulie, don't you worry. Your family is here for you." Morgan handed her a bottle.

As she fed her Jim said, "You sprung a leak there! Do you want to keep the leak?"

She replied, "No thanks! Dry these puppies up. Tune me up, pal."

Jim sat beside her and said, "Before I do the fine tuning, I want to sever the fallopian tubes, so you are done with kids."

"Make it so number one. And I want perky boobies like Bev's please."

"You got it, Sis."

"How much does she weigh?"

"Four pounds, 9 ounces."

"Can we go home now?"

Thar approached and smiled, "Yes, and you can take Paulie with you as long as you keep her in a monitored incubator for Dr. Cay, and she and I both want to swing by once a day. We will bring you across in the bed. I don't want you up. You have a catheter in for your bladder. We will take that out in a couple days. I would feel better doing the hysterectomy again, but let's get you recovered from all this first."

14

Coming To Terms

The next day, they again worked on cracking the White House china code. This time, Olzing came over to help. He explained he had been looking at the symbols for each element and since they didn't know for sure if it was all numbers, they might want to take the symbols into consideration just in case.

Jim remarked he would have never looked at it like that, then reminded them the presidential seal had arrows which pointed up, which by itself could represent the element of iron. Jim told Bev and Marsha that Olzing, he and Morgan along with Aggie would be going this afternoon to look at the Hall of Archives, Mt. Baker, and the Skinwalker Ranch.

Marsha looked panicked. "No, first you have to go to the Serpent Mound, and somehow that seems to scare me."

"You have Lassie, Wolfie, and Lazy Bones, although I personally believe that little killer rat terrier could probably pull off the face of anyone who came near you, or anyone else in this room for that matter. Don stays with you. We have sharp shooters with all kinds of weapons on the roofs of both houses as well as in a perimeter surrounding both houses."

"Thar and Dr. Cay will be over twice today, and you have the emergency button. Bitty will stay in the room with you and will run errands for both you and Bev."

"Kiki will be here shortly and, though Frieda is miffed that she has to walk through the gate, the x-ray, and the metal detectors, she has agreed to do the overwatch with the drones."

Jim then reminded them to keep looking for clues on the china itself. Jim and Morgan both could see Marsha's panic level rising, though they knew she certainly had good reason to feel the way she did.

As Omar wandered into the room, Marsha cried, "Morgan, what in the Sam HELL is wrong with you? A lion cut—really?"

Wolfie and Lassie stood in unison, casting low, throaty warning growls in Omar's direction. Morgan grabbed Omar's collar and redirected him upstairs.

"Poor Liam will have a meltdown, again! Every time you do this, he tells me the dog cries and is both humiliated and embarrassed. Please let this poor dog's hair grow back out!"

Liam had remarked that Toodles liked her hair pink, so he had no issue with Toodles.

She sighed heavily, then suddenly began to shake. She looked directly at Jim and said, "It was just one, right?"

In the brief internal it took Morgan to run to the bed, she had begun shaking almost to the point of verbal confusion. Jim laid her back flat and her breathing became heavy, even with her eyes closed.

"It was just one, right?" Jim looked at Morgan as he strode over and pushed the emergency button. Marsha started screaming again and tried to jump off the bed into Morgan's arms.

Jim snapped, "Back on the bed with her, Morgan!"

"Too late to move her—this baby is coming out right now!" He deflated the catheter and pulled it out. Marsha was both pushing and screaming at the same time. She sat up to push harder and as it was born, she saw it was a Blue—a hideous monster. She screamed!

Morgan laid her back and Thar gave her meds to put her completely out. Morgan said, "She saw it."

The monster snapped at everyone. Its teeth were two-inch long fangs and his deadly claws were six inches long.

They cut the cord and Marsha screamed, "Kill that thing! If you don't, I will!"

Thar grabbed a large scalpel and dispatched the aberration. Bev was now screaming as well, saying, "That woman was a Blue! You have to test her! Marsha could have eggs all through her body!"

She became frightened and hysterical as well, so Morgan grabbed the med gun and gave her enough to stop her hysteria. Then the team took all of them to the lab. They checked each and every person for Blue eggs or DNA. Thankfully, Marsha was the only one infected, but she had hundreds of eggs.

Morgan said, "I am staying! You guys go on, but I am staying right here!"

Jim approached Morgan, "You have to go! I think you are on the verge of the breakthrough we need. Facetime me, if you must, but I am staying with the girls!" He gave Morgan a quick hug.

Olzing told him he was sending a security team plus Aggie as well with him and he was staying behind to obtain DNA samples from that "lady" who had infected Marsha.

The security team as well as Aggie and Morgan left for the ships. Jim knew Bev would be out through the night, but Marsha always fought every med they gave her. "I'll be lucky if that lasts two hours," he grumbled to himself.

Dr. Cay brought little Paulie over to the nursery. Jim sat in the chair next to Marsha working on the formula when he heard her stir. Thar wanted to strap her down, but Jim countermanded him. He put his tablet down and went to lie on the bed beside her, putting his leg over her along with his arm.

She opened her eyes, and immediately they went wide with fear. She jumped from sleep into full panic, melt-down mode. He spoke to her softly, reassuring her, "You're safe; I am here with you and security is all around us as well."

"Did that horrid thing come from me?"

He sat up; since she seemed in control and leaned across her chest. He looked her straight in the eye, and said, "Yes."

"Please, Jim, just kill me! I never want to produce another thing like that, please!"

He told her that he would not even consider anything like that and the bed was cleaning out all the eggs inside her. "They came from the woman who cut you. She was actually a Blue."

"I would rather be dead than to keep going through this!"

Jim held her tight. "Please don't say that, Marsha! You have all of us here to support you."

"Did you see that demon?" she screamed as she began to beg, "Let me go, please, just let me die!"

Thar heard what she was pleading for, and quickly loaded medications into the gun. He told her it was the shock of seeing what a male Blue child looked like. "You will have no eggs left after this. The bed is programmed to clean out all remaining eggs. In the morning, when Morgan gets back, we will do a hysterectomy."

She sat up and demanded, "You will do that this very minute, damn it! RIGHT DAMNED NOW!"

Jim hesitated for a moment. Marsha demanded, "Get up and do it, Jim, NOW! Not one second longer am I going to be fertile for demons." She started screaming over and over, "DO IT NOW! DO IT NOW!"

Jim sat and pulled her to him, holding her tight. "I want to wait for Morgan." She screamed "NO! You Facetime him now, right this minute, and tell him." Her breathing had become both rapid and labored.

Thar approached her again with meds, but she shoved him away. "Only Jim touches me, GOT IT??"

Reluctantly Jim reached Morgan on Facetime. Marsha grabbed the phone out of his hand.

"MORGAN KING, YOU TELL JIM TO DO THIS HYSTERECTOMY RIGHT NOW! NOT ONE MORE MINUTE WILL I BE FERTILE FOR THESE DEMONS!!! TELL HIM NOW!" With that, she gave the phone back to Jim and again repeated, "NOW!"

Morgan lowered his head and told him to do it now. Jim hung up and instructed the bed to sterilize everything including the patient, Thar and himself."

Marsha sat up and demanded, "YOU, JIM—ONLY YOU! You got that?"

"Okay, now lie back and let us put you under," urged Jim.

"You are doing a breathing tube thing?"

He nodded yes.

"THEN YOU DO IT! Your face better be the last thing I see, buster!"

He laid the three syringes on her chest and grabbed the kit.

"Nothing left, Jim! You make sure of that." She began to shake and moaned, "Oh, God, not another one, NO, NO, NO! Jim, please, NO."

Thar pushed the first drug and Jim told her to close her eyes.

She refused, saying, "NO, I need to see your eyes!" even as she began to drift off.

Jim stood up, leaned over and held her face, saying, "I am right here, Marsha! Feel my hands on your face." He injected the second syringe and sat down to intubate her.

As Thar injected the third, another hideous Blue male fetus slid out and Thar immediately skewered it with a scalpel and destroyed it in the incinerator.

A nurse moved the surgical unit over to Jim. Immediately they saw five other babies ready to be born: all male. Jim dissected her uterus and fallopian tubes free and pulled the organs out with the fetuses still inside. Thar programmed the disintegrator to destroy everything on the tray.

"She has eggs all along the incision where she was cut." They took the laser to all the ones they could see, quickly zapping them out of existence.

Jim said, "All the babies, including Bev's, need to be checked for Blue DNA. There is sure to be an attempt today or tomorrow by the Blue to retrieve these babies. We need all the children and all of us to be in the insulation room in the bunker. Check each and every animal for Blue DNA. I want everyone to move in the next hour!"

"Check Bitty, too. She has been outside with the animals. Make sure she has not been impregnated with Blue eggs. I also want Morgan and I checked because we delivered Marsha, and anyone who even touched the baby or Marsha needs to be checked. And, just to be sure, you'd better check any surface Marsha, or the fetus touched, as well."

"I am beginning to wonder if coming home was worth it. We were all safer in your mountain bunker."

Jim sat beside Marsha. He knew she would awaken soon. Everyone had been gathered into the bunker and security was extremely tight. All cameras were recording and light-bending technology was deployed.

Jim glanced down as Marsha moved her hand. He sat on the bed and leaned across her. She opened her eyes. He smiled, "Good morning, sunshine."

"Did you get it—all of those nasty things?" she asked through dry lips. He nodded his head.

"Did you have to kill more of them?" He put his finger to her mouth and whispered, "Shhhh, no more talk! You are clear of everything."

She blinked and glanced around. "It is so dark and grey here. Where the heck are we?"

He told her they had moved everyone into the bunker for the time being. She closed her eyes and scrunched her face as she grimaced in pain. "Number, Marsha?"

"I am okay."

"Good, now you will answer my question!" She shook her head back and forth. "Stop fighting me and give me a number or I will just put you under for a full 24 hours!"

She clenched her teeth and through them hissed, "Ten. But Jim, don't knock me out. I need you to talk to me. I burn down there."

"May I look?"

She nodded her agreement. "Bed, rig for pelvic exam," he instructed, pulling on the surgical gloves.

The entire area was inflamed. He asked for the topical pain spray and gave her a generous coating. He put her back down and stripped off his gloves.

She was already yelling his name. "Marsha, I am right here! I can hear you!"

"Where is Morgan?"

"They should be back in about an hour." He pulled the cover down and gave her a shot of heparin.

She asked, "What was that?" He told her it was to prevent clots.

Noticing her chest, she lit up and looked happy. "You gave me perky, stand-up boobies!"

"Your wish is my command." Marsha closed her eyes and drifted back into sleep.

Later, he pulled the curtain back to check on her. She had her eyes closed and was dreaming. It was clearly a nightmare. He sat down on the bed and touched her. She pushed him back, as she rolled onto her side and screamed, rolling side to side in pain, then curling into a fetal position.

"Jim, you promised me that this was over!" She cried and was breathing heavily. "You promised!"

He instructed the bed to ready itself for a pelvic exam. He flipped her over, telling her to stay put. He told the bed to expand and make the light brighter. And there it was, hanging on the anterior abdominal wall, a half human and half Blue female fetus. Only the blue curl gave her away, unless you counted that she was screaming at the top of her lungs.

Dr. Cay came running. She looked over Jim's shoulders and urged, "Pull it out now. This is gonna hurt, Marsha!"

He reached up with his fingers and grabbed the leg to slide her down and out. She was tiny but her voice protested loudly.

Dr. Cay ran with her as Marsha was crying and screaming hysterically. He put Marsha under and then finished pulling the fetus out. He looked again and this time, even with as much pain as this would cause, it became clear to him he had to laser her entire interior abdominal cavity.

Marsha would need to stay under for three days. No one could withstand that level of pain. As he finished, there was no doubt in his mind the Blue would hunt them down for this female. He hooked Marsha to monitors with audible alarms and sat beside her.

An hour later, Dr. Cay came back and looked at Marsha. "She looks just awful. The baby will make it and we dialed her DNA back to 100% human; however, like Marsha she is still good for breeding. They will continue to hunt Marsha, her, and Bev down. They have proven they can produce Blue babies."

"As for a name for her; how about Mickie? Marsha likes that kind of name."

Morgan came back later that night and told him, "For sure the Hall of Archives is a site, as is Skinwalker Ranch. It has all the

Egyptian hieroglyphs, and both had the number 12 all over them."

"How is Marsha?"

Jim sat down as did Morgan. "She did quite well with the hysterectomy; however, she still gave birth to another Blue, this time a female."

"Oh, God, they will hunt all of us down."

"Dr. Cay has her dialed back to 100% human. I named her Mickie. We need to rerun for eggs every hour. I missed this one because they are growing at a rate that is astonishing and unbelievable! I had just done the hysterectomy five hours before and didn't see it."

Marsha began to stir. "I lasered her abdominal cavity. I don't think she can withstand it, but let's see." They let her come into consciousness, and she reached for Morgan. The veins in her forehead and neck were bulging, so her blood pressure was clearly sky high, and she was tachycardia. Jim quickly put her back under.

"No way can she be allowed to be conscious again for two more days."

"We should do a pelvic tomorrow to see where we are at," said Morgan.

Jim said, "No, every hour, Morgan, to make absolutely sure we have no others."

Morgan looked nonplussed but nodded and told him to sleep and that he would take the next five hours. He sat beside her working out various locations. He was sure there were more than Giza, Teotihuacan, the Hall of Archives, Skinwalker Ranch, Malta, Rosslyn Chapel, and the Cauldrons in Russia's Valley of Death.

His watch alarm went off and he asked for the pelvic exam, wide and bright. She was bright red but scabbing over in some spots. There were no babies that he could see. He told the bed to lay her flat again and scan for eggs; happily, it returned negative.

Her cover slid off and as he went to cover her, he noticed her new boobies. He laughed and said out loud, "I can't believe she talked him into this." He shook his head. Lassie in came and jumped on the bed with her, lying quietly beside her, nestling her head below her knee.

———

Sitting down, Morgan wrote a careful outline of what had transpired and what had been done to Marsha. If anything further happened, there needed to be a record to trace backwards. He hoped to God all scans remained negative and this would never happen to another human being.

Thar approached and asked how she was doing. He said, "Holding her own."

Thar pulled a chair around facing him and said, "Perhaps we should consider going back to our mountain base where everyone is safe. We will need to expand it, certainly, but it has more extensive barriers and is more solidly fortified and gives a lot more security."

Morgan nodded his head, saying, "Yes, maybe that is a wise choice, so we are not putting all your people in danger as well."

"I hate having to hide; this is not really living! It is cowering in fear. Let me run it by everybody, and I'll let you know our decision tomorrow."

Thar said, "We have enough staff that the necessities can be picked up and gone in a matter of hours—just leaving this place as is to come back to."

The alarm went off on Morgan's watch. He stood and asked for a pelvic exam, wide and bright. She still looked clear, and he reset his watch.

All his exams remained negative. Jim came strolling down the hall with his nose buried in his tablet. He looked up and asked how she was.

"So far, all negative."

He told Morgan that three bays down they had a bed set up for him. Morgan patted Jim on the back and went to bed.

The alarm dinged and Jim asked for a pelvic exam and bright light. She was not nearly as red, and several areas were scabbing over.

On a hunch, he decided to slide a catheter back in. He had just finished with her when something caught his eye. It was a seed sliding down the side of the wall. He watched to see what would happen.

It found a spot fairly close to a pink area showing good blood supply and sprouted roots like a plant, appearing to grab on. He lasered that spot and cleaned it off.

Then he spoke to the computer controlling the bed and told it, in different words, to obliterate any eggs of the Blue Alien by telling it anything alien was to be destroyed.

Twenty minutes later, the bed reported that over 400 alien eggs along with Blue DNA had been destroyed. He was aghast at that number, so thought of another way to rephrase his request for any alien debris and/or microbes to be identified and destroyed. Fifteen minutes later, it reported back that 57 additional alien microbes had been located and destroyed. He asked again for a pelvic exam and expansion with light. She was looking a bit pinker, less red, but thankfully no alien life forms.

As she began to stir, he put her flat and decided to let her come out of sedation. She opened her eyes and seemed to be handling it. All her vitals looked stable. He sat on the bed and leaned into her so she could see him. Tears ran down from the corners of her eyes.

He asked if the pain was manageable, and she nodded. "Shall we try this without the tube?" Again, she nodded yes. He untapped her and removed it. She didn't talk. He came back around the bed and sat down again and leaned over her. "Are you doing okay?" he asked.

She nodded yes but swallowed carefully. "Is your throat sore?" She closed her eyes and nodded yes. He walked over to the supply cabinet and brought a throat spray. He was about to spray and thought, nope, look first. He asked her to stick out her tongue and let him look. It was coated with eggs. He had to think fast to prevent any escaping. Coke was high in an acid that eats things off corrosively. He grabbed a bottle and told her, "I want you to gargle with this. Can you do that?" She nodded.

She sat up and gargled for three minutes. They were both shocked to see the number of dead eggs. He told her to do it again. She did and many more came out.

He said, "Let's keep doing this." Fewer came out the next time and only a couple on the next, and none the last two gargles. He said, "I am going to give you twilight and look down with a tube."

She nodded. He injected her and inserted the scope. It was clear completely down and through the stomach. He withdrew the tube and Marsha opened her eyes. Jim leaned across her and asked if that was better.

She said, "Yes, much better."

"I want you drinking Coke until it is running out of your ears; hear me?" She nodded.

They settled back onto St. Pierre Island in Newfoundland. The tunnel went deeper into the mountain and their quarters had been expanded. They were now situated even further down in the tunnel, and sunlight lamp bulbs had been added to simulate daylight. There was plenty of earth shielding them now.

Marsha was still recuperating and found it difficult to do much of anything due to her residual effects in breathing.

There was a nurse for every two kids. Each nurse was tasked with scanning every day for Blue. Additionally, Marsha had a nurse with her every day. Anyone coming into their quarters had to be scanned prior to entering.

Bat and Emma were actively considering going back in time, at least for now, with Charlie and Wyatt for the safety of their children.

15

The China

The taskforce was concentrating on the Monroe presidential china. They gathered in the family pod, exchanging ideas. They had covered all the sites except Cambodia, and that was planned for the next day. Jim glanced over at Marsha who had her head lying on the sofa arm. Her eyes were closed, and she curled her legs under her. Her tablet was in her other hand.

She wore a mobile sensor that pinged them when her blood pressure was too high or low, or her sugar was off and, most importantly, when her oxygen levels dropped. Jim stood and put an electric blanket over her.

They listed everything about the Monroe china. Marsha hastily lifted her head to scribble the additions to the conversation.

Stylized starburst

Gold

Arrows pointing up, symbolizing the element of iron

The three stars of Orion belt with Betelgeuse, the star Merlin had warned was going to go supernova

Star field

Forty-eight gold points

Gold circle

Gold circle rim

Napoleonic eagle

Secretary of State during the War of 1812

Five vignettes inside the dark red border, representing agriculture, strength, commerce, science and arts.

Fifth president

Two terms

Mississippi (1817)

Illinois (1818)

Alabama (1818)

Maine (1820)

Missouri (1821)

His was a complicated plate and they would break it down further in the morning. Morgan ran to help feed crying babies. Bev went to Marsha and put her hand on her shoulder. "Did I miss much?"

"No, not really," Bev told her. Marsha stood and Jim could see she was clearly not going to make it to her bed. Jim asked if she just wanted to stay under the electric blanket and stay on the sofa. She didn't answer but just laid her head back down.

Bev looked at Jim, "No, she is not staying here if I have to drag her myself. Get her up." Jim pulled the blanket back and turned it off. She didn't budge. Bev asked how much she was being medicated, adding, "This is not living, Jim!" He asked Marsha to stand and she told him, "I can do it."

"No, I don't think so, Marsha," Don picked her up and carried her into her bedroom. Bev pulled back the covers and Don laid her in the bed. She rolled on her side and nearly fell out of the bed. Bev steadied her as Jim covered her.

"It has been two weeks since we got back here. This is awful. This is not what she would ever want."

Jim looked at her and said, "You are right. It's time we saw our spitfire Hellcat. No meds tomorrow except for blood pressure and insulin."

Morgan walked into the bedroom and stood by Jim and Bev. Jim told him, "We can't let this go on, Morgan."

"You know this is not what she would want," said Bev.

Morgan asked when her last exam on the lab med unit was. "While she is like this, we could get a good exam." They asked Don to carry her to their lab. Morgan ran ahead and got the bed warming. Don laid her on the table. Marsha tried to turn on her side and Jim moved her back over. He asked the bed for a pelvic exam. Morgan held her arm to help keep her on her back.

Jim looked at the diagnostic screens and remarked, "What a freaking mess," he said. "I have never seen scar tissue like this. It looks like a mass of spider webs! Jesus, Morgan, come look."

"Oh, my God, Jim. Her colon is completely enveloped with scar tissue!" They told the bed to set up for 3-D imaging. "Her intestines are a total mess, Morgan! All of her organs are encapsulated in this scar tissue. Tomorrow we ask Thar to look at this for his recommendations." Don carried her back to bed.

The next morning Morgan asked her to get up for breakfast. She turned over and never stirred. He pushed her hair back and sat next to her. He told her he had to go check out a site and would be back around 1:00 PM.

Jim was working on a few things and when he looked up, he saw Marsha was not out in the family pod at 10:30 AM. He wanted to finish Monroe today but went into her bedroom and saw she was still in bed. He sat beside her, calling to her and finally she rolled toward him.

"Marsha let's get up." He helped her sit up and she pushed her hair back. "I am dizzy," she told him.

"Yes, you are dehydrated. Let's go back to the lab and access your port so I can give you some fluids."

She stood and said, "Let's go." Jim knew she was really sick to not resist going to the lab. He put his arm around her waist, and she leaned into him. She laid on the bed and he brought up the temperature, turning on the sun bulbs.

He got her accessed and the fluids running. Then he told her , "Let's go work on the code." He helped her to the sofa and gave her the tablet. By noon she seemed more alert and asked for a cup of tea. The chef brought it in with cookies. She sipped the tea and ate a cookie.

"I need to go pee," but she stood and promptly dropped to her knees. "I am good," she mumbled, then stood and stumbled into the bedroom. Jim and Bev eyed her, glancing from her to each other. Jim stood and walked over to the bedroom door. He heard a thud and went through their bedroom into the bathroom to see Marsha lying sprawled on the floor, unresponsive. He slapped the medical emergency button.

Jim splashed cold water on her. Thar's team picked her up and put her on a gurney. Jim held onto the gurney and ran beside her. She turned her head to see Jim.

She blinked and said, "Help me, Jim, please!" He transferred her to the bed. Thar went through the screens. Jim told them to hold all medications until they could figure out why she was not functioning.

Thar turned to him and said, "I have never in my career seen scar tissue like this! It is attacking her organs, completely choking them off." He called for Dr. Mid, their vascular surgeon.

As he glanced through the diagnostic screens, his eyes opened wide and his eyebrows shot up. "How is this patient even alive? She needs to be on one of our beds."

Jim turned and asked, "You have your own beds?"

Dr. Mid replied, "Yes, our cardiovascular system is similar to what I'm seeing from this girl. We can do away with this scar tissue using our beds. First, we break it up with a special ultrasound. Then the bed dissolves it."

Jim blinked and retorted, "Why are we talking? Let's go."

Thar muttered, "Prime directive."

Dr. Mid exclaimed, "To hell with that, Thar! We are so far past that with this family. Get your team to transfer her to my bed and let's get started saving her life!"

They told Jim they would come get him after the treatment. He said, "That's a no! I'll stay with her." Dr. Mid ran the ultrasound over her; it took almost two hours. They had her strapped down and restrained but Jim stayed beside her stroking her hair and telling her she was okay. She was on the last leg of dissolving the scar tissue when she murmured, "I can't breathe." Dr. Mid and Thar pulled up the diagnostic. Dr.

Mid looked down and told her, "You are having a panic attack; calm yourself! Unstrap her right now." Thar took the restraints off as Jim grabbed her arm and put it on his chest. He told her, "Now follow me, one breath in, hold it, and now out. Follow me Marsha, in, hold, and then blow it all out. Dr. Mid asked why he was coddling the patient. Jim looked at him and said, "Because we are human and not Nordic." Dr. Mid looked at him, looked chagrined, and said, "You're right, I am sorry, please forgive my sharp tongue."

He then asked Jim to stand and look at the screen, it read 95% cleared. "She will experience pain for maybe a week because of her human physique, but considering she was nearly dead, this is a miracle."

Marsha reached for Jim. "I am scared; where am I?" Dr. Mid told her she was in the Nordic treatment bay. "This is the type of medical beds we use for the Nordic race." He told her she had lots of scar tissue that had been causing her body big issues. "We have resolved it as we speak. You are free to go back to your pod and rest. Please come see me in two days so we can see where we are." He helped her sit up. She swung her legs over the side of the table and Dr. Mid lowered the table.

Jim walked her back to their pod. "May I sit out in the family pod?" Jim told her that was okay but the minute she felt tired he wanted her in bed. She pulled up the subject of Monroe on her table, and she and Bev discussed what they had deduced from the Monroe china. She asked where the War of 1812 took place, as she laid down with her head on the arm of the sofa.

Jim got up and sat by her, covering her with the electric blanket. She rolled on her side and closed her eyes. "Don't make me go in there by myself please. Stay with me, you guys. I am so scared, and I don't know why." She grabbed Jim's arm and said, "Really, I truly feel scared." She drew her legs up in a ball, then sat up and almost burrowed herself in the arm of the sofa. Jim looked at Bev. She signaled with her head to scoot over to her. "I am so, so scared. What is wrong with me?"

Jim moved over and started by telling her, "You have been through so much in the last three weeks." She looked at him and asked, "What have I been through?" Bev moved over and scooted her over a bit and wiggled in between the sofa and her. Jim and Bev sat tight against her.

When Marsha began to cry, Bev glanced at Jim. "Marsha, do you remember giving birth?"

Marsha looked puzzled, and told her, "No." "Do you remember me delivering babies?" She said "No."

"Well, nothing to worry about, Marsha. You just let Bev and I hold you."

She laid her head on Bev's shoulder. "Why am I here?" she asked. Bev looked at Jim. Marsha curled herself into a tighter ball and covered her eyes. "That giant hairy man Merlin, don't let him get to me."

Jim shot a glance at Bev and yelled, "Run and get behind our door now!" Bev ran and slammed the door.

Merlin appeared with no swirls or time-displacement waves. "Let her remember. Your time is short! You have but three more days! Listen to her! She has your answer." He walked over to Marsha and Jim jumped between Merlin and Marsha.

Merlin shoved him aside, briefly touched her head, and then simply vanished before their eyes. Jim could hear her wheezing, as she rocked and cried with every ounce of her body trying to force itself into the cushion to get away from him.

Bev activated the intruder alert button and security arrived at a dead run. Don jumped in front of Jim and Marsha. Olzing arrived and Jim told him as he held Marsha who wouldn't look at anyone. Jim yelled, "Merlin just paid us a visit. There were no time displacement waves or swirls. He shoved me out of the way and touched her head." Don helped get Marsha to her bed with Jim on her other side.

Don asked when Morgan would return. Olzing told him not until the following day. Bev came out of her room and went directly into Marsha's room. They both laid beside her, holding her tight as Marsha mumbled incoherently. Bev looked at him, shaking her head.

Jim turned Marsha toward Bev. "Are we going to die because of me?"

"No, absolutely not, Marsha." She started mumbling again, "12, 1, iron symbol, 2—stop, it hurts, it hurts, make it stop!" He took Marsha's chin and lifted it toward him.

"Marsha, open your eyes."

She pushed his hand away, "I don't want to see the hairy man. Please make him leave me alone."

"He is gone now, Marsha, look at me!" She opened her eyes and almost jumped on top of Jim. Bev moved toward Jim as well. She laid her head on him with her hair cascading off his shoulder.

Jim asked Bev to go get the med gun. She got up and left for the lab. He laid Marsha flat on the bed. "I think we should go to the lab."

She cried out, "Don't leave me. Where is Morgan? Is he in the lab?" She slid out of the bed. Jim wanted her in the lab and preferred not having to fight her to go there, so he suggested, "Let's go see." He regretted telling her the lie but rationalized the end result would be positive. She nearly collapsed from exhaustion and dehydration along the way.

She looked and inquired, "Morgan?" Jim took her hand and guided her to a bed.

"I need to access your port for fluids." She backed against the wall and then slid down the wall, sitting with her legs up under her chin. Jim sat down in front of her. She would not look at him so he waited like Morgan would have. After 40 minutes she turned to him and said, "You always win."

She stuck her hand out to him and he helped her up. "You start it here and then we go to my bedroom."

He smiled, "You've got a deal." He accessed her port and gave her meds for anxiety and pain. He held the bag up as they walked to the bedroom. He scooted her over into the middle of the bed and Bev laid on one side with Jim on the other. She snuggled into Jim and Bev moved in closer. In mere seconds, Marsha was asleep. Jim watched her and Bev as they both slept. Bev had her arm over Marsha. Marsha rolled on her side toward Jim. He looked at her as she murmured, "Hold me tight and make me stop shaking." He put his arm around her and pulled her close. She closed her eyes. "Morgan," she called out. Over and over she called to him.

Jim finally told her to just go to sleep. Within a few minutes, he felt her body begin to relax. He rolled her over toward Bev so he could get up and add another bag of fluids. He wished he had slid in a catheter. He got a catheter kit to see if he could get it in without disturbing her. He came back and pulled the covers back and moved her legs apart and he was able to get her legs up. He slid it right in and inflated the balloon, then covered her back up.

Jim then picked up his tablet to work on the answer. Time was ticking. Merlin seemed to think Marsha had the secrets. He looked over the notes Marsha had made. He got up and decided an antibiotic could be a protocol for taking down adhesions. He brought in Vanco and hung it, then went back to what Marsha had said during the sessions she attended and was awake and alert.

Jim fell asleep holding Marsha. Morgan walked in and laughed at the three sleepers, "Now, this is a Kodak moment!"

He touched Jim's shoulder, telling him, "Trade you."

Jim got up and Morgan slid in holding her tight to him. Jim squeezed in beside Morgan and fell back to sleep.

At 9:00 AM Marsha sat up. Bev, Morgan and Jim were still asleep. She tried getting out of bed, but saw she had a catheter in. She covered back up and stared at Morgan.

Suddenly, she began thinking of Merlin and the shaking started. Morgan stirred and turned over. She closed her eyes and tried to control her breathing. Her knees were pulled up under her chin as she began rocking back and forth. Jim felt it and sat up. He got up and climbed on the bed in front of Marsha. He pulled her up to him, holding her tight and letting her rock. Morgan sat up. He got behind her and pulled her back against him. She turned around and straddled him and wouldn't let go. She held him so tight she was nearly choking him.

Jim pulled one arm up off his neck and laid her back against the pillow as Morgan slid in behind her. Jim laid down between Bev and Marsha. He moved in tight.

Morgan looked at Marsha who murmured, "Particle beam with satellite mirrors for the access point 12, 1, 2, 12, 15, 50, alchemical iron symbol… and the fire symbol in alchemy. Gold, silver, mercury in the beam." Then she conked out again.

Morgan grabbed the tablet and typed the sequence out. Marsha didn't move, but Jim sat up and called her name.

"Gold, silver, mercury with an iron base on satellites with copper." Morgan got that written down.

Then… "Don't leave me, hold me, I need to feel you." Jim grabbed her and held on tight as he could.

"Copper on the reflective mirrors." Marsha laid her head on Jim's shoulder, but her nose began to bleed almost immediately. Morgan got up, wrung a rag out in cool water, and put it behind her neck. She then roused and asked if she was going to die. Morgan told her "No, just sleep."

"I feel sick." He grabbed the gun and gave her anti-nausea meds. He told her to relax now and for her to just let them hold her.

"Can you feel us holding you?"

She said again, "Cooper on the mirrors or it won't work." Jim held her tight. "Don't forget the place at Rosslyn Chapel You need the fleur de lis cufflinks of 45 to put in the access as the last step. Don't forget, baby."

Morgan carefully wrote it all down. She said, "I have to pee, too. Help me to the bathroom."

"You go ahead and pee," Morgan told her. "I am going to go work the launch out and how many to make it work. We need to talk to the Pleiadeans to get their particle beam technology."

"Hold her," she told him. "Adams has the Eye of Horus. Take that."

Morgan looked back in to hear her talking to Caci. "I am so afraid of Blue. They are after us. They're all dead."

Morgan became alarmed as he watched Jim trying to wake her. Morgan moved back to the bed and held onto her, as well. "Marsha, They are safe."

"Caci. Dead, all dead."

Jim finally got her to open her eyes. She buried her head in his shoulder and cried hard, hanging onto him for dear life and Morgan could not pry her away.

"The fleur de lis of 45, you have to have that cufflink; it is the last step. It is the key to launch. Don't forget, baby."

Morgan looked hard at her, "Forty-five, you mean Trump? He wears fleur de lis?" He pulled it up and saw he actually did. Then she was calling for Caci again.

Jim couldn't get her loose. Bev asked if he wanted her to try. Jim said to Bev, "She would crush you. Let's see if chai tea will entice her. Her shaking has me concerned about maybe..." Morgan put the tablet down. "Let's go! right now!"

Morgan yelled for Don. "Take her to the lab!"

Don pulled on her and managed to pry Jim free. Don told Jim, "Those will be beauties when the bruises pop up." They ran back to the bed. "Restrain the patient." Morgan ran the screen diagnostics while Jim said. "Pelvic exam. Light and expand."

Marsha fought back, yelling, "Stop—help me stop!" He told him to lay across her pelvic area so he could see. He laid his weight on her holding onto the bed as leverage and finally got her to lie still.

Jim said, "Damn it! She grew back the damn uterus! Have you had sex, Morgan?"

"Only once. Damn, hold her while I feel for it." Morgan touched her softly. "Of course, there ya' go. Congrats again!"

Morgan passed out, slumping to the floor. Jim asked Don to get a cold pack from the freezer and put it behind his neck, then get a wet washcloth, run it under cold water and put it on his forehead. Don followed his instructions.

As Morgan came to and sat up, "Tell me you didn't say what I think you did."

"Well, Morgan I could say that, but it would be a lie. Just one is all I feel. Since she was on the Nordic bed, we need to find out their cycle."

Don overheard and told them it was 11 months. "Good to know."

Marsha was dripping with cold sweat. Her sugar was low, and Jim gave her the rescue pen. Bev came in with a cup of chai tea.

Bev told Marsha, "I have a nice cup of tea for you." Marsha opened her eyes as Jim sat her up. She took the cup from Bev and leaned over and kissed her cheek.

"Caci said all the females are dead," she said offhandedly. Morgan felt his knees going weak. Jim walked over and sat next to her. "Their race will be dead soon, then we will be free."

Marsha sat straight up with a total look of fear and what little color she had was gone. Jim turned to her. Her mouth was open.

"Bev, right now! Run to the lab and shut the door till I come to get you! NOW, baby!"

She ran with Don right behind her, telling her to lock it as he ran back.

It was Merlin, "Take heed! You have all the clues. This is my last opportunity to implore you to follow what she says if humanity is to survive! I can't travel safely again." He reached for Marsha and Don pulled the trigger. Merlin faced Don and roared as he pulled the trigger a second time. Bat came running in with both pistols out, firing. The alarms sounded, "Weapon discharge in Dr. Kings' pod."

"You're wasting ammo, gentleman!" Morgan continued, "He is an immortal—no way to kill him," as he was also trying to lay Marsha back. She was frozen. Morgan rubbed her breastbone hard. That brought her around and he laid her back.

"Keep him away, please keep him away, please, please, please!" Each please got louder and louder until she was screaming at the top of her lungs. Thar went straight to the bed and put her to sleep. "Merlin again. Jim, oh God, Bev!"

Two agents went back, with Don entering first. Bev was hiding in the corner behind a corner cupboard. Don held out his hand and helped her up. "He is gone." Bev threw her arms around him and cried, emerging and wiping her tears. She ran to Jim.

"Okay, we've gotta focus to save our planet!" said Morgan. He sat next to Marsha who was cuddled up in the electric blanket with her head on his shoulder. Bev was bracketed with Dallas on one side and Liam on the other. Jim sat on the love seat with Finch beside him with Tig on the floor in front of Jim with Omar the Lion as he called him. Lassie had sprawled out in front of Marsha and Droopy was laying in the middle of the room with Toodles cuddled up into him.

Droopy had claimed Toodles as his puppy and they were inseparable. Wolfie had assumed the role of guard dog and posted himself by the door. Giles sat in Liam's lap with Lazy Bones on the other side of Tig, They were best buds. The girls had the little dogs except for Toodles who barked and whined until she got to be with Droopy. "Gage, what are you doing in here? Better yet, how did you manage to escape?" asked Morgan.

He was sucking his thumb, carrying his blanket and rubbing his eyes. Marsha started to pick him up, but he laid down and cuddled with Lassie, who curled around him with her head on his chest. He closed his eyes. Morgan looked down and then looked at Marsha with a smile of satisfaction.

Marsha looked around the room, smiled, and closed her eyes. The nurse came in and Morgan told her to leave Gage and that he was fine where he was. She apologized, somewhat chagrined one of her charges had managed to escape. Morgan heard loud giggling and squealing. Marsha was asleep. He got up to go check on the girls. Dorothy-Alice, El, Zoey, Rue and Emmi had dressed up the rat terrier, beagle and the mini pin in doll clothes and were pushing the baby doll buggies, racing them up and down the hallway. Morgan came around the corner, surprising them, and asked, "What are my princesses doing with the three dogs?"

"We are having dog races."

Morgan asked to see them. He sat on the floor and watched as they lined them all up and gave them a push. The rat terrier would not stay in the buggy, but jumped out and ran, so El would have to go get him and bring him back.

Morgan laughed and the girls all piled on him. Jim poked his head out to see down the hall and laughed. El had decorated Morgan with a pink boa, and Rue parked a pink sparkly hat on his shock of white hair. Emmi had put a pink wand in his hand, and Zoey told him he looked like a pretty princess. Jim laughed and told "pretty princess" to come back and get to work.

Morgan shook his head and said, "Sorry, my young ladies, no more dog races tonight. You might accidentally hurt one of the dogs and I know you don't want to do that! You take them into the playroom. Morgan picked up the beagle and asked, "Who put lipstick on this poor puppy… never mind, please someone wash it off," and handed the dog to Zoey.

Liam suddenly yelled out, "Look Daddy, LOOK! Two of Jupiter's moons are being pulled towards Betelgeuse."

Jim and Morgan jumped up to cast his tablet onto the big screen. "OH, EXCELLENT FIND!!"

Finch went on to tell them that Mars had shifted its axis toward Betelgeuse. "Boys, you don't know what a wonderful discovery this is!"

Dallas muttered, "Just saying, look! That black hole is bigger!"

They spent the rest of the afternoon readjusting their plan. That evening, the Nordics and the Pleiadeans met together to map the launch of the copper satellites and the particle beam accelerator. They were still working on the correct mix of gold, silver, iron and mercury.

The Pleiadeans assumed the testing of the different mixes in their labs. They now had to take into consideration the reversal of gravitational pull.

Liam pointed out that the star Mintaka in the belt of Orion had shifted on its axis by 18 percent. That alone could take out Betelgeuse all by itself.

Dallas questioned if the supernova, with the help of the particle beam and the tilt of the planet, could potentially have a reversal effect. One of the Pleiadeans answered, "No, that is not possible, but it might push it into that black hole."

Then Dallas asked why they had not looked at King Arthur's old castle and the Lady of the Lake as a planetary protection access point.

The adults looked at each other in surprise and shock. Morgan told Dallas, "You and I will go look tomorrow, if Olzing can arrange it."

The meeting adjourned at 11:00 PM and Jim told the boys to go to bed. After they all filed out, he told Morgan, "We have some super smart kids." Morgan was clearly shaken and interrupted Jim, "Yeah, Yeah, I know! But good night. Tomorrow's gonna be a busy, busy day!"

Morgan laughed and went to his bedroom. Marsha was already in bed. Morgan tried to be quiet as he crawled in bed. It had been a very long day. He turned on his side toward Marsha looking at her. She opened her eyes, scooted toward him, nuzzling into him and closed her eyes again.

At 7:00 AM, Morgan got up and showered. Marsha sat up and Morgan joined her on the bed, asking how she felt. She pulled him on top of her and said, "You tell me."

He laughed and replied, "You know the rules, none of that until you pass the first trimester."

"Why can't you?"

He sat up and slid off the bed. "Nope, but nice try."

"Morgan, I have been dizzy all night. When I turn over, I am dizzy." "What is your sugar?" She said, "115." He turned to her and said, "Let's go."

"NO, MORGAN. We'll play it by ear."

He stood there with his hands on his hips, thinking about how to get her into the lab. She turned and he caught her off guard, grabbed her by the arm and pulled her down the hall.

"Morgan, stop!"

"Let's go! No complaining." He pulled her into the lab. "Get on that bed this second!"

Jim walked down the hall with his cup of tea. He saw what was happening, stomped up to Marsha and yelled, "SIT!"

She sat down, then he commanded, "Lie down!" They both turned their attention to the screens as they paged through them.

"You are having hormonal swings, my dear. That means this could actually be a normal pregnancy for you."

Jim looked at Morgan, "No sex, right?"

He said, "Yep, none."

"I need to do a pelvic, let's have a look and see where we are."

Marsha tried to sit up but Jim set his cup down and leaned across her. "We want this to be a successful, regular pregnancy, right? We will look as often as we see fit, or we could ask Thar to look."

"NO THAR!"

"All right, then." He pulled his gloves on and instructed the bed to position for a pelvic exam.

Jim said, "Well lookie here! Is that underwear? That'd be a new addition for Marsha!" Both laughed as she rolled her eyes.

"Get it over with, boys!" She said as Morgan slipped off her panties.

"Light and expand," said Jim. They said nothing for almost a minute. "Okay, you are going to feel a pinch. I need you to stay still."

"WHY?"

"Because I want a tissue sample."

"FINE! OUCH!"

Jim made a face and told her, "You will live. I am going to say this once again: no sex or hanky panky of any kind, and stay off your feet today. You may see some spotting. No panic, it is from the biopsy. No picking up dogs or kids today. You will stay in the family pod with us."

"Not this crap again," she shot him a dirty look as she sat up.

Jim retorted, "Yes, this crap again!" He washed his hands and picked up his cup. Morgan was already looking at the biopsy.

She told them, "I am going to shower and dress. Can I have my panties back?"

"Only if you promise to wear that cute bright yellow dress of yours. It makes everything so much more cheery." He handed them to her and said, "Good job and they are pretty, too."

She walked down the hall and showed her butt. He laughed and went right to Morgan. "What do you think?"

"I am going with mixed Nordic DNA, so I bet the baby has some, too."

As they congregated in the family pod, Dallas, Finch, Tig and Liam had the big screen up mapping trajectories of the new positions of planets, and where they would be during perihelion. The dogs had staked out their usual territories. Marsha accused poor Giles of being a methane factory and showed him to the door by Wolfie.

Morgan held the Rutherford Hayes ornament. He was studying it, and Marsha suddenly leaned over and said, "Look! A white horse means victory, courageousness, trustworthy, and masters of knowledge and faith. Helios the Sun God! Morgan, what are the elements in the sun?"

The words had scarcely left her mouth then Dallas was pulling it up and cast it to the big screen. "Hydrogen 91.2 and helium 8.7. Daddy, it also has other elements in it, too. Look at this, iron, nickel, magnesium and silicon."

"Good find, boys! Marsha, this is an important find and we would never have found this without you!" exclaimed Jim. "You win a prize, so go surprise us."

She went into her bedroom and came out dressed in her gown from the first Nobel prize ceremony she attended. She held a statue in her hand. The boys all turned around with smiles on their faces. "I have something for each of you that from now on will be known as the King Prize."

She looked at Jim and continued, "We will not start until the party pooper Jim stands." He laughed and put down his tablet, then stood and faced her. She set down the statue and said, "When I call each of your names, come forward."

"Dr. Jim Mottice." He moved forward. She opened a small box revealing the small crown with all his kids; and Bev's stones on the points like she had made for Morgan. She pinned it on him. He gave her a tight hug and kiss.

She said, "Please you're rumpling my gown!" He laughed.

"Bev Grissom, please come forward. For your uncompromising faith and contribution," she pinned one like Jim's on her.

"Dallas and Finch, would you please step forward? This award is for your contributions to save humanity." Theirs had each of their names and their birthstones around it. They both gave her a hug.

"Liam and Tig, please come forward. Ditto on saving humanity." She pinned their medals on their chests. "Dr. Morgan King."

He stepped up and his pin had all the new babies arrayed in a star field. She pinned it on him and said, "May I have this dance?" Morgan asked Tig to find *May I Have This Dance*. He found it and turned the volume up and they danced. Then Morgan took Bev's hand and Marsha pulled Jim up. Then Bev took Finch and Dallas for a swing around the floor. Marsha did the same, then Bev and Jim, and Morgan and Marsha danced again.

Finally, Tig turned it off and said, "Enough of this gooey gunk."

They laughed. Bev and Jim stood close to Morgan and Marsha. Bev had tears streaming down her face as she thanked Marsha.

"Okay, shall we get back to work? Oh, and, by the way, still no sex for you two."

Morgan expelled the word, "WELL!" as they laughed. Marsha kissed Morgan very passionately, but the boys all yelled, "EWWWWW!" Marsha went in to change. She slipped on her PJs and laid down as she snuggled under the covers.

Jim had been reworking the particle beam and said, "We should break for lunch. It is 1:00." He looked over at Morgan who was still working and asked where Marsha was. Morgan jumped up and went into the bedroom with Jim right behind. Morgan sat on the bed and called her name.

She didn't respond, so Jim reached over and felt her neck for a pulse because she appeared ghostly white. She slapped his hand away.

"Go away people, I can't catch a break."

They looked at each other and laughed in relief.

Jim whipped back the covers and said, "Oh, look, she even has real clothing on."

Morgan pulled her into a sitting position, saying "LUNCH." Jim grabbed her arm and they pulled her up. Her hair was every which way but combed back. She shook her head to clear the cobwebs, and drug herself into the kitchen where the four of them sat.

Lunch was on the table self-serve style. She sat beside them, disheveled and closed her eyes. Jim glanced at Morgan, then back at her. Bev stood and took Marsha back to bed. She told them she thought it was pitiful to drag her into the kitchen like that.

When they finished eating, Bev made her a tray. Jim looked over to Morgan as she left with the tray. Jim said, "Not like this. My gut is yelling danger, Will Robinson, danger!" Bev came back out and picked up her tablet to study the china of Madison.

Morgan asked, "Did she eat?"

Bev said, "Nope. So I can guess what is next. The boys and I will keep working."

Morgan got up and put his hands on Bev's cheeks, giving her a kiss. She retorted, "Please, I am a married woman!" But she grinned.

Jim walked into Marsha's room and sat down. He rolled her over and said, "You eat, or we drop an NG tube and access your port for fluids." She weakly pushed at him and rolled over.

He rolled her right back and asked if that was her final answer. "Shut up! This is not Jeopardy!" She rolled back over.

Morgan got Don, who scooped her up and carried her down the hall.

Even the boys were laughing. Bev giggled, too. Tig said, "Man, I cannot eat! And, I am always starving."

Dallas said, "Me, too. Guess we'll just be fat when we are older."

Tig said, "As long as I am not bald!" Bev laughed so hard she was coughing.

Marsha fought Don the entire way back to the lab. He laid her on the table and Jim instructed, "Restrain the patient."

Neither talked to her, just got out the supplies necessary. She kept screaming at them to let her up. Then she laid back quietly as they laid out the supplies and pushed them over to her.

Morgan accessed the port as she lay there without protest but with her eyes closed.

Jim paged through the screens, "Yep, dehydrated and short on C and D." Morgan told him to give her B for some energy as well. He then raised the head of the bed up. She turned from him.

Morgan said, "Okay, missy show time." He lowered the upper body restraints but left the one for the lap and legs. Jim slid the tube down quickly.

Jim said, "Got it. Let's lay her back."

Jim stood and walked across the lab getting the suction ready for her. Morgan kept kissing her and said, "Let's get that suction on." They laid her back and put the restraints on again, so she did not yank things out.

"Okay, let's let the boys keep working trajectories on the big screen and we work in here." Morgan leaned over and kissed her, and told her nighty-night, then gave her meds. Jim told him he would hang the feeding for 12 hours.

16

The Maze

Marsha was dreaming. She waited and listened, yet as she listened her mind was searching out the maze before her. She turned left and suddenly saw Merlin. From here on out she decided every turn must be carefully chosen. It was such a labyrinth and she feared she would lose herself forever. She glanced at her watch and felt sick. She started forward, but then shrank back.

Someone was coming! She said, "A long path before here." Someone was drawing nearer and with each step, she backed further into the shadows of the alcove. She looked around her and saw death lay all around her. She was expecting Merlin and waited, ready to stab him.

She told herself, "I have to get out of here." At that moment, a book with a map fell from a shelf. It looked very old. Was it a forbidden map that had been tucked away? She realized staring at it, that it depicted the Orion Nebula. She looked around the room and over the door it said Hall of the Archives.

There appeared a table with three chairs. They were all made of stone and elk horns. There was a sword lying across the table that said Sword of Destiny and braced against the table was the Spear Of Destiny.

Quickly, she grabbed all three and ran down the passage and into an opening in the maze. The Sword and Spear stuck into the Rock of Destiny and blocked the interloper from following. She saw another opening that was below her. She descended the steps as she tucked the map into her shirt. Hearing movement behind her. She ducked behind a door.

She heard a shot from a pistol that reverberated through the hall. It was Bat! He smiled and told her to follow him. She turned to him sharply. "I need to take you to safety. Let me guide you." He put his hand out toward her. "You will not be alone; I am with you. Come, I will save you from death." The place they were in was dank and musty. The long halls were empty.

She asked where the ruins were? He told her they were beyond the desert. She was disturbed and felt irritated.

"We have to make the next turn, or we will loop back." She followed and told him they could not fail. He told her to stay with him regardless of anything. They ran down a long passage. She gave Bat the fleur de lis cufflink and told him that was their key. He inserted it, and the door opened revealing it was full of particles of gold and silver. Unleashed by the opening of the door, it rushed by them and hit the planet and pushed it into the great black hole.

The particles stopped and she said, "No, it will come back out and explode!" The beam came back on with more gold particles surrounding earth. She could see the light bouncing from one copper dish to another. Bat told her to stay with him. A door opened revealing there was a golden beam shining into the darkness.

Then she saw a flashlight and heard someone say, "She is back!" She opened her eyes and she saw Bat was there with her. She closed her eyes.

He said, "Marsha, you must open your eyes and stay with me." She opened them, then realized she had a breathing tube in and reached for it. Bat took her hand. She turned her head and saw Jim and Morgan working the screens and Thar was beside Bat. She closed her eyes again and heard someone say, "She is having other rhythm issues." She closed her eyes… and was suddenly back in the room which was alongside some kind of guardroom. She stepped in and saw she faced two doors. She hesitated but went to the door on her left. She took another key that had an Eagle holding arrows and made of iron and put it in the door where Bat stood with his arm outstretched. He was smiling as she took his hand and felt him pulling her.

She again heard, "She is back." And somewhere Bat said, "I got ya', girl." She even felt his solid grip. She could not open her eyes but drifted off to sleep.

Later, she awoke to see Bat still holding her hand and Jim sat on the bed next to her. "Welcome back, princess. The tube is out."

She told them, "I have another puzzle piece. You need one more key. It has an iron presidential seal. It was in a guardroom. I saw the whole thing in a maze I went through. Don't stop the beam. You must keep it going so the planet does not pop out and explode. But you have to have that key."

Jim quickly typed out a text which he sent to everyone working on the project. She turned to Bat and told him how he had saved her. "You came and got me."

He told her to rest and he would stay right here beside her. "My chest hurts, Jim."

He put the tablet down and gave her light symptomatic meds. He also put an aloe topical cream on the burns from the paddles. Bat asked if that was better. Being Marsha, she asked if they had ruined her perky boobies.

They laughed and said they had not. Then Morgan came running into the room in his PJ's. Bat stood up and let go of her hand. Morgan sat down and kissed her. "I just went to bed. You scared all of us to death."

"I was in the maze and Merlin was chasing me," Marsha told them. "I was so lost and scared, and thought I was going to die. Bat came and got me."

Morgan looked at Bat. "He was right there with you when you decided to code on us three times, my little Princess," Jim told her. "We will have no more of that! I have never been so scared, Marsha!" Jim told her.

She began to cry for Morgan. Jim and Bat each touched her as she looked at Jim and asked, "My baby?"

"SHE is fine. But that was touch and go as well; but for now she is fine."

"A girl? We'll name her Galyn."

Morgan laughed and said, "Okay, how do you come up with names so quick?"

She responded, "With whatever pops in my mind! I know that is a gift from God and that is to be her name." Morgan leaned into her which she knew meant a lecture, so she turned her head away with her eyes closed. He did his usual patient wait.

Finally, she turned toward him and told him she was sorry. He smiled with warmth and love.

He said, "You will stay in the lab on this bed for maybe the rest of the pregnancy. No bartering, no arguing, only listening to orders and obeying them." He leaned down and kissed her.

"I was so scared, Marsha. I never want to feel like that ever again. Jim even had to medicate me when you stabilized. And you know Dr. Snip-Snip! He took great joy in medicating me." They laughed.

Then Jim started with, "Now, you sleep, and I want to hear if anything hurts, cramps or stings. Got it?"

She smiled and replied, "Got it!" Then, a worried look crossed her face and she told them, "You need the key and there is another access point at Mount Saint Catherine at Mount Sinai. I looked over and saw the beam from where I stood in the maze." Jim promptly texted that out to their team.

Morgan told her to rest now, and to stop thinking about this! They had the plan nearly laid out. He kissed her again as Jim administered the medication. Morgan slid the facemask for oxygen on Marsha and turned it on. Jim told Morgan and Bat to go get some rest since they had a second shift and that started in five hours.

Marsha woke to the bright lights of the lab. Morgan walked over to her. "My sunshine! How about some tea if you can sit up?"

"My chest burns and hurts!"

"I am sure it does. We had to use the paddles on you four times, my princess." He took the topical numbing med and sprayed it on her chest and then rubbed an aloe lotion on top. He pulled the blanket up and asked the bed to come up 40 percent. He walked over to the breakfast bar and brewed her tea. "You feel up to holding this? If not, I can get you a straw."

She smiled and said, "Let me try." She was shocked at how weak she felt. She looked at him and began to cry.

"It's okay; you've been through a bunch. I will hold it and you sip it with a straw. Your strength will come back."

"I feel like a wet dish rag."

"Stop thinking about it. We will have physical therapy come in in a couple days and work with you. For now, let me be your man!"

She took a sip and told him, "My throat is really sore."

"Yeah, I imagine that will clear up." She laid her head back against the pillow.

"I am done."

Morgan said, "Oh, no you're not! We will not have a repeat of scaring your husband to total white hair!" She smiled and reached for his hair. He grabbed her hand and kissed it.

"I am tired, Morgan."

"Baby, you must finish this cup of tea!"

She took another sip and told him, "I have to pee."

"You're hooked up, go ahead." She closed her eyes, and he laid her back, letting her sleep.

When she awakened, Bat was holding her hand. Jim noticed, and walked over, smiling, "Hey, pretty princess, you slept all day long. How about I make some tea for you?"

She gazed at him and said, "I feel awful."

Jim pushed the button for Morgan and Thar, and she closed her eyes.

"No, you don't, little missy," Bat told her. "You open those eyes and look at me." She opened her eyes. "Now you are not going anywhere! I need you to stay awake and focus on little ole' me.

Your very first love!" She laughed and tried to turn over but couldn't move.

Bat grabbed her chin, saying, "Nope you stay with me."

"I am so tired and feel terrible." A medical team came streaming in and Marsha closed her eyes again.

She was back in the maze. "You're wasting your time," she heard.

"I am being watched," she thought. She found herself running on Iron Mountain along the Love Dead River. She saw a steamer to the north, then saw the river port on Mars. She heard, "Try to understand the circumstances of things." The voice was familiar to her. She heard the train conductor say, "Next stop, Iron Mountain. To save the world, return and tell them." There was no sound or movement. She felt arms pulling at her. She said, "Show me the way, Bat!"

"I am here! Take the opportunity and run to me before it closes." She glanced around and saw Bat signaling her to come toward him. "The map!" She turned and picked up the map and it burned her chest when she tried to tuck it in her shirt. She saw the earth beneath her sliding away, and Bat was yelling to her, "Jump!" signaling he would catch her. She let go of the fiery map and jumped into his arms. She could hear some kind of commotion and then someone said, "We got her!"

She opened her eyes and noticed it was almost dark. She moaned; the pain was that bad. Jim sat on the bed and said, "Number!" She told him 10, so he gave her meds. Her tears ran down her cheeks and Jim wiped them away.

She managed to get out of Iron Mountain and some sort of port on Mars. "Fire—it burns!" He pulled the blanket down and sprayed her, then put the aloe on her chest. "My baby?"

"She is fine. You, however, have a long way to go."

She told him, "Iron Mountain is an old riverbed and port on Mars." He walked over and picked up the tablet and sent the text to the working team. Then, returned and sat down next to her.

"How are you feeling and TRUTH, now."

"Like I've been through a war zone."

He said, "You have." She tried to reach for him but fell back. He picked up her hand.

"Lie next to me," she begged.

He swung his legs up and told the bed, "Two humans, one male, one female."

"I need to feel you against me, please?" as she began to cry. He got under the covers with her and pulled her to him. She closed her eyes and drifted off into sleep. As soon as he was sure she was asleep, he jumped up and began texting.

The satellites had been deployed. They still could not find the eagle key. "Guard house, Iron Mountain," he texted everyone. "Steamship?" What was that, he mused.

Liam snuck in and whispered, "Steamships can travel against currents. There is a colony on Mars that needs immediate evacuation on a ship like a steamship that can still speed along against a current, which is the pull of the black hole." Jim hugged him and texted that information to the working group.

Liam went over and looked at his mom who was sleeping. He began to cry and asked if she would live. Jim immediately turned to him and told him, "This much I know for sure: she is a fighter and will fight to stay with us." Liam looked up at Jim and with a longing glance at his Mom, he turned and walked away.

If Marsha only knew how much she helped the plan with decoding the china plates and keys, and the ship. And now, rescuing a trapped colony whose ship could not break free of the gravitational pull of the black hole.

Bat walked in. Jim asked him to take off his coat and get into bed with Marsha to hold her tight against him. Bat stood still, looking perplexed.

"Come on! I am not asking you to sleep with her, just get under the covers with her and hold her. She is naked." Jim looked at him and said, "Just do it, please! She needs to be held by someone she knows and loves."

Bat said, "That was a long time ago—literally!" and laughed. He removed his coat and slid under the covers pulling her tight against him. She nuzzled her head in the crook of his neck. He said nothing and she slept.

Morgan walked in and nonchalantly exclaimed, "Oh, I see you got roped in, too. Continue."

He turned to Jim. Today was the day of the perihelium. They had found the old iron key at Iron Mountain; it had been the key to Andy Jackson's personal home.

"Don is taking lead on activation and entering that sequence." Marsha opened her eyes, moaning. Jim approached as did Morgan. Jim asked for a number, and she muttered 10 plus. He gave her appropriate meds. She looked at Bat and laid her head back down on his shoulder.

He looked at Morgan who told him, "Okay, up ya' go and let me jump in for a bit." Bat was visibly relieved to be up and away from that situation. Morgan just laughed. As Bat put on his coat and walked away, Morgan said, "Poor Bat, he will never adjust to this century."

Marsha murmured, "I did something with the Bat?" He laughed and answered, "No, baby." She rolled to her side; it was the first time she had felt able to move.

Morgan looked at Jim, suggesting, "Try touching her." He slipped his hand down with no response. "That would be our barometer, for sure." Without warning, she threw up all over Morgan.

Jim exclaimed, "EWWWW—gross!" He rolled out of the bed, grabbed the med gun and gave her meds.

Morgan shrugged, "I'll be back after I shower and change."

Morgan came back wearing only scrubs this time. "I learn fast." Both laughed. "Let's look at the plans and all the steps."

"We know the Washington china code:

Fleur de lis cufflink key

Twelve for the universal number

One for the gold element

Two for the silver element

Fifteen for points on the gold china starburst

Fifteen for the states around the china plate.

Four life path number of Washington

Ten representing circle and completion

The symbol for iron element: The arrows pointing up

The symbol for fire element: A triangle filled in

Napoleon's iron eagle with arrows pointing up: an iron key."

Abruptly, Marsha awakened and told Morgan she had forgotten to tell them that on Monroe's plate it is a Bigfoot holding the starfield and pointing. "You can see the right arm and the head sitting forward. He is pointing to the west. What is to the west? Sirius. I sure hope they have planetary defense shields!"

Morgan messaged Olzing to notify Sirius. He added that Venus had outposts, but they had been evacuated and the defense shields were up on Orion's belt always. "They must take Aggie. The Bigfoot is on there for a reason."

She broke off, crying out, "I hurt, oh, God, I hurt."

Jim came over and Morgan stood by her side. "I hurt; do you hear me? I hurt!" Morgan told him not yet. "Let's not mask her symptoms." They put in a call for Thar.

"I hurt, please! I hurt!" Morgan got in her face, telling her to hold on for a minute. Thar arrived at a run, went directly to the screen and flipped through the screens, drilling down into screens Jim had never seen before. That showed her now as Nordic DNA, with Human DNA, and pieces of leftover Blue DNA that were all competing.

"I hurt, oh, GOD! Help me!"

"What do we do?"

"Nothing, or it will harm the baby or even abort the baby."

Marsha heard that and screamed the loudest they had ever heard her, "NO, YOU WILL NOT!"

Thar glanced at her and then turned toward Morgan. "If she were mine, that baby would be gone by now."

"NO, Morgan! NO!"

Jim looked over at Morgan. He told Thar, "We will let you know." Morgan told them not to start anything but suggested asking Dr. Mid for a second opinion. He phoned Dr. Cay, asking her to bring Dr. Mid to their lab.

Marsha's blood pressure was high, and she could not tolerate this kind of pain. Both came right away. Dr. Mid took one look at her and told them, "She needs to be on the Nordic bed. We need to dial up the Nordic DNA just for now until the baby comes, then we can dial her back down. If we don't, she will lose the baby and most probably her life."

Dr. Mid called for his staff to come and get her. "We will take her down on this bed and bring her back on this bed. It will only take about 35 minutes." Dr. Mid grabbed the medical gun and gave her a bit of pain meds and told them, "She will sleep through the entire thing."

Morgan became angry, clenching his jaw.

"I will go. Morgan, you stay here and make sure Aggie is on that ship," said Jim. He walked with Drs. Mid and Cay. She assured him the baby was doing fine. Thar saw them and approached both Dr. Cay and Dr. Mid, "This is against the prime directive."

"Shut up you fool! They are saving the universe, and us as well! Don't you think we owe them that?" Dr. Mid retorted.

Thar looked down and admitted, "Of course." He grabbed a hold and helped move the bed.

Dr. Mid told him, "You need to be a bit more bendable, Thar, particularly if you ever want to be promoted to be head of the medical units for all of the Nordic Galactic Fleet. You have it in you, I see it. But I also see rigidity in your process." That hit home for Jim, he was a lot like Thar.

Morgan was more like Dr. Mid and Dr. Cay.

"How is that, Marsha?"

"I do feel a lot better."

"Good, now Jim and Morgan can go save all of us!"

They walked her back and told them, "You will see she is sitting at 63%." That is all he said. Jim thanked him.

"Please keep her calm with sedation for the next couple weeks until her system has time to assimilate."

Marsha had drifted back into sleep. They put the bed in place in the lab. "I will see to it that three beds are moved into the lab so you and Morgan can sleep while keeping an eye on her. I will come tomorrow as will Dr. Cay to check her."

"Thank you."

Morgan's eyebrows raised and he said, "Well?"

"I learned a lot, Morgan," said Jim. "I need to not be so rigid in my thinking. It was kind of a refresher course in doctor 101."

Marsha called out to Morgan. He climbed in bed and Jim gave her some light sleep meds. As soon as she was sleeping soundly, he got up.

The radio was now busy with chatter. The ship took off for their first stop, Serpent Mound. They only needed the fleur de lis. The blue beam came up. This will be the proving ground if the beam activates."

Liam, Tig, Dallas and Finch were all in the lab crowded around and listening with Morgan and Jim. Liam got up in bed with Marsha and snuggled into her. He told Morgan he did not want her to feel all alone.

Tig shot rubber bands at Dallas across the room. A look of concentration crossed his face as he stopped, turning toward Morgan, "Dad, we have to have that piece of Bat's stone in his cane! It will control the quantum fluctuations within the black hole. The quantum signal will be the amplifier it needs for the black matter. Dad! They need those planet shields around Venus,

Mars and the belt planets in Orion. Someone needs to run that to them, like now."

He texted it to everyone for confirmation. Morgan walked up to him, holding out his hand. It only took five minutes for the Pleiadeans to confirm it as well as the Nordics.

Bat was already down the hall giving the stone to Olzing. Tig walked over to Morgan, putting the rubber band in his dad's outstretched palm. Morgan continued standing by Tig with his hand out until he was certain all the rubber bands had been surrendered.

Tig leaned against the desk and asked if he could go to the Nordic College on their planet for the upcoming semester. Morgan sat back in his chair and said, "Tig! You're still playing with rubber bands! How do you think you're anywhere near qualified now?"

"Jeez, Dad! All four of us are ready. We want to learn, we're ready. You still see us as little kids, maybe we are physically but mentally we are college students."

"This is not the time, Tig. After this crisis, we can all talk about it as a family."

"Why am I the only one with balls enough to ask?"

Jim stood straight up. "You do not use that language young man! I will not tolerate that! Now, what do you think you should do as a consequence of such obnoxious behavior?"

Tig moved a stool over and stood on it, so he was eye to eye with Jim. "I am talking to you as a man," said Tig. "I believe we are all stressed out today and need a little leeway at this moment."

Jim broke into a loud laugh and said, "Tig you need to be a lawyer or a politician."

Morgan popped up off his chair and said with vigor, "That's My Boy! And, being my boy, I decide who gets leeway and who does not. You, my boy, do NOT!" He stuck his hand out for the tablet.

"But, Dad…" Tig handed it to him and called him a big meanie.

"Oh, yeah, that is some college-level language for sure!" Jim laughed.

17

Saving A Galaxy

They stood and Morgan said, "Let's all go back to the pod with Marsha and Bat, and the doctors who have supported us." They walked back to the pod. Bev stood waiting for them holding Mae. The kids aligned themselves along the side of the lab with their teachers and nurses. Each child had items they loved keeping them seated and busy.

The room was packed full. Charlie and Wyatt sported new arm casts and Marsha was sitting up feeding Paulie. Emmi cried for her daddy. Morgan went over and picked her up. He noticed she had Toodles snuggled in her robe. Morgan laughed and went over to Marsha.

Jim scooped up Helen who was screaming and Bat held Ed while Emma held Sarah. Thar's family was with them as was Kron, Virg and their kids, Mottice and Grissom. Liam had crawled up and sat next to his mom. He had smuggled all the dogs into the bay. Tig sat down and put a hand on Omar's back who was still growing out his lion cut. Morgan lifted Droopy and Giles up on the bed and they lay at the feet of Liam. El held her rat terrier, Gertie, and Dallas had the beagle, Stanley. Wolfie stood next to Olzing and Lassie lay on the floor next to Marsha's bed.

They all understood the next radio broadcast they heard would determine their fate, either a shockwave and massive debris would be incoming or, hopefully, total success. Morgan looked at Marsha and saw she was approaching full melt down. He told Liam to slide down by Giles and Droopy so he could sit with his mom.

Jim saw the shuffle and moved him along with Bev over to Marsha. He sat down next to Marsha, still holding Helen. Bev held onto his shoulder. Morgan and Jim moved in close to Marsha. Emmi crawled down and sat next to Liam, letting Toodles cuddle up to Droopy. Morgan held her tight. Thar took Paulie who was fast asleep.

Dr. Cay started singing Bev's favorite prayer and hymn and all voices joined in.

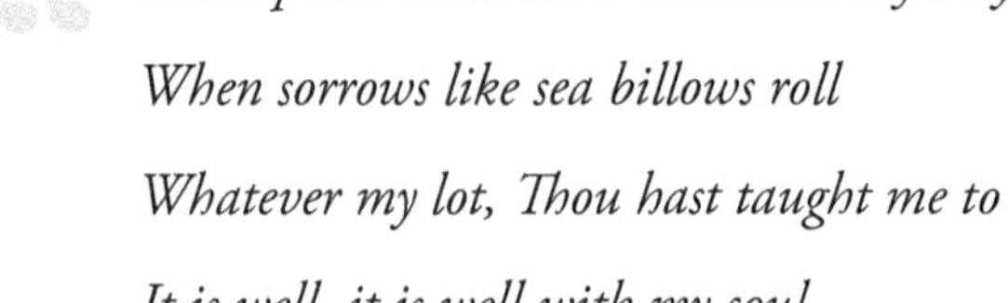

When peace like a river attendeth my way

When sorrows like sea billows roll

Whatever my lot, Thou hast taught me to say

It is well, it is well with my soul

Though Satan should buffet, though trials should come

Let this blest assurance control

That Christ hath regarded my helpless estate

And hath shed His own blood for my soul

It is well with my soul

It is well, it is well with my soul

My sin, oh, the bliss of this glorious thought

My sin, not in part but the whole

Is nailed to the cross, and I bear it no more

Praise the Lord, it is well with my soul

It is well with my soul

It is well, it is well with my soul

And Lord, haste the day when my faith shall be sight

The clouds be rolled back as a scroll

The trumpet shall resound, and the Lord shall descend

Even so, it is well with my soul

It is well with my soul

It is well, it is well with my soul

It is well, it is well with my soul

You could hear Bev and Dr. Cays' voices leading everyone in this beautiful moment together as they all awaited their fate. They had sung it through twice when they heard the crackle of the radio. Everyone went quiet except Bev and Dr. Cay. Both stood with their eyes closed humming the song softly.

"On Planet Earth, we have been rescued by Dr. Morgan King and his family, Dr. Jim Mottice and his family. We recognize the miraculous gift of themselves to save the Planet Earth as well as other planets and outposts."

"President Charlotte Kennedy and President Victor Ramirez of Earth along with their brave pilot, Falig, of the Planet Sirius who gave the ultimate sacrifice of their lives, to save this galaxy by imploding the black hole with their ship and the dark matter carried inside the compartments of their ship."

"There is no greater sacrifice than to lay your life down to save not only humanity but every species in the galaxy. Godspeed to them."

Don continued. "Now, may we all bow our heads in prayer:

"Holy One, you are our comfort and strength in times of sudden crisis. Surround us now with your grace and peace through this storm and the crisis our galaxy has faced with such bravery.

"Compassionate Lord, we pray for all those who have been devastated by this recent crisis with a remembrance of those that have so suddenly lost their lives. Help us hold in our hearts those families forever changed by loss. Bless those who have survived and heal their memories of trauma. May they have the courage to face the long road ahead. Bless the work of the relief agencies and those who provided assistance. May their work be guided by the grace and strength that comes from you alone."

"Help us to respond with generosity in prayer, in assistance, and in aid to the best of our abilities. Keep our hearts focused on the needs of those affected, especially after this crisis is over. You are rock and redeemer. We ask this in Jesus' name. Amen."

There was not a dry eye in the pod; instead a sense of love, gratitude and happiness filled the pod that night. It had been a miraculous manifestation of the entire group's work.

"Morgan King's incontrovertible voice of unity, discovery and humility in the search for the clues needed to save the planet rested squarely on his shoulders with the most able assistance of Jim Moticce, Liam, Tig, Dallas, and Finch. Much of the help came from Marsha's will and determination to move forward, even with the threat of death from the Blue and Merlin to relay important clues to the puzzle. Bev had the innate ability to correlate items for the overall plan."

The Kings—Morgan, Marsha, Tig and Liam; The Mottices—Jim, Bev, Dallas and Finch; Thar, Olzing and Don Scrodel all received the Congressional Medal Of Honor at a private ceremony at the White House. It was decided that would accommodate Marsha's fears of the press.

Additionally, the Nobel Prize went to Dr. Morgan King, Tig King, and Dr. James Mottice. There would be no escaping the press for the Nobel Prize with Tig being one of the youngest ever recipients.

This time, for the Nobel ceremony, they devised a different plan: they would shop in the USA in New York at a famous bridal shop where they knew they could find the gowns the ladies wanted. It would be at night with the stores closed so they could be the only shoppers in the store. Security would be the tightest. Don would inspect each gown they wanted to try on for chemical or foreign devices.

Once in Paris, they planned to give out a false schedule to try to throw the press off. They were going to take the Nordic ship to Orly airport telling reporters they would come into de Gaulle that afternoon when, in fact, they arrived at 5:00 AM with heavy security overseen by the Nordics and Pleiadeans.

Leaving from the hotel would be the usual press gauntlet, and Marsha was determined to not deprive Tig, Morgan or Jim their due acclimations.

They arrived in New York at the Pleiadean base just outside the city. Tight security had already been at the location looking through every square inch of the place, scanning with all their most advanced equipment. Only four associates were permitted to assist them, and they had to pass extensive background checks.

Their motorcade was not that unusual for New York City. Security formed a barrier for them to exit the SUV's. Morgan and Jim were excited to watch Bev and Marsha shop. Thar, Dr. Cay, and Dr. Mid joined them this time. Dr. Cay was excited to shop for a gown as well. Emma wanted to wear her gown from last year but warned Bat she might need some new accessories. The men had already been fit for their formal wear, including Wyatt and Charlie.

Both Bev and Marsha tried on 12 gowns each. Bev found one of Randy's gowns that had a deep blue tight bodice with the bottom all tulle decorated with clear sparkly sequins. It was a beautiful halter style ball gown. Bev got even more daring, and her gown was cut just below her breasts and exposed a good portion of them. Dr Cay was remarkably daring. Her dress was nearly see through with just crystals on the nude fabric designed strategically to cover the essentials. Marsha loved the gown on her, and thought she was breathtaking.

As usual, Marsha took her time. She let no one but Bev and Dr. Cay see what she looked like in each gown. As Don handed her each gown, he would point to his watch for Dr. Cay. She was watching Marsha closely.

Finally Marsha stepped out for all to see in a sheer white gown flowing over one shoulder. The silk was like butter and the front had a slit nearly all the way up to her womanly area. It flowed in sweet billows as she walked. The upper bodice stuck like glue to her body and was relatively see through on the top. If you looked closely, there was no hiding her breasts and her shoes had six-inch heels. She chose long sparkly earrings and her hair was drawn up in a high ponytail. She looked like a Grecian goddess.

Jim and Morgan both stood as she walked out. Morgan ran to her with his eyes big and sparkling with excitement. Jim sidled up to her and said, "I certainly did a great job on your boobs!"

Morgan looked at her and remarked, "Marsha, we agreed you would stay dressed. She looked down and told him, "I am covered; can I help if it is sheer?" Morgan directed the associate to add another layer of fabric to the breast area, so it was not so revealing. Marsha looked at Morgan and called him a big party pooper.

The associate told her it would be gorgeous on her body and not to worry. Jim told her to get the gown off so they could get going. When she left to change, he instructed the associate to stitch the slit closed two more inches. He did not want an unseemly great reveal at the function.

Morgan, Jim, and Dr. Cay lined up at the checkout to pay. Jim went first. His hand shook as he tried to hand the cashier his card, but somehow his hand wouldn't let go of it. Morgan slapped him on the back, laughing so hard he had tears and advised the clerk he would pay for all three, including alterations. Morgan made sure no one saw the grand total but him. Jim was still at the counter with the card in his hand. Morgan patted him on the back and said, "Come on, brave one. Let's go eat."

As they left, a throng of reporters appeared, with cameras flashing bright lights. Security tightened around them with their shields up and batons in hand. Olzing led in the front and Don squeezed in close behind Marsha; Jim and Morgan both tightened on either side of her.

Dr. Cay got in first, turning the bed on to warm it. Bev was in next with Olzing going around the vehicle to the other side. Morgan got in, while Don helped pull Marsha in and at the same time Olzing jumped in on his side to get her onto the mat. Jim jumped in and off they sped down the road.

Olzing looked up and could see the Pleiadean ship above them with a jamming device rendering the motor useless in any type of vehicle that intended to chase them.

Jim and Dr. Cay turned directly to the diagnostics and Morgan had already given her sedatives. Dr. Cay told Morgan she needed to be on the more powerful med bed on the ship. Dr. Cay asked Morgan to give her enough to put her to sleep. Don called out, "Twelve minutes ETA to ship."

Olzing instructed Don to get the Pleiadians to land and take the party to their base because it would only be a 10-minute ride from there. Don switched frequencies and they swerved off road, into what looked like a bare field. The ship was cloaked; however, with light-bending glasses they could all clearly see the ship with the ramp dropped. Don grabbed Marsha and ran for the ship as did Morgan and Jim with Bev as Olzing and Dr. Cay ran close on their heels. The ship started rising into the air as Dr. Cay jumped on and the ramp came up.

Thankfully, they had a full medical bed onboard. Their doctor did the read outs because Dr. Cay could not read the Pleiadean language. He translated for them. They gave her blood pressure meds and oxygen. Don radioed ahead for a gurney and for them to ready the trauma team. The ship made it in eight minutes flat and landed right next to the entrance.

The team came flying out and pulled the medical bed into their bay. The Pleiadeans brought the ship into the dock which then transferred them to the lower level.

Dr. Mid and Thar both met them in the bay. She opened her eyes. She was eye-locked to Morgan. "Did I get my gown, baby?"

"Yes, you did, and I might say you took my breath away."

"Good, it matches my breath right now."

Thar cued right in on her words. "Okay, truth now; how are you feeling?"

She turned to him, locked eyes and admitted, "Like I got run over."

"Okay, now, TRUTH! What else?" asked Jim.

"Am I having a baby?" Morgan swayed and Don moved in behind him, poised to add a steading hand should it be needed. Jim looked over at Morgan.

"I don't think so," Jim said, "But, should I look?"

She closed her eyes, but Jim pulled her chin around to him and demanded, "Open your eyes right now, little missy!"

She opened them. "Do you think you are, and can I look?"

"Morgan told me to keep my clothes on."

Hearing that answer, Dr. Cay began slicing her clothes off. Marsha protested, "Hey, those are my good jeans!"

Dr. Cay just shot her a wry look and kept cutting. Jim pulled his gloves on and asked for the pelvic position. Dr. Cay stood behind him so she could see if an incubator would be required. When he illuminated and expanded, Dr. Cay said, "Nordic."

Jim turned and eyed her, then asked her to do this exam. She felt, and quickly said, "Yes, pregnant, but it is a true Nordic pregnancy. You can tell by the elongation of the uterus and the triple plug. She will, in theory of course, go 11 months. This is her body adjusting and that is what she feels right now. She must have sat on the bed AGAIN, and somehow it regenerated while we were waiting for the success of the codes to be announced. None of us even thought about it. We were all just caught up in do we live or die? Instead we got a new life."

Thar was already busy giving her regular meds. Dr. Cay told them, "We will set her up on a regimen of meds and foods she will need to eat. She has not been dialed back to 100% human and is still registering 62% Nordic. The good news is, I do not detect any Blue at all in her DNA. But she must come in here twice a week for a check up."

Jim laughed and said, "I wish you luck with that!"

Dr. Cay went on, "Morgan, it is a little girl and only one." Jim said, "You have to name her 'Star' because of when she was conceived." Morgan asked if he could get in bed with her.

Thar told him please do, adding they needed to take care of him, too.

Morgan got in and pulled her toward him. Thar said, "Look at that high blood pressure! Woooeeee!" and shot him in the neck.

Morgan rolled over and said, "Thanks buddy!"

They laughed, then Thar told him his blood sugar was low. "Couldn't be the thought of another kid, could it?" which caused ripples of laughter.

Jim retrieved an orange juice, and demanded he sit up and drink it. Morgan did, draining the container, then asked to go back to his pod and get Marsha into bed.

Thar along with Dr. Cay, Morgan and Jim helped get her into bed. Dr. Cay put a night gown on her and told him to press the button if they needed anything, then handed them both bracelets to put on so they could monitor both through the night.

Morgan crawled into bed, awakening about 6:30 AM. Marsha still slept. He got up and jumped in the shower, then headed straight for the lab after giving Marsha another check. Jim was already in the lab. He took one glance at Morgan and directed him to "Get on the damned bed!"

"Ok, Dr. Snip-Snip, shall we do this dance again? That's why I am here bright eyed and bushy tailed."

"I knew you would be up and seeking my services," said Jim. "So, Let's do this one more time!" Morgan stretched out on the bed after slipping out of his scrub pants. "Thanks for warming the bed!"

Without warning, Jim picked up the med gun and medicated him with it. Morgan had zero time to react, then he was off to sleep.

Morgan awakened again, and it was 10:10 AM. "Jeez, you could have told me first!" Jim laughed. Morgan sat up and asked if Marsha had been in.

Jim said, "Nope, haven't seen her yet. Not really sure how she is going to take this, Jim. She told us repeatedly she was done and wanted no more. We need to go have the discussion; what are your bets for this one?

Morgan grinned, and said "Four." Jim said, "I am going with three plus a throw." Morgan opened the door to find she was still asleep. He went in and sat on the bed beside her.

She rolled over and told him, "Not now, Morgan, I am tired!

Jim laughed and remarked, "Well, that's a first."

"You get bonus points," added Morgan.

Marsha gathered enough energy to heave a pillow at Jim.

"Mark that down! There's my throw!" Jim crowed.

Marsha sat up in bed. "What do you want? Get out!"

Jim remarked, "One and a throw! Appears I am right on track."

She looked at Morgan and asked what time it was. Morgan told her it was around 10:30. She laid back down and told them to call her at noon, "If you know what I mean."

Jim laughed, then they both got up and left her. "Let's get us some breakfast! I'm hungry." They went to the breakfast bar. Morgan had his usual as did Jim.

"So, what did you think of our girls' gowns?" Jim told Morgan that Dr. Cays' gown was downright shocking to the point of almost being obscene. Bev's gown was even quite revealing, especially for her. Then he added, "And do we have to say anything about Marsha wanting to literally show off her boobs!" Just about that time Thar came waltzing in. He poured a cup of coffee and sat down. "Shall we talk about Tig now?"

Morgan sat forward, "What now? I hope he didn't glue Omar's hair on again."

Jim laughed and shot back, "Wouldn't that be a pretty sight for the ceremony!"

Thar nearly spit out his coffee, laughing hard. "No, your son is to receive his Congressional Medal of Honor in a private ceremony with all the kids in Vaughn present." Thar pulled the paperwork from his pocket. "He thought Vaughn was far more deserving, because he wanted to feed the Galaxy!"

Morgan felt tears well up in his eyes as Jim looked over at him. He did not know what to say to Morgan. Morgan closed the medal in Thar's hand and choked out, "Tig is his own man now, and if that is what he and all the kids want, so be it!" Morgan got his emotions under control and told them he was so proud of Tig and how much he had matured in the last several months.

"I am just so darn proud!" Morgan's tears finally spilled over. Jim's eyes glistened with moisture as well.

Thar shook his head, "We can't accept this!"

"We don't get to vote on it," said Morgan. "This is up to Tig and, apparently, all the rest of the kids." Thar stood and rounded the table to give him a hug. He threw in thanks for what he had done for him and his family. Marsha flung open the door and demanded to know who was making all the racket.

Thar laughed and told her, "It's 11:00 AM! Glad you could join us for the day! And, before you start your day, get into the lab this second!"

"Oh, really? I have been a good girl." He laughed and grabbed her by the arm and guided her firmly down the hall toward the lab but she put on the brakes and slumped to the floor outside the lab door. Thar put his hands on his hips and said, "Gee, Marsha, so predictable! Being pregnant, I would have expected you to act a bit more mature."

Jim and Morgan immediately cringed. Both shook their heads, waiting for her next remark. Thar thought to himself, "I guess I've let that cat out of the bag." She pulled her legs up to her chin and began rocking.

Morgan dropped down to her level and said, "Jim and I came in a bit ago to tell you, however, you wanted to sleep. Thar had no idea we had not told you."

Marsha stood and got face to face with Thar. Morgan was trying to pull her back. She yanked her arm away from Morgan. She said, "Thar, you better make damn sure I don't miss this ceremony. When is it due?"

Thar answered, "She is due in 10 months."

"I am not missing my man nor my kid getting their statue!" Jim said thanks to Marsha or him as she pointed.

Jim and Morgan both laughed. "You can start by calling her by her name, Charlotte Kennedy King. Got it everyone. Pass the word!" Morgan wrapped his arms around her and asked if she was okay?"

She said, "Oh, HELL YES! The more the merrier. I will get on the table willingly if you promise boom-boom when I am done."

Thar turned her to him and faced her nose-to-nose. "Absolutely, positively NOT! Do I need to keep you with my family to keep temptation out of your way for a month?" Jim and Morgan shot each other a look of surprise how far Thar had acclimated to Marsha's less-than-normal moral code.

Thar continued, "No? And you, Morgan, would you like to stay with my family to keep your hands off the merchandise?"

Morgan barely contained his laughter as he choked out a semi-squeaky, "No."

"Good! Now, Jim, you are on official night duty with these two for two weeks until we leave for the ceremony! Got it?"

"Yep, I got it! I want a bed back in their bedroom pod. And, you can include the same routine for the panic attacks sure to ensue with the prego mood swings."

"Marsha, you will adhere to the food and drink schedule I will send you."

She looked at him through her eyelashes, and said, "TRUTH?"

Thar said, "Oh, yeah, let's have it all!"

"I can never drink enough during the first trimester to stay hydrated. Jim accesses a port and keeps a bag hanging."

"Okay, and you must eat! No letting your sugar bottom out!" "Looks like you are a full-time physician with spare time on your hands."

Jim laughed and told him, "You got it."

"I still want her drinking or attempting it throughout the day. Make sure Lassie and Wolfie are both with her except for their potty breaks."

"Last thing before you get on the table, Bitty is wandering off again into the woods. She was with a group of Bigfoot. Please talk to her and make sure she is not putting off cycle pheromones."

"Now, Missy, shall we?"

She jumped on the table and Thar read the diagnostics, "High blood pressure, sugar is 30, and pulse 110."

Jim mixed up the rescue pen and pulled up her nightgown and gave the shot to her. He then gave her another shot with the med gun.

Thar said, "She stays medicated for anxiety and so does Morgan. Next, pelvic exam."

Jim leaned over and gave him two injections, and another for Marsha. Thar put on gloves and felt, "Yep, just one for a change. And this so far is not accelerated."

Jim walked down the hall and came back with Bev. "She is next." Morgan shot a glance at him and Jim told him, "Ours was planned, Morgan."

Marsha jumped down and Jim told the bed to sterilize everything as Bev and Marsha hugged each other. Thar informed

Bev she was early at just about a week. "And you are all cut off for the next month."

Jim gave himself a shot and Bev. "You are also having a girl."

She smiled and said "Star!" Marsha grinned at her, "I love it, Bev. Good call!"

Marsha was feeding Sparrow while Morgan tended to Galyn-Aggie and in their slings, Paulie and Heidi, while Bitty held Idell. They were contentedly rocking, feeding, and watching TV.

Morgan and Marsha with Jim right behind them appeared on the news screen. Marsha groused, "Ugg, my makeup is awful!" The reporter said they were hiding from humanity because of Morgan's drunk and uncontrollable wife, Marsha. Bitty immediately chucked the bottle at the TV and yelled, "Lies! No listen to lies!"

Marsha laughed and said "Bitty, I do not care what those losers say. As long as my family loves me for ME, I am good!"

She moved over close to Morgan and put her head on his shoulder. The nurse came down and gathered Sparrow and Galyn. She asked Bitty to come up to get Idena and Iris, "And, oh, Emmi is calling for you, Dr. King; she's pulling her at her ears again."

Marsha said, "I thought you and Jim were supposed to put tubes in!"

He asked the nurse to bring her down while he got his bag. Morgan retrieved his bag from the bedroom as Emmi came down sucking her thumb with Toodles in her arms.

Marsha asked Emmi if she could hold Toodles, so Morgan put Emmi in his lap and said, "Let's take a look, princess. Oh, YUCKY! My princess is sick and it feels like she has a fever."

Marsha put the dog down and put her hand on Emmi's forehead. "Yep, a fever for sure." Marsha got up and knocked on the door of Jim and Bev's pod.

Jim answered and Marsha told them, "Princess Emmi is sick with the ear thing and fever. You guys want to walk her over to the pediatric bay in case she needs an IV?" Jim came out and sat beside her and felt her head.

"Oh, boy, would I say a fever!" Morgan stood and told her they should go get medicine for her. She started to scream just like Marsha and reached her hands up to her.

Jim and Morgan turned and shot a look at Marsha who looked mortified. She took a deep breath and said, "Give her to me." They all walked to the pediatric bay.

Dr. Cay greeted them with a smile at Marsha. Marsha told her, "Princess is sick with a fever and yucky ears."

Dr. Cay could see the shivering start and suggested, "Let's bring her in and put her on the bed. Why don't you sit with her, Marsha?"

Emmi would not allow Dr. Cay to touch her ears. Morgan told her, "They are cruddy. We would like to put tubes in tomorrow."

Marsha looked at him and asked, "Surgery?"

Dr. Cay told her that it is really almost not like that anymore. Marsha turned her head away from Emmi with tears in her eyes.

"Temp is 103.2." Dr. Cay gave the med gun to Jim. "Can Uncle Jim give you some medicine?"

She shook her head. Morgan walked to the other side of the table as Jim gave her the meds and she quickly fell back, asleep.

"Let's get an IV in her." Dr. Cay handed them the kit and told her she would keep her asleep tonight. We'll start the antibiotics."

Marsha refused to leave Emmi in the bay alone. She laid down on the table with her and told Morgan he knew where to find her. Morgan and Jim walked out with Dr. Cay as Marsha stretched out on the bed with Emmi.

Dr. Cay looked excited. "She carried Emmi back and is staying on a bed with her. What a giant leap for Marsha!"

Jim slapped Morgan on the back and said, "Finally—some real progress!"

Jim and Morgan returned to the pediatric bay promptly at 6:00 AM. Dr. Cay asked Marsha to go to the other bed which she had warmed for her and cover up while they put in Emmi's tubes. Marsha did it with no fuss. Putting in the tubes took less than 15 minutes and they were done.

They would not let Marsha back on the bed until Emmi awakened. She sat right by the bed holding Emmi's hand. Morgan stayed with Marsha and Emmi, while Jim went back to bed. Marsha did not talk. Morgan and Dr. Cay noticed she was shaking. Thar arrived and was afraid Marsha was on overload. He refused to wait another second, and walked in to ask, "What is this we have here?"

Dr. Cay said, "Just tubes for Emmi's ears." He walked over to Marsha who was solely focused on Emmi. He put his hand on Marsha's shoulder and signaled Morgan to come over. Her body had progressed to violent shaking so Thar silently held his hand out for the medical gun and gave her light meds for anxiety.

He asked Dr. Cay to get Dr. Mid, and he arrived almost immediately from his bay. He could see Marsha as he rounded the pediatric bay. Dr. Mid went right up to her and called her name. She did not look up. She stood holding Emmi's hand. Emmi began to stir, and Marsha sat down with her, holding her close. She rocked back and forth with her as she cried. She looked up at Morgan and said, "Pain meds. Morgan gave Emmi just enough so she would sleep. He took her from Marsha and laid her back down, telling them all that she needed to sleep the rest of the day here.

He said, "Let's go get something to eat. She froze at the door looking out on the lab bay. "Not the lab, no. not the lab!" Thar grabbed one side and Morgan the other and they pulled in tight to her and walked her back to her bedroom. She crawled in bed and Thar picked up her med bracelet and slid it on and told her nighty-night. Morgan laughed and told him that was copyright infringement. Thar laughed and walked back to his pod.

Liam came running to Morgan and asked if he had seen Toodles and mentioned she had been missing since yesterday. Morgan looked down and said, "No, but she can't have gone far." They searched the family pod and then went back to the lab. And there she was, under Jim's chair on the rug with five puppies brand new puppies which looked suspiciously like the mini pin. Morgan said, "She must have been on my damn table."

Of course, Liam was ecstatic. "Puppies!" He yelled to anyone who would listen. Morgan was a bit less enthusiastic, but said, "Yippee!" as he rolled his eyes. Then he thought, oh God, Lassie had been on that same table. "Hope that mini pin did not get to her, too!"

Around 9:00 PM, Jim wandered down the hall, and spotted Liam and Morgan. Jim asked what was going on. Liam excitedly said, "We have puppies! Toodles and Tiny had puppies." Liam pointed beneath Jim's chair.

Jim said, "Well, I'll be—and under my chair of all places." Jim told Liam to go get Toodles' bed for the pups and an old blanket. It took Liam no time and he was back. Jim put the blanket in the bed and picked up Toodles and each baby, putting them in the bed with Toodles. "Do you have pee pads Liam?"

Liam said, "Yes."

"Okay, let's take Toodles up and since you want to be a vet, they are all yours to care for. Make sure she has water and food. Let me carry them upstairs for you."

Later, Jim was back downstairs and in the lab. He broke out in laughter several times. Morgan said, "I hope that damn mini pin did not get Lassie because she has been on the bed with Marsha."

Jim suggested naming them after the stars in Orion, and he laughed again at Morgan.

"Bedtime my friend. I got things to do."

"Well, according to Thar, I've got some assignments of my own." Morgan put down his pen and stood. "Uh, how much do I owe you for Bev's gown? I vaguely remember the bill being $22,350."

"Yeah, Bitty the Brave you are not." But he did think it funny to watch.

"All right, let's go, funny man. To the bedroom we go! Is Marsha there? Yep!"

"Oh, this should be fun; BETS?"

Morgan shook his head. He opened the door to find Marsha sitting up watching TV. Morgan went up to her and gave her a kiss. She wrapped her arms around his neck and gave him a long passionate kiss. But Morgan knew it was a test to see how far she could push Jim, so he stood there and waited. She pulled Morgan down on the bed on top of her.

Jim shook his head as Marsha tried to undress Morgan. Morgan pulled up and said, "Baby, we promised."

"But baby, I need you."

Finally, Jim stepped in, grabbed her arm and gave her just enough meds and helped her over to the medical bed. He raised the temp by 25 percent and covered her. Morgan slipped into bed and Jim told him he had his hands full with Marsha. He asked if he could leave the TV on so he could work on his speech. Morgan told him to go for it, and Jim gave him a bit of sedation. Morgan said nothing but rolled over.

Around 3:00 AM, the bed pinged. Jim heard the audible sound, but jumped up and looked at it. PVC's, "UGG," he groaned. He knew Thar would be down immediately with Dr. Mid. He leaned over on the bed and gave Morgan a light boost in sedation to keep him asleep through the commotion he knew was about to happen.

Sure enough they ran in. Jim had already told the lights to come up. Dr. Mid carried the pacemaker adjustment device. He tweaked it and put the heart monitor on Marsha. Thar told him she was pushing too hard. "Keep the wildcat in bed tomorrow. We will be in several times to take inventory of where she is. Access the port and give her the meds as ordered on her chart. Keep her sleeping if you can but we realize she fights the meds every time."

Thar asked if he wanted him to sit with her for a while. He told him to watch her while he went and got supplies. Jim came back with everything just in case. Thar grumbled this would be easier on all of them if she would just come to their lab.

Jim shook his head and said he would try to get her to consider it. Thar turned and left. Jim accessed the port, ran fluids along with the heart meds. He slid a catheter in so she would stay in bed. He also slid another monitor on for the baby. She still did not look accelerated.

At 9:30 AM, Morgan sat up. He asked what time it was, and Jim told him 9:30. He looked over at Marsha. He literally jumped over Jim onto the bed with her. "What is going on? Why didn't you wake me up?"

Thar answered as he walked in, "She was throwing PVCs, so she stays asleep. Jim had a good call on the monitor for the baby and the catheter. She may NOT get out of the bed today. I have a nurse on her way over. In fact, the next two weeks prior to the ceremony she is to be at complete and total bedrest. I would prefer having her over in our lab for 24/7 care. It would be wonderful if you could talk her into that."

Morgan looked at Thar and asked, "How about if I tell her I have to have it and I want her to come be with me. That way, Jim can sleep and be with his family. Jim will still be your primary physician, so he still pulls night shifts including for our traumas."

Jim looked at him and said, "ME?"

Thar told him, "You are as good as any of our primary care doctors. You just take your turn in rotation and Morgan, you will too when we get the ceremony behind us." Both Jim and Morgan's eyebrows went up in unison.

"Oh, ye of little faith!" grumbled Thar. "It is also time for the two of you to begin planning your next project so we can enter it in our planner and assign lab assistance for you. We are a community and not separate pods. We all pull our weight in this community. We are all family here. We need Bev to teach home economics and cooking. Once Marsha delivers, she will be in charge of sports and physical education. We all have jobs starting today."

Morgan smiled as did Jim who said, "Then you will from this day forward allow us to contribute to the community financially."

Thar looked at both of them and said, "No need. We are funded by our government to work with you and serve as a medical outpost for our soldiers. So your financial input is not necessary. We have vast uranium mines on our planet and sell them to planets for their heating needs. We are also part of the Galactic Police Force and funded by such. You will continue to be shielded and protected. We do not want to give away your position so we will maintain secrecy on a need-to-know basis which, of course, is virtually nobody."

"Last piece of business: Aggie is pregnant by one of the Bigfoot on the island. She will tell you when she is ready. If I were you, I would prepare for her to be with him and move from the cozy family you have given her for all these years. We, of course, will fill in her gap with two additional nurses. We are also adding an additional pre-school teacher and digging another pod for that. It should be complete tomorrow."

Jim left and went to bed while Morgan worked in the bedroom and helped the nurse care for Marsha. Fortunately, the meds were keeping her under for a change. Morgan gave her a sponge bath. He loved caring for her. He got up in bed with her and pulled her to him. She stirred and snuggled into his shoulder. He told the nurse to go have lunch and he would have his when she returned. She never stirred from his shoulder.

When the nurse came back, Morgan got up. Thar came in, adjusted her meds, and told Morgan to hang her heart meds. He also advised Morgan he looked like he needed more sleep time. He would be back at 4:30 AM.

"I want you to have eaten and be in bed. I will be in to medicate you and her, too. I will stay till 9:00 AM when Jim takes over. This is not negotiable." He turned and left.

Morgan tried to start on his new project outline and loosely summarize it. At 3:00 he went to the doctor's mess and had dinner. He brought back his hot vanilla latte, then went upstairs with the kids. Liam showed him the puppies. Toodles turned out to be an excellent mother and cleaned up after all her babies. She was nursing them when he looked in. Only one had the white poodle fur and color. The others looked exactly like Tiny the mini pin.

Tig and Dallas were showing Wyatt and Charlie how to play Fortnight. They played with each other and with Vaughn and Lang. Sometimes Dr. Cay and Thar played. Wyatt and Charlie would be returning in four days. The boys loved talking to them and hearing their stories. Morgan checked on Emmi who was by herself and lost without Toodles. Morgan texted Olzing and told him he needed another fixed mini poodle dyed pink pronto for Emmi. Then he asked Emmi how her ears felt. She just nodded her head up and down. Morgan gave her the stuffed dog Toodles for her to hold. She crawled up in her bed and laid down.

Morgan went right down to Emma and asked her to get Emmi and let her stay with them for now. Emma smiled and kissed Morgan and went up and picked her and her Poodle backpack with clothing and brought her down to stay with Grandma.

He was just coming out of Bat's pod when Thar came around the corner. Thar asked if there was a problem. He said only with Emmi. "She is lost without Toodles," explained Morgan. "I asked Olzing to find her another mini poodle dyed pink pronto and, of course one that is fixed and checked out. Emmi will be staying with Grandma and Grandpa.

"Okay, let's go; you look exhausted. Tomorrow, I will be over when you wake up and we will wake Marsha, and you both will be moving over tomorrow."

"Just FYI, Jim hides his well and I'm going to suggest you look at him as well. It was a long time to hold the fate of the planet on both of our shoulders. I've already prepared the order for him to take a 12-day rest."

"Okay, rest time for you," and he gave Morgan a light dose.

Jim came in at 9:00 and was surprised to see Thar with his tablet waiting for him. He told Thar it was a pleasant and unexpected surprise. Thar said, "Yeah, I bet. Effective tomorrow, I will be here at 10:00 AM to take Marsha, Morgan and you over to our bay. You will remain there on bed rest for 12 days. You will do what we say, when we say. And NO arguing if you want clearance to attend the ceremony."

"Now, I want to know about Bev. Right now! Let's have it. Should she be on bed rest too?"

Jim fell silent for almost five minutes, thinking through the question. He finally looked directly at Thar and said, "We both will be ready. I need you to sit here for an hour to prepare her, and I will be back after that."

Thar told him that was the best decision ever!

At 10:00, they waited for Thar. He brought four assistants with him. Thar said, "Good morning. Today is the start of your rest vacation you have all earned as a group."

"We will take Marsha in the bed and not wake her just yet. Shall we go to the medical bay, my lovely patients!"

As they walked, Thar told them they found a poodle that checked out and was currently being made pink. "Sorry, but it is a standard size dog; that's the best we could do on short notice. Her name is Greer. Emmi will have her after school."

"In addition, all the Nordic ponies have been brought back and we have a riding ring inside for the kids. Since you all have your tablets, you can watch TV on them. NO GAMING! That would drive your BP up. We also have an entire library online which includes medical journals. NO NEWS SHOWS! Is everybody clear?"

They all responded yes. Bev asked what they had for reading that she would like. "The nurse will show you where to look.

"Morgan, first bed. Marsha will slide in right here. Jim and Bev, you are one divider down. Bev, we will start an IV to give you fluids since you are dehydrated. That is not good for the baby. We will continue to access Marsha's port. I would like to keep her asleep for another couple days, if possible. If we see her come up, we will restrain her until she calms down. Is everyone clear?"

Morgan said "Yes, Captain Klink!"

They all laughed; however, Thar did not. Morgan cleared his throat. "Okay, in bed everyone. I will be by in a second to medicate each of you. And no hiding things from me, I always find out! And, if I can steal a line from Morgan and Jim as they lectured Tig on the hair-gluing fiasco, 'consequences for your choices.'" An embarrassed twitter of laughter spread, but quickly died.

He actually started with diagnostics on Jim. Thar looked at him and said "Hmmm, anything you want to tell me?" He stood looking down at Jim.

Jim laughed, "Okay, okay, bladder infection."

"…And…" Jim said nothing.

"…AND…" Thar said.

"Okay, AND a bunion on my left foot."

"BINGO, pupil gets a star! Nurse, IV for my man, Jim, and start antibiotics on his chart, and scheduled him for the orthopedic doctor in the morning." He medicated him and Jim quickly drifted off to sleep.

He moved to Bev and immediately the softer side of him was revealed. He asked if she had morning sickness, she nodded, yes. "Okay, we will fix that. Any strange cravings we can get for you?"

Bev asked for oranges and jellybeans. Thar laughed and told her, "You got it. I know the exact shop to get those at. And chai tea latte, right?"

She nodded. He told her, "We will keep an eye on her blood pressure. For now she was just dehydrated." They would start an IV while she slept and run fluids overnight. I would like you in bed so we will also put a catheter in so you can stay in bed."

She asked about a shower. He said twice a week. The other days she would need to settle for the nurse and a sponge bath. She asked if she could have her sweet pea lotion. He told her that someone would run over to their pod and bring it back for her.

"Now, how about a good night's sleep. Why don't you scoot down in the bed and lay back on the pillow?" She did that and thanked him for his kindness and caring for them. He smiled and gave her meds for a 12-hour sleep.

He came to Morgan's bed and said "The Mottices are out for the night; how about you?"

Morgan nodded. Thar gave him his meds and said, "Nighty-night." Morgan smiled and drifted off to sleep.

The 12 days went fast. Mostly Thar kept them sleeping. Toward the end, they all appeared much healthier and less stressed. Even the hellcat Marsha was tamer. She had only spent one day in restraints. She would not leave the bed at all. She began to shake each time she tried. She felt safe in the bed.

Thar told them he would be over to the pod to review the schedule for the trip. "FYI, Lassie had four puppies and is fixed again. They all look like her but are smaller." Marsha clapped her hands and exclaimed, "PUPPIES!" Thar laughed.

"In addition, Charlie and Wyatt have gone back. We were sorry they had to go, however, they were at the very end of their time in this century."

"Now, I would like to take you to the riding ring to watch a 20-minute lesson with Morgan-Barclay, Dorothy-Alice, Dallas and Finch."

They all looked at each other in amazement at the giant round pen and that each of the kids had an instructor teaching them how to saddle a pony, how to brush, and pick out the hooves.

Dorothy-Alice had an incident when her pony bit her. She turned around and promptly kicked the pony. Marsha asked if she could say, "That's my girl!" They all laughed.

Liam ran out to the ring and grabbed Morgan's hand and asked him to demonstrate how to use the stethoscope on an animal. Morgan showed him the way to know the earpieces are correct and how to hold the piece to the heart. He showed Liam where to put it on the pony. Liam looked so determined. When he heard it, he smiled and ran around in a circle doing a happy dance. They laughed and Morgan rejoined the group as they walked back into the pod and Thar told them he would see them later.

18

The Nobel Prize

The schedule looked amazing. Olzing and Don walked them through it. The Pleiadians and Nordics had thought of everything down to shielding the entire venue. Their guards were equipped with shields and batons as well as side weapons. Each person had a bodyguard, front and rear. "Jim and Morgan holding up Marsha, Thar will stand directly behind her. Tig stands between Bat and Emma with security surrounding them. Additional security will flank each side of the group."

Olzing looked at Marsha and said, "Thar in your car and Dr. Cay in Bat, Emma and Tig's car. All cars have med mats. There will be a Pleiadean ship on top of the venue, cloaked of course.

"Should anyone—and I mean anyone—get into an issue, we all go to the ship. You will be pushed, carried or dragged into that ship, your choice, of course. We have 12 medical beds onboard. There will be four Pleiadean doctors as well as Dr. Mid, in addition to three nurses. We are covered."

"In the presidential suite there will be four mats, two in each bedroom. You will sleep on those mats so that we can monitor you. We will have four cots in the living room for myself, Dr.

Cay, Olzing and Don. We will all bring our black suits to wear. Dr. Cay has her gown covered."

Marsha burst out laughing. He said, "Oh, excuse me, Marsha, we have you covered for anything and everything. You don't worry one bit!"

"The variable is Tig and how he will react. Kids are unpredictable. We will not medicate him since he is giving a speech. We will have no way to measure how much of a reaction we can expect. We will eat in the hotel for every meal. Our own chef will prepare your meals and bring them to your room. Don will deploy shields over every window that can withstand the blast from just about anything. Any questions?"

Marsha piped up, "I have one."

Olzing said, "Yes, go ahead, Marsha."

"Can we please NOT cut off my gown this go around?"

He laughed and told her they would make every effort for that to not happen this time.

"Ladies, in your gowns just below your left breast will be a button to press which immediately deploys a shield all around you. You press that if you see anything not right or feel dizzy. Both of you will have a tracker and microphone in the hair clip that you will wear. Jim, Morgan and Tig will have the same thing, only on their lapel."

"Sorry, Marsha, no pin this year. Those clips must be worn. We leave here at 3:30 AM to arrive at 4:30 PM. SUV's will be ready, and we will unload in their delivery bay where you will see extensive security. Have your bags outside the pod tonight except what you will carry on. We have a nurse who will assist Tig in case he is still sleeping. See you all in the morning. And don't forget to print off your speeches as well as Tig's!"

Everyone was onboard. Tig was still sound asleep in his PJ's. They brought clothing for him to change into later. They arrived and loaded into the SUVs, and still Tig slept. He slept in Bat's arms, no one spoke but many smiled. They could see apprehension on Marsha's face. They arrived at the hotel and pulled into the bay. So far all was going on schedule and on plan. Security got them to the lobby where hordes of reporters were camped out.

The moment they walked into the lobby, the camera flashes began, and people screamed at them. Bat pulled Tig in close as he began to cry. Bat guided him with one hand and kept the other hand on his pistol. Emma had her hand on hers beneath her coat and held his collar with the other. Four guards moved in tight around Bat, Tig and Emma. They all deployed their clear shields.

Morgan and Jim squeezed in close, and Marsha screamed, "NO… NO…." Five broke through pushing and carried by the mass of a group in a large surge forward. Security had batons with lasers but those did not seem to faze the surge. One person snatched Morgan's coat out of his hands as he tried to turn to get away. Marsha fell to the floor and one woman took her shoe and pulled her necklace off. Two guards immediately surrounded Jim and Bev, deploying their shields.

Two jumped in front of Thar and Dr. Cay. Don pulled Marsha across the floor with one hand and pushed Morgan into the elevator with the other. Marsha screamed for Tig. Morgan was on the floor of the elevator with Marsha telling her to calm down, that he was right here with her, and that Bat had Tig.

Don called for a medical emergency at the elevator getting off at the penthouse with Morgan who had been assaulted and Marsha had been pushed to the ground and assaulted before she was pulled to safety from the mass of pushing and surging humanity. They had been the two closest to the surge.

Don looked out the window to see the Pleiadian ship rising each floor with them. Morgan caught sight of it, too. Don told him the Pleiadeans would blast the first person that tried anything further.

"They will also blast out a window should it be necessary for us to board their ship." Morgan asked why all those people had been allowed into the lobby.

"The government allowed it. We did not expect our schedule to be compromised by the French government!" They arrived on the penthouse floor with the Pleiadean ship at the window and the ramp already extended to the window. The window almost magically dissolved, and Dr. Mid followed by two Pleiadean doctors ran through; security picked up Marsha with Morgan close behind.

Don opened the door to the penthouse. They laid both on med beds pulling diagnostic screens. Dr. Mid gave Marsha a light dose of meds, then turned to Morgan, giving him meds as the other doctor began healing scraped skin with the wand. Thar ran in, telling him not to heal the skin until they had been checked for Blue DNA. The wounds were scanned, and all came back clean. Thar then let the doctor repair it. Marsha had a scratch, too, and hers also returned as clean.

Don seemed so perplexed that there was such a mass, that they had surged forward with zero time to react to that tsunami of people.

"We will go to plan B," said Olzing as he walked in with Bat carrying Tig and Emma following behind. Dr. Cay gave Tig medicine to sleep.

"Everyone was just shaken up with a few scratches. Marsha will need time on the bed. Morgan you, too. We will take the Pleiadian ship to the venue, and then take the elevator down to the ceremony floor. The ship will remain to take us back to the hotel; however, all security from here forward will have their shields up and deployed. We will tune the lasers to wound severely. We do not come out of the elevator until the crowd is cleared, including all reporters."

Morgan and Marsha were both medicated. They also medicated Jim and Bev. Tig slept with Bat and Emma. Thar, Dr. Cay and Olzing along with Don slept on the cots in the family room. The Pleiadian ship remained at the window with the ramp extended.

The next morning, Jim and Bev were awake as was Thar, Dr. Cay, Olzing and Don. They ordered breakfast as Tig wandered out of Bat and Emma's room. Jim went right to him. Tig asked where his mommy and daddy were. Jim told him they were still sleeping. He asked Tig if he was okay. He knew that was a lot of people.

Tig admitted to being scared but "Grandpa picked me up and pulled his gun and so did Grandma! I didn't know she carried a gun, too." Jim asked if he still wanted to go to the ceremony. He looked straight at Jim and said, "Hell, yes!" Bev walked around the table and asked who taught him that language?

"Uncle Wyatt!" he admitted.

"No more or there will be consequences for that language," Bev told him. "Now, come sit down and eat breakfast." He saw the donuts, grabbed three and put them on his plate. As he turned to get milk, Jim swiftly removed two, replacing them with scrambled eggs and a banana.

"Aw! Can't I catch a break even today?" complained Tig.

Jim pointed to his plate and said, "EAT."

Jim sat beside him and told him, "Tig, just so you know, Don has orders to search you before you go on stage. There will be no funny business during the ceremony."

Tig rolled his eyes and complained, "You people treat me like I am three!"

"Did I not see rubber bands just yesterday?" asked Jim.

Tig mumbled just loud enough to be heard, "Caught and guilty as charged."

Everyone laughed but then Tig pulled his frog out of his bathrobe pocket. Jim looked at him and said, "Really? Tig!"

Tig shrugged and asked if he could put water in the tub and let his frog swim because he has never been to France.

Dr. Cay and Thar just shook their heads.

Jim said, "I will go check on Morgan and Marsha while Tig lets the frog swim in our bathtub."

Finally, everyone was up and done eating. Don helped Tig rehearse his speech while Jim and Morgan worked on their own speeches. Bev and Marsha sat on the sofa chatting when they were interrupted by a loud knock on the window. They turned and saw three people and a reporter had repelled down the building.

Don and Olzing quickly radioed the ship, which promptly decloaked and grabbed all four. Tig came out of the bathroom and remarked "That was super cool."

Unfortunately, Marsha was shaking and had gone into a panic attack. Morgan and Jim ran to her, with Morgan behind and Jim in front of her. Emma coached her to follow her breathing pattern. Thar approached to give her meds.

"Why won't they leave us this just one day to enjoy? Why is that so hard?"

Tig said, "Mom, we sort of saved the world, you know, all of us. People want to see us and know we are real. Some are on the crazy side, but most are not. Gotta take the good with the not so good.

"You know, I was scared yesterday, too. Grandpa picked me up and pulled his gun and did you know Grandma carries one, too? How cool is it to have a pistol-packing Grandma!" he said with evident pride.

Marsha laid her head back on the sofa just as there was bullet fire against the windows. Marsha grabbed Tig and pulled him down. Olzing told everyone to get down and stay down.

Bat and Emma had their weapons in their hands. They could all see the Pleiadean ship as it fired on another ship. They watched Olzing as well as Don speaking into the cuff of their shirt sleeves.

Next thing they saw was a blazing fireball falling to the ground as they stood in shock and awe. The windows had held.

Tig said, "Grandpa, that was just like Star Wars!"

They told him to go play with his frog. "And no reconnaissance, Tig! Just play with your frog."

Emma went in with Tig and shut the door behind them.

Olzing said, "We have an issue. That was a Blue's ship."

Morgan announced, "That is it; we are not safe here. We get on that ship and go back home. No stupid statue is worth this." Sadly, Olzing and Don both agreed. Marsha could not talk; her shaking was at the full bore, near seizure level.

Thar gave her light meds to help her sleep and they boarded the ship back to home base, where they got Marsha onto the bed. Morgan anxiously asked about the baby. Dr. Cay assured him she was safe as a bug in a rug and not accelerated.

They were home in an hour and took Marsha directly to the medical bay. They strongly recommended Bev stay overnight in the medical bay for observation. They all knew leaving would not be optional at any time soon.

Morgan, Tig and Jim delivered their speeches that day via scrambled and encrypted video. The Nordics set up a TV studio but masked its location. They set a table long enough to seat Morgan, Tig, Jim, Marsha, Bev, Finch, Dallas and Liam. Everyone dressed in their tuxedos and gowns with hair and makeup. Dr. Cay was also in her gown and Thar was in his tux but not seated at the table. There was plenty of seating for everyone else, so it looked like there was a large audience. They wanted nothing to give their location away. With the display of force by the Pleiadeans at the hotel in addition to the Tellites, anyone looking for them would turn their focus to the species helping Morgan and Jim first.

Tig was first to speak. He sat at the table with a microphone in front of him. Every speaker had their own microphone to talk into. That arrangement allowed each person speaking to read their speech from a teleprompter.

"Good morning, everyone. My name is Tig King. It is a privilege to accept this highest Award and Honor for something which every person I know would do. It just takes letting your mind be free and bringing the spirit of helping planet Earth to the project."

"My mom and dad encourage all of us kids to nurture our talents with hard work and dedication to win the project race. In my family, each of our goals every day are to always be the best we can be with confidence that with our work and participation, we will help make this planet better. We start with a task and take each challenge with the thought of never saying 'no' when we're told to TRY!"

"Yes, we do sometimes fail. You can't be afraid of that. Heck, one time I glued my dogs' cut off hair to my head thinking how good I would look with long hair by taking a shortcut and gluing his hair on my head. Obviously, for many reasons that was not a correct hypothesis as my Uncle Jim pointed out. But the point is, I tried!"

"Success is a result of hard work, and my Grandpa has taught me NOT to take shortcuts. Let's all help each other to reach the destination we each desire to make this a better place to live. My cousin Finch and my friend Vaughn say be creative and don't be afraid to do things in different ways."

"We all have talents to make each challenge smoother with our hard work. Dad and Uncle Jim did not receive their success with one night of hard work. It was about trying, thinking outside the box, and giving the highest quality to their work which is reflected in their quality of service to humanity."

"Through teamwork, we knew we would have to have the courage to stand back up every time we failed and face the problem with hope, and all give it our very best effort."

"God uses trials like saving our planet to strengthen our faith. When trials come, we should keep the long view and remember he has our best in mind. My cousin Finch said he knew through our family's faith that we were all shielded by God's power. Our faith, for many on this planet now, understands what is of greater worth than gold, which will perish even though refined by fire."

"Our genuine love for God and each and every person on this planet can help us find the strength to grow toward maturity and love for one another as well as our Heavenly Father. We trust in hard times, trust God in all difficult times, He has a plan for all of us and knows infinitely more than we do. Our family found trusting God through trials, means trusting him and his plan!"

"So in overcoming all the storms of life, they all have one thing in common, Trust!"

I will leave you with this thought: Trust in the Lord forever; he is your everlasting rock. We are the bright hope of the future. Let's walk down this path together and show our parents' and grandparents' generations what we will do next for our planet and our galaxy. Let's be the superstars they hope and believe we can be. Thank you."

The entire pod erupted in applause and cheering, and someone yelled to Tig, "That was beautiful." Olzing cut the feed until it was time for Morgan and then Jim.

Tig went right to Finch and Vaughn and hugged both. He told them he could not have done the speech without them. He asked if he could start on the Feed the World project with them tomorrow.

Jim grinned at Tig and told him he loved that he had thrown in the dog hair bit. Then, he picked him up and gave him a long hug. Marsha and Morgan waited for their turns. Marsha knelt down in front of Tig and told him no mother could be more proud of her boy this very minute. "And thank you for telling all of your hair episodes. It made you look like just a typical boy."

Morgan told him that he could not have given a speech any more true or encouraging, and with some funny and oh-so-Tig mixed in.

Tig asked his Dad what his next project was? Marsha stood and looked at Morgan as he said, "I am writing a book about work, family and love."

Tig's face lit up, "Wow, you have a great copy with all I have done!" He ran off laughing.

Morgan put his arms around Marsha and told her, "No, I will not be using the picture of Tig with Omar's hair glued on as the cover."

Next to speak was Morgan, and he kept his speech short as did Jim. The announcer thanked everyone for listening and then they cut the feed.

Morgan went right to Marsha and asked her how she was doing because she looked tired. She looked at him and said, "I am the proudest woman on this planet and probably off planet, too!

"With that said, I would love to lie down in my warm snuggly bed for an hour."

He asked if she wanted him to come in and she said, "You wish, my handsome Teddy Bear!" He laughed and walked her to the bedroom pod. He turned as he shut the door and told her not to wrinkle her gown.

The party went on for an hour and all kids were told that it was bedtime, and 10:00 PM was way past time for bed. The nurses and nannies took all the kids to their pods. Marsha got up and joined the adults, just in time to sit down to a candlelight dinner. Everyone had a wonderful time. They shared stories— many by Bat—and Marsha's getting to wear and keep her gown on this year.

Everyone laughed and relaxed, finally. She looked at Jim and told him she had cut the two inches of stitching he added to close the slit. "AND I took out the extra fabric panel in the boobie area."

Morgan and Jim just looked and shook their heads. Marsha stood and asked all what they thought. She grabbed Dr. Cay, Emma and Bev and they danced and twirled together in their lovely gowns.

The good food and wine along with the love of each for the others in their tight-knit community could not be a more fitting end to this chapter and crisis. Everyone was looking forward to the next project which would require all their cooperation and mutual skillsets to overcome.

About the Author

Beth Ann Roose was born in Northampton, Ohio. Her ancestors farmed what is now the Cuyahoga Valley National Park. Beth has an appreciation for the beauty and magic within the park boundaries. Her stories embraces much of the folk lore that is still told to this day. Beth takes a "flash" forward approach to her books. Drawing on universal themes, like good versus evil and family, Beth is developing original content combining folk lore and fiction in her creative projects. In addition, she is an award winning animation writer and director. She continues to expand her creative base, with new avenues in Reality TV shows.

Also by Beth Roose

Forest Guardians Chronicles

A Matter Of Humanity

Christmas in Cuyahoga Valley

Blue's War

Awakening of the Olympians

Elf Sparkle Series

Elf Sparkle And The Christmas Train

Elf Sparkle And The Christmas Ribbons

Christmas Magic On The Cuyahoga

www.ingramcontent.com/pod-product-compliance
Lightning Source LLC
Chambersburg PA
CBHW060615100726
47907CB00006B/1636